Christmas of Hope

An Anthology of 7 Christian Inspirational Holiday Stories

Darlene Panzera, Debby Lee, Carol Caldwell, Jeri Stockdale,

Beverly Basile, Julianne M. Haag, Robin Gueswel

ISBN-13: 978-1539598510

ISBN-10: 1539598519

Note: Scripture quoted in the story is taken from the New King James Inspirational Study Bible.

TABLE OF CONTENTS

Homespun Christmas

by

Darlene Panzera

Dedication:

For all who have ever questioned their place in this world

Acknowledgement:

I want to thank God for the inspiration for this anthology, and for the friendships I've made along the way. Julie, Robin, Carol, Debby, Jeri, and Beverly: The seven of us have laughed, cried, prayed, but we also grew in our faith and our writing skills, and have undoubtedly made bonds I'm sure will last a lifetime.
I also thank my family for their patience and my daughter, Samantha, for helping us put this entire anthology together. We couldn't have done it without you. You're awesome!

Note: Scripture quoted in the story is taken from the New King James Inspirational Study Bible.

CHAPTER 1

There it was—the perfect gift for her mother—sitting high on a shelf in the Collectibles section of the upscale New York City department store. A tiny, white, porcelain bird cage with an exquisitely detailed feathered replica of a yellow parakeet perched on a swing within its interior. Her mother *loved* birds, almost more than people, or so it seemed with all the bird feeders hanging around the family farm in Pennsylvania. Cassie Sutherland flipped over the price tag to see how much the figurine cost. More than she'd planned, but on Christmas morning, when she saw the look of appreciation on her mother's face, it would be worth it.

Absolutely, completely, one-hundred-percent worth it.

With a smile upon her lips, she sighed, dreaming of the appreciative looks on *each* of her family members faces when they saw what she had bought them. For her dad, she'd purchased the latest high definition TV, for her older brother, Tim—a circular saw. She'd spent fifty dollars on a bottle of perfume for Tim's wife, Eileen, and twice that amount on toys for their two kids, Amber and Timmy Jr. She'd also found a plethora of baby items for her younger sister, Sarah, and her husband, Rick, who were expecting their first child in just a few days on December twentieth.

In the past, Cassie hadn't been as successful at finding the right Christmas gifts to please her family. But *this year*, it would be a merry Christmas indeed!

After paying for the boxed birdcage figurine to be gift-wrapped in shiny, green, wrapping paper and tied with a big, red, velveteen bow, she slipped the item into one of her many shopping bags. Then, strolling out the door, she sang the first three lines of the carol, *"I'll Be Home For Christmas,"* which was being played by three rag-tag street violinists who had set up stage by the curb.

A strong-scented waft from the corner stand brought visions of roasted chestnuts and doughy, giant-sized, salted hot pretzels to mind and her stomach growled with sudden longing. She'd been so busy shopping, she'd forgotten to eat lunch. However, before she could approach the vendor, she was stopped up short by a bell ringer for the Salvation Army.

"Do you have any change for the poor?" the bell ringer asked.

With the handles of three large shopping bags in each of her hands, Cassie couldn't reach into the purse hanging from her shoulder, even if she'd wanted to. "Sorry," she said, giving the teenage girl wearing the snowman print hat and scarf an apologetic look. "I don't have any cash."

The bell ringer glanced down at the shopping bags loaded with colorful packages and gave her a sardonic look that said, *"Obviously."* Cassie's cheeked burned, despite the cold outside, and when the teen reminded her that she could always donate online, she realized she couldn't do that either, because she'd already maxed out her credit cards.

Eager to escape from the girl's line of sight, Cassie hurried through the crowd and around the next block, sneaking occasional peeks back over her shoulder as she went.

Wham! Maybe that's why she didn't see the woman standing in front of The Doll Shop.

"Excuse me," Cassie said, straightening after their hard-impact collision. "I didn't mean to bump into you. Are you all right?"

"Yes, of course," the stick-thin woman assured her, but Cassie noticed she had tears in her eyes.

First she'd offended the bell ringer, now this woman. "I *am* sorry," Cassie said, trying to swallow the lump of guilt lodged in her throat. "I didn't mean to make you cry."

"You didn't. These tears are for my daughter." The woman sniffed and nodded toward the doll display in the storefront window. "She wanted one of these fancy 18-inch dolls for Christmas so she'd fit in with the other girls in her class. They all have one except her. I didn't think it was such a big deal but now the girls have started having overnight doll parties and—my little Susanna isn't invited."

Cassie swallowed hard and remembered the Christmas long ago when her mother set up that horrible miniature tree in front of the bay window of the dining room. Every award ribbon from her family of super-achievers had been hung on it. Everyone's except *hers*, because she didn't have any. And as a result, she'd felt...the same way this woman's daughter must also feel.

Left out. Alone. Like she wasn't good enough...or belong with the rest of them.

"I'd give anything to buy one of these dolls for Susanna," the woman said, a catch in her voice as she gazed longingly at the dolls in the window. "But I—I just can't afford it."

Cassie set down her bags and this time she *did* dig into her purse. "I think I can help," she told the mother beside her. "The Doll Shop is one of my clients. I'm designing an ad for their online marketing campaign and they gave me a store credit as a holiday bonus."

The forlorn mother took the voucher from Cassie's outstretched hand and her brows shot upward. "But this card is for two hundred dollars!"

Cassie smiled and nodded, her heart swelling as she imagined the delight on the daughter's face when she was finally accepted into the group with the other girls. "There's even enough for you to buy the doll a few extra outfits."

"Thank you, but I—I couldn't," the mother said, shaking her head. "It's too much money."

The woman proceeded to hand the voucher back but Cassie refused to take it. "Please," she said, her voice coming out more than a little bit desperate. "Your daughter needs a doll a whole lot more than I do, and I'd hate for the voucher to go to waste."

The mother's eyes filled with tears a second time as she clutched the voucher to her chest and exclaimed, "You, my dear, are an answer to prayer."

Cassie smiled politely in response to the remark, but as she walked away she attributed their meet to coincidence more than anything else. The woman wanted to give her daughter a doll and she had a free voucher. Simple as that.

For if there *was* a God who answered prayer, why hadn't he answered any of *hers?*

Twenty minutes later, Ned Doherty met her in front of the advertising agency where they both worked and escorted her into his slick, Monsoon Gray Audi Coupe to drive her back to her apartment.

"Where were you?" Ned asked, checking his gold Rolodex watch.

Cassie held up her shopping bags to point out the obvious. "I took the afternoon off to buy gifts for my family."

Thanks to her move to the city and her promotion to the graphic arts department in a high-profile marketing agency, she could afford good ones this year, gifts she normally wouldn't have been able to afford.

"Any for me?" Ned teased, trying to peek into the packages as he helped her put them in the trunk of his car.

"Maybe," Cassie conceded, climbing into the passenger seat.

Ned jumped in behind the wheel and arched a brow. "Something great?"

She stopped breathing for half a second as the pressure to buy the perfect gifts caught up with her. "I bought a porcelain bird cage for my mom. What do you think? Should I have bought her something else? What did you buy for your mom?"

Ned's eyes lit up. "I got lucky. One of my client's gave me an engraved ball point pen."

"A *pen?* That's what you are giving your mother for Christmas?"

"It's an expensive pen and comes with a velveteen lined wooden box."

Cassie laughed. "You're joking."

"No. I'm not." He looked at her, scowled, and shook his head. "You don't approve."

"It's just that...it's not very personal. It's not like she's a writer or likes to journal, does she?"

"No," he admitted. "It's just a gift that she will probably re-gift to somebody else. See? In the long run, I'll be saving her money too."

"But—"

Ned pulled the car into the long line of traffic and leaned on the horn when a yellow taxi whizzed past and cut him off. "Who does that guy think he is?"

Cassie took her hand off the dashboard and tightened her seat belt. "He had the right of way. You didn't see him."

"He came out of nowhere."

Cassie was beginning to think their relationship was going nowhere. When she'd first moved to the city two years before and didn't know anyone, she'd met handsome, dark haired Ned in a coffee shop when he barreled through the door and bumped into her. Impressed by her ability to brainstorm an idea for his latest marketing assignment, he'd been quick to recommend her for the opening in the graphic arts department of the advertising agency. Ned had leverage in the firm because of the gleaming credentials on his resume, and because of his initial helpfulness, she'd thought he'd make a great boyfriend too. But the more she really got to know him, the more she realized he was a whole lot better on paper, than he was in person.

She glanced over at him and realized he held the steering wheel with only the pinky finger of one hand, with his cell phone wedged tight between his thumb and forefinger. His other hand played with the car stereo. She opened her mouth to urge him to drive with both hands on the wheel, but he caught her gaze and stopped her words with another scowl.

"What?" he demanded.

"You've got your phone in your hand."

He shrugged. "I'm expecting a call."

She hated to nag, but he'd got them both into an accident just six months before. At that time he'd also been distracted by his phone. "It's illegal to text and drive."

"I'm not texting. And if the phone rings I'll only be on for just a few seconds."

A few seconds of danger was all it took. "You don't need it," she said, clutching the armrest as he swerved around the next corner. "Just put it down and relax."

"Stop being so paranoid. What's with you? Always complaining about the way I drive."

"I don't like it."

She *did* seem to be complaining a lot lately. She loved her job but the long hours were wearing her out. It would be good to go home and take a mini-vacation. Then she'd come back to New York recharged and ready to take on the company's next project.

Ned grimaced and set the phone down. "There. Happy?"

She wasn't, but nodded anyway.

"See what I do for you?" Ned asked. "Because it's always all about you, right? Always about what *you* want."

She rolled her eyes. He wasn't always a jerk, but what she wanted more than anything at that moment was to get away from him.

"How long are you going to blame me for that accident?" he continued. "I told you it wasn't my fault."

"It never is, is it?" She was tired of him always playing the victim and never owning up to his own mistakes. In fact she was tired period. Maybe she needed a mini-vacation from *him* too.

"What is that supposed to mean?" he asked, taking his eyes off the road to glance at her. "You're perfect and I'm not?"

She shook her head. That wasn't it at all. She *knew* that she wasn't perfect. "Just forget it."

Ned pounded a fist against the wheel, making the car swerve once more. "No, I don't want to forget it."

Cassie tried to focus on the thick green garlands decorating the various store windows as they drove past, but the thought of how her family might react to Ned's winning personality stuck in her mind. She'd been waffling back and forth, wondering if she should introduce him, but their present car conversation made the decision ever-so-clear.

"Ned," she said, looking him straight in the eye once he parked in front of her apartment building. "I'm going home for Christmas. *Alone*."

The muscle in Ned's jaw tightened. "I thought we agreed I'd go with you so I could meet your family?"

She held his gaze. "Not this time."

"Are you breaking up with me?"

For a moment, the expression on Ned's face flickered with uncertainty, and reminded her once again how he'd believed in her when she really *needed* someone to believe in her. She *still* needed someone to believe in her. She also didn't want to be impulsive and throw away two years of dating because she was over-tired.

Cassie forced a smile. "No, I—I just need some time to think."

His face paled. "You *are* breaking up with me."

Cassie shook her head and took out her cell phone. After bringing up her latest text message, she said, "I wasn't supposed to tell you for a few more days, but Skip and Joey asked me if I'd be okay with you going with them on a snowboard trip to Vail, Colorado over the holidays."

Ned sucked in his breath, his expression hopeful. "And you said yes?"

Discretely typing in her reply and pushing the 'send' button, she put her phone away and nodded. "My Christmas gift to you is a set of lift tickets."

Ned's mouth curved up into a broad grin as he leaned toward her. "Forgive me for what I said earlier. You *are* the best!" Then after placing a quick kiss on her lips, he added, "I got you something too—something great—"

She doubted that. By the way he hesitated, she knew he was lying. She'd seen him do it a thousand times over when schmoozing a new marketing client. But he still had a full week to buy her a gift. And maybe it *would* be great.

Ned took her hand. "But...is it okay if we celebrate Christmas together when we both get back? After all, the exact day we exchange gifts doesn't matter does it?"

Christmas used to hold more of a religious meaning for her, back when she trusted that God did indeed listen and would work everything out in her life for good. Now it just seemed like another endless day on the calendar.

"No," she agreed. "The exact day doesn't matter."

CHAPTER 2

Early the next morning, Cassie carefully packed all the expensive, store-bought gifts into the back of her metallic, lunar blue painted Mercedes Sedan, and left the city to make her way back to her family. The drive took two hours, not bad for a Saturday, especially since the rolling hills outside of New Hope, Pennsylvania were covered in snow. The sign for Sutherland Farm came into view and with an anxious flutter at play in her stomach, she realized—she was home.

Her thoughts skittered toward her parents, brother, and sister. Would they like her new car? And the gifts? Congratulate her on her new promotion at work? She knew it was wrong to pride herself on her accomplishments, but this was the year she secretly hoped to impress them, to show her Christian family of super-achieving super-servers that she too could be a raving success.

The car tires crunched over the snow-covered gravel in the driveway, announcing her arrival, and as she got out, she looked toward the front of the large, brown shingled, two-story farmhouse to see if anyone was there to greet her. A couple of snow figures stood on either side of the entrance.

One was made of three round snowballs forming your typical snowman with two charcoal eyes, an orange carrot for the nose, and a bright teal scarf, no doubt hand-knit by her mother. The other greeter had been shaped like one of the farm's resident llamas, with intricately carved grooves outlining the body and legs, a pillar of packed snow for the neck, and a small snowball for the head on which someone had placed a red and white Santa Claus hat.

Cassie smiled. It looked like she had a young niece or nephew who might grow up to be a sculptor. No one had claimed that illustrious title yet.

Leaving the multitude of wrapped packages in the back of her car, she pinched the collar of her wool coat closed to ward off the twenty-seven degree chill, and eyed the snowman's scarf with envy as she made her way to the front door.

She squeezed the handle but it wouldn't budge. Was she locked out? Frowning, she raised her hand and rapped on the knotted wood with her gloved hand. For several seconds she stared at the decorative evergreen wreath which faced her at eye level, as she waited to be welcomed in, and another anxious flutter coursed up her spine. Then the door opened and the exuberant, smiling face of her mother appeared.

Except her mom held a phone to her ear, was busy chatting with whoever was on the other end of the line, and Cassie wasn't sure the smile had been meant for her. Grace Sutherland was always helping someone, either by talking on the phone or in person, the go-to woman in the neighborhood when anyone needed anything. From the sound of her mother's voice, it appeared she was organizing details for the church's upcoming Christmas Eve service.

Cassie would have loved to have been wrapped in a big hug upon her arrival, but she understood—as always—her mother was busy doing what she did best. However, her mother did whisper an apology as she motioned her in, and then shut the door before they let in any more cold air.

The house smelled wonderful. As Cassie stepped over the threshold, pungent scents of cinnamon and nutmeg greeted her nose. And it was easy to see why. Her younger sister, Sarah, and sister-in-law, Eileen, stood behind the kitchen counter, decorating gingerbread men and an assortment of sugar cookies cut out in various shapes. Some of them had been frosted with thick, colorful icing.

"Cassie!" Sarah exclaimed, setting down a small container of candy sprinkles. "So glad you're here. You can help us with the cookies. Eileen's recipe won first place in the holiday contest at the community center and the organizers asked if we could bake more to hand out to the people picking up gifts at the Giving Tree event this afternoon."

Eileen's recipe won first place? Cassie forced a smile as she took off her coat and hung it on one of the wooden pegs lining the wall by the entrance. "That's wonderful."

"Of course, if you want to help you'll have to change out of those fancy clothes," Eileen said, eyeing her pearl white cashmere sweater and navy blue slacks. "And—oh dear! Watch out for the kids!"

Before Cassie could blink, her five-year-old niece and seven-year-old nephew, chased each other around the counter, their fingers coated with what looked to be bright red and green frosting, and...they ran straight into her arms, nearly knocking her over.

"Aunt Cass!" Amber exclaimed, tugging on her sleeve and slathering the sugary mess all over her. "Guess what? I get to be an angel in the church play!"

"I'm going to be a shepherd," Timmy Jr. informed her, grabbing her other arm.

Cassie was excited to see them too. She just wished they'd washed their hands first. Now she really would have to change her clothes. And her father and brother hadn't even *seen* her yet.

"Both of you, to the sink, right now," Eileen commanded the children. Then she gave Cassie an apologetic look. "Sorry about your sweater. Do you want me to put it in the wash?"

Cassie shook her head. Cashmere was special and needed to be treated as such. "No thanks. I'll take care of it."

Great. Now she'd have to hand wash the thing with lukewarm water and roll it up in a towel to dry so it wouldn't lose its shape. Served her right for wanting to show off by wearing something expensive.

Eileen dried her children's wet hands with a dishcloth and teased Sarah, "See what you have to look forward to?"

Sarah grinned and patted her bulging stomach. "The doctor says the baby can come any day."

"Hopefully it comes before Christmas Eve," Cassie's mother said, hanging up the phone. "Sarah is playing the role of Mary in the live nativity play at church and her baby is supposed to play the part of baby Jesus—if it arrives on time."

Of course, Sarah would get a leading role. Her popular, blond haired, blue eyed younger sister had won many local beauty queen pageants, was president of several different clubs, and had her own column in the town newspaper. Who wouldn't pick her?

"We don't know if the baby is a boy or a girl," Sarah told Cassie with a wink. "But I think Mom's hoping for a boy so it doesn't mess up her plans. She's in charge of the play."

Their mother laughed. "I'll be happy no matter what. Even if it is a girl, the baby can still play the part of baby Jesus. We all know who the baby is *supposed* to be."

"Your mother has a part for you, too," Eileen said, giving Cassie a broad grin.

Cassie's heart leapt in her chest and she looked at her mother with surprise. "You do?"

Her mother finally gave her that hug she'd been waiting for, and nodded. "We figured you might like to dress like one of the wise men and lead a camel."

"But..." Cassie frowned. "We don't have any camels."

"The llamas," her mother explained. "We're using the llamas as camels."

"Great," Cassie said, trying to hide her disappointment. She'd always dreamed of being on stage, just not with the llamas—who were sometimes known to spit. But she'd come home determined not to let anything ruin *this* Christmas, so she swallowed hard and told her mother, "I'd love to be in the play."

"Your brother is also going to be one of the wise men, along with his friend, Logan Whittaker," Cassie's mom continued. "You can stand next to him. Logan is quite a fine catch."

"I have a boyfriend," Cassie reminded her.

"He didn't come with you?" her mother asked, raising her brow.

"No. Not this time."

Her mother's mouth curved up into a grin and she wiggled her brows. "Like I said, Logan Whittaker is a fine catch!"

Cassie rolled her eyes. Her parents had married young, when they were just twenty. Cassie's older brother had also married when he was twenty. And in an inexplicable twist of fate, her younger sister had been twenty when she married too. But here *she* was, the awkward middle child, who was almost *thirty*, and she still hadn't married.

"Ned Doherty is also a fine catch," Cassie said defensively. "He's the best ad designer in the agency with a client list a mile long. He's handsome, he's got money, and he...he just helped me get a big promotion at work."

"Did you get your own office?" her mother asked.

Cassie shook her head. "No, but I got a raise, and oh! Just wait until you see what I bought Dad for Christmas! He's going to be so surprised."

Her mother hesitated. "You *bought* your father a present?"

"Of course!" Cassie said, hardly able to contain her excitement. "All my Christmas gifts for everyone are still out in the car but—" She broke off as she watched her mother exchange a worried glance with both Sarah and Eileen.

Then her mother frowned. "I told you that we were only going to exchange *handmade* gifts this year."

The disappointment in her mother's voice twisted her gut. Cassie stared at her and fought valiantly to keep her own disappointment at bay. "I thought you were *joking.* We—we always buy each other presents at Christmas."

"That's not true," her sister reminded her. "Remember the year Grandma knitted us those matching sweaters?"

"And the time Sarah gave us handmade llama ornaments?" Eileen added. "And your mother handed out pints of her award-winning raspberry jam?"

"Don't forget the wooden candlestick holders your brother carved last Christmas," Mom said with a nod. "And the planter boxes and wind chimes your father created for everyone."

"Well okay, yes, we've had *some* handmade gifts over the years," Cassie admitted, her face growing hot. "But—"

"We figured with your father and I going into semi-retirement, Sarah and Rick's baby on the way, and Tim and Eileen and their kids moving into a new house," her mother continued, cutting her off, "that it would be best to cut expenses this year. And certainly with your promotion, fancy clothes, and shiny new car, you don't need anything."

Cassie raised her brows. "You saw my new car? What do you think?"

"It must have cost a fortune," her mother said, pursing her lips. "Enough money to feed an entire community for a full year."

Cassie's shoulders slumped. Not the response she had been looking for.

"Can you get your money back?" her mother asked, her expression hopeful.

"For the car? No. The gifts, yes," Cassie told her. "I kept all the receipts and can take them back to the store after the holidays."

Her mother's face brightened and she clapped her hands. "Thank God! Crises averted. Now we can all have a festive, homespun Christmas just like we wanted."

"Except...I'm not *like* the rest of you," Cassie said, her throat painfully tight as she forced out the admission. "What will I do for gifts? I'm—I'm not very good at making crafts. I always mess up when I try to bake, and I don't know how to can jam, sew, spin wool, or build things with wood." Her stomach turned queasy as she envisioned everyone opening gifts on Christmas morning that would once again showcase their talents. "What can *I* do?"

Her mother smiled. "I'm sure you will come up with something."

"You might get some ideas if you come help me distribute gifts at the community center this afternoon," her hulking six-foot-four giant of a brother said with a welcoming grin. He and their father came in through the front door and carried a fresh-cut pine scented tree into the house. "Many of the items brought in for the poor are handmade."

"I don't know, Tim," Cassie said, shooting him a pleading look to try to help him understand her dilemma. "Even if I *do* find some ideas for handmade Christmas presents, I still have to *make* them."

"You still have plenty of time," her mother assured her.

Her father, who always believed in the positive, gave her a firm nod and agreed. "You've got a whole week."

CHAPTER 3

She had one week. But even if she had a whole year, Cassie didn't think she'd be able to come up with any gifts—not the kind that would impress her family.

The only artistic thing she'd ever done was draw pictures of the farm animals. She'd sketched rough images of the dog, chickens, goats, cow, horse, and especially the two llamas. As a teenager she'd curl up with a pencil and pad of paper in the field outside their paddock fascinated by their tall, woolly bodies with their long necks, big watchful eyes, and adorable banana shaped ears. However, Cassie was sure her young niece's crayon drawings were better than anything she could do now.

Maybe her brother was right. Maybe if she accompanied him to the Giving Tree at the community center, she'd find some ideas for gifts. Besides, it would be nice to spend alone time with Tim. They hardly ever talked one-on-one anymore. Not since he married Eileen and had kids. He was always too busy working. And she hated to bother him and take him away from "family time" unless it was for something important.

After she'd properly washed and dried her cashmere sweater, and changed into jeans and a holiday sweatshirt, Cassie jumped into the passenger seat of Tim's pickup with the six tins of homemade cookies Eileen and Sarah had baked for the Giving Tree event.

"Please don't drop them," Sarah pleaded.

"I won't," Cassie promised, stung by the reminder that at times, *yes*, she could be clumsy. Especially when she was put into an awkward situation, like the time their mother had assigned her the task of taking a pie to their neighbors', the Knapp family, who lived down the street.

She'd been fourteen and terribly in love with her friend Bridget Knapp's older brother, Pete. But when she turned into their driveway and saw him kissing the same girl who told everyone in their biology class that 'Cassie Sutherland smells like a llama's mama'—well, she'd dropped the pie, turned tail, and run home. Crying the entire way. She'd cried even more when she had to face her mother—who stood in the midst of an entire group of friends—and explain why the beautifully latticed, blue-ribbon blueberry pastry now lay face down in the dirt.

Cassie told them she'd been startled by a snake, which she figured wasn't too far from the truth, and promised her mother nothing like that would ever happen again. But a few years later, she'd also dropped a batch of her younger sister's warm, gooey, homemade chocolate fudge all over the dining room carpet when she caught her first glimpse of the infamous award-laden Christmas tree.

Sarah had called her clumsy, and unable to put into words what had caused her sudden bout of clumsiness, Cassie just let it go...and asked her sister to forgive her.

But those events had happened years ago and Cassie hadn't had cause for a clumsy moment since. She was an adult now, more confident in herself, not as easily shaken. Moving to New York and landing the job in marketing had boosted her self-esteem and turned her into a steady achiever, someone others valued and depended on to get the job done.

She wouldn't let her sister down.

Holding her head high, she picked up the cookie tins and followed her brother into the spacious room the community center used to host special events. Then after she deposited the cookies on the goody table, Tim introduced her to a couple of the other people in charge, and led her toward the piles of presents which lay on fifteen rectangle tables waiting to be wrapped.

"Each gift gets tagged with the number beside each family on the list," he said, handing her a clipboard.

Cassie's gaze fell to the bottom of the page. "Seventy-five names? There's so many of them. How long do you think this will take?"

"First we have to wrap the gifts," he informed her. "Then we'll break for lunch served by the hospitality team. At two o'clock the families will start showing up and we'll be here for at least another four hours handing out the gifts."

"But—" Her jaw dropped. When Tim suggested she come to get ideas for handmade gifts she had no idea it would be an all day event. "I take it you were all short on help today? Is that the real reason you asked me to come?"

Her brother grinned. "We need you."

She eyed him skeptically. "You do?"

"Of course we do, Cass. You know how hard it is to find volunteers?"

"Well...hopefully I'll find the ideas I'm looking for," she said, reconciling herself with the notion that her brother was *also* depending on her. She wouldn't let him down, either. Picking up a red and green holly berry tube of wrapping paper, she scanned the donated gifts on the table next to her.

There were handmade items all right. Someone had made a cabin block quilt with tiny blue flowers stitched around the edges. Beautiful, but not something she had the talent to make.

Someone else had made cinnamon scented candles which had her mouth-watering for some of her mother's iced cinnamon rolls. Yet candles were messy, took time, and she doubted she'd be able to use the stove to melt wax since her sister-in-law was hogging the kitchen with all her baking.

Her brother showed her the birdhouses, Noah's ark figurines, and ring toss toys he'd fashioned out of wood. However, the last time she tried to use a hammer, she hit her thumb so hard it turned her nail black and blue for over a month. No, she'd leave the carpentry to Tim.

An hour later, after all the gifts on her table had been wrapped, her shoulders slumped as she walked to the next table and let out a sigh. All the other gifts were either beyond her skill level to make or had been bought from the store.

"Tired from all the wrapping?" a friendly male voice asked.

"Just anxious to finish," she replied, glancing at the guy who reached across the table to borrow her scissors.

He wasn't as tall as her brother. Not many men were. But he did have attractive medium-brown hair long enough from behind to touch the back of his shirt collar. He also had a handsome face with blue eyes, a straight nose, and...a killer smile.

"I'm anxious to finish wrapping too," he said, cutting through his roll of Christmas paper and laying the scissors down again, "so we can hand out the gifts. I can't wait to see the parents' eyes light up when they see what we have for their children."

"Yeah," Cassie said, and hesitated. "That's exactly what I was thinking."

It wasn't, but she wasn't going to admit to the truth. Not to him. What would he think if he knew she'd only been thinking of herself? A pang of guilt weaseled its way into her gut, giving her a gnawing, uneasy queasy feeling which only increased ten-fold when the parents finally arrived. The long line of people who filed through the door looked like a lot more than the seventy-five families they'd prepared presents for.

She was right. As the parents came toward the decorated tree in the middle of the room to receive gifts for their children, Cassie matched their names with the tags attached to each gift. Her heart went out to each one of them as they told her how many kids they had, how they just weren't able to make ends meet with the income their jobs provided, and how these donated gifts would make a world of difference. Except there were still a handful of people left in line when the gifts were gone.

"I'm sure my name is on the list," a struggling single mother said earnestly. "Please check the clipboard again."

Cassie's stomach wrenched tighter as she did check it again, a second and then a third time. All the boxes had been checked off and the woman's name was not on it. Neither was the name of the other four people behind her who also said they'd signed up to receive gifts for their children.

What was she to do?

Cassie glanced over at the handsome man she'd met while wrapping gifts and saw him take out his wallet and hand three people a twenty dollar bill. Cassie didn't have any twenties to hand out. She had a wallet full of credit cards, but no cash. But...maybe she had something better.

"Wait here," she told the single mom. "I have to make a phone call, but I'll be right back."

Setting the clipboard aside, she took out her cell phone and walked outside. Her sister answered on the second ring and after Cassie explained the situation going on at the community center, she asked, "Can you drive my car over here? The keys are on the kitchen counter beside the flour canister."

Sarah gasped. "You want *me* to drive your car? I've never driven anything that fancy!"

"It drives the same as yours," Cassie assured her. "Just smoother."

Her sister arrived in ten minutes, with a huge grin on her face. "Think I can talk Rick into buying me one of these for Christmas?"

"Doubt it," Cassie teased, knowing her sister's husband couldn't afford it. "Not with a baby on the way. Besides, this year we're all having a *homespun Christmas.*"

"Well then maybe you'll let me borrow it again sometime," Sarah mused.

"You can drive my car back home," Cassie offered, "after we're done delivering gifts for the day."

Cassie went back into the room with all the people and waved her hand to get her brother's attention. He saw her, as did the handsome do-gooder she'd conversed with earlier, and she motioned them both to follow her outside. Since her family didn't want the store bought gifts, she might as well give them to someone who did.

"What are you doing?" Tim asked, as she opened the trunk.

Cassie took out an armload of gifts and nodded toward the bigger box, the TV she'd originally bought for their dad. "Give me a hand?"

Her brother met her gaze. "Are you sure?"

She swallowed hard as she took out the package containing the porcelain birdcage she'd intended to give her mother. "Yeah. It will save me the trouble of returning them."

"Oh, Cass," Sarah said, wide-eyed as she came around the back of the car to join them. "Just look at how God is using you to bless others!"

Cassie wasn't so sure about that, but pushed the conversation aside when the handsome, brown-haired guy asked, "What can I do to help?"

She smiled. "Tell me your name?"

"Sorry, we've been so busy I forgot to introduce myself. I'm Logan."

"Whittaker?"

He nodded and his mouth curved into another killer smile. Well, her mother had been right about one thing. He was one fine catch. For someone. Not her. Because she had a boyfriend. At least until she figured things out in her head.

"I'm Cassie. Nice to meet you, Logan. You can help by grabbing as many of the gifts as you can carry."

After two more trips back to her car, they handed out the wrapped toys Cassie had intended for her niece and nephew to the remaining families. Then as the single mom was about to leave, Cassie pointed her toward the large box her brother had brought in. "Could you also use a TV?"

To Cassie's surprise the woman burst into tears and blurted, "How did you know?"

"Know what?" Cassie asked, alarmed.

"Our TV broke a week ago," the woman explained, her voice choked.

"I—I didn't know," Cassie admitted.

"But God did," Tim said, beaming at her with what looked like...*pride?* "Everything happens for a reason."

"Like me not following Mom's directions and buying gifts anyway?" Cassie prompted.

"Even that," her brother assured her. "You did good, Cass."

Cassie was still reeling from the unexpected praise and questioning whether it was really deserved, when the single mom touched her arm.

"Thank you for your kindness," the woman said, no longer teary-eyed but smiling. "I'll never forget this."

Cassie was sure that *she* would never forget this either. A two week paycheck full of gifts had just walked out the door. With her okay. What was she crazy? Maybe the long drive from New York had addled her brain.

Either that or the way Logan Whittaker kept looking at her. With a jolt of awareness jumping up her spine, she drew in a quick breath as he drew closer.

"You saved the day," Logan said, his tone sinfully playful. "Will you be at church tomorrow with your family?"

"I—" Cassie's mouth fell open as she thought of the last time she'd attended church. It had been a while. Nearly two years. But it was the holiday season. Her family would expect her to go. "Yes, I—I'll be there."

"Good." He flashed her another killer smile. A smile that lit up his whole face and left her in a stunned stupor for several seconds. "I'll see you tomorrow then, at church."

Cassie's breath caught in her chest. Did she dare tell him she already had a boyfriend? Even if she was on the verge of telling Ned Dougherty to take a hike?

She smiled back at Logan, unwilling to break away from his mesmerizing gaze, and just nodded. "See you tomorrow."

After all, Logan hadn't actually asked her out on a date. *Not yet.*

CHAPTER 4

The seats in the church were nearly filled by the time Cassie and her family arrived on Sunday. Her sister had an unusual bout of third trimester morning sickness which had tied up the use of the family's only bathroom, and Tim and Eileen's kids had been too distracted by the new dusting of snow the farm had received overnight to get dressed. Cassie had been distracted as well, thinking of hot cocoa and sleigh rides, until she remembered who awaited her.

As she followed her family to a row of open chairs on the far left side of the worship center, she strained her neck to see past the heads of those already in attendance.

"Who are you looking for?" Sarah whispered.

Cassie's gaze continued to sweep the room. "A—a friend."

"Bridget Knapp probably won't be here today. Her son is in the hospital recovering from appendicitis."

"Oh no, right before Christmas?" Cassie imagined how sad it must be for Bridget and her seven-year-old son, Isaac, to be trapped within the hospital's sterile white walls, unable to participate in any fun holiday activities. "I should go visit them."

"We can go together," Sarah offered. "After church I'm delivering gifts to the kids in the pediatric ward."

"What kind of gifts?"

"The toy lambs that Mom and I made from the llama wool."

Cassie nodded. Yes, during their last three phone calls, she'd listened to her mother go on and on about the stuffed animals she and Sarah had sewn together.

"Yes, I'll go with you," Cassie said, glancing around the room once again.

Sarah laughed. "But Bridget isn't the one you were looking for?"

When Cassie didn't answer, her sister teased, "Logan Whittaker seemed very impressed with you yesterday over at the community center."

Heat flooded Cassie's cheeks as she confessed, "He asked if I would be here today and I said...yes."

Sarah frowned. "Well, why wouldn't you be?"

"I haven't attended church in a long while," Cassie said, dropping her voice so their mother wouldn't hear. "Now I fear I'm here for the wrong reasons."

Sarah nudged her with her shoulder and smiled. "Not if it's all part of God's plan."

"You think God is using Logan to bring me back to church?"

Sarah's smile widened. "I think God will use whatever it takes to bring his loved ones back into a relationship with him."

Cassie shook her head and noticed the music had begun. As everyone stood to sing, a chorus of voices rose in unison to mouth the lyrics to the popular Christmas hymn, *"Joy To The World."* Except one robust voice, a clear male tenor, sang out louder and more enthusiastically than all the rest. In all her years of attending church, she'd never heard anyone sing with such *passion* and she wondered who it could be.

First she looked at the praise team up on the stage who held microphones and were in charge of leading the music portion of the service. There were a few new faces since she'd been here last, but as she studied the movement of their mouths she realized the special voice that had caught her attention had not come from any of them.

She searched the lips of the people standing in the front of the church, then those who stood to the far right. The voice certainly hadn't come from anyone on the left side near her. Then as she continued to listen, she realized the voice came from the *back* of the room. Without making it too obvious, she turned her head and cast a quick glance in that direction...and found him.

There was no mistake. The owner of the engaging, soulful voice stood in the very back row with his hands uplifted, not high enough to draw attention to himself, but with his palms face up before him. His eyes too, were cast upward, as if he were singing directly to God himself. Cassie supposed that's how it should be, but for many, the passion had fallen prey to routine.

There were over three hundred people in the room, a third more than normal due to the holiday which always brought in strays. *Like her.* But only one who sang with his whole heart.

Logan Whittaker.

He was sandwiched between a man and a woman, and as Cassie continued to cast sneak peeks back at him, she watched the woman's expression to see if her relationship with Logan went beyond friendship.

"He's single," her sister confided, after the service ended. "Every available woman under thirty has tried to catch his attention, but ever since his parents and younger brother were killed in a car accident fifteen months ago, he devotes most of his free time helping the church."

"In other words, he's *not* looking for a relationship," Cassie mused.

"Oh, I don't know about that," Sarah said, a note of teasing reentering her voice. "There's one woman who may have turned his head. He's coming straight toward you."

"Sarah, you know I have a boyfriend!"

Her sister waddled her large pregnant belly into the aisle to follow the departing crowd, and shot her a sideways look over her shoulder. "Cass, if you and Ned were serious about each other, he would have come home with you for Christmas."

Cassie's mouth fell open but she failed to say anything in response...because what Sarah said was true. She knew it, her sister knew it, and from the comments she'd received upon her arrival it was a good assumption that the rest of her family knew it too.

"Hi Cassie."

She stiffened as Logan Whittaker approached. He wasn't her type, not by a long shot. In fact, the two of them were polar opposites when it came to showing their emotions. His faith was real, unencumbered by restraints or worries about how he might be perceived. While she...well, she did care an awful lot about what others thought of her. That's why she hadn't brought Ned home. She'd been worried he wouldn't make her look good. No wonder her prayers went unanswered. She was only focused on herself.

"A bunch of us are going into the woods to pick greens for the wreath making party tonight," Logan said, following her through the wide double doors and down the church steps. "Would you like to join us?"

Oh! Why did he have to be so nice? And handsome? *And single?* It was such a shame to have to turn him down.

"I'm sorry, Logan, but I promised my sister I'd help her hand out toy lambs at the hospital."

"What about the rest of the week?" he asked, giving her a heartwarming look surely meant to melt her resolve. "Do you have plans?"

"I'm afraid I'm going to be busy making crafts. Or trying to. You see I messed up. I didn't believe my mother was serious when she told me my family was only exchanging handmade gifts this Christmas. I *bought* gifts—the gifts I gave away last night at the community center. Now I only have a few days to come up with new *handmade* gifts for my family and I have no idea what to make."

Logan grinned. "I bet I can help with that. We're having a craft day tomorrow at my place, Whittaker's Garden Shop. We'll have all the supplies you need to make pinecone wreaths and birdseed ornaments."

"My mother loves birds," Cassie said, raising her brows. "I'm sure she'd like a birdseed ornament to hang outside in the tree for them."

Logan nodded. "She's always feeding them every time I'm around."

"You've been to my house?"

"Many times," Logan said with another grin. "Your mother seems to think I'll starve if I have to cook for myself. She's always inviting me to dinner or sending me home from church with a mound of cookies."

"Yeah, that's her," Cassie agreed. "Always concerned about helping everyone in the neighborhood."

"Seems like you take after her."

"No, I—I'm not like my mother at all."

"Why is that?" He gave her a curious look, then when she hesitated he teased, "You don't like birds?"

Cassie laughed. "No, I—well, for one thing, I can't bake cookies without burning them."

Logan shrugged. "No one's perfect."

"Especially not me," she confided. "Just wait until you see me try to make crafts."

"I'll look forward to it," he promised. "Come by my shop tomorrow around noon?"

Cassie hummed the hymn *"Joy To The World"* all the way to the hospital wondering if maybe there was a chance she and Logan weren't so different after all. She didn't devote herself to helping others like he presumed, but she didn't mind helping her sister hand out the stuffed toy lambs to the children stuck in the hospital wing. Especially when she got to the room her friend Bridget's son was in.

"Cassie, I've missed you!" Bridget said, flinging her arms around her for a big hug. "How long are you in town?"

"Just until after Christmas." She sat on the edge of Isaac's bed. "How are you feeling?"

"Okay." The seven-year-old took the lamb she handed him and asked, "Is this made from Marshmallow's wool?"

"Isaac loves the llamas on your family's farm," Bridget explained. "Marshmallow is his favorite."

Cassie ran her hand over the soft white fiber and said, "It looks like Marshmallow's wool, doesn't it? He's my favorite too. I used to draw pictures of him all the time."

"Will you draw me one?" Isaac asked, sitting up straighter in the bed. "Please?"

She hadn't drawn a llama in a long time, but she didn't think he'd mind if she didn't get it exactly right. "Bridget, do you think the nurse can give me a sheet of paper?"

Her friend left the room and returned a moment later with an entire notepad. "The other kids asked what you are doing and want to know if you'll draw a llama for them too."

Cassie turned her head to see other children, dressed in their tiny hospital gowns, peering at her expectantly through the doorways of their rooms. How could she turn down such a hopeful array of sweet, innocent faces?

"Of course I will, if they want me to," she said with a nod.

Cassie took the newly sharpened pencil and pad of paper from Bridget's hands and stared at the blank page before her wondering how to start. But once she sketched the first few lines, her imagination swept her away with an exhilaration she hadn't felt in a very long time, and her fingers *raced* to capture the images in her head, each picture filled with more and more vivid detail.

She drew llamas, goats, dogs, horses, chickens...all the animals living at her family's farm. Then on later drafts, she added people into the background with houses, trees, barns, fences, and fields of snow. She'd always had a weakness for drawing landscapes behind her focal subjects. The background setting always seemed to make the llamas look so real. *Complete.*

Her heart beat rapidly in her chest and even after she'd finished the last picture she held the pencil tight, almost as if she couldn't let go. Glancing at the clock above the nurses' station in the hall, Cassie realized that instead of an hour, she'd spent the entire afternoon with the children, visiting each room and letting them watch her work to bring the animals to life.

"I'm sorry, I didn't realize the time," Cassie apologized when she looked up to see her sister beside her. "I didn't mean to keep you from getting back home to your husband."

"Rick will understand," Sarah said, smiling. "Besides, I get a kick out of seeing you draw again. I always thought you had real talent."

"Not enough to win awards," Cassie reminded her.

"You don't need awards," Sarah said, nodding toward the children's smiling faces as they walked down the hall toward the elevator. "You make people happy."

"Seeing the excitement on the kids' faces made me happy too," Cassie admitted.

"Maybe you could draw pictures for everyone this Christmas?" Sarah suggested.

She'd already done that, years ago, and her drawings hadn't garnered the appreciation she'd hoped for. They'd been overshadowed by Tim's wood carved ducks and Sarah's cute little hand sewn mice.

"No," Cassie said, thinking of the sure-to-please birdseed ornament she'd make for her mother at Whittaker's Garden Shop. "I have a different plan in mind."

CHAPTER 5

For some reason, Cassie had thought she'd have Logan's undivided attention when she arrived at Whittaker's Garden shop the next day. Maybe it was because of the way he'd looked at her, a look that made her pulse race and made her brain turn into unintelligible mush. Yeah, that must have been it. Because now, as she glanced about the bustling shop filled with customers and festive greenery waiting to be shipped, it was perfectly understandable why he'd hired someone else to lead the craft session he'd mentioned.

Of course, Cassie reminded herself, she wasn't here for *him*. She was here to make crafts for her family. And it was high time she got started.

Sitting down at one of the wooden picnic tables set in the back of the shop beside a stand of pine scented garland and flocked Christmas trees, she took the large pinecone the female instructor gave her and prepared to create the best birdseed ornament her mother had ever seen.

First Cassie and the other participants tied a thin red ribbon loop to the top of the pinecone so that it could hang from a tree. Next the instructor distributed butter knives and placed a jar of peanut butter on each table. Then they were told to spread the peanut butter over the pinecone and dip them in the bag of birdseed, also on each table.

That was it?

Cassie held hers up and frowned. It didn't look like much. In fact, she could almost remember making one of these when she was in kindergarten. Glancing around at the other tables, she realized a lot of the other crafters looked like they *were* in kindergarten. And worse, their ornaments appeared to have turned out a whole lot nicer than her own. While theirs were fully coated with beautiful golden round seeds, hers had gaps where peanut butter leaked through.

"Here's a wet cloth for your hands," the instructor said, giving her a smile.

Cassie glanced down at her fingers and gasped when she discovered she also had peanut butter on her shirt, her jeans, and even a couple globs stuck to the ends of her hair!

"Would you like to make another one?" the instructor asked.

"No," Cassie said, glancing around the shop to make sure Logan *hadn't* seen her. "I think I'm done with this one. Isn't there another craft?"

The woman nodded. "Yes, we're decorating wreaths next."

Cassie perked up. She could decorate. She loved decorating the tree each Christmas and putting up strings of lights, and tying ribbons and shiny colorful balls onto fence posts and railings around the farm. The instructor just didn't tell her they'd have to *make* the wreaths first.

She took a sprig of greens and wrapped the end with thin wire. But when she went to attach it to the metal hoop, the sprig fell apart. Even after she managed to affix some of the greenery, her sparse, misshapen wreath came out looking more like something the llamas had chewed on rather than a beautiful Christmas decoration.

Her last hope rested in the stenciling of 3-inch sliced wood rounds. Holes had been pre-drilled near the top of the round so tying a ribbon on was easy. It was the stenciling that got messy. Cassie pressed her stencil of a reindeer on the flat side of the round with one hand and took a thin brush and coated the opening with brown paint. When she removed the stencil she was supposed to have the perfect image of a reindeer, right?

Cassie held up the wood round ornament and frowned. Her reindeer was...well, it didn't look anything like a reindeer, that's for sure. Maybe she could repaint the whole thing brown, dab on two eyes, and tell her mother it was an owl?

Someone came up beside her and asked, "How's it coming?"

Logan.

Cassie jumped in her seat, afraid to look at him. "Not good. I told you I wasn't very crafty."

"You could always offer to buy an ornament off someone else," he suggested, with a wink.

"Nope. No buying," Cassie reminded him. "I need gifts that are handmade, by *me*."

"Aaaah, an *honest* crafter. Maybe a steaming cup of spiced hot apple cider might help you come up with some ideas?"

"Logan, that's it! The perfect gift for my sister-in-law, Eileen! She's always doing something in the kitchen and she'd love it if I put together homemade satchels of spiced apple cider mix. All I'd have to do is combine all the ingredients. I wouldn't even have to cook. Or worry that I might burn it."

"It's hard to burn a dry mix," Logan agreed.

Cassie laughed and caught his lingering gaze. "That's why it's perfect."

"What about a cup of hot apple cider for you?" he pressed. "We have a big pot on the portable stove by the front counter."

"Do you have cinnamon stirring sticks?" she teased.

"Of *course*," he said, feigning offense, and the corners of his mouth lifted into a grin. "What guy would offer a gal spiced hot apple cider *without* cinnamon stirring sticks?"

Cassie laughed again, enjoying the banter, the rich sound of his voice, the sparkle in his eyes when they locked gazes. "What guy, indeed?"

Early the next morning Cassie rose early before anyone else in her family was awake, and tiptoed down to the kitchen hoping no one would discover what she was up to. She only had five days left before Christmas but at least she'd come up with a gift idea for her sister-in-law. She'd found the recipe on the internet, a spiced hot apple cider mix that had garnered rave reviews.

After taking several small glass jars from the spice cabinet, Cassie combined measured amounts of dried cloves, allspice berries, peppercorns, orange peel, cardamom, anise, and candied ginger into a bowl with a couple broken cinnamon sticks. Then she spooned the mixture into a square of white cheesecloth she'd found in the pantry and tied the bundle closed with a red ribbon she'd found in her mother's sewing box the night before.

Cassie raised the spiced sachet to her nose and breathed in the flavorful scent, then took a final look and realized the gift needed a name tag. Retrieving a pencil and a piece of paper from the center island drawer, Cassie sketched a picture of a steaming kettle on a stove top, and wrote the words, 'Eileen's Kitchen.'

Footsteps padded down the stairs and Cassie scrambled to clean the counter and put everything back in place.

"You're up mighty early," her father said, doing a double take when he spotted her.

"Just trying to make some 'homespun' Christmas gifts," Cassie told him.

Her sleepy-eyed father nodded. "I'm having trouble coming up with some of them myself."

"You are?"

"Your mother thinks everyone has the same amount of free time that she has," he said, and then chuckled. "But with all the chores, and helping your brother build a wood stable backdrop for the nativity play at church, there's not much time for me to make gifts."

"So I'm not the only one? But you always have great ideas," Cassie confided. "How about I help you feed the animals and you help me do a little brainstorming?"

"I've always thought *you* had the better imagination," her father said, giving her a hug. "But I *would* appreciate your help."

Cassie hadn't helped with the farm chores in a long while. She'd forgotten how much time it could take to scoop out the grain for the feed buckets, and break the ice that had formed overnight in the water troughs and refill them with warm water so the animals would have something to drink. By the time she and her father had finished, Amber had come into the barn to join them.

"Aunt Cass, can you draw me a llama?" the little girl asked, holding out a coloring book and a box of crayons. "Aunt Sarah said you drew llamas for the kids in the hospital."

"Is that so?" Cassie's father said, raising his brows.

Cassie smiled. "I couldn't say no."

Sitting down on a hay bale, she pulled her niece onto her lap so they could look at the coloring book together. "Looks like you've already colored a lot of animals in your book."

Amber bobbed her head. "Yeah, Grandma says I'm going to grow up to be an artist."

Cassie had once had the same dream for herself. Except she didn't think drawing could bring in enough income to pay the bills. She pointed to a scribbled drawing of a four-legged figure in purple crayon. "Is that a llama?"

"No," Amber corrected, looking up at her. "It's a pony. The one I'm getting for Christmas."

Cassie gasped. "How do you know you're getting a pony?"

"I pray for a pony every night," Amber said, her tone matter-of-fact. "And God answers people's prayers."

Cassie met her father's gaze. "Does Tim know about this?"

"He does," he assured her with an exasperated grin.

"My brother says I won't get one because a pony isn't handmade," Amber continued. "But I told him it is too handmade because God makes ponies."

"She has a point," Cassie's father said, his face beaming.

No doubt her niece would get a pony for Christmas, and all other gifts, including the one *she* came up with to give to her, would be pushed to the wayside.

"What is your pony's name?" Cassie asked, glancing back at the crayon drawing.

Amber wiggled on her lap. "I don't know."

"Well, what is he doing?" Cassie took a crayon from her box and sketched a few lines into the background. "It looks like he's in a barn. Who are his friends at the barn?"

The little girl giggled. "A llama?"

"Yes," Cassie agreed. "If there was a pony at this barn, he'd be friends with a llama. How about a goat. Can a goat be his friend too? And the dog?"

Amber shook her head. "Not the dog. He barks too much."

"Then maybe we should put earmuffs on the pony," Cassie said, adding a few more sketches on her niece's drawing. "So he can sleep at night without hearing the dog."

"That's silly," Amber said, and laughed.

"No," Cassie said, her thoughts spinning. "What is silly is that the dog doesn't *really* bark but croaks like a bullfrog."

"I told you that you had a better imagination than me," Cassie's father teased.

"Not sure what I can do with it, though," she admitted.

Her father frowned and nodded toward the coloring book. "You can keep doing what you're already doing."

Cassie glanced down at the embellishments she'd made to the central character. "Create children's books? You mean for Christmas gifts?"

Her father gave her a broad grin. "Sounds like an idea to me."

Excited by the prospect of creating children's books for Amber, Timmy Jr., and Sarah's unborn baby, Cassie found some paper in her father's study, set herself up by the warm, crackling fireplace in the living room, and sketched images for the children the rest of the day.

Her first goal was to pencil out some rough ideas. Later, if she scanned the pages into the computer and added embellishments via the illustrator tablet she used to create marketing ads, she could make it look even more professional. And include her niece and nephew's names on the front.

Now if only she could come up with gifts for her brother, sister, and parents. But she wouldn't worry about that just yet. She'd made good progress so far and she still had four more days.

The smell of turkey drifted in from the kitchen. Her mother had mentioned earlier that they might have a guest over for dinner and had set to work cooking the bird with all the fixings. Cassie heard pots and cooking utensils rattling around the kitchen all afternoon but just after she finished the final page she was working on, there was the sound of a door opening, then a murmur of voices.

"*Cassie!*" Sarah hissed, her expression tense as she ran into the room.

Cassie set her artwork aside and sat up straight. "What is it?" Glancing at her sister's belly, she asked, "Are you having the baby?"

"*No,*" Sarah said with a scowl. "Your *boyfriend* is here!"

"*Ned?* He's *here?*"

Sarah nodded her head vigorously. "Yes. And so is *Logan!*"

CHAPTER 6

Cassie followed her sister into the dining room where everyone else in her family—and Logan Whittaker—had already gathered for dinner.

Her mother gave her a pensive look, pursed her lips, then announced, "It seems we have a surprise visitor."

Cassie's gaze shot toward the archway between the kitchen and dining room where Ned Doherty, dressed meticulously in a Christian Dior three piece navy blue suit, waited to be introduced. *What was he doing here?*

Logan looked up from the table where he sat between her father and brother, and from his curious expression, Cassie imagined he must be thinking the same thing. She also couldn't help notice how different the two men were. In stark contrast to Ned, Logan wore a green flannel over a white t-shirt and faded jeans...and looked the better for it. His appearance exemplified comfort, simplicity, peace. A longing for peace in her own life pulled at Cassie's heartstrings. All too often lately she'd found her stomach tied up in a fretful knot. Never more so than *now.*

Avoiding Logan's gaze, she turned and gave her mom a weak smile. Then she took Ned's arm and pulled him back around the corner into the empty kitchen.

"Why didn't you tell me you were coming?" she whispered.

Ned placed a quick kiss on her cheek. "Thought I'd surprise you. I had a couple days free before I take off on the snowboarding trip with Skip and Joey and I felt bad about not being able to come meet your family. Then I thought to myself, why not do both?"

Cassie suppressed an inward groan. *Yes, why not, indeed?*

She swallowed hard as her heart rate tripled and her palms began to sweat. "This isn't a good time."

"Looks like the perfect time to me," Ned said, oblivious to her discomfort, and laughed. "I'm just in time for dinner."

Cassie hesitated. "I'm—I'm not sure if my mother fixed enough food."

"Nonsense! It looks like she fixed a feast."

She searched her brain for a plausible excuse, one that would offer a quick escape, away from everyone else's scrutinizing gaze. "But there are a lot of people in our family. Maybe we should go out to eat."

"I'm sure there's room for one more," Ned insisted. "In fact, I already saw your mother add one more plate to the table."

Frowning, he stepped back and held her at arm's length, his gaze perusing her from head to toe. Then the corners of his mouth twisted into a smirk and he let out another laugh.

"What's so funny?" Cassie demanded.

Ned grinned. "You're wearing *flannel!*"

Her gaze dipped down toward her blue plaid shirt. "Most everyone in my family wears flannel this time of year. It's warm, soft, and perfect for helping out with the chores around the farm."

Ned's eyes widened. "They make you do chores?"

"I volunteered. But yes, as long as I'm here, I'm expected to help pitch in."

"If I were you," Ned said with another smirk, "I would have stayed at the nearest Sheraton."

Cassie stared at the snooty expression on his face, and said softly, "You're not me."

Unable to avoid the inevitable, Cassie drew in a deep breath and introduced Ned to her family one by one. But when she got to Logan, she stopped, and after a moment's pause, explained to Ned, "He's a family friend."

"Not *too* friendly, I hope," Ned warned, giving Logan an ominous look.

Cassie froze, unable to breathe, as Logan, seemingly unaffected by the threat, smiled and replied, "Well, we are kind of tight-knit around here. Especially around the holidays."

Ned slid his arm around Cassie's shoulders and pulled her tight to his side. "In my experience, too much time around family leads to nothing but trouble."

"*Trouble!*" her mother exclaimed. "It seems to me the opposite is true. It's when one *doesn't* spend enough time with family that they lose their way and find themselves in a heap of trouble."

Cassie pulled away from Ned and took a seat before her knees hit the floor. She'd had reservations about him meeting her family, but had never imagined it would play out like this.

"Ned's been very helpful," she said, hoping to move the conversation along as he sat down beside her. "He's the one who helped me get the job at the advertising agency in New York."

"I always thought Cassie should draw for a living," her mother said, glaring at him.

What? Cassie cut her mother a sharp glance. Her mom had never mentioned anything like that before.

"She *does* draw," Ned said, defending her. "Her logos on the computer are top notch."

"I meant draw by hand," her mother corrected. "That way she could stay here at home, attend church on a regular basis—"

Who told her mother she hadn't been attending church?

"—and marry a good Christian man," her mother finished.

Cassie gasped and shot a look at Logan, who met her gaze and looked just as surprised as she was. Is *that* why her mother had invited him to dinner? To play matchmaker and fix them up as a couple?

"*Mom!*" Cassie pleaded. "I'm *good* at creating marketing ads."

Her mother shook her head. "*I* certainly wouldn't want to sit cooped up in some cubicle at the computer all day."

No, her mother wouldn't. But she wasn't like her mother. She'd found *her* success in a different way. It wasn't a dream job, but it gained her respect.

"She makes good money," Ned assured her family.

"Money isn't everything," her mother insisted. "Isn't that right, John?"

"That's right," her father agreed. "Which is why we need to thank God for our blessings."

As the others around the table bowed their heads and listened to her father pray, Cassie fervently sent up a silent prayer of her own.

Dear God, I know I haven't talked to you much lately, but if you're there, I'm sorry. And I could really use your help right now. Please don't let my mother embarrass me further. Or Ned. Or Logan.

Her face flushed hot as she cast a quick glance toward their hometown dinner guest wondering what *he* thought of all this. Now that Logan knew she had a boyfriend, would he ever look at her the same way again?

If only she had broken off her relationship with Ned *before* she came back home for the holidays. Too late now. She'd have to suffer the consequences. Which seemed to include disappointing her mother once again.

Why wasn't anything she ever did good enough?

After dinner Ned didn't need much encouraging to make his way out the door.

"Now I know why you didn't want me to meet them," he joked, taking his car keys from his pocket.

Cassie nodded. "I'm sorry."

"No need to apologize to me," Ned told her. "I understand."

Yes, he did. Despite his worst faults, he understood. That's why she'd stayed with him as long as she had.

"I'll see you back in New York?" Ned asked, opening the door to his Audi Coupe.

Cassie hesitated. If she didn't intend to continue their relationship, then she needed to tell him now. She hadn't wanted to ruin his Christmas, but she couldn't lay her true feelings aside any longer. Without a doubt, she now knew he was *not* the man for her. Not because her mother thought so, but because she couldn't picture herself marrying someone who could be so haughty and talk back to her family the way he had.

"Ned, I—we need to talk."

"Of course," he said, jumping into the driver's seat and starting the engine. "As soon as I get back from my snowboarding trip. I'll see you New Year's Eve."

"But—"

Too late. Ned had already closed the door.

With a ragged sigh, Cassie reentered the house and hoped to slip into her room unnoticed but unfortunately her mother came chasing after her like a cat on a field mouse.

"Did he leave?" her mother demanded.

Cassie nodded, lowering her gaze.

"I didn't mean to embarrass you, honey," her mother soothed. "I just want what's best for you."

"How do you know what's best for me?" Cassie asked, her voice coming out as a high-pitched squeak. "You don't even *know* me."

"What do you mean? I'm your mother. Of *course* I know you."

Cassie gulped back a sob, not wanting to resort to tears. Not in front of her. "You might not approve of Ned, but you don't know how hard I've worked to get that job in New York. Yes, it took me away from the family farm, but I've proven I can be successful there. Don't you *want* me to be a success?"

"I want you to be *happy*," her mother said quietly. "God gave you a passion to draw and it breaks my heart that you aren't making better use of the talent he gave you."

Talent? What talent? There were a half million artists on the east coast alone who could probably draw better than her.

"No one wants to buy my drawings, Mom." The admission constricted her chest and hurt her lungs, making it hard to breathe.

"How do you know?" her mother challenged. "Have you ever really given it a fair shot?"

"In high school—"

"I'm not talking about high school," her mother said, cutting her off. "After college, after taking all those art classes, did you ever go all-in and give a hundred percent effort into selling your sketches?"

Not exactly. She'd gone straight for the higher paying career. Avoiding her mother's gaze, she turned away and asked, "Did Logan leave?"

Her mother gave her a compassionate look and nodded. "He slipped out the back while you and Ned were saying goodbye."

"Even if Ned and I weren't together anymore, it wouldn't change the fact that Logan isn't interested in a relationship, Mom," Cassie said, swallowing what was left of her pride. "Sarah said so. And now he never will be—not with me."

Her mother shook her head. "Don't be too sure about that. *'With God all things are possible.'*"

Was it possible her mother could ever just love her for who she was instead of always wishing she were something more?

CHAPTER 7

Two days later, Cassie spent the morning working on the children's book she'd scanned into the computer in her father's den. She'd been skeptical at first, wondering how it would look when it was done. But as she smoothed out the rough edges with the different brushes available on Photoshop her confidence grew. It wasn't perfect, but as her imagination took flight, she found the pictures and words made her laugh. Hopefully, the children would find it just as funny.

Glancing at the clock, she bit her lip and closed down the program. She'd promised her mother she'd meet her at the church at ten o'clock for the live nativity play practice. Tim, Eileen, her mother, and the kids had left early to set up props, and Sarah and Rick had taken their own car in case she went into labor. Cassie's mother was still optimistic that they would have a real baby to play the part of Jesus on Christmas Eve, but Amber was prepared to let them use her doll if the need arose.

While Cassie wished she could stay home to work on her homespun Christmas gifts, she *had* promised she'd take part in the play and after the dinner fiasco, she didn't want her mother's disappointment in her to deepen any further.

Scooping up her keys she donned a coat, scarf, gloves, hat, and pulled on her boots to go out the door. Once outside, she glanced up wondering if the sun would ever come out. The sky had remained a constant cloudy grey ever since she arrived. The chill in the air hadn't lessened either.

Good thing her shiny new Mercedes Sedan had good heat. She turned the dial to full blast as soon as she started the engine. She also turned on the radio and the song *"There's No Place Like Home for the Holidays"* rang out loud and clear. Not sure if she shared that sediment at the moment, she changed the channel and hummed along to upbeat tinkling tune of *"Sleigh Ride."*

Cassie loved whisking across glistening new fallen snow in a horse drawn sleigh. Her father used to have one when she was little but the metal strips had broken off the wood runners a few years back and he'd been unable to replace them. She hadn't been on a sleigh ride since.

Twenty minutes later she approached the Van Sant one-lane covered bridge. Historically known as one of the county's "kissing bridges," for the privacy the structure offered, the Van Sant seemed to fit right in with the holidays with its distinctive cranberry red paint, white side trim, and crisscrossed wooden trusses.

She slowed her car, to make sure no one was coming from the other direction before she entered and when she came out the other side, she spotted a lone figure standing by the stone curb staring out at the river.

Bridget?

Pulling her car into park along the side of the road, Cassie jumped out to join her friend. Except Bridget didn't seem to be in the mood for company. She barely turned to acknowledge her and Cassie could clearly see she was distraught.

"What's wrong?" Cassie asked with alarm. "Is Isaac okay?"

"He's fine," Bridget assured her. "The hospital released him last night. He's home sleeping. My mom is watching over him so I could take a break. I just had to...get out of there for a little while. I didn't want Isaac to see my tears. And this place...always seems so peaceful."

Cassie nodded. "We used to come here to tell each other our secrets. Do you remember?"

Bridget spun around and gave her a fierce hug. "Yes, I remember."

"So..." Cassie said, giving her friend a direct look when she released her. "Are you going to tell me what's troubling you?"

Bridget sniffed, wiped her eyes, and gushed, "I just got the hospital bill for Isaac's surgery. It's far more than I can ever pay."

"Don't you have health insurance?"

Bridget shook her head. "When Michael died he left behind a lot of debt. I had to cancel our insurance, cancel the lease on the place we were renting, and move in with my parents."

Cassie's heart wrenched as she recalled how Bridget's husband had been crushed by a piece of heavy machinery in a factory accident three years before. Isaac was only four years old at the time, and chances are the young boy would never remember him.

"I know you hate the idea of being indebted to them," she said, softly, "but can't your parents help cover the bill?"

"They don't have the money either," Bridget said, her voice shrill.

"What about a payment plan?"

Bridget sniffed again and more tears streamed down her cheeks. "We still wouldn't be able to afford it."

Dear God, what will she do? Is there no hope?

Cassie looked past her friend, the very best friend she'd ever had—mainly because they *both* had parents who didn't understand them, and her gaze fell on her metallic blue Mercedes Sedan. How could she possibly walk over and get into a car like that when Bridget stood here in such desperate need?

Her guilt followed her all the way to the church where as one of the "wise men" she stood alongside Logan and Tim during practice for the live Nativity play. And since the llamas wouldn't arrive to act as camels until the real performance, her mother had stuck them with the task of holding onto the ropes that raised several angels and the illuminating Christmas star up into the air.

"I see you survived dinner the other night," Logan teased, giving her a sideways glance. "For a minute there, I wasn't sure you were going to make it. I'm sorry your mother came down hard on you."

Cassie grimaced. "My mother is never pleased. The only reason I left the farm and went to New York was so I could get a good job and make her proud of me. Obviously, that didn't work."

"Have you ever told her how you feel?"

Cassie shook her head.

Logan took a step closer and asked, "Why not?"

"I'm not sure it would do any good."

"Expressing how you really feel is *always* good."

"Easy for *you*," she countered.

Logan laughed. "What do you mean by that?"

"I see how you are when you sing in church," she accused. "You sing your heart out."

"You had your eye on me?" he teased, lifting a brow.

Heat flooded over her as she met his gaze. "When I heard you singing above everyone else...yes, I—I had to look."

"Careful, Cassie," he warned, his tone lighthearted and playful. "You don't want to get me in trouble with your boyfriend."

"I'm so sorry, Logan. I—I didn't know he was going to show up."

"Well, I guess it's a good thing he did," Logan said with a grin, "before I embarrassed myself by asking you out."

Logan wanted to ask her out? On a date?

Cassie sucked in her breath, her heart hammering as he winked at her and moved to the other side of the stage. She would have really liked that date...*very much.*

After the nativity play practice, Logan disappeared out the side door with everyone else, leaving Cassie alone with her mother.

"Mom, do you think we can go out for lunch, just the two of us, so we can talk?" she ventured.

"Sorry, Cassie," her mother said, gathering up her purse. "I've got to bring Mrs. Woodward some of my homemade chicken noodle soup. She hasn't been feeling well, poor thing, right before the holidays too. And I have to deliver a few jars of raspberry jam to the crippled elderly couple up the street. Then at two o'clock I have a group of women from church coming over to the farm to pick up their orders of hand-dyed wool. I've been teaching them how to spin so we can knit scarves for the homeless and they all agree that the wool from *our* llamas makes a superior yarn."

"Okay," Cassie said, pulling on her coat. "Another time then."

Except she wasn't sure when 'another time' would ever come. Her mother was always serving, serving, serving. Cassie knew it was good to help others in need. Isn't that what God *wanted* them to do?

But her mother was so busy serving God and other people, she didn't have enough time to blink twice in *her* direction...unless she won a multitude of trophies and award ribbons like her brother and sister. Maybe that was the reason Cassie had always felt she needed to do something significant to win her attention.

Maybe that was also the real reason she'd drifted away from God.

All her thoughts about serving others brought Cassie up short when she stepped outside and took another look at her superior, salary-sucking new car. Her mother might not have time for her. But Bridget always had. How could she not do something to help her?

Driving straight toward Franklin's Car Auction, she steeled her resolve and handed the owner, her keys. "I'd like to trade in my car for another one," she told him.

"I'm not sure I have any cars that would suit you," B.J. said, walking around to admire her vehicle.

Cassie scanned the lot and pointed to the far corner. "How about *that* one?"

"Are you pulling my leg?" B.J. scoffed. "You want to trade a new Mercedes Sedan in for a ten-year-old Jeep Grand Cherokee?"

"Does it run?"

"Of course it runs," he said, scratching his chin. "But it has a hundred-and-seventy-five miles on it."

"I'll take it," Cassie told him. "But I'll need you to make up the difference in value in cash."

"Pay *you?* You expect me to part with that kind of money right before Christmas? You've got to be kidding."

"I'm not. Bridget Knapp's son was in the hospital for appendicitis and I'd like to help her out by paying the bill."

B.J. reached a hand up to scratch his chin again. "I heard about Isaac from his grandfather. He and I play chess together each week. Sure is a shame, the misfortune that family has had."

"And this is how we can help them," Cassie encouraged. "Don't you think you could resell the Sedan for what it's worth?"

"Of course, I could," B.J. boasted. "I'm the best auctioneer in the business."

"Well?" she prompted.

He looked her straight in the eye, took a deep breath, held it a moment, then exhaled. "I'm going to have to ask you a favor in return. You see, I also heard you drew a bunch of pictures for the kids in the hospital and I'd like you to draw a picture for me to give my wife for Christmas. She lost her mother not too long ago and I'm sure she'd be thrilled if you were to sketch a portrait of her from one of our old photographs."

Cassie gasped. "You...want me to draw a picture of a real person?"

"Don't you think you can do it?" he challenged.

She'd drawn people in the background of her farm sketches before, and if it meant being able to help Bridget, then...

Cassie stuck out her hand and smiled. "You've got yourself a deal."

CHAPTER 8

Inspired by the spiced, hot apple cider mix sachet she'd made for Eileen, Cassie went back to the kitchen to put together a dry hot cocoa mix for Sarah's husband, Rick. She attached a hand-drawn logo on his gift tag too.

Then with only two days to go, Cassie put the finishing touches on the children's books, printed them out using the computer equipment in her father's den, punched three holes along the left margin, then bound the pages together with a pretty red ribbon. At least her brother and sister's significant others and the gifts for the kids were taken care of.

But she still didn't have a clue what to make for her immediate family. Christmas carols seemed to fill the house day and night, and at the moment the tune happened to be *"The Little Drummer Boy."* The line, *"I have no gift to bring, pa-rum-pum-pum pum,"* seemed especially appropriate since she was in the same situation.

What could *she* give?

Continuing to think about the animated cartoon story of *"The Little Drummer Boy"* which she had seen as a child on TV, she realized the boy did the only thing he *could* do because he didn't have anything else to give. His drumming wasn't anything special, but the boy did his best before the Lord and it made people happy. And while her drawings might not be award winners, it was all *she* could do. Hopefully, it would make her family happy too. At least she'd have *something* to give them. And her mother had made it clear she wanted her to take up drawing again.

The night before, Cassie had gone into her room to find her old sketchpad laying on the middle of her bed. No doubt her mother had put it there. Which Cassie found odd, because it had never been her mother who supported her drawings when she was younger, but her *grandmother*.

It was Grandma Sutherland, her father's mom, who had given her the sketchpad for Christmas one year in the first place. The gift had come with a new set of artist's pencils and a note telling her that there wasn't anything she couldn't do if she put her mind to it. Afterward, Cassie had spent countless hours drawing in the book with her grandmother by her side, spinning llama wool and wrapping it into skeins.

She missed her grandma. She missed her understanding and support. But she'd passed away several years back not long after her grandfather, and her other grandparents lived far away on the other side of the country.

Cassie sat down at her bedroom desk, picked up a sharpened pencil, and opened her sketchpad. But before she could start drawing pictures for Tim, Sarah, and her parents, she needed to finish the image she'd already started of the auctioneer's mother-in-law. Taking out the photograph he'd given her, Cassie compared it to her drawing. To her surprise, the likeness between the two wasn't bad.

The fact the woman she had drawn a picture of was deceased made her think of Logan's family. If B.J.'s wife was sure to treasure the sketch of her late mother, wouldn't Logan appreciate a sketch of *his* deceased family too? Especially at Christmas when he was all alone?

As her mind wandered, she began outlining Logan's face from memory, her pencil moving across her sketchpad slowly at first, then picking up speed as his topsy-turvy brown hair, bright eyes, strong jaw, and wide grin appeared with brilliant clarity on the page before her.

"Why are you smiling?" Sarah asked, pausing by the frame of her open door.

Cassie glanced up at her sister, back at Logan, then lied, "No reason."

"I just wanted to let you know we leave for church in two hours for the Christmas Eve service. Mom wants us there early so we can put on our costumes for the nativity play."

"What about the llamas?"

"Dad's going to load them into the trailer and bring them over later."

Two hours. Time was ticking away and having to be in the play with the rest of her family was going to take away even more of it. She'd have to stay up late in order to finish her gifts. But instead of diving in to work on them, she kept sketching the one she'd started. On the internet she searched for photos of Logan's family and found one of the four of them together on an old Facebook account that had not been closed down.

Logan's younger brother had looked just like him, and while they shared features similar to both their mother and their father, it was clear they mostly took after their father with their sparkling gaze and similar smiles. The entry on the Facebook page contained the date of the crash that had taken the lives of the trio Logan had lost with a simple added tribute from him saying, "Love you forever. See you in Heaven."

Dear God, that must have hurt. She couldn't imagine losing a member of her family no matter how much they aggravated her at times. No wonder he hadn't dated since then. He was probably frightened to get close to anyone. And yet, he *did* want to be close to others or he wouldn't spend so much time serving the community.

Glancing back and forth between the photo and her sketchpad, Cassie quickly sketched Logan's family in behind him. It was the least she could do to make up for Ned's demeanor at dinner earlier that week.

The doors of the single story historic white church with the tall pointed steeple were adorned with beautiful green wreaths with red bows donated by Whittaker's Garden Shop. Cassie knew it was Logan who had donated them because it was mentioned in the printed bulletin the greeter handed her as she walked in. The donation was in honor of his family.

Cassie searched for him as she followed her family into the back room to don their costumes, and her breath quickened the moment she saw him. The last time they were together he'd winked at her and made the joke about dating.

She'd convinced herself it *must* have been a joke, because he knew she wasn't here to stay. Tomorrow, after her family opened their gifts and ate the noon meal, Cassie would need to return to New York to get to work the next day.

"Wise men," Cassie's mother said, handing each of them a colorful gold trimmed robe and a glittery paper crown. "Put these on and after the pastor finishes the closing prayer at the end of the service, lead the procession to the outdoor stage. The llamas should already be there and all you'll need to do is stand beside them and hold on to their lead rope. Amber, Timmy, after your mother helps you get your angel and shepherd costumes on, you can sit up front and when the wise men go out the door you can follow them."

Amber nodded, anxious to get her 'angel' wings, while Timmy Jr. twirled the stick he was using for a shepherd's staff around like a sword.

Cassie's mother held up the next costume and said, "Mary—"

But Sarah wasn't there.

"Where's our 'Mary?'" their mother called.

Cassie turned her head and saw her sister, her face pale as a ghost, sitting down in a chair halfway down the aisle. Her husband, Rick, stood beside her.

"Mom," Sarah said, doubling over as she stood with her arm wrapped around her middle. "It's time."

Their mother stared at her, without comprehending. *"What?"*

"The *baby*," Cassie said to enlighten her. "The baby is coming."

Their mother sucked in her breath, then ordered, "Rick, what are doing just standing there? Take her to the hospital! We'll meet you there as soon as the play is over. And—and...Cassie and Logan, I'll need you to take their place as our new 'Mary' and 'Joseph.'"

"Mom! I can't!" Cassie protested, and shot a quick glance at Logan who met her gaze.

"You're all we've got," her mother said, shaking her head. "Just do the best that you can."

Cassie couldn't stop fidgeting throughout the entire service. The giant red-leafed poinsettias decorating the front of the church were lovely. The songs were more joyous than any she'd ever heard, thanks in part, to Logan's melodious contribution. And after the pastor read from the passages in the Bible that told the story of Jesus' birth, the candles were lit as they sang *"Silent Night,"* a timeless tradition she'd always enjoyed. But still her mind, God help her, kept straying toward the fact that at the *end* of the service everyone would go outside and she would have to act out a starring role in a play she'd never rehearsed. And she'd have to do it with Logan as her 'pretend' husband to boot!

She'd always dreamed of landing a starring role in a play like her sister had in high school. But when the time came for her to take her place up on the stage, and she looked out over the crowd...her stomach clenched, her palms began to sweat, and her head felt dizzy as if at any moment she might *faint*.

"Don't worry, I've got you," Logan said, grabbing hold of her arm. "You can do this."

Cassie refocused her gaze on his face and his concern for her helped slow her rapid breathing. She wondered if the *real* 'Joseph' had been this concerned over his expectant wife or had looked as handsome as Logan did in the brown hooded robe he wore with a belt of rope tied about his waist.

Amber twirled about, showing off her white wire and nylon wings, then handed her a doll, and exclaimed, "Behold! A baby!"

"Just as it was told to us in the fields," Timmy Jr. said, drawing near with his shepherd staff.

Now it was Cassie's turn. She knew the line. It was one of the first verses she'd ever memorized in Sunday School. "*'For—for God so loved the world, that He...He...'*" She swallowed hard, unable to go on, her mind a complete blank.

Beside her, Logan put his arm around her and whispered, "*'—gave His only begotten Son—'*"

She repeated after him, loud enough for the crowd, then stopped again...unable to recall what words came next.

"*'—that whoever believes in Him should not perish but have everlasting life,'*" Logan prompted.

She repeated after him a third time, then she took a step across the makeshift platform her brother had built to lay the baby Jesus in the manger, but one of the llamas nudged another who then bumped into her side. She stumbled, and in a split second knew without a doubt...that she was going down.

Worse! As she flung out her arm to brace herself, she realized the doll— *the baby*— had slipped from her fingers.

Dear God! She'd let go of Jesus!

However, after her initial panic, she *was* able to catch him by the hand. She also became aware that someone had grabbed *her*, but she must have thrown him off balance because a moment later, both she and Logan, and the 'baby' landed on top of each other in a heap on the floor.

"I don't think that was supposed to happen," Amber said with a frown.

The crowd giggled and Cassie caught a glimpse of her mother covering her face with her hands. Picking herself up, Cassie wished she could cover her own face with her hands. Instead of a full grown adult, she felt like she was back in grade school. Why had she ever agreed to do this? She wasn't an actress. She wasn't *meant* to be in the spotlight!

For once, she *wanted* to be invisible. Especially when the play ended and she had to face her mother.

"I'm sorry I ruined the play," she said, fearing she'd disappointed her yet again.

But her mom surprised her with a smile. "It's okay. Everyone had a good laugh."

"That's right," Bridget said loyally, as she drew near.

"I forgot the words to John 3:16," Cassie said, her voice coming out an octave higher than normal. "Who forgets the words to John 3:16!"

"Lots of people get stage fright," her mother soothed. "And God loves us despite our mistakes."

"The only mistake I see," Bridget said, her eyes shining with tears, "is that they should have cast you as an angel. The hospital called today to tell me Isaac's bill had been paid in full. How can I ever repay you for what you've done?"

Cassie hesitated and suddenly the message behind the lines she'd recited in the nativity play and what the promised Messiah had done for her hit home with a poignancy that ached her heart. Jesus had not been recognized for who he was during his time on earth either. Was it true that an almighty God could recognize her—even if her own family couldn't—and *love* her despite all her shortcomings? Enough to send his own Son into the world as a baby only to grow up and die on the cross for her sins? All so that she could have a *relationship* with Him and live with Him forever in eternity? Wasn't that a debt that *she* could never repay?

"Don't thank me," Cassie said softly. "Thank God."

"I'm going to thank you both," Bridget said, wrapping her in a hug. "And I'm going to pray that in return, God blesses you more than you could ever imagine."

"Hey Cassie," Logan's voice called over to her from a short distance away. "We're going for a sleigh ride around town. Do you want to come?"

A sleigh ride? Oh how she did love a good sleigh ride...and she hadn't had one in so long.

But when she turned toward him she saw that he wasn't alone. A throng of smiling young women surrounded her handsome 'Joseph.' One of them was even so bold as to loop her arms through his and lean her head on his shoulder, a very pretty women who made it clear she intended to compete for his attention.

Her initial excitement plummeting, Cassie shook her head. "Sorry, Logan. I appreciate the offer but I need to head home."

Cassie handed off the drawing she'd promised to B.J. Franklin before leaving the church, then climbed into her cold, dark, Jeep Grand Cherokee and realized the interior overhead lights didn't work. But the engine *did*, and that was all that mattered.

Once she was back at the farm, she drew the four remaining pictures she needed for her parents and siblings as Tim and Eileen struggled to settle the kids down and get them to bed. Finally the house quieted, but just when she was about to shut off her own light, there was a knock on her bedroom door.

"Cass, are you awake?" her brother called out in a muffled whisper.

Crossing the room, she opened the door to let him in. "What's the matter?"

Tim let out a groan and rubbed his hand across his face. "I don't know what to do. I still need a gift for Mom and Dad."

Cassie gasped. "What? It's nearly midnight! We open gifts in another eight hours."

Her brother winced. "I *know*."

Apparently she wasn't the only one who had trouble coming up with homemade gifts. First her father, now Tim? The revelation made her smile. Maybe she wasn't so different from the rest of her family after all.

"Your imagination is always running," Tim said, and gave her an earnest look. "I thought you might help me come up with something?"

Cassie's gaze fell on her sketchpad.

"You could go out to the shed and make wooden frames for the pictures I just drew. We'll tell Mom and Dad we combined our gifts this year."

Her brother nodded. "Perfect."

"But Tim? When you make the frames, don't just make two, make three." Thinking of the photo she'd drawn of Logan's family, she said, "I'm going to need one more."

CHAPTER 9

"Sarah had a girl!" Cassie's mom announced when she came down the stairs early the next morning. "She, Rick, and the baby will be home from the hospital later this morning."

"Merry Christmas, Mom," Cassie said, wiping the sleep from her eyes.

"Oh yes! I forgot! Merry Christmas to you, too, Cassie." Her mother hurried to the kitchen to whisk on an apron. "I suppose I should make coffee and get out the cinnamon rolls before the kids come down and want to open their stockings."

The pitter-patter of little feet echoed behind them and Cassie smiled. "Too late."

Both Amber and Timmy Jr. ran into the living room, stopped up short in front of the fifteen-foot-tall Christmas tree, and stared in amazement for a moment at all the packages. Since it was a 'homespun' Christmas, none of the gifts had been decorated with store bought paper, but looked just as pretty.

Some had been wrapped in beige burlap and tied with colorful bows. Some had been stuffed inside hand sewn "Rudolph" and "Santa" sacks, and tied off at the top with string. A few were in polished wooden cases of various sizes. And some, like Cassie's, had been covered with fabric and lace, with a few golden jingle bells added.

"Grandma, come look what I got," Amber squealed, dumping the contents of her stocking out on the floor. "Christmas Candy!"

Cassie had seen her mother fill up the stockings the night before, and assumed everyone had baggies of her mother's famous homemade caramels, fudge, gum drops, and chocolate-covered toffee in their stockings.

Timmy Jr. didn't bother with his stocking. His gaze went straight toward the new bike standing in the corner. "Is that for me?"

As Cassie's brother and his wife joined them, Cassie's mom frowned. "I thought we said we were only giving out gifts that were handmade!"

Tim grinned as he walked over to his son. "I put the entire thing together with my own two hands," he told her. "The bike came in a kit."

"If he got a bike," Amber said, dropping her stocking to look out the window, "does that mean I'm going to get my pony?"

Right on cue, Cassie's father brought a brown and white miniature pony, just three-feet-high, through the front door. Around its neck was tied a huge red bow.

"My *pony!*" Amber squealed, her voice even louder this time, as she ran over to give the animal a hug.

"Handmade?" Cassie's mother asked, quirking a brow at Cassie's father.

"Indeed!" her father said defensively, handing his wee granddaughter the green-striped lead rope. "Made by the hand of God Himself!"

"The gifts are supposed to be made by *you*," Cassie's mom scolded him. "What did *you* do?"

He gestured toward the pony's bow and grinned. "I added the decorations. Doesn't that count?"

Cassie's mother finally broke down and laughed. "Yes," she said. "I suppose that does."

Cassie was about to give her mother the framed drawings from her and Tim, but the door opened and her mother rushed toward it when she saw Sarah and Rick.

"Oh my! Look at all the hair!" her mother exclaimed. "Isn't she the sweetest thing ever?"

Cassie congratulated her sister and brother-in-law and agreed. Baby Madeline was the perfect Christmas gift, one her family would treasure forever. Taking a seat by the fireplace, Cassie wondered why she'd ever worried about coming up with gifts at all. The best gift was that they were all here together, laughing, smiling, joking. It was times like this when memories were made. Which is why she chose to make the gifts for Sarah, Tim, and her parents that she did.

Realizing her family—and the whole town for that matter—would likely never forget the spill she'd taken up on stage during the play, she'd wanted to give them a few *different* memories this year. Hand-drawn memories of other times that were less embarrassing. Times that were *good.*

And when Cassie's mother finally opened the gift she'd made for her later that day, she cried. "I always knew you had talent," she said, a catch in her voice. "But *this* means more to me than any of the other sketches you have ever done."

"You—you mean you really like it?" Cassie asked, her heart skipping a beat.

"I *love* it, Cassie." Her mother wiped her eyes with her hand. "Why wouldn't I?"

"It's just that—" Cassie swallowed hard and recalled how Logan said she should open up to her. "I never thought you were impressed with any of my sketches before."

Her mother gasped. "Why would you think that?"

Cassie shrugged. "I've never heard you say much about them."

"Who do you think encouraged you to take up drawing in the first place?" her mother demanded.

"Grandma gave me the sketchpad and—"

Her mother's eyes filled with tears again. "Your grandmother never knew what to get you and so she asked *me* to buy the gifts she gave you. She just wasn't much of a shopper."

"But the note—" Cassie said, staring at her. "That was from you too?"

Her mother nodded.

"But whenever anyone else won a trophy or brought home a blue ribbon you would *ooh* and *aah*. You never did that with me."

"Of course I did. Maybe you just chose not to hear it," her mother shot back.

"Or maybe you were just too busy," Cassie challenged. "You are always taking soup to this person, taking cookies to another, helping out at the church, talking on the phone. I've been here a whole week and we haven't had a chance to sit down alone together. Not once."

Her mother's mouth fell open as if she was going to say something but nothing came out.

"I'm sorry," Cassie said, hanging her head. "I shouldn't have said that."

"I'm glad you did," her mother said slowly. "You're right. I've been too busy. So busy serving others that I failed to see the needs sitting right in front of me. *Your* needs, Cass. I never knew you felt this way. You always seem to be so independent that I guess I thought you didn't *need* me. I'm sorry."

Taking her hand, Cassie's mother told her to get on her boots. "Now it's time for your father and I to give you *our* gift."

What kind of a gift would they have for her outside?

She followed her parents down the snow covered path past the barn and the tool shed, past the penned pastures, to the old stone garden shed by the pond.

"Go in," her mother said, her eyes gleaming as she motioned her toward the door.

Cassie stepped through and for a moment she couldn't breathe. The garden equipment had been removed and the interior walls had all been freshly painted. A bed, a couch, a plush oversized chair, and a desk had all been brought in. But it was the new cork bulletin boards that had been nailed to the walls that drew her attention. Pinned to each one were her sketches. Dozens and dozens of them. Drawings she'd done since she was a child right up until the present day.

Her mother had even keep sketches she hadn't been aware of. Like the doodles she'd done on the back of the bulletins at church, the animals she'd drawn on napkins when they ate at restaurants, and the landscapes she'd penciled on old thin scraps of wood.

"We made you your own art studio," her father said proudly.

She hesitated. "It's—*beautiful*. But I—I live in New York."

"Any chance we can get you to stay?" her mother asked.

Cassie shook her head. "I have a life in the city, a job where people are depending on me. As much as I love sketching, I still don't think I can turn that skill into a career that would bring in enough money for me to support myself."

"Well, you can still use this studio whenever you come to visit," her father told her. "It will be here for you whenever you want it."

"Which we hope is *often*," her mother added. "You have to come back so we can go out to lunch. Just the two of us."

"I'd like that," Cassie said with a smile, and overcome with emotion, she ran into their outstretched arms and gave them each a hug.

The rest of the day was just as exciting as the kids opened the books she created, and sat on her lap demanding she read to them over and over. They especially liked the fact that she had used their names for some of the characters in the stories.

Eileen and Rick loved the dry mixes she'd made and the logos she'd sketched onto the tags. Eileen even asked if she could use the stovetop logo for her new made-from-scratch baking business.

And Tim and Sarah had laughed good and hard when they received their sketches of the time they went ice skating and Tim slid into a snowman on the edge of the pond, and the time they went on a picnic and Sarah kept feeding her sandwich to the raccoon under the table, thinking it was the family dog.

It was such a wonderful Christmas that Cassie hated to have to leave.

"Are you sure you can't stay a little longer?" her mother asked. "Logan's coming over for dinner."

"I have to get to work early tomorrow," Cassie said, and handed her mother the drawing of Logan's family that she had slipped into one of Tim's frames and wrapped with brown paper. "Can you give this to him?"

"I'm sure he'd appreciate it if you gave it to him yourself," her mother insisted.

Cassie smiled. "Tell Logan I said goodbye and that...it was nice to meet him."

CHAPTER 10

On Monday morning Cassie sat behind her desk in the six-by-six-foot cubicle, one of twenty-four such cubicles on the eighteenth floor of the building where she worked, her mind on a conversation she'd had with her mother the week before.

"Your office—in New York—" her mother had said hesitantly. "Does it have a window?"

She'd had to admit, "No, I have an interior office space."

"I'd be unhappy if I couldn't at least look outside."

"There's a window in the lunch room," Cassie told her.

"Just one?"

For some reason Cassie couldn't get the earnest look on her mother's face out of her head.

The phone rang, interrupting her reverie, and sitting up straight, she answered the call. "Hello?"

"Hi. It's Logan. I wanted to thank you for the gift. It really meant a lot to me, Cass."

Cass. It was the first time she'd heard him use the shortened version of her name like her brother and sister did. But didn't he tell Ned at dinner that they were all pretty 'tight-knit?' The memory, and the fact Logan had taken the time to call her, put a smile on her lips.

"I thought you might be thinking of your family this time of year and then I sketched off a photo I found online. I'm...I'm glad you like it."

"It's the best gift anyone could possibly give me," he said, his tone soft. "You're very talented. And I'm not the only one who thinks so. Mrs. Franklin showed Mrs. Woodward the drawing you did of her mother and now *she* wants one. She wants to know how much you charge."

Cassie gasped. "She wants to pay me?"

"And everyone is talking about the drawings you did for the kids at the hospital," Logan continued.

"I made children's books for Amber and Timmy Jr. for Christmas," she said, her gaze straying toward the macaroni necklaces on the edge of her desk that the kids had given her in return.

Logan laughed. "I know. Last night at dinner they couldn't wait to show me. Have you thought of having the books published?"

"Are you serious?"

"Why not? I think they'd be a hit."

"I'll think about it," she promised. "Thank you for calling, Logan. It's nice to hear your voice."

"You haven't heard enough of it echoing off the walls at church?" he teased.

Cassie laughed. "Maybe *you* should think about producing your own music CD."

The person in the cubicle next to her frowned and raised a finger to her lips and Cassie groaned. "I have to get back to work."

"I understand. Thanks again for the gift," Logan said, then after a brief pause added, "I hope to see you next time you come around."

Me too, Cassie thought as she hung up the phone. But she had no idea when that might be.

Her heart suddenly yearning for home, she left her cubicle, walked into the lunchroom, and opening the window, stuck her head out as far as she could. The frosty air stung her face as she glanced up at the endless overcast sky then out over the vast network of roads, bridges, and buildings below.

"Hey, you're going to jack up the heating bill by letting all the cold air in," one of her co-workers yelled, pushing her back and slamming the window closed. "What are you doing in here anyway? Lunch isn't for another hour. Do you *want* to work here?"

At the moment, Cassie wasn't sure. Mumbling an apology, she went back to her cubicle and found a new file had been sent to the inbox on her computer. Upon opening it, her heart skipped a beat and she gasped. *Was this God's doing?*

For her next assignment she'd be working with the editor of a publishing house.

New Year's Eve came all too quickly. Cassie had tried to call Ned several times to cancel their date, but he didn't respond except to tell her to meet him at 8 pm in front of the Hard Rock Cafe at Times Square for a special surprise.

"Cassie!" he greeted, kissing her cheek. "Let me introduce you to my new friends, Phil and Steve."

He brought friends? Cassie hadn't even wanted to come out tonight and now she'd have to wait until after the evening was over before she could talk to Ned alone?

Four hours later the two million people in the crowd—packed in tighter than a herd of cattle—cheered as the clock struck midnight and they watched the shiny LED lit ball drop one-hundred-and-forty-one feet down the pole on top of the New York Times Tower. Shouts of "Happy New Year!" rang out in nearly every direction, except Cassie wasn't feeling all too happy. Partly because of the company she was keeping and partly because she was wishing she were someplace else.

As a series of loud, obnoxious horns tooted in her ears, and invasive party poppers shot string and confetti past her face, Ned, oblivious to her despondent mood, grabbed her hand and shouted, "Isn't this great?"

She shook her head, but he didn't seem to notice. Instead, he pulled a small jeweler's box from his pocket. *Dear God, was he going to propose?*

Cassie sucked in her breath, dread racing up her spine. But when he opened the lid, it wasn't a ring that lay tucked inside, but a bracelet with a gold heart meant for engraving. Except her "boyfriend" hadn't had it personalized. Maybe he hadn't had time or maybe...he'd left it blank intentionally in case she hadn't returned from the farm and he had to take it back.

"Well, what do you think of your Christmas present?" Ned prompted.

"The heart is blank," she said, catching his gaze to watch his expression.

Ned shrugged. "I thought it was prettier that way." Scanning the crowd, he high-fived his two friends and shouted a second time, "Isn't this fun?"

No. It wasn't. Luxury was great. But all the glitter, champagne, and excitement in the world couldn't take the place of being in the company of those she loved—and who loved her. With sudden clarity all the events of the past two weeks joined together to show her she was *meant* to go home, *meant* to reconnect with her family, *meant* to pick up her sketchpad again, and...maybe even meant to meet Logan. Surely it couldn't have all come about by coincidence.

God? Are you there, God? I know now that you are *there for me. You always have been. I just didn't see it.*

With a sudden giddiness that matched the crowd she knew what she had to do. Thanking Ned for the gift, she told him it was too beautiful a piece for her to accept and asked he give it to his mother, who surely deserved much more than the pen he'd given her.

Then she wished him a Happy New Year and bid him goodbye.

The following morning she called her boss on his private number—since it was a holiday—to put in her two weeks' notice. And after canceling the lease on her apartment, packing her belongings, and loading her car, she turned her old beat up Jeep back onto the road for home.

Everything transpired smoothly, as if it had all been pre-planned...except for the snowflakes that first floated down in tiny white flakes, then fell harder and faster until the hilly Pennsylvania road was covered by several inches. The good news was that there was a snowplow in front of her. The bad news was that the vehicle was moving slow, delaying her trip while the storm grew worse.

After what seemed an eternity later, the snowplow turned off onto a different path, but her relief was soon short lived when her vehicle lost traction on the slick road. Hadn't she put it into four wheel drive?

God, I thought you wanted *me to come home. Wasn't that your plan for me? Did I misread the memo or something? Was I supposed to wait and come on a different day?*

Holding tight to the steering wheel, she held her breath as her car skidded into a snow bank right beside the entrance to the Van Sant Bridge. Luckily she hadn't driven straight into the river.

Unable to back up, she turned off the engine and got out. Her car was so full of snow she doubted anyone would notice her. Not good.

What do I do, Lord?

Making her way through the barrage of white wintery flakes, she stepped under the cover and protection of the bridge hoping to flag down the next car to come through.

Except the next vehicle wasn't a car, it was a sleigh!

And if her eyes did not deceive her, *Logan Whittaker* was the one driving it, his hands on the reins of the horses in front of him. She blinked three times to make sure she was right. After all—what were the chances? But as the horse-drawn sleigh drew closer, her doubts fled and all she was left with was a happy smile.

Thank you, God!

Logan appeared just as surprised to see *her.* "Cassie Sutherland, what are you doing here?"

"Waiting for you, apparently," she said, and laughed. "My car got stuck. Care to give me a ride?"

"I'd love to," he said with a grin. "As long as your boyfriend doesn't find out."

"I don't have a boyfriend," Cassie told him. "I've left everything in New York behind and have come home to stay."

"Well then," Logan said, as he reached toward her. "In that case, let me give you a hand."

He told her that earlier in the day he'd been at the church for a potluck celebration and had been on his way back toward his own place when he'd found her. He attributed it to good timing, but she knew better. It had been God's *perfect* timing.

A short while later, Logan turned the team of horses into her driveway. And this time when she arrived home, the door opened and both her parents came out to greet her before she even made it to the front step.

"Cassie!" her mother exclaimed. "Why didn't you tell me you were coming? And how are you with Logan? Where is your car?"

After she filled them in on the details, they all went inside, where the rest of her family—who had an equal number of questions—were gathered in the living room around the warm, cozy fire.

"I gave the advertising agency two weeks' notice but I don't have to go back to the office," Cassie told them. Glancing at Logan, she added, "My latest client is an editor for a publishing house and she said I can email her back and forth from my computer here at home."

Logan held her gaze. "Do they publish children's books?"

"As a matter of fact," Cassie said, unable to stop her emotions from welling to the surface and spilling over in a huge smile, "they *do.*"

"But what convinced you to come back?" her mother asked, staring at her in disbelief.

Logan arched a brow to show *he* was interested in hearing the answer to that question too, but with so many eyes on her, all she could say was, "*Mom*, my office didn't have any windows!"

Her family had themselves a good laugh. However, later that day, when Cassie stood to follow the rest of her family into the dining room for dinner, Logan held her back and repeated the question. "Why *did* you come home, Cass?"

Mustering her courage, she looked into his eyes and said, "I realized that God has a plan for me and that this is where I belong."

"Any other reason?" he asked, his expression hopeful.

Cassie smiled. "I like you, Logan."

He grinned at her in return. "I like you too. I'm sorry we didn't get to spend Christmas together."

"Well, I'm here now," she said, her cheeks growing warm.

Logan glanced up at the ceiling. "Yes, you are."

She followed his gaze, spotted the mistletoe hanging above them, and her heart skipped a beat, or maybe several, as Logan took her in his arms, leaned his head toward her, and brushed a warm, gentle kiss against her lips.

"Merry Christmas, Cassie," he said, his eyes twinkling.

Breathless, she whispered back, "Merry Christmas, Logan."

A timeless second passed between them during which Cassie didn't think she'd ever been happier. Then Logan's grin widened and he asked, "Will you go out with me after church next Sunday?"

"You mean like a date?" she teased. "Not an invitation to help out at a community event, or to make crafts, or go on a sleigh ride with a gaggle of girls?"

"Yes, a real date," Logan assured her, and let out a chuckle. "And no gaggle. Just the two of us, I promise."

"Well, that's an offer I can't pass up," Cassie admitted, and pressed a hand to his heart. "To new beginnings?"

"Yes, Cass," he said, giving her a wink. "And a whole lot more, if your mother has anything to do with it."

She laughed and glanced into the dining room where her mother had left two seats at the table open for them side by side. "My mother *does* have a good time trying to play matchmaker, don't you think?"

Logan nodded. "Let's not disappoint her."

"No, let's not," Cassie agreed, but as she and Logan walked into the dining room arm in arm, she wasn't really worried about pleasing her mother.

For she knew that no matter what the future held, she was valued by One who would never be disappointed in her. And with that knowledge came a joyous peace that flooded her entire being. A peace that could only come from the highest heavens.

And from a heart of love.

About the Author:

Darlene Panzera is a multi-published author, speaker, and writing coach of both sweet contemporary and Christian inspirational romance. Her career launched with *THE BET,* included in a volume along with bestselling author Debbie Macomber's *FAMILY AFFAIR.* Darlene is also a member of Romance Writers of America and the Northwest Christian Writers Association, and says she loves writing stories that *"inspire people to laugh, value relationships, and pursue their dreams."* When not writing, she loves camping and hiking with her family, rooting for the Seattle Seahawks, and feeding her horse carrots.

Learn more about Darlene at her website: **www.darlenepanzera.com**

Spiced Hot Apple Cider Mix Sachets

One of the homemade gifts Cassie makes in my novella, *Homespun Christmas*, is a sachet of spiced, hot apple cider mix for her sister-in-law, Eileen. It made me thirsty just writing about it. Here's the recipe! —Darlene Panzera

Combine together in a bowl:

4 cloves

4 allspice berries

4 peppercorns

2 cinnamon sticks broken into pieces

1/2 tbsp dried orange peel

2 cardamom pods

2 star anise pods

1/2 tsp candied ginger

Directions:

Place all the ingredients in the center of a 6"by 6" square of cheesecloth. Fold the corners together and tie with baker's string. When ready to make the hot drink, place the sachet in a large pot with 1 to 2 quarts of apple cider and let simmer for at least a half hour. Pour into mugs, top with whip cream, and enjoy!

A Christmas Shot

by

Julianne M. Haag

Dedication:

To my Mom, who always supported my crazy dreams and adventures and encouraged me the entire way.

Acknowledgements:

I would like to thank Darlene, my teacher, who guided me and showed me the way. Samantha, who was our elbow grease to get the anthology launched and our biggest supporter. Finally, my fellow anthology authors who helped me form, shape, and mold my story and always had my back. Thank you!

CHAPTER 1

Click. Snap. "Okay. Beautiful. Aren't you a gorgeous baby? Come on. Smile for the camera." Elise Forstner cooed at the leaf covered infant surrounded by pumpkins on the floor. One hand held the camera steady while the other tightened around a squeaky toy dog in an attempt to make the child smile. *Is this really all I'm going to do with my life?*

Within thirty minutes Elise had the photo shoot wrapped up and the parent and child escorted out of Benson's Photography Studio. She sat down in the reception chair and rubbed her temples. When she was a young girl and dreamed about what she wanted to do when she grew up, working in a mall photography studio had not been on the list. Granted, it paid her bills and left her enough time on the side to run her own photography business, but what she would give to see a world outside of her hometown!

Grabbing her new edition of *Adventure Magazine* off the reception desk, she eagerly perused the articles and photographs for work done by professional photographer Janell Grayson, whom she admired. As she thumbed through the pages, she also made sure to bookmark the columns written by Mr. Adessi, the top travel journalist of *Adventure Magazine*. She had been following his career ever since they graduated high school.

Violent vibrations on her thigh startled her. She shoved the magazine into a drawer and wrestled to free the phone from her pocket. A heavy sigh escaped her mouth at the name on the caller I.D. What did her mom want her to do this time?

"Hello, Mom."

"Elise, dear." Mary Forstner's voice rang through the phone. "It's been so long since we last had a little chat. How are you?"

She tried to reply, "I—"

"I have a favor to ask. You have the evening of December the fifteenth free, am I correct? I noticed the blank date in your planner which is perfect since I really need a photographer for my tea party. Would you be a dear and spend it with us?"

"How did you get my planner?"

"You left it here when you came over for dinner the other night. Which reminds me, I have some mail for you. But you really should get your own post office box. I threw out some things that looked like junk mail, if that's all right by you. I don't know why those travel magazines have our address but you should call and tell them to stop sending those things. They're cluttering up my house."

"Mom, I pay for those." Elise had started buying them in high school when Tom, her ex-boyfriend, bought one for her. She had been hooked ever since.

"I thought you stopped after you broke up with that wild boyfriend of yours. You know, the one who almost took you to Timbuktu with him." Her mom's voice took on a suspicious edge. "Don't tell me you're planning on going somewhere."

"Well... No... I..."

"You simply can't leave. Thanksgiving is almost here and then it's Christmas season; you know how busy our tree farm gets. With your father growing older, we need more help around the farm. And after Christmas, your brother Matthew is getting married and they will need a photographer. It's lucky we have you, so much cheaper. Anyway, this time of year is not safe to travel. Americans are always targeted overseas. Do you understand?"

Elise bowed her head. "Yes."

"Good. Now please get here around four o'clock on the fifteenth to help with the preparations. Also, please wear something acceptable and bright, not that dreary look you favor. And don't forget about Thanksgiving next week. I expect you to help out with the cooking. Ta Ta."

The call ended and she slipped the phone into her pocket. Why did her mother need a photographer for a tea party anyway? Then again, if she didn't go, 'hell hath no fury like a mother scorned.' Elise was sure even God was afraid of her mother. Heck, her mother was probably the one who ingrained the Ten Commandments into his head, especially the 'honor thy father and mother' part. No, she'd better go.

A wail echoed through the air. Looking out, Elise saw a determined woman with a red faced toddler headed straight for her. *Oh no! Not another one!* She stood and rapped her knuckles on the back door before poking her head through. "Hey, Jen. Just wanted to let you know I'm taking my lunch break. See you later."

*　　　*　　　*

Elise's favorite time of day was lunch break. The café was only a short walk away from the studio in the mall and always had freshly brewed coffee and warm gooey cinnamon rolls. On good days, the smells drifted to her workplace.

During the week the café wasn't as busy and she went straight up to the register to order a hot chocolate with a shot of espresso and a flaky granola muffin. When the barista called her name, she collected her order and sat at a small corner table with a view of the entire room. It was the perfect place to watch the customers come and flow through the shop, and Elise often imagined different photoshoots for each individual.

A young child's bubbling laugh rang through the café and Elise spotted a young girl whose spools of hair flopped with each skip. *Bright colors: yellow and pink. She should have a party scene with balloons,* Elise determined. The girl waved impatiently to a man outside the entrance. *Probably her father.*

"Wait up. I'm not as fast as you." The voice of the child's 'father' created a surge of recognition that punched Elise's stomach. Her eyes snapped to attention on the two in front of her again.

The muffin crumbled like ash in Elise's mouth as she watched a young man with messy black hair catch up to the girl. He laughed at the girl's excitement and his face confirmed her fears: Tom Adessi was back. She glanced again at the child. *His?*

An elderly gentleman walked up to him, and Elise could hear the man thank Tom for buying his granddaughter hot chocolate. *Guess he's doing a Good Samaritan act again.*

As discreetly as possible, she gathered up her belongings, thankful she had sat near the back of the café. *Don't notice me, don't notice me. I am invisible.* When she had exited the café side entrance, she shot straight for Benson's.

In a matter of minutes she returned to the studio and went into the back room, attempting to slow her quick, staccato heartbeat. *He didn't see me…I'm sure of it. Calm down.*

"Hey Elise. Are you done with lunch already?" Jennifer popped her head through the door. "Cool, then I'm going to take my lunch break now if that's okay."

Without waiting for a response, Jennifer grabbed her bag and jacket and left. Elise welcomed the unexpected privacy and focused on taking deep breaths.

Ding! Ding! The bell from the front desk chimed, alerting her that a customer was there. She took another deep breath before she snatched her unfinished muffin and walked outside. "Hello. Welcome to Benson's Photog—"

"Hey Elise. It's been a while."

She froze, then tried to muster a smile which probably ended up looking more like a grimace. "Hi Tom."

Silence fell and her gaze dropped to her new favorite sight — her plain black shoes. "Is there anything I can do for you?"

"I just wanted to say 'hi.' I saw you in the café." Tom walked around the interior of the studio. "Not much has changed in the ten years since you started working here. It's almost as if this place is frozen in time."

"Yeah, it can seem that way," she answered slowly, "but if you look closer you can see a lot of differences."

Tom faced her. "Is that so?"

"I started my own photography business. It's not much, but growing." Talking about her business always helped her to smile. While it didn't satisfy her dream of being a travel photographer, she was still proud of her work. "What have you been up to?"

"I just got back from Southeast Asia. *Adventure Magazine* hired me to write about my experiences. But now I'm taking a short break. Thought I'd spend part of the year in America before going off to travel the world again."

So he was able to achieve his dream. If only I had... She cut the thought from her head and swallowed hard. "How long are you here in Washington?"

His head tilted, as if to scrutinize her. "About two months. Depends on if one of my friends in Italy gets married or not."

Numbers quickly added in her head. *He'll be here until after Christmas.*

"So you'll be seeing me around, if that's okay." He hesitated and rubbed the back of his neck. "Can I ask you to do a photography session with me? I want to send updated pictures out to friends and family. I'm also thinking of sending them to my financial supporters."

His earnest, crystal green eyes studied her and the scent of his exotic spice cologne must have addled her senses because she asked, "You want to schedule a photography appointment?"

"Yeah, I was thinking a Christmas theme would be appropriate."

Inwardly, she groaned. He wanted to *be* the subject of her work, *in* her lens. *No way, I can't, not again.* There was no way she could say 'no' to a customer, but she could get him in and out of the studio as fast as possible. She went over to grab some 3-ring binders with head shot and holiday theme samples.

"Benson's takes walk-ins and, as you can see, we are currently not busy. Why don't we get those photos out of the way right now? It'll only take a few minutes. If you would like a different outfit, Benson has an excellent sale on men's shirts"

"Elise." He took the books out of her hands and laid them on the counter. "I don't want copy and paste photos. That's not who I am and that's not the quality of photos you take. I've seen your pictures. I know what you can do."

She avoided his gaze as he spoke. Of course he wouldn't take the bait. It was her own photography that had drawn them together in the first place.

"I want to make an appointment with your *personal* photography business and have a one-on-one session with you. What do you say?"

"It's not cheap."

"Good photography never is."

Blinking a few times, she moved away to collect her thoughts. "Honestly, I don't know if the timing will work. Christmas is the busiest season and my schedule is booked with baby and family portraits. I also have a few weddings coming up. I don't think I can squeeze you in before you leave."

"Wow, sounds like your business is doing great."

At his impressed look she preened a bit with pride. *I may not be following my dream, but I have a good business here and he can see it.*

"It's a good thing I don't have a departure date for Washington." Tom continued, "I can wait 'til after Christmas and just make the pictures a winter theme or something. No problem."

Stuck for words, she nodded.

"Great!" His enthusiastic agreement was punctuated by a sharpie pen he pulled from his coat. He grabbed her hand and pushed her black sleeve up to scribble a number on her arm. "That's my phone number. I've got to go meet a pastor for some coffee soon so I gotta run." Next, he lifted up his hand in a two fingered salute and, before she could utter another word, disappeared out the door.

Elise simply stood there, unable to comprehend what just happened or decide what to do next. It was as if a tornado had just left the room. Finally, she sat down to finish her muffin and collect her thoughts. She was about to take a bite when a rap on the entrance wall to the studio got her attention. He was back.

"Elise, I was just thinking… I'm only meeting the pastor for, like, thirty minutes to an hour. Why don't I stop by after you finish your shift so we can hash out the details over dinner? I'll pay. See you in a bit." Another salute accompanied by a cheerful whistle signaled his exit.

Oh good Lord. Elise thumped her head down repeatedly upon the counter to try to smack sense back into herself. *What have I gotten myself into?*

CHAPTER 2

She was grateful that Jackson's Burger Joint was a lively family restaurant. Childish laughter and boisterous chatter in the background made the restaurant a safe place to eat with Tom. 'Deep' or 'personal' conversation was nearly impossible which was why she chose it. She wanted to get in and out as quickly as possible.

Her stomach rumbled as steaming onion burgers were carried past them and her fingers tapped out an impatient beat on the table.

Tom looked at them and laughed. "Don't worry. The food will be here soon."

At his response, she self-consciously withdrew her hands and folded them in her lap. Clearing her throat a few times, she asked, "Since we're here to discuss your photo shoot, why don't you tell me what you're looking for? I understand you want a 'Christmas' theme, or at least 'winter,' but that's a little vague. Are you going for a certain look or feel? Do you have a location in mind?"

"I want to do a few head shots to put into my newsletter. Nothing fancy. I would also like to give other pictures as gifts to family and friends so, yeah, a 'Christmas' or 'winter' theme would be great. I'd prefer to be outdoors so maybe in front of the Silverdale Christmas tree or on the waterfront would be nice. Hey!" Tom's hands suddenly gripped the table as he leaned toward her.

"What?"

"I just had a fantastic idea. Why don't we take the photos at your family's tree farm? That's definitely the 'Christmas' feel and image. The picture would be perfect if it snowed. And I'd love to see your dad again."

"No." She shook her head. "I'm sorry, but we can't take photos at the tree farm."

He sighed. "Lemme guess. Your mom still doesn't like me, huh?"

"Tom, what happened was a long time ago. Let's drop it, ok?"

He crossed his arms, but stayed silent. She twitched nervously until he finally spoke again.

"You know what I'd really like in the photos? It's not the setting or what I'm doing that really matters to me. What I want is a photo that makes the viewer 'feel.' Where the unspoken message reaches out to them. You know what I mean don't you?"

"I think so. Like the photo of the monk on fire or of the lone man standing in front of a long line of tanks." Those were the kind of images that always spoke to her. They told a story much deeper than the picture. The kind she longed to take herself.

"Those photos definitely spoke, but they're intended to get a message across. What I want are pictures that you can't stop staring at even though there doesn't seem to be anything special. The ones so simple, yet profound. Like the one of your brother and his girlfriend you took in high school."

A rock formed in her throat. The portrait had been of John, before he was deployed overseas, and Penny. Those two had been inseparable. In the black and white portrait, they had embraced each other. Her back was to the camera with his arms wrapped around her, his face buried in her neck. It was Elise's favorite photo of her late brother.

The photo was also how she met Tom. She had submitted the image to a photography contest and won second place. When Tom saw the picture on display, he did whatever he could to meet the photographer, *her*.

"Why don't you take photos like that anymore?"

She tensed at his soft question. "Since this is a general picture for all your supporters I think a photo with the town's Christmas tree will be perfect. You get a Christmas theme and we can do it quickly—"

"Can I ask your Dad if I can help at the farm for one day, like old times? Maybe we could get a shot then?"

"Tom—"

"We could do the photo shoot when your mom's gone. I still have your dad's cell number on my phone. I'll give him a call right now."

"Tom, wait—" She reached out to grab his arm but it was too late. The number had already been dialed.

"Jack? Hi, this is Tom Adessi. Remember me? It's been a while… Yeah, I just got back from overseas and I plan to be in the area for a little bit. Hey, I was wondering, could I help out at the farm this year?"

She held her breath.

"Really? That'd be great." Tom winked at her and gave a thumbs up.

Her heart dropped.

"I would love to get some pictures taken while I'm there. Elise is helping me out with that... Don't worry, we're fine. Can't wait to see you again. I will call you back later for the details... Ok. See you later."

He put the phone in his pocket and grinned at her. "There we go. Problem solved. So, when are you free to spend a day with me?"

A waiter arrived with her wrapped burger, but she didn't notice. Why did Tom still have her dad's number? And why did her dad agree? This had to stop. Who did Tom think he was? Ten years had passed and she was fine. Now he was taking control of everything. *No way.*

She looked him in the eye. "If daddy said you can help out at the farm, then that's fine. But if you want to keep working with me, please have a little consideration for my feelings. I don't appreciate my words being dismissed." She stood up and grabbed her burger. "I'll see you at work."

Elise turned and walked to the front door with her head held high. He wasn't going to jerk her around anymore.

*   *   *

Two days later, Elise's studio resembled a miniature NFL football game. "Ok, guys. Give me some real football star poses. Yeah. That's great." Elise moved fast to capture the three young boys in purple uniforms. She tried unsuccessfully to keep them from re-enacting yesterday's game in the studio. "Please don't push your brother. Give me five minutes and then we're done." *Lord, please keep them safe.*

The youngest started to shove his brothers into the backdrop behind them.

"You might hurt one another," she warned, but much to her dismay, a wrestling match broke out.

"Please stop. You might break my—" She gasped as one of the boys rolled into a light stand, which wobbled and tipped. Her feet fumbled over each other as she reached out to stop the light from falling on him. *"No!"*

Tom appeared from behind her and caught the falling guillotine. He lifted the stand back into place and pinned the shocked boys with a stern gaze. "Careful guys. If this had fallen on you, you'd be on the bench for the rest of the season." He looked at her. "Is this where it goes?"

She nodded and watched as Tom spoke to them. While she couldn't quite hear what he said, the boys' eyes lit up with excitement and they all eagerly nodded. He strolled over to her with a small smile.

"Thank you," she whispered.

He inclined his head and turned to the sport stars. "Now guys, give me your best defensive positions."

They all bent low and glared at Elise as if they were about to tackle her to the ground. She shivered and moved quickly to finish the photos. "That was great boys. You made me think I was actually going to be sacked."

They all laughed and boasted about their sport prowess until they left.

"You need help cleaning up?" Tom walked up to her, rubbing the back of his neck.

She nodded. He had helped her many times before in the past and didn't need direction. Anyway, she wasn't in the mood to talk to him. Their dinner conversation still ate at her nerves.

"Look, Elise. I just… I came here to say sorry for the other night."

Her head snapped up. *Was he apologizing? Tom never does that. This can't be right.*

"I went over the conversation we had. I guess I kind of pushed you into everything and didn't ask you. I'm sorry."

He looked like a kicked puppy. This was not the same guy she knew in high school. Would it be safe for her to work with him again?

"I get it if you don't want to take the pictures anymore," he continued. "We don't have to do them. I kinda threw those on you. So I'm sorry." He looked at her for a moment then shrugged and turned. "I guess I'll get going."

Elise stared at his receding back and panicked. Her mind flickered back to a similar sight from ten years ago. Except at that time his eyes were red and her mother had stood between, blocking his access to her. Then he left and all she did was watch from the living room window. Was this how it was going to end? Was he going to disappear a second time? What about her? Was she going to let him leave again?

"Tom, wait." She rushed to the door and turned him around to face her. "I'm sorry for being abrupt with you that night and I want to thank you for helping me today." She took a deep breath and continued, "I would really like to take those pictures for you. Do you think we can meet Wednesday this week? Before Thanksgiving?"

His grin made her heart flutter into overdrive. *Dear Lord, is this the right thing to do?*

*   *   *

I need the money. I need the money. That's why I agreed to do this. Two days later Elise mentally repeated the mantra to herself as she waited for Tom in the studio. Maybe if she repeated it enough the phrase might even come true. *A new camera* would *be helpful.*

Her reflection flashed on the studio's glass wall as she paced the corridor. She looked like a nervous wreck. *Calm down. We can be friends. I can do this.*

"Elise."

She spun around, her heel squeaking on the tile. Tom stopped in front of her. His eyebrows knit together and he looked at his worn leather watch with a frown. "I'm not late, am I?"

"No. No. I was just—" Heat flared up her neck as she remembered her attempt to wear a hole into the floor moments before. "I was just working off some energy. My last appointment went faster than expected. Why don't we get your headshots started?"

She opened the door to the glass studio on the right. He set down his backpack and sat on the stool, waiting for her. His tanned face and thick black hair filled her camera viewfinder. Chilling green eyes stood out among his dark features as if he could see straight through her. She shivered a bit.

Tom started to get up. "Are you cold?"

"No, no, please sit down. I need to make a few adjustments to your pose." She walked over to him and readjusted his posture, raised and tilted his chin, and shifted the torso away from the camera. Stepping back to view her work, she nodded with finality.

"All right, Tom." She moved behind her camera and gazed through the lens. "Smile."

A cocky smirk slipped onto his face. *My goodness.* She snapped a photo. *He's still a natural in front of a camera.*

"Kinda reminds me of old times." Tom's words echoed her thoughts.

"Hold still. The only time you're allowed to talk is when you're changing your pose."

He chuckled. "Yes ma'am."

After a couple more shots she stepped away from the camera. "You were always asking me to take pictures of you in high school." The memory made her smile as she went to move Tom into a different pose. "Plays, sports, portraits, even just hanging out. I wonder if you have narcissistic tendencies," she teased.

"Yes. That's the answer. Someone finally knows my secret."

Elise laughed as she checked his new stance in the camera. "Seriously, though. Why did you want all those pictures back then?"

His face became serious and she seized the opportunity to capture a few photos.

"Truth be told, I never cared about the pictures. I asked you to take them because that was the only time you ever looked directly at me."

She stilled. Slowly lifting her head, her gaze met his.

He smiled. "Ah, there it is. I knew there was fire in your eyes."

Jerking, she broke eye contact. *Fire? But they're a plain, overcast gray.*

Tom rose from the stool. "I'm pretty sure one of the shots you took will work." He rummaged through his frayed patch-covered backpack to produce a checkbook.

After he filled out the amount owed, he turned toward her. "Hey, I heard something from work I think you would be interested in. *Adventure Magazine* is hosting a photography contest this Christmas. You can submit through December first and winners are announced December fifteenth. The grand prize is a two week all expenses paid trip to Brazil with Janell Greyson who will give you one-on-one mentoring."

"Janell Greyson?" Renewed energy shot through every fiber of her being. "She won Travel Photographer of the Year three times in a row. Is the prize really an internship with her in Brazil? Just imagine what the trip would be like. The places you'd see, the people you'd meet." She let out a wistful sigh. "I would love to go."

"You should apply. I think you've got a good chance. You're extremely talented."

"I…I don't know. Christmas is always busy for me." She turned away to take down the camera.

"Don't you have a photography portfolio or something? Maybe we can find a photo that would work."

"I'm not sure if I have one. I haven't touched my portfolio in years."

"What about the picture of your brother and that girl—"

"I'll think about it."

He studied her, then placed his check on the stool. "I should get going. I need to buy some food for Thanksgiving tomorrow. Thanks for the photos."

Her stomach clenched as he exited the studio, his disappointment by her response evident in his tight expression. After a quick grab for the check, she followed Tom out into the lobby to make amends. "Who are you spending Thanksgiving with? Didn't your grandma move away?"

"Yeah, Nana now lives on a cruise ship in the Mediterranean. I don't understand how she gets away with that." He swung his backpack onto his shoulder. "I'm going to spend Thanksgiving watching the football game in my hotel room. Not too different from last year."

"Tom, that's no way to spend Thanksgiving. You know that." She had a new thought, then hesitated. "I… uh… would you like to spend Thanksgiving with my family at the farm? We could look at some of my old photographs at home to see if they would work for your magazine's contest."

His eyes widened and blinked owlishly at her. "Really? Are you sure your mom won't mind?"

She snorted. "Mom's a genteel woman at heart, trained to be hospitable and gracious to all who bless her with their presence."

"Are *you* sure about this?"

She nodded. "I would really love it if you would come."

That trademark grin flashed once again. "I'll be there."

CHAPTER 3

Thanksgiving Day arrived all too soon. Elise wrapped her scarf around her neck as she led Tom through the woods.

"Lord, I know I said I would love for it to snow, but I meant for my photo shoot," Tom grumbled as he tightened his coat and trudged through the thick, fresh powder.

The light of the full moon reflected off the white crystals in the blue night. Two sets of footprints led away from the dark car on the side of the road to her and Tom. Her family's brightly lit farmhouse in the distance beckoned to them.

"I am so sorry," Elise mumbled.

He shrugged his shoulders. "No worries. Your car is old and I guess the snowy hill was too much for the engine. At least the car died on the outskirts of your family tree farm. Anyways, right now is the perfect time for a nighttime stroll."

They walked in silence, her camera bag hitting her hip with each step, until they came upon a fir tree covered in burgundy garlands and bright bells.

"Wow." Tom stopped to appreciate the tree.

"My family used to do this every year," she explained. "Decorate a tree outside on Thanksgiving. One of us kids would choose the tree and Mom would bring steaming hot chocolate and crisp apple cider to keep us warm. Dad always placed the star on top while my brothers and I would cover the tree in silver bells, ornaments, garlands, and tinsel." She rang a silver bell on one bough. "When John died in Iraq, we just stopped. I guess Dad still comes out every year to decorate a tree. I can't imagine Mom or Matthew doing it."

"Your brother was a good man. I read about his death in the local papers."

Guilt filled her. "I'm sorry. You should have heard the details about John's death from me."

"Yeah, well, we were different back then. I understand what happened now. Before John died, all of us were happy. Your mom and I tolerated each other, your dad was like a father to me, and I looked up to John. Matthew, though, not so much."

She laughed in agreement.

"You and I, we were going to live our dream, go out and see the world," Tom continued. "I already bought our tickets to Belize. I was going to write the stories and you were going to capture them on camera."

"We were so young and naïve."

"Yeah, your brother's death was a hard blow. I hadn't heard from any of you in days so I came over to figure out what happened. I never suspected John was killed. His death hurt. He was the brother I never had. And then you told me you weren't going to leave, ever."

Their argument from that time echoed through her head. When her family had received news from the Marines that her brother had been killed overseas, everyone seemed to shut down. Her dad hadn't left the barn for days and Matthew delved into his studies, his temper becoming short and quick. Elise drifted around the house in a daze.

Her mother, though, spent the first day crying. From the second onward, she went back into her normal daily routine with only a few changes. She'd placed John's picture on display and his flag from the military, along with his medals, were hidden in the attic. Mary also started to spend more time with her daughter, comforting Elise as well as herself.

"John was such a good son. Too good, at times. That's why I knew he would excel in the military. He liked to help others. It was his dream and he always volunteered to go on tours overseas. I told him it was dangerous. I warned him—" Her mother choked up a moment before continuing. "But he didn't listen. I am proud of him, so proud, but now he's gone. He's left us forever. I don't understand why he wouldn't listen to me. We needed him here where he would've been safe. Elise, my dear, I love you so much. You're such a good daughter. You would listen to me, wouldn't you? Promise me you'll stay safe."

Elise agreed with her promise.

Tom had shown up a few days later and she tried to break the news about her brother to him gently. Of course he took it hard but when she told him her decision to stay home, that was what broke them. He couldn't understand why she wouldn't still travel, to pursue her dreams. She couldn't understand why he didn't realize the importance of being with her family that year. Their argument escalated into shouting and crying until her mother came out onto the porch and shooed Elise back in so she could face Tom herself. Elise could only watch through the screen door as her mother spoke to Tom with an icy chill, taking him to task for not only causing her daughter to cry, but also for still trying to convince her to travel when her brother just died overseas. When her mom ordered him off their property, Elise rushed to the window and watched him turn and fade down the road, not to see him again for a decade.

She released a deep exhale. "My family needed me at the time. You just kept pushing me and pushing me to go. I wanted to, I really did want to go with you. But I couldn't. My responsibility was at home."

"I understand. I really understood when your mom came out to explain for you. I had never seen her so angry before."

"I'm sorry."

"Don't be. Seriously, stop apologizing. You do that way too much. We've forgiven each other and that's what matters." He patted her shoulders. "I'm surprised, though, that after ten years, you're still here. You wanted to see the world, capture life in your viewfinder."

An invisible weight settled on her shoulders. "I still want to. But it's expensive to travel and now I have my own place and car. I work two jobs, Matthew's wedding is coming up, and mom wants me to help around the farm. I have a life here. I can't just go."

"Those are easy to fix. Sell the car and end your lease, then you'll have the money to travel. Quit your jobs and you'll have plenty of time and less responsibility. The wedding I understand, but doesn't Matthew and your cousin, Mark, help around the farm?"

"Well, they do, but still—"

He grabbed her hands. "Elise. Is this the life you want to live? This 'American Dream'? Your dream is to photograph the world and God definitely gave you the gift to do so. Why are you still here?"

"I have a duty here. A responsibility. I think God understands that." She tried to shrug off his hands, but they remained fixed upon hers.

"I believe God gave you your gifts and desires for a reason. Tell me honestly. What do you want to do?"

What do I really want? Elise stared into his earnest face. *Do I really want my current life? Am I actually happy? Is this 'American Dream' mine or what's expected of me?* Tears crept to the corners of her eyes. "I want to go."

Tom's face lit up. "Then take the first step. Even if it's only a baby step, at least you're headed somewhere. Why don't you submit to the photography contest?"

"But what about my family?"

Tom thought for a moment, then nodded. "Ok, how about this. Let's make a Christmas wish. Why don't we ask God what you should do?"

"A Christmas wish? But it's Thanksgiving."

He flung his arms wide and gestured around him. "It's snowing and there's a Christmas tree. Come on." Tom clasped her hands in his again. "Let's pray."

"Here? Now?"

"Yup."

While she had prayed out loud before, they were only generic prayers at family meals. Intimate prayers were often silent, once a week deals. "I don't really know what to do. What do I say?"

"Tell God what's on your heart. He already knows, but He just wants you to talk with Him. Tell Him your concerns and ask Him whether or not you should go. Prayer is easy. You're just talking to a friend." Tom raised a victory fist in support, then closed his eyes.

Elise stood in the quiet for a moment. Soft plumps could be heard in the background as snow fell off the trees. She glanced at Tom, then her feet, and lastly at the star on the tree. *A Christmas wish…huh? What could happen?*

"God. It's me, Elise. I haven't talked to you in a while. But God, if you can hear me, I really, really want to travel the world. I want to take pictures and share stories. I want to live this life you created. I don't want to stay here." An image of her mother flashed through her mind. "But, God, what do you think? Don't I have a responsibility here? You said to honor your Father and Mother and they want me to stay. What should I do? Should I apply to the photography contest? Please, let me know. I don't want to get my hopes up if the answer is 'no.' Please. In Jesus' name I pray, Amen."

"Amen," echoed Tom. He squeezed her hands once before letting go. "We should head in."

She nodded and followed him toward her parent's house, head high and light on her feet.

*   *   *

The red farmhouse was situated on top of a hill and overlooked the whole property. Golden light that emanated from the windows spoke of warmth and was accompanied by the smell of roasting turkey. Elise and Tom rushed to open the door to escape the chill and caused the bell above the door to chime in greeting.

"Elise. Welcome home, sugar-bug." A gray haired middle-aged man with a heavy mustache stood in the entry way. His eyes crinkled as he took them in.

"Daddy." Elise slipped effortlessly into Jack Forstner's arms and held on tight. Her father always smelled like the trees he worked with and she buried her nose into his chest to capture the memory of the scent.

"Tom, welcome home." Her dad reached out past her and shook his hand. "I'm glad you could come to dinner. Feels like old times."

"Jack, thanks. I have definitely missed being here. Does Mary know?"

Her dad shook his head.

Elise drew back. "Daddy—"

"Don't you worry. I'll handle your mother. I'm just happy to have you here again, Tom."

"Me too, sir."

"Daddy, I want to look through my old portfolios and photographs. Do you know where they are?" she asked.

"I stored them in my office for safe keeping. The boxes should be labeled with your name."

"Is that my daughter? Elise!" a bright voice charmed. Her mother, wearing a holly red tea dress, bustled around the corner holding a tray of golden cornbread. "I'm glad you're here, dear. It was getting rather late and when you didn't come early to help cook like I expected, I was worried. I'm so happy to learn I worried for noth—" The tray of cornbread fell with a loud *clang* and scattered the yellow pieces across the floor.

"Hello, Mrs. Forstner. I'm glad to see you're as lovely as ever." Tom nodded at the shocked older woman and bent to pick up the rolls. Elise and her father quickly followed.

Her mother smiled as she bent down to help. "Oh, how clumsy of me. I'm sorry you had to see that, Tom. I'm just so surprised to see you here. Elise hadn't told me you were in town." The hard gaze her mother sent belied the warmth in her words.

"I only got back in town this week and dropped by the mall studio to see if she still worked there." Tom stood with the tray of cornbread. "Should I bring these to the kitchen or the table?"

"The table would be grand. There is already a basket made up for them." Mary gripped her elbow tight. "Elise, dear, I would love to speak to you for a moment."

Elise began to panic until her father intervened.

"I need some help carving the turkey. Why don't you leave these two to say 'hi' to Matthew and Marie?" Jack said, guiding her mother to the kitchen.

Tom looked confused. "Marie?"

"My brother's fiancée."

When the rolls were disposed of, Elise escorted Tom into the living room where Matthew was seated on the couch with a demure petite woman who had shockingly red hair. Marie sat quiet with a smile as she listened to Matthew regale her with tales about an event at his law firm.

When Marie caught sight of them, she stood up to hug her future sister-in-law. "It's so good to see you again. Who is your friend?"

Before Elise had time to introduce Tom, Matthew decided to greet them as well.

"So, you've returned, Tom. I thought you were off consorting with some half-dressed natives somewhere." Matthew gripped Tom's hand. "What a surprise to see you here."

"Yes, well, after spending some time with the Dalai Lama in Dharamshala, India, I felt the desire to return home and visit old friends. Nice to see you too."

Neither one's smile reached their eyes and Elise began to wonder if this was such a good idea after all.

The dinner conversation was all politeness and regal airs. Rearrangement of seating situated Tom between Elise and her father. Her mother's eyes accused Tom the entire meal. Marie sat in obvious confusion about the coldness in behavior and tried to bring warmth into the conversation without success.

When dinner was over, Elise rushed to her father's office which was decorated with old photographs and vintage cameras. She collected the box labeled with her name. *The night's almost done. We've almost made it through.* At a slight rap on the office door, Elise looked up to find Marie.

"Please excuse me. I'm not quite sure what's going on tonight. Your friend seems kind. But I thought you should know that Mary is…well, she's seems to be very angry with him at the moment."

Elise stood up and tucked the box under her arm. "Thank you, Marie. I mean it."

Marie nodded and she headed out. Her mother's raised voice carried up the stairs.

"I don't know why you're here and I don't care, but I don't want you hanging around my daughter anymore. She's not your play toy or comfort thing to cart off around the world with you. She's too good for that."

Heat flooded Elise's face at her mother's words.

"Mary!" her father's voice intervened.

"I have only the highest respect for your daughter, ma'am. She is a very good friend of mine." Tom's voice was calm and low.

"Don't you dare think you can take her away from here again. I don't want her to follow you to God-knows-where and end up dying from God-knows-what. You're a good-for-nothing vagabond and if you try to take her away, I will do anything to keep you from succeeding."

"Mother!" Never had Elise felt more disgusted by her own mother's words and actions. "How could you speak to him that way? Tom has never done anything but support and respect me."

"Elise, honey, I am doing this for your own good. I know what's best for you but this two-bit slacker has no idea. He wouldn't be able to take care of you and would probably ditch you at the first opportunity. He's already done it once."

"If I recall correctly, Mother, both you and I drove him off last time. We forced him to leave and I will not do that again. Tom is a good friend and a well-respected writer of *Adventure Magazine*. I respect Tom and the work he has done. Not only has he forgiven me for my harsh words and actions ten years ago, but he's even given me the opportunity to enter a photography contest. I could win one-on-one mentoring with a professional photographer and an all-expenses paid trip to Brazil. I am submitting to this contest and I promise you, I will win to get away from you." Elise stormed over to her coat and camera and slipped them on.

As Tom walked out the front door, Elise turned to address the room one last time. "Good night, Dad, Matthew, and Marie. I had a wonderful evening. Happy Thanksgiving." With that, she slammed the front door as the bell rang again to announce her exit.

*   *   *

Elise stomped through the snow as she followed their old set of footprints. "Please tell me you can get the car to start when we get there. I need to hear you say this."

"A few hours have passed since the car died, so the battery's had time to rest up a bit. Since the transmission is a manual and we're facing up a hill, we can try to turn the car around and head down the hill to jump start the engine. I think we've got a good shot."

"Good," Elise mumbled and pressed on for a few more minutes. "What my mom said was inexcusable."

"I'm fine. I've heard far worse out there. I did enjoy seeing you stand up for yourself. You really have changed."

"I was so mad. Someone had to draw a line."

Tom slung an arm around her shoulders and drew her against his side. "Thank you."

His response was barely a whisper but the words made Elise's heart grow warm. They walked like that in companionable silence for a while. Then as they neared the outside Christmas tree, Elise gasped and pulled Tom behind another tree, the closest one she could find.

"Elise? What is—"

She quieted him with a finger on his lips and he looked to see what caught her attention. There, at the Christmas tree, was a large elk bathed in blue moonlight. The elk's antlers were almost as high as the star on top of the Douglas fir and the animal nudged the ornaments and bells with his muzzle.

Silently, Elise pulled her camera out of the case and adjusted the settings. She wasn't about to miss this shot. As she raised the lens, she focused in on the buck and snapped a few pictures. The elk lifted his mighty head toward a bell just above his crown and breathed a cloud of mist onto the ornament. She caught the moment on camera and exhaled in awe herself. The animal seemed done with his inspection and wandered off deeper into the trees.

"Did you get that? Please tell me you got that."

She smiled and nodded. "I think I did."

They examined the digital screen on the camera. There was the picture. Bathed in moonlight, with a backdrop of blue night, the elk's mighty antlers were bent back as a breath of life enveloped the silver bell.

"Elise. This is your picture."

She didn't even have to look at Tom to understand what he meant. This was the picture for the contest. This was the winning photograph. Strange assurance and confidence foreign to her settled deep inside with a rush of exhilaration. She knew this was the path she had to pursue.

God, thank you.

CHAPTER 4

Crunch, crunch, hop. Elise flew down the snowy driveway of her parents' home with a skip to her step. Today was the day. December fifteenth. Two weeks of nail-biting and nervous pacing were over. Soon a letter would arrive telling her whether or not she had won the *Adventure Magazine* photography contest.

She had a good feeling about this. The photo she had taken of the elk had been a photo of a lifetime. It was even more beautiful in print. The colors vividly popped out and the elk's fur was defined. She had submitted her photograph Thanksgiving weekend, just before the first. Since then she had spruced up her portfolio, renewed her passport, and submitted past and recent photos to local photography contests. The more she won, the more she knew this was the right path. It had been a long time since she had felt so proud of her work.

To her right, behind families and recently cut trees, were her father and Tom. They waved to get her attention. With a turn of her heel, she swerved toward them and wove through the crowd. The crisp air soothed her tired lungs when she reached them.

"Daddy." Elise wrapped her father up in a huge hug.

"Hey, sugar-bug. I hear you're going to steal my best employee for a bit."

"Best employee? Don't exaggerate." Tom shook his head. "Your nephew Mark is doing more work than the both of us combined. He could probably carry five trees at once if you let him. Plus, he's a natural around your horses. They all bite me at least once a day no matter how many carrots I give them. Look." He rolled up his coat sleeve to reveal a large purple and black bruise.

"Ouch. You ok?" she asked.

"Yeah, I've had worse. I think the horses just don't like me. They get along with everyone else around here."

"I got a picture of it." Her dad held up a camera for her to see. In the picture, Blackie's large teeth had caught Tom by the arm. His panicked face was priceless.

"Dad, I didn't know you started taking pictures again."

He shrugged. "All this talk about photo shoots and contests rubbed off on me, I guess. But it's late afternoon and the light is starting to fade. You should probably get your pictures done now before your mother's tea party tonight."

She smacked her head. "Thanks for reminding me. I'd almost forgotten. Thank goodness I keep extra gear in my car. Okay, Tom. Let's get going."

For the next hour, Elise and Tom walked all over the tree farm. She shadowed as he worked. There were several shots of him as he helped cut and haul trees for families. Later, she had him pose in the snow and among the trees. They finally ended in the barn where treats and drinks were made available for the customers.

When they passed the hot chocolate stand, Elise took a break to have some. Tom downed several cups. After he finished his third, she couldn't contain her giggle at the foam mustache on his upper lip. Her giggle turned into full blown laughter as he retaliated with a mini marshmallow fight.

She tried to hold her own against the onslaught of fluffy white treats. As she reached behind her to grab more marshmallows, she didn't notice when she grabbed a handful of sawdust instead and chucked it all over him and his drink.

He froze and looked down at his cup covered with small wooden chips that slowly sank to the bottom of his beverage. "My hot chocolate…" His eyes shot up with a teasing sharp glare. "It was innocent. How could you?"

"I'm sorry." Try as she might, she couldn't stop her giggles.

"You think this is funny? Oh, it's on."

He grabbed a fistful of sawdust and advanced. Elise, desperate to save her own drink, ran out of the barn into the snow. His footsteps thundered close behind her and she pumped her legs faster but didn't see the rock hidden under the frozen powder. She tripped and flew face first into the bank, her hot chocolate lost.

As she scrambled into an upright position, Tom loomed above her with a mad grin accompanied by a very large snowball. "No—" *Smack!* White powder hit her in the face. "Why you—"

A snowball fight broke out between them. Neither party seemed to be the victor as the game went on. Both were equally covered in snow and laughed uncontrollably. Without warning, Tom suddenly tackled her. With hardly a fight, he wrapped her tight in his arms before he deposited snow down the collar of her coat. She shrieked at the icy chill running down her spine. Quickly, she shoved a half formed snowball into his mouth and giggled.

"You know…" *Snap.* "You two might be scaring the customers away with your screaming." Her father looked down at the digital screen on his camera. "Nice."

Tom spat out the snow and helped Elise to her feet. "They probably just wished they joined in."

"Yeah." She nodded. "Why don't we invite them all to a snowball fight and—"

"Elise." Her mother's sharp voice cut her off. She stood a few feet away, her face drawn tight with a stern expression. "It's almost five o'clock and you're drenched. Did you forget about the tea party?"

"No, Mom. Don't worry, I have a few clothes here I can change into. I'll head right up."

Her mother nodded. When she saw Tom, she stopped for a moment, scowled, and then walked to the house.

"Okay, Tom." Elise sighed, pulling away from him. "I'll send you copies of your photos through email. Let me know which one you'd like."

She waved goodbye and was gifted with a cheeky grin from Tom, which lit a flame inside her and kept her warm as she followed her mother home.

*   *   *

Her feet *ached*. Why did she have to wear high heels? If slippers were out of the question at a tea party, at least bare feet would've been better. After standing for a few hours with her feet raised at the two inch awkward angle, Elise was certain that high heels were a device designed to torture women. Once the guests had left, she couldn't limp to her old bedroom to remove the horrible things quickly enough. As she rubbed her sore foot muscles, a soft rap echoed from her door.

"It's open."

Her mother's head poked around the corner. "Hello, dear. May I come in?"

Elise nodded. Hopefully this would be quick.

Her mother entered with a white envelope in her hand and sat down on the bed next to her. "I wanted to thank you for your help this evening. Your photos are a big help in promoting our farm."

Elise frowned. Her mother rarely thanked her for her photography. "Th-thank you."

"I have always admired your pictures." She smiled and patted her daughter's hand. "Did you think I'd let just anybody photograph my tea parties?"

"But didn't you always ask me so you didn't have to pay a lot of money?"

"Dear, when it matters, I choose quality over cost. You didn't win all those contests for nothing."

Her heart lifted. For years she had wanted her mom's approval. "That really means a lot to me."

Her mother nodded. "Whatever you choose to do with your life, wherever you decide to go, I fully support you one hundred percent. You know that don't you?"

"Yeah. Of course."

Almost absent-mindedly, her mother brushed a lock of hair away from Elise's face. "I brought you some mail. This came earlier today." She handed her the white envelope she had carried in. "I think this is what you've been waiting for."

The envelope was addressed from *Adventure Magazine*. At the sight of the company name, Elise's heart leaped to her throat. This was it. Inside that white slip was the answer to her dream. Was she ready? *Of course. I've been ready for years.* A fine tremor shook her hands as she carefully opened the envelope and unfolded the letter. Her eager eyes took in every word.

> *"Dear Ms. Forstner,*
> *Thank you for sending your submission to Adventure Magazine's annual Christmas photography contest. We appreciate the quality of excellence and unique creativity your submission possessed. However, your entry has not been selected as a finalist. It was a difficult decision…"*

The words started to blur and bleed. Like an underground spring, sobs erupted from within her.

"Elise, what's wrong?"

She shook her head, unable to speak past the tears.

Her mother snatched up the paper and quickly scanned the contents. A second later the letter floated to the floor as her mother embraced her. "Oh, I'm so sorry dear," her mother whispered as she rubbed her back.

Elise buried her head into her mother's chest, her dreams shattered.

CHAPTER 5

Brrrt. Brrrt. Brrrrrrt. Her phone vibrated across the nightstand beside her. The glow from the screen filled the room and Elise groggily covered her eyes from the sudden light. She should really just turn her phone off. Three days had gone by since her photo was rejected and she hadn't left her parent's house, every phone call ignored. He should really take a hint.

With a slight reach to pick up the phone, the caller ID confirmed her suspicions. Tom. Guilt slammed into her again and she curled up into a ball. He deserved to hear the contest result. He was the one who had encouraged her to apply.

The phone died down in her hands and indicated she had received another voice mail. *I guess we'll talk another day. Good. I can't really handle his happy-go-lucky attitude right now.* When she leaned over to place the phone back on the nightstand, the screen lit up again accompanied by another set of vibrations. *Tom.*

Elise gazed at the name for a moment. Then, without a second thought, she ignored the call and turned off her phone. *It's his fault I'm in this mess anyway. I should've never listened to him.*

*   *   *

"Elise." The front door shook beneath the rapid pounding of Tom's knock. The sound carried throughout the farmhouse to her bedroom. "Come on. Open up. It's been five days. Please talk to me."

She sat on the edge of her bed and stared down at her feet. Was she ready to face him?

"Would you like me to talk to him for you?" Her mother stood in her room's entrance, arms folded with a defiant look on her face.

She shook her head. "No. I need to do this." Elise wiped her sweaty palms on her jeans and stood. "This is my decision. He needs to know that."

Her mother nodded. "I understand. Just remember, I'm here to support you in any way. If you need my help again."

"Thanks."

The walk from her bedroom, down the stairs, to the entry was hazy and surreal. She could see Tom's shadow through the front windows and his pleas filled her ears. The scene's familiarity teased her like a sense of déjà vu.

In a matter of minutes she was at the door and opened it. Relief flooded Tom's face at her appearance.

"Elise. How are you? Where've ya been?"

For a few moments, she stared up at him from inside. Her hand clutched the frame, unwilling to let go and leave the shelter of the house.

"Sorry. I should've called you back. This week's been very hard for me. I got a rejection letter from *Adventure Magazine* and I—"

"What? You were rejected? That's not—"

"Tom. Please stop. I'm having a hard enough time already."

"But Elise, I work for *Adventure Magazine* and I will be a part of the trip to Brazil. I know who—"

"Stop it," she shouted. Fury flamed inside her. "Just stop. I won't have you pulling strings for me or skewing the results. That's not how this works. I lost fair and square. I am done."

At her outburst, he froze on the deck and glared at her. Finally, he breathed out a long gush of air and crossed his arms. "Okay. You lost the contest. So what? Why don't you still go out and travel the world on your own? You don't need a contest to go. You told me you have enough money saved up. A friend just invited me to his wedding in Italy this New Year's Eve. Why don't you join me?"

Frustration trembled through her like a volcano. "You don't get it, do you?"

"I am trying to help you. You have so many options and paths open to you."

"We prayed about it," she exploded. Elise moved from the door and prodded him in the chest with her index finger. "We prayed and asked God whether He wanted me to go or stay with my family. I thought because of that stupid elk picture I was supposed to go."

As she went on, her words sped up and her finger drove Tom to the edge of the porch. "I thought He gave me a way out, an escape. I thought He really did want me to be a travel photographer, that what I wanted to do above all else wasn't wrong."

Elise paused, then deflated. Her arm dropped and her head lowered to hide her tears. "I was wrong. I lost. God doesn't want me to go. My place is here."

She turned around and headed back to the door. When she arrived at the frame, Elise looked over her shoulder. "I'm done, Tom. I'm staying. Don't ask me again."

He looked broken, lost. Unable to stand the sight, she looked away.

"Elise, wait," he called out.

She hesitated.

"Please," his voice cracked. "Don't do this again."

For the final time she looked into his alluring green eyes, then shut the door.

CHAPTER 6

Two days before Christmas, Elise sat in the living room bay window seat of her parents' house nestled tight in a thick quilt. The lights in the house were off to allow the view outside to shine through. Night had already claimed the sky and frost had begun to crystalize the glass panes where Elise rested her head. Lanterns lined the path from the house down the hill to the red barn. Tree shoppers had gathered to drink hot beverages and to listen to the local high school choir sing Christmas carols. All these which had once been so bright and joyful for her were now a painful reminder of everything she had lost. *Happiness.*

She exhaled listlessly, her hot breath clouding the window. For three days she had replayed her fight with Tom non-stop in her head, her heart heavy with regret.

When the door had closed between them, Elise had leaned against it and listened to the soft gravel crunch from Tom's fading footsteps. Then the tension that had built inside her, wound tight like a coil, snapped. She'd cried out, hunched over, and covered her mouth.

"Elise, dear."

Her mother had stood with open arms. With a wail, she'd rushed into her mother's embrace that offered the comfort and acceptance she needed.

Her mother had stroked her hair. "I'm so proud of you, dear. So proud."

In that moment, Elise felt closer to her mother than she had in a long time. Her mother had been her support these last few days and helped her make it through, always reconfirming that she had made the right decision. But if it was the right choice, why did she feel so awful?

A soft rap sounded at the door. "Come in."

Her father peeked around the door and smiled. "Hey sugar-bug. May I sit with you a while?" At her nod he moved to sit by her. "You don't want to come down to listen to the carolers?"

"No. I hear enough carols at the mall. They play non-stop."

He chuckled. "Yeah. I suppose that would be annoying."

They sat quietly for a while, drinking in the night scene. Elise loved these moments with her dad. In silence they could communicate more than in a thousand words. Peace settled over her and somehow she knew everything would end up alright.

Her dad reached into his coat and pulled out a small red envelope, laying it on his lap in such a way that the light reflected off and grabbed her attention.

She frowned. "Another Christmas card?"

"Hmm? Oh yeah. I thought you might be interested in this one." He held it out to her.

She slid the card from his fingers. Turning it over, she paused at the sender's name. "I didn't think Tom would send one. Especially since I forgot to send him his photos."

She pulled the card out. A sprig of mistletoe graced the front. Flipping the cover open, she was surprised to see a photo in addition to a letter drop onto her blanket. She picked the picture up. Underneath a printed '*Merry Christmas!*' sat a couple covered in snow. Tom held her tightly in his grasp, doing his best impression of a young boy's pout with snow stuffed in his face. Elise herself had been caught laughing. *I look...happy.* Tears filled her eyes, and her throat tightened as she asked, "When did he get this?"

"I sent the photo to Tom the day after the shoot. Seems like he decided to use it for his newsletter."

She tucked the photo back into the card and then into the envelope. "He probably regrets sending those out now."

"Who knows? He left for Italy yesterday."

Her head snapped up. "He left?"

"Says so in the letter. Are you going to read it?"

She shook her head. "No, I don't think I will. Here." She handed the card back to her dad. "You took a really nice photo, Dad. If I didn't know better, I'd say you were a professional."

"Thanks. I did win a few contests in my day."

That was news to her. "You used to enter photography contests?"

"Yeah. I started back in Vietnam. I used to send photos to my parents and they even passed a few to the paper. When I came home from the war I kept taking them. I made quite a few bucks too."

Elise's mouth fell open. "I never knew this. Why did you stop?"

He shrugged. "There was never one reason why. Life got in the way. My father had an accident so I took over running the tree farm. Soon after, I met your mother, and then you kids started to come around. There were bills to pay, farm expenses, and school expenses. Photography was an expensive hobby back then, not like today with all your smartphones. Soon, I was too busy and too old to start a new career."

She shivered and pulled her blanket tighter around her. "Do you ever regret it? Giving up photography?"

Her dad sat a while before he answered. "That's a tough question, sugar-bug. I love your mother very much. I wouldn't have traded you or your brothers for the world and I do love this farm. I don't regret any of that or being there for my father when he needed me. But, it took me a long time to get over the 'what ifs.' A very long time."

The 'what ifs.' She knew those very well. For the past ten years she had been plagued with them. When she had finally gotten those wild thoughts under control, Tom came back and reignited the dying embers of her dreams. But reality was cruel and Tom left again, leaving more 'what ifs' in his wake. *Is this what the rest of my life is going to look like?* Her inner being rebelled and she felt like she was going to throw up.

Her father grabbed her hand. "What's wrong, sugar-bug?"

"Daddy," she sobbed, "I don't want to live a 'what if' life. I'm tired of it. I wanna go, Daddy. I wanna be a travel photographer."

"What's holding you back?"

"God."

Her father jerked back. "What?"

"I prayed and asked God if I was supposed to be a travel photographer. I asked if I could go and He said 'no.' I lost the contest, Daddy."

"Sugar-bug," her father said, pulling her into a hug. "Are you saying that the contest result was His answer?"

She nodded.

"How?"

"Because I asked Him for a sign to show me if I was supposed to travel the world. When I took that photo of the elk I was sure that was the answer. I had never been surer about anything in my life. But then I didn't even place."

"Okay, let me get this straight. You asked for a sign, right? Then you took that once in a lifetime shot of the elk. Next, your passport came within four weeks of applying before Christmas. Also, you have been saving up all these years and have more than enough to pay for the trip on your own, right?"

Elise nodded at each statement he made.

"With everything else falling into place, why is whether or not you win His answer?"

"Because, it was an all-expenses paid trip…" Elise faltered. "Because I would go overseas and Janell Greyson would tutor me." She sniffed and broke down. "Because I wanted to win. I wanted a definite 'yes' from someone. I wanted to be told I was good enough."

He pulled her into a tight hug.

"I'm tired of always feeling sorry for myself and never doing anything about it. If I stay, it's only going to get worse. I need to go."

"So go."

She looked up at her dad. "But God said 'no.'"

"Did He? Look at everything, Elise. If all the signs point to 'yes' except for the contest, do you think that maybe God wants you to go but in a different way?"

A small hope lit inside her. "You think that God wants me to travel, just not with *Adventure Magazine*? Like another magazine?"

"Could be. Or maybe you could go out and create your own adventure. You have everything you need to go off traveling tomorrow, don't you? You just need to cancel your lease."

"Just go tomorrow…" she rubbed her lips absent-mindedly. No plan, no schedule, just go where and when she wanted to. She liked plans and schedules, their familiarity and security. But something about the idea of complete and utter freedom called to her. The small flame inside her burned brighter and her skin started to tingle with excitement.

"Daddy, do you know the visa requirements for Italy? Like if I need one and how soon I could get it?"

"Not sure, sugar-bug, but I could ask my good friend Google. You gonna go to Italy?"

She nodded and took back the Christmas card from her father. "There's someone I really want to see."

Her dad stood up and offered her a hand. "Need help canceling your lease?" Elise hopped to her feet, a smile on her face. "No, I've got this."

CHAPTER 7

The crackle of fire accompanied carols crooning from the stereo. Elise and her family sat around their Christmas tree adorned with red spheres and hand-made ornaments. On the center of the tree hung a framed picture of John, a place of honor and remembrance.

Everyone shared tales from work and laughed as they waited for midnight to ring in Christmas Day. Even though many holiday traditions had been lost since John died, staying up with the family until morning and opening one gift each was still a welcome custom.

Elise looked from one family member to the next: Father, Mother, Matthew, and Marie. Tonight was the night she would announce her trip to everyone. Her dad already knew, but soon it would be official. How would each react? Her fingers worried a thread loose from the couch blanket.

"A toast."

Her mother rose with a crystal goblet in hand and a bottle of sparkling apple cider in the other. Everyone quickly offered their glasses so she could pour the fizzing amber liquid and rose to stand with her.

Setting down the bottle, her mother raised her crystal cup high and the rest followed her example. "To a happy Christmas and a wonderful New Year. I am so glad we are all home together, safe and sound. The Lord has blessed each and every one of us this year and I'm sure he will continue to do so into the next. I want to thank Him for a profitable season on the farm and for you two's upcoming nuptials," her mother added, nodding to Marie and Matthew. "I pray that Elise will follow their example."

Matthew chuckled as Marie turned red. Elise only offered a small smile in return.

Her mother continued with a triumphant note in her voice, "May God help us see the paths He's laid out for our lives and give us courage to walk them."

"Cheers!" Glasses clinked against one another as the clock started to chime, announcing midnight. Elise stared, the last words of the toast reverberating through her heart in time with the heralding gongs. *Lord, please give me some of your courage.*

"It's time for us to open a present." Matthew started to dig under the tree and presented a small box to their mother. "Here, Mom, you can open my gift tonight."

Marie gave a gift to Matthew as her mother gave a gift to her father. That was the tradition. Each person gave one gift and opened one from someone different. Elise had framed a picture of her elk shot and wrapped it for Marie. Despite being her future sister-in-law, she had never spent time with her brother's fiancée. Hopefully, her picture was a safe bet.

As everyone fawned over their gifts, her father leaned over and placed a bulky brown paper sack with a huge red bow in her lap. He winked at her and said, "I thought you could use it when you go."

Reaching in, Elise pulled out a large green bag. It was huge with a couple of straps to slip arms through and no identifiable features except for the words 'C.P.L. Forstner' printed in black.

"What is it?" she asked, examining the bag.

"My old duffle from my time in Vietnam. I know it's not the prettiest and doesn't have wheels, but you can fit more in that bag than one of those fancy wheeling ones. It's also really durable, lasted through many fights without a tear or hole. This bag is easy to transport and should last you until you get a decent backpack of your own."

"Daddy." Elise smoothed the wrinkled bag out and touched the printed words. "Thank you."

He nodded.

"Jack, what is that thing doing out?" her mother's voice cut through their conversation. Her eyes glared at the military duffle in Elise's lap.

She clutched the bag to her chest. "Daddy gave it to me. It's my Christmas gift."

Her mother sighed and shook her head. "Really, Jack? You couldn't have thought of something better than that old thing?"

"I like it, it's perfect," Elise defended.

"Perfect?" Matthew poked at the duffle with a distasteful look on his face. "For what?"

She froze. Everyone in the room was staring at her and her heart started to pound. *I guess it's now or never.*

Clearing her throat, she rose to address them. "Everyone, I have an announcement to make. These last few days I've been praying and thinking things over, and I have finally come to a decision. Even though I lost the photography contest, I am still going to go on a trip of my own. I'm leaving for Italy in two days."

After a few seconds of silence, Matthew jumped to his feet. "What? You can't be serious. Dad, say something," he pleaded with her father.

"Did you already get the plane ticket?" Marie looked at Elise with a strange expression on her face. Was that…longing?

Elise nodded and looked at her mother, who gazed at her silently with lips pressed into an almost non-existent smear of red, before turning and walking up the stairs.

Her heart sank. *Of course she wouldn't approve.*

"Elise, what are you thinking?" Matthew came over and gripped her shoulders. "Are you at least going to be back in time to photograph my wedding?"

She shrugged him away. "I don't know, Matthew. I'm sorry."

"Did you even think about any of us when you made your decision?"

Everyone stilled at her mother's icy words. She had returned to the stairway without anyone noticing and held a small slip of paper in her hand. Her face was as smooth as marble except for a single raised eyebrow. Her gaze seemed fixed on Elise as she descended and held up her prize. "Is this your plane ticket?"

Elise tried to swallow the lump in her throat and nodded again. "Mom, may I please have—" She gasped as her mother promptly ripped her ticket in half. The rest of the family stood in shocked silence.

"There, now that's the end of that discussion," her mother declared. "Why don't we all head to bed and clean up the living room in the morning?"

Elise's hands clenched into fists. "How could you? That was mine and you had no right to tear it apart. I paid for that."

"A wasted expense, my dear." Her mother's cool voice cut deep. "I raised you to know better than to travel on your own. You will end up hurt. I am saving you from a foolish decision."

"It is my choice whether or not I travel, not yours. It is my choice whether or not to spend that money, and it is my choice whether or not I'll be hurt. You don't make those decisions for me."

"Are you serious? Haven't you heard the stories of young women who go alone? Do you not care about how your selfish decision will affect us, will affect me?"

Her mouth dropped open. "Selfish? I'm sorry if my *selfish* decision will ruin your cheap wedding plans for Matt. I'm sorry if my *selfish* decision will ruin your tea party promotions. Oh yes, I am terrible, indeed, for finally taking a step forward to live my dream instead of staying at home to be at your beck and call."

"Do you realize how much I have sacrificed for you? For all of us to be here together? And now you want to throw everything away so you can prance around with some savages in the middle of nowhere."

There's no way. She won't listen at all. She'll never approve. The fight inside Elise died, replaced by an eerie calm.

Without another word, she bent down to pick up her ripped ticket. She could probably get a replacement at the airport.

"What are you doing?"

Ignoring her mother, she walked past the rest of her family and headed upstairs to her room. She started grabbing her clothes out of her drawers and shoving them into the duffle.

"Didn't you hear what I said? Are you listening?" Her mother's voice rose as she followed her to her room.

"Yes, Mother. However, I regret to inform you that it has not changed my decision. I am supposed to go."

"What do you mean you're 'supposed to go'?" her mother demanded.

She sighed and moved to her closet, pulling more clothes and shoes out. "I've prayed and prayed about it, Mother. And you know what? When I finally decided to go, that was the first time in my life I felt at peace. Staying here has made me feel horrible about myself." She finished up with her closet and went to her bedside table, pulling her passport out of its drawer. "Then this Christmas, when I took those contest photos and got ready to leave, I was the happiest I've been in ten years. I believe God gave me a passion for photography and travel for a reason and that He wants me to use them. I'm going to go to find out how. I'll stay at a friend's house until I go since you can't accept that."

Elise headed back downstairs with her bag and mother in tow.

"You think that God wants you to leave your friends, your family, and your home?" her mother exclaimed. "That He wants you to put yourself in harm's way? You can take your pictures here. I will not lose another child."

Everyone stared at them as Mary puffed heavily on the stairs, her face red.

"Mom, I'm not John," Elise whispered.

"I know that," her mother snapped bitterly. "Fine. Do what you want. But if you walk out that door, don't think you have a place to come home to."

What? The ultimatum rang in Elise's ears and she faltered.

"Mom, what are you saying?" Matthew whispered.

A heavy hand rested on Elise's shoulder. She looked up to see her father holding her coat. "You should go on your trip, sugar-bug. Why don't you finish packing another day?"

"Jack?" her mother looked at her father in disbelief.

"Mary, I'm going to take Elise to the airport the day she flies out. She will always have a home here."

Elise's eyes watered and her mother broke down on the stairs. Matthew hurried over to comfort her.

"Would you like to stay with me until you go, Elise? I've got an extra room." Marie walked up to her, pulling on a pastel blue pea coat and some mittens.

She nodded, grateful. This wasn't how she wanted to end things, but Elise doubted anything she could say now would make things better.

They had just opened the door to leave when her mother cried out, "Elise, wait. Please don't go!" She ran up, and grabbing the duffle in Elise's hand, tugged hard.

Reflexively, Elise let go of the bag, releasing her mother who stumbled back and fell into the Christmas tree. The tree tipped under the sudden weight and crashed against the bay window behind it, dropping its fragile baubles. John's picture swung precariously on its branch before flying off onto the ground, shattering the glass.

Her mother cried out and knelt, scrambling to pick up the pieces while pushing Matthew and her father away. Elise stared down at her, her heart clenching at the sight, then picked up her bag and walked out the door.

CHAPTER 8

Elise checked her watch. Thirty more minutes until the ticket counters opened at five A.M. She had wandered the airport for the last five and a half hours. People were now lining up in front of the ticket counters. *Maybe I should get in line too. Getting here at eleven at night wasn't my best idea but the thought of driving here at three in the morning was even more ridiculous.*

Marie had become a true friend the last few days. Though they only spent a short time together, Elise came to really appreciate her brother's fiancé. Marie had even hung her gift as the centerpiece in her living room. While Matthew's character had room for improvement, he had chosen a wonderful woman to join their family and Marie had accompanied her future sister and father-in-law to the airport. Matthew had stayed behind to support their mother.

No matter how many times she tried, Elise couldn't think of another way her talk with her mom could have gone. Even if she hadn't goaded her, her mother would still have been on a war path.

If you walk out that door, don't think you have a place to come home to.' The words repeated like a broken record in her mind. Her father made it quite clear that she still was welcome to come home, but her mother's last words cut her. *I didn't want to say goodbye like that. I didn't want to start my adventure like this.*

Buck up, Elise. She stood and rolled her shoulders. *New life awaits. Maybe Mom will have a more open mind when I come home. Just a few more minutes until my adventure begins.*

Bending over, she picked up her duffle bag. *God, thank you for being patient with me. Thank you for opening my eyes. Thank you for pushing me out the door. Please, help me with Mom. Help her accept that traveling is what I'm meant to do.*

"Elise."

She stiffened at the familiar voice behind her and turned around to find her mother standing there in the airport aisle, her expression tight. She could see Matthew lingering in the background, stuffing car keys in his pocket. *Wow, God, that was fast.*

Her mother stood before her with red rimmed eyes and in sweat clothes. Red blotches covered her face, unadorned by make-up, and her hair was pulled back in a hap hazard bun. The last time Elise had seen her mother like this was after John had died.

"I'm not going home with you."

Her mother nodded. "I know." She sat down and patted the seat next to her, an unspoken command which Elise obliged. Several times, her mother opened her mouth only to close it again and wring her fingers. Elise waited patiently. This was her last time with her mother before she left and she refused to repeat Christmas.

Finally, her mother spoke. "You know, years ago, I used to want to travel like you do. I wanted to see the world, do impossible things. However, in my family's social circle, proper young ladies didn't do such things. That was for older folk. I thought I could wait until you kids grew up or I retired. I never questioned that unspoken rule. I did what I was told to do. The only time I ever rebelled was when I married your father. My parents didn't approve of Jack. He wasn't a proper, rich, social elite boy."

Elise snorted. Her father definitely wasn't that. He was more like a backwoods man.

"Your father is a good man. I love him, I really do, but I would be lying if I said my current life with him is what I used to dream about as a kid. It's more hard work, more compromise, and less money, but I think we've managed.

"While life hasn't been all bells and whistles, I had you and your brothers. You three brightened up my life. One of my proudest moments was when John joined the Marines. When he left on that last deployment to Iraq, I never thought it would be the last time that I saw him. I mean, I knew there was a possibility he could die in battle and I warned him, but I never suspected him to be blown up during leave." Her mother choked and tried to push back tears. "He was only in the local market, wearing civilian clothes and he was blown up. For what?" Tremors shook her mother's shoulders as she desperately questioned her son's purpose. "Was he targeted or was it a coincidence? What was the point of his death? Was his life a waste?"

"Mom…"

"I know." Mary nodded. "I know there's some greater scheme. I know he must've made a difference over there, but his death is still hard to accept."

She turned to Elise and gripped her hand. "Do you really have to go?"

Elise squeezed back. "I'm not going to die, Mom. It's not even a combat zone. But if I did, I wouldn't regret going. I'd be happy knowing I followed my dream instead of staying safe at home. Anyway, Tom's there. He doesn't know I'm coming, but I hope I can apologize to him. He deserves that at least."

Her mother nodded. "He really is a good boy. I'm sorry for how I treated him. Please, would you…?"

"Yeah, Mom. I'll let him know."

The noise level of the terminal rose. People hastily got to their feet around Elise and her mother to get in line for the ticket counters as attendants opened up for business.

"I should get going and say goodbye to you and Matthew." Elise stood and helped her mother rise. "I'm sure I have one of the first flights out of here and that line is getting long." As she hugged her mom, a heavy weight on her shoulders disappeared. Now *this* was the goodbye she wanted.

"I'm sorry but there's one more thing I need to tell you." Her mother dug through her pockets until she produced a torn envelope. "This is yours. What I did was very wrong. I hope you can forgive me."

"What is it?" Elise took the envelope and read the letter she pulled out.

"Dear Ms. Forstner,
Thank you for sending your submission to Adventure Magazine's
Christmas photography contest. We want to congratulate you for
being selected as the top finalist for this contest. Your submission
possessed a quality of excellence and unique creativity with
startling clarity. As the winner of this contest you will receive as a
prize a two week…"

Tremors in Elise's fingers shook the letter, her mind barely able to comprehend the words. "I…won?"

Her mother nodded.

"Then the other letter…?"

Her mother looked ashamed. "I forged it. I shouldn't have. Please forgive me?"

Frustration knotted in her heart as she looked sharply at her mother. Ready to lash out at her, Elise suddenly remembered how she had attacked Tom. Taking a few deep breaths, she instead reached out and grabbed her mother's hand. "I still love you, Mom."

"I love you, too, dear. There's still time to accept the prize."

She bit her lip, then nodded. "I'm going to Italy."

"Still?"

"Yup, already paid and I want to see Tom. I'll email *Adventure Magazine* once I get past security. I'm sure I can head to Brazil afterward."

"You're going to do both?"

Elise couldn't stop the laughter from bursting out of her as she stood. "Yeah. I'm going to go to Italy and Brazil. Wow, God is good." She slung her duffle bag on her back and hugged her mother one more time.

"You forgive me?"

"Yes. Yes I do. Give my love to everyone."

Her mother nodded and squeezed her.

Elise waved to Matthew who came up and gave her a hug. When they let go, he pressed several bills into her hands. "I thought you could use this. Have a safe trip."

She nodded and tucked the money into her coat.

With a kiss, her mom and Matthew turned around and headed out of the airport. As they disappeared through the automatic doors, Elise eagerly proceeded to the ticket counter, ticket in hand.

*　　　*　　　*

A white tent stood out against the inky black of the night, illuminated on the outside by sporadic bursts of kaleidoscope colors from New Year's Eve fireworks. Inside, every nook and cranny was filled with bouquets and ribbons, draped along chairs, tables, and the ceiling. Waiters attended to the tables, dropping off the last course of food along with little bomboniere boxes filled with sugar coated almonds. Accordion music, accompanied by tambourines and guitars, blared across the dance floor. Wedding guests, joined by their hands in a large circle, spun faster and faster to the music, reversing direction as the tempo increased. Spectators clapped in time and toasted with cheers of "evviva gli sposi!"

In the middle of the dance floor, a peculiar couple stood out. A tall young man in a black suit guided a little girl in pink around the dance hall. She giggled every time he did a turn or a hop. He grinned at her enthusiasm and then hooked her arm in his to spin rapidly in circles. The child squealed in delight and, with a raised arm, shouted, "La tarantella!"

Click. Snap.

Tom looked from his dance partner toward the photographer and slowed to a stop.

Elise lowered her camera and smiled at him. "Now there's a photo of a lifetime."

He blinked once. Twice. Then, slowly, he grinned back at her. Leaning over, he whispered to the girl in his arms and she nodded before running off toward the tables.

Tom turned back to Elise. "Look up."

She glanced at the ceiling to find leafy-green boughs filled with berries. "Mistletoe?"

"It's tradition here, to kiss underneath mistletoe at midnight on New Year's Eve. You should be careful, or else you might end up kissing a complete stranger."

"Oh? And what do you suggest I do?" Elise crossed her arms and arched a brow, smiling.

Tom's eyes twinkled. "Kiss me, of course."

Elise laughed as she moved toward him, not planning to wait until midnight. After all, she'd waited for this moment *long enough*.

About the Author:

Julianne M. Haag is a member of the Northwest Christian Writers Association and of Romance Writers of America. Raised in a Christian home, her family taught her about the love of Jesus Christ and gave her a heart to travel, two important aspects of her life that she incorporates into her inspirational romance, historical, paranormal, and fantasy fiction writing.

To learn more about Julianne M. Haag, you can visit her Facebook page at: **https://www.facebook.com/juliannemhaag**

The inspiration for "*A Christmas Shot*" actually came from my own life. I had just returned from an eleven month mission trip with Adventures in Missions (AIM). The mission trip ("The World Race") took me to eleven different countries where I served and helped the local ministries. It was an amazing year filled with vastly different cultures bright personalities, crazy and funny stories, growth in my Christian walk, and a fantastic community. When I returned home, everyone always asked "what was your favorite place?" Well, after a year of miracles, of new sights to see, of beautiful people, and inspirational stories, how can one answer that? You try to summarize it in a few sentences but once you start going, it all comes pouring out.

By the time I was done talking, everyone would sigh and say "I wish I could do that, but…" and give a variety of reasons. Honestly, I could not understand. If you truly wish to do something, why let anything hold you back? I found the mission trip by doing a simple Google search and then dropped everything and left. I took a chance, and I wasn't the only one. The people I traveled with sold their homes and cars, quit their jobs, gave away their pets, released everything because they were called to go and they answered. It's scary to leave the life you built behind, but it'll be the greatest adventure you'll ever go on. It's not just in the movies. It can actually happen to you if you have the faith and courage to walk out your front door. This story came about as a way to motivate and encourage you to do the crazy and unthinkable. To trust God will work everything out if He calls you to go.

(Photo description: Month 10 of the World Race. Mbidi Lodge, South Africa. I got to pet and kiss the Cheetahs up close! One of the most exciting experiences of my life!) – Julianne

Silver Lining

by

Robin Gueswel

Dedication:

This is for my three wonderful boys. Your dreams are worth working for.

Acknowledgement:

I want to thank everyone who has stood by me while I worked my way to this point. I have had an incredible support group, some of them are published here with me. I have learned so much from them about writing and about faith. I also want to thank my parents who endured years of my story telling.

CHAPTER 1

Anita Crispin stood in the back room of the salon, tearing foils into perfect rectangles and humming along with Bing Crosby. She loved the holiday music and the fact it was gently snowing outside lifted her spirit to a new height. Someday she would be getting ready for Christmas in her own salon.

She could almost see it, elegant black chairs and silver stations. Her product displays of Chi and Biosilk would be wonderful and clean. She would have antique styling tools hanging on the walls, and if she could get her hands on one, a perm machine from the early 1940's. Anita planned to dedicate the old fashioned decorations to her grandparents with a special plaque befitting the elderly couple who had faithfully supported her through the years. She sighed wistfully.

If only they were alive to see my dream come to fruition.

Her first appointment of the day was with Noelle, who needed a color lowlight. Anita had been Noelle's stylist for a little over a year now and she completely understood how Noelle felt about her appearance. The woman's hair was a natural pale blonde color, but she had started getting a warm caramel lowlight about nine months ago. She loved it, and Anita thought it gave Noelle's wispy layers more depth.

Glancing out the back door, Anita caught a glimpse of Bernie. She stood bundled up in her heavy parka and fur lined snow boots puffing on a cigarette. Anita had worked for Bernie for four years and now her boss was looking for a partner. It cut her to the quick to think that after all this time, Bernie didn't think she was ready step up to the challenge.

Anita always worked hard, whenever Bernie told her to be there, she arrived at least ten minutes early. Styling hair was her life. She loved what she did, making people feel good and look good always made her smile.

Just as Anita decided she had a good stack of foils ready for her color, she heard the cheery tinkle of the front doorbell and the sound of feet stomping on the welcome rug. "Hello, Noelle. Go ahead and hang up your coat. I will be right there."

Doing a color service for a client was always a thrill, depending on the tube of color and the developer she used; the dye that was applied could come out in many different ways. Taking a deep breath, she grabbed her cart loaded with boxes of color, a bottle of developer, a stack of stained towels, and the foils, and she headed up to her station where her client was getting comfortable. Anita had an overload of clients scheduled right now with everyone preparing for the big Mallard, Colorado party the Sunday evening before the 25th of December.

"Ready for the party?" Anita asked, while she wrapped a towel around Noelle's neck.

"Almost there. I need this little break from all the holiday hubbub."

"I can only imagine. Please tell me you are bringing that wonderful apple strudel of yours?" Anita asked as she divided the hair into five even sections.

"Ha, do you really think they will let me in the door without it?" Noelle watched as Anita carefully squeezed the bright yellow hair color into the bowl.

"Good, that stuff is amazing. I love the strudel topping, I mean it is all good, but that is my favorite part." Anita set the empty tube down before carefully measuring the 20-volume developer and pouring it over the vibrant gold color paste already in the bowl. After mixing the two chemicals together, Anita grabbed her foiling comb with its long metal tail and the first foil and went to work.

Looking in the mirror to see how Noelle was doing, Anita saw Bernie watching with a sour look on her face. *Oh God, if you are ever going to help me, help me now. Please don't let her come over here and say anything. I can't afford to lose Noelle. She is my best client.*

Anita used the tail on her comb to pick up a thin section of hair, and then wove the tail up and down to thin the section even more. Her stomach churned as she looked at Bernie's reflection. *The last time she interfered, I lost an entire family of clients.*

Anita grabbed a rectangle of foil off the cart and laid the section of hair on top of it. Using the comb's metal tail to hold the foil against Noelle's head, Anita grabbed the color brush with a small pile of the color and brushed the chemicals onto the separated hair. Then she cast another quick glance toward the mirror.

Please God, don't let Bernie come this way. Anita saw the subtle shift in her posture that said Bernie was definitely going to interrupt.

"Anita, if I may, you will get better results with this foil if you take a finer weave. You don't want to make it obvious that Noelle had her hair colored. It needs to be subtle." Bernie reached for Anita's foiling comb, but she pulled the comb out of Bernie's reach.

"Thank you for your input," Anita said with a smile. "But I think I am doing fine." Glancing in the mirror Anita saw Noelle's eyes widen, and her waxed and flawlessly lined eyebrows arched almost to her hairline. *Oh, Lord, please take Bernie to another room. If Bernie says anything else Noelle is going to freak out.*

Bernie spoke sharply, "I am trying to help here, Anita."

"I understand that Bernie, but this isn't the time to do this," she warned hoping Noelle couldn't hear the desperation in her voice. She continued to weave the fine hair and place foils in her client's hair. Noelle sat stiffly in the chair, no longer reading the magazine she held white knuckled in her lap. Oh no, she *did* notice.

"Ok, Noelle, that is the last, well placed, foil," she said, her voice rising to an unnatural pitch. "I set the time for 30 minutes. I'm going to go wash the bowl and then I will be right back." Anita placed her hand on Noelle's shoulder and squeezed, hoping to reassure her friend. She could only hope that Noelle knew she would take good care of her hair.

Anita pushed her cart of supplies to the back room. Her grip was so tight that the plastic edges cut into her fingers. *How could Bernie call her out in front of a client like that? Didn't she understand that Noelle might not ever come back because of their tense exchange out on the salon floor?*

"Anita, if you are not going to listen to advice, then how are you ever going to improve? I am just trying to help," Bernie whispered following along behind.

She was stunned. Bernie had always been somewhat controlling, but lately it had been getting worse. Now she was following her just to berate her. "I won the Color Zoom contest two years in a row. I can do a lowlight foil." Anita's voice trembled and her hands shook as she put her tools away. She knew that Bernie wanted to retire, but did she need to be so nasty?

"Winning is wonderful, however day to day color is different. Our clients have to live with the color and style we give them. Every person that walks out that door is an advertisement for this salon. I want every person to be happy." Bernie glared at her. "And if that means I tell you how to do a color, then I will. If you are doing something wrong, I will take over."

Her jaw dropped as Bernie bundled up and headed out for another cigarette. The older woman may have been doing hair longer, but Anita was good at what she did. While she was in school, she'd taken extra classes when different product companies offered them. Even now she continued to learn the newest techniques; she read every hairstyling magazine and attended any hair show she could get to.

The trill of the timer brought Anita's thoughts back to the present and the fact that she had a client waiting. "Ok, Noelle, let's get you rinsed!" she called as she walked out of the back room, hoping that her client hadn't run out the door.

CHAPTER 2

Later that night Anita and Jojo Gella, her best friend since kindergarten, were getting a head start on cookies for the Christmas party.

"I can't believe she did that, I mean in front of a client." Anita rolled her eyes and shook her head as she put the cookie sheet in the oven. "She has tried to correct me before. Remember when I lost the Anderson family? So unprofessional."

"Bernie has been doing hair for a long time, she may have some tricks to teach you. On the other hand you could just go find another place," JoJo said.

Turning back around, Anita watched as JoJo licked the holly berry red icing off her fingers, then looked at all the Christmas cookies the two had already covered in bright and colorful frosting.

"Yeah, sure. Only that isn't so easy to do here in Mallard. There aren't too many salons looking for a stylist." Anita dried her hands on a towel and leaned on her kitchen counter. "Maybe it's time for me to open my own place? I could rent that little shop on the strip."

"Before you make any other calls, I have an offer for you." JoJo stopped piping white frosting onto the latest batch of red and green cookies and looked Anita right in the eye. "My manager, Karen, is leaving to have her baby and won't be coming back. How about you take her place?"

Work for JoJo? Anita's heart skipped a beat as she stared at her friend. To become the manager in JoJo's salon would be, well, fun. However, JoJo's business was located an hour away and she only had her lease for another year. After that she'd most likely have to downsize and change locations. JoJo was a great stylist but the competition over in Estes Park was hard and she was having trouble making ends meet. On top of that, Anita didn't want to have to ask her clients to relocate twice. She also didn't want to hurt her friend's feelings, especially when she was just trying to help.

"Wow, thank you JoJo. Can I think about it?"

"We used to talk about it all the time. Imagine owning a shop together." JoJo sounded a little hurt at Anita's reluctance. "This is our chance."

PING, the timer on the last batch of cookies went off, saving Anita from answering right away. She stooped to pull the lightly browned sugar cookies out of the oven.

"JoJo, I know we always talked about it. While we were in beauty school it was our dream. I just don't think being partners would work for us now. My business is established here and I don't want to start over."

JoJo playfully stuck her tongue out at her. "If you really want your own shop, call that new realtor in town. He took Steve and I to look at some places for my new shop over in Estes last week."

JoJo had been dating Steve since they'd graduated from beauty school. He had been her client and when she cut his ear, and he didn't yell at her, she fell hard for him.

"The realtor's name is Gabriel Brecht and he is new in town," JoJo continued. "You should call and see if he can show you some available locations and maybe you can get him to ask you out."

JoJo pulled a business card out of her purse and wiggled her eyebrows as she handed it to her. Anita hadn't been on a date in ages. While it would be nice to have a boyfriend, even a date every now and then *would* be nice. Tapping the card in her palm, she looked at the decorated cookies and decided yes—it was time.

*   *   *

Two days later, Anita waited to meet her realtor, Gabriel, outside the vacant storefront she'd had her eye on. She watched him walk toward her with a folder under his arm and a steaming cup in each hand.

"I thought as cold as it is, you might like something warm to drink while we look inside." Gabe handed her one cup before taking a sip of his own. "I wasn't sure how you liked your coffee so I got you peppermint hot chocolate."

She smiled, and met his warm gaze. "Peppermint hot chocolate is perfect."

As he unlocked the door, she took a sip, thinking how nice it was of him to bring her something. And since she had never liked the taste of coffee, this new man had scored some major points with her.

She stood inside the vacant shop on Main Street with the realtor. Located in a little strip mall across the street from both the bank and the cafe in the center of town, the storefront had a great central location for a new salon. The church Anita went to and where the party would be in two short weeks was just down the street, behind the new shop.

"The space is 700 square feet, and has Internet , phone and cable available. This is a great location, but it would need to have the plumbing updated to meet code for a salon." Gabriel continued to spout out information as they walked around the inside of the large open space.

Anita fell in love. The room was perfect; or rather it would be, with a few minor changes. As the realtor said, the plumbing would need to be redone. She wanted three sinks, but right now the only plumbing sat in the bathroom next to the back door. Anita could see the potential of the storefront area. It had wonderful picture windows and the walls had been painted the perfect color of creamy yellow.

"How much is the monthly rent? Do you know the average for utilities for something this size?" Anita asked the realtor as she wandered around the room.

She was so glad she had called, for more than one reason. Jojo was right about the handsome man standing next to her. He might make the perfect date. Gabe was slightly taller than her. His shoulder was just where she could, in theory, lean her head against him without slumping. His smooth, caramel skin and dark, chocolate eyes made her weak in the knees.

"Let me see," he replied, looking over his notes. When he glanced back up, butterflies danced in her stomach as their eyes locked. "The monthly rent is going to be $1.18 per square foot, and we really don't have an average on the monthly utilities since it has been unoccupied. However, the spaces on either side both show moderate cost for electric and water."

Gabe cleared his throat and Anita thought he looked flustered as he read from the pages in his hands.

"I have been praying for this for so long. This space is perfect," she said, heat rushing into her face as he caught her staring at him. "Do you think the owner will pay for the renovations I need done here?"

Gabe choked back a laugh before responding, "Normally that is up to the person renting. But before you get any of that started, you'll need to make sure the owners approve of any changes you want to make."

"I don't know if I can afford everything needed to get the salon ready." Anita turned and walked toward the front windows and trailed her fingers along the windows edge. Gabe followed and stood close enough for his shoulder to brush against hers. "I may be able to negotiate the monthly price per square foot down."

"Do you think they would really lower the monthly price? That would be great." Anita spoke softly, not wanting the moment to end. For $826 a month, she could have her dream shop. She would finally be out from under Bernie's critical eye, overbearing style, and heavy-handed rules.

Anita was more than ready to be in charge, to put all the skills and knowledge she had learned to good use. Before long, she would be managing other stylists in her salon. She could almost smell the hairspray and minty freshness of her special shampoo when she closed her eyes.

Gabe ushered Anita out onto the snowy sidewalk and locked the door behind them. "Well, I can definitely take this to the owner and see what they have to say."

"Great!" Anita bounced on her toes. Her enthusiasm radiated off of her in waves. "I will go to the bank tomorrow and apply for the loan."

"Would you do me a favor?"

"Sure, anything." Not only did she like the shop, she liked him. Hopefully, he liked her too.

"I am still learning my way around here. Can you tell me a good place to get some lunch?"

Anita could hardly refuse. When she had moved to Ft. Collins six years ago for school, she had been the new kid in town and looking for help. "Let me treat you this time," she told him, "the café across the street is wonderful."

Anita decided this day couldn't get any better. Gabe appeared to be an amazing guy and she couldn't wait to get to know him better.

CHAPTER 3

The following day Anita studied her reflection in the full-length mirror in her bedroom at home. She needed to look like a business professional but also wanted to appear bold and maybe show a little of her sassy side. In the end, she'd decided to wear the purple and black pinstripe skirt with the purple tank top. Her bolero jacket finished the look and the trendy colors gave her a confidence boost. Surely the loan officer would take one look at her and her business plan and think she was worth the $100,000 she needed, wouldn't he?

Her nerves were strung taunt. Sweat beaded her brow and she decided to powder her face again. Applying a second dose of antiperspirant to her armpits wouldn't hurt either. Her hands were shaking so hard she dropped her brush on the floor when she set her compact down. Anita closed her eyes and prayed.

God, please help me today. You know how long I have wanted this and how important it is for me. Give me the strength to handle whatever happens.

Anita marched into the bank confident she would walk out with her loan approval. She carried all her paperwork in the soft leather bag her Grandpa had given her when she graduated from community college with a small business degree and she'd pinned her grandmother's favorite opal broach to her blouse. It was almost like they were going to be with her while she met with Mr. Anders, the loan officer.

"Good morning," Anita greeted the silver haired gentleman politely.

"Hello, Anita. How can I help you today?" Mr. Anders asked, peering over the top of his trifocal glasses.

"I need a loan so I can open my own hair salon," she blurted out. Plunking down in the hard chair across from him, she hoped her nerves didn't make her voice shake. "I have the last two years of tax returns, as well as the last six months of receipts showing an increase in my monthly income, and here is my business plan."

She laid the paperwork out on the desk between them and Mr. Anders read it over. Her stomach tightened leaving her slightly nauseas when he frowned at the numbers on the page. She knew the income was variable, but surely he could see she had more good months than bad. She bounced her knee and drummed her fingers against her thigh while he laid the income form aside and began to read over her carefully created business plan.

"My dear girl." He laid the paperwork on his desk, and looked at her in earnest. "I am afraid your income is not sufficient for the type of loan you are asking for. The numbers are all over the place. For a loan this large your monthly salary has to be higher and more consistent."

"My client base has been steadily building, Mr. Anders. My income will only get better. I know I can do this," Anita pleaded, tears welling up in her eyes. "Please reconsider."

"I am sorry. There is no way we can give you a loan at this time."

Mr. Anders tone let Anita know that her appointment was over. It was pointless to argue. With tears blinding her vision she stumbled out of the bank, her mind reeling. *What am I going to do now?*

*   *   *

Anita was just walking in her front door after a long day in the salon when her new ring tone, *Amazing Grace,* chimed from her purse. Taking her coat off with one hand, she pressed the green button on her cell and answered, "Hello?"

"Anita, I have some news on the space we looked at last week." A shot of electricity shot straight through her upon hearing Gabe's voice on the other end of the line. She picked up on the excitement in his voice, he sounded so happy. It must be good news.

"Great, so when do I hire a plumber or meet with the owners to go over the changes I want to make?" She forced a little laugh. The bank might have fallen through but she would find another way to finance her dream.

"I have something I would like to discuss with you," Gabe replied. "Can you meet me for lunch?"

Anita really enjoyed the last lunch they'd had together. After they ate they had driven around town and she'd pointed out the church where the party would be. She was hoping that Gabe would ask her to go with him as his date. He was the kind of guy her grandpa would have liked, steady with good Christian values. Her grandpa had always been a good judge of character.

"Sounds great. I will meet you at the café on Main at 11:30." Anita did a little happy dance, grateful he couldn't see her. This time *he* had asked *her*. That meant something right?

After hanging up, Anita ran upstairs to get ready. It may have been nine a.m. but she was sure if she hurried she would be ready to go by eleven o'clock.

*   *   *

Anita arrived at the café early. The red and green lights twinkled on the tree in the corner, the tinsel around the front windows glittered and the lilting music of Elvis crooning out *Silver Bells* made the room feel like Christmas. It was a season of anticipation for her.

Something about the snow had her looking for new and exciting changes. She loved the way the lights, even the taillights on the cars sparkled against the fresh snow that seemed to fall all month. Opening gifts had always been fun, but she preferred to watch as her friends and family opened the gifts she had given. The look of joy on their faces always gave her warm memories that she could carry with her all year long.

Anita checked her pocket mirror to make sure her lipstick was ok and that her hair still had some body. She worked on her appearance, just like she worked hard on everything she did. She wanted her clients, both current and potential, to know that she cared about looking good. After all she was a walking billboard for her business.

She sat at the table facing the door. She loved watching the people as they entered the cafe. She was good at what she did, isn't that what all her instructors and all the judges told her? She knew how much a good cut and color could give someone a boost of courage for a job interview or… a trip to the bank for a loan.

Anita smiled as she saw Gabe walk through the door and stomp the snow from his boots. While she wanted other people to see her as a stylist, she didn't want Gabe as a client. She was hoping for more. She waved him over to the table.

"I'm so glad you could make it," Gabe said as he shrugged out of his coat and took the seat next to her at the table for four. He opened his menu, barely glancing at it before the waitress brought them each a glass of water.

"I was so happy to hear from you. It was great to see you in church on Sunday." Anita tried not to gush, but couldn't help it. Hopefully he wouldn't notice.

"I enjoyed the service, too." Gabe grinned, "This is such a wonderful time of the year. It always brings home how much God loves us."

Anita was a little confused. "What do you mean?"

"Christmas to me is a reminder of a fresh start."

Anita accepted her cup of cocoa and took a sip. She had never thought much about Christmas in the way Gabe did. Anita was a Christian, but her faith was more abstract. Something she could call on when she needed help, but otherwise she left it on the shelf. Christmas had always just been a time to give gifts and have parties.

Absently she wadded up the wrapper from her straw and used it to soak up a drip of water from the glass.

"Are you getting settled in, finding your way around our big ol' town?" she asked, trying to be silly and hoping to change the subject.

"Yeah, I think I am, thanks to you. I now know where the grocery is and the best place to eat." He grinned at her and her heart gave a little jump. Then he cleared his throat, and his smile disappeared. "But I'm afraid I have some bad news."

Her stomach dropped. Would he tell her he had a girlfriend or that he wasn't staying?

"The space is no longer available. The owners had an offer from another to take it as is, and they snapped it up." He leaned in and picked her hand up off the table. "But I think I may have a solution for you. I know someone in town who is looking for a partner for her salon. She could really use some help and I think the two of you would be great together."

Anita pulled her hand away from him, and leaned back in her chair, her dream fading. She didn't get her loan and now it looked like she wouldn't get her dream space either. Maybe she could still work with JoJo, and start over. Although if she was going to partner with someone, maybe she could find out who Gabe was talking about.

It was a small enough town that she thought she knew everyone, but perhaps this other person was new in town or had space in a garage or something like that. A terrifying thought hit her, surely it couldn't be…

"Actually, she should be here any time now. I invited her to join us."

Anita gasped. He had invited someone else to join them? So this still wasn't a date. "Why didn't you ask me first?"

"I sent you a text and you replied yes. Did I misunderstand?" Gabe looked confused.

Anita pulled out her phone and read the text from him. Sure enough, there it was. "I'm sorry, I didn't read the text right." She was a little disappointed. She wanted Gabe to ask her out, not invite someone to join them for lunch.

"I have done that myself. It can be really embarrassing." Just as he finished speaking, the bus boy dropped a plate on the floor and it shattered into hundreds of little sharp pieces. Like her heart.

"I guess we should wait to order until she gets here then?"

Gabe smiled wide. "No need, here she is now."

Anita looked to the door and her stomach dropped. She recognized the heavy parka and clunky snow boots. The woman Gabe wanted Anita to partner with was Bernie. Anita froze as Bernie walked up to the table and sat down.

Bernie wore a sardonic glare. "When my nephew told me he had someone he wanted me to consider partnering with, I suspected it was you. How long have you been planning on leaving me high and dry?"

Gabe looked back and forth between the them, and Anita felt the blood drain out of her face.

"I gave you a job, young lady, when you were fresh out of beauty school and didn't know which way was up. You are so wrapped up in yourself that you don't pay attention to what people say. You don't listen and as a result you hurt people. I have had several of your clients come to me. Not because you messed up, but because you didn't do what they wanted." Bernie grabbed Gabe's untouched glass of water and took a long drink. "I won't be staying for lunch, Gabe."

Before Anita could utter a word in response, the older woman stood, turned on her heel and stormed out the door. Anita shot a glance at Gabe. He looked as shocked as she felt, his face flushed deep red and his eyes wide.

"Anita, I am so very sorry. I had no idea that you worked for my aunt." Gabe gave her an apologetic look. "I didn't mention her before because I didn't want you to think I wouldn't do my best to get you your own location."

Anita knew everyone in the café, and they were looking straight at her. Bernie hadn't exactly kept her voice down. Overwhelmed, tears spilled from Anita's eyes, and it broke loose a damn deep within making her whole body shake.

"What am I going to do? She was already so critical of my work. She seems to enjoy pointing out any mistake, real or imagined, I make." Anita held her head in her hands, trying to cover the mascara streaks from the rest of the room.

"That sounds like my aunt." He pushed the glass of water Bernie had sipped away from him. "She has been like that for years. When my uncle died they had only been married nine months. She kind of gave up on life I think. She never found anyone that made her feel the way my uncle did. The older she got, the more critical she became."

Anita had known Bernie for a long time but she had never considered the woman wasn't single by choice.

"I love my aunt, that is why I moved here. I didn't want her to be alone anymore, but I can't excuse what she just did. I promise to help you out of this mess." Gabe took her hand and held it tight. She needed to believe him, to trust that he meant what he said.

Chapter 4

The next day, Anita sat in her truck staring at the shop she had worked in for the last four years. All she had ever wanted was to help people feel good. She didn't want to leave her home, but she couldn't stay here without a job. She picked at her steering wheel cover and wondered if Bernie would come in today. Normally she had the day off, but after the mess yesterday at the café, Anita didn't know what to expect from the older woman.

She walked to the shop the way a condemned person walks into a courtroom. She struggled to keep the tears from streaming down her cheeks. Today, Sarah, the lovely pastor's wife, had an appointment with Anita to freshen her color for the holiday. Anita took a deep breath and squared her shoulders. *Dear Lord, I need you. I don't know what is going to happen today, but you do and I can lean on You. Give me strength.*

Normally the pastor's wife was Bernie's client, but Bernie didn't have time to see her before the party on Sunday. So Anita took the appointment for her.

She moved around the salon, turning on the overhead lights and the sparkling multicolored bulbs on the Christmas tree before heading to the back room to turn on the radio. Anita used this time to mentally prepare. While she worked, she made a point to focus on her client. Her troubles could wait. Her clients trusted her to do her best and she hated the thought of letting anyone down.

She looked over Sarah's color card, the record of all the color that Bernie had used on her, when the woman walked in.

"Thank you so much for getting me in, Anita." Sarah hung her coat on one of the hooks in the waiting room. "I don't want to stand up in front of all those people with my roots showing." The older woman chuckled as she climbed into Anita's chair.

"I am glad to help you. I know how good it feels after a good style and color." Anita draped her color cape over her arm and grabbed the towel off the counter. "Did you want the same as last time or are we doing something different today?"

"Oh, the same as last time." She scooted back in the chair, making herself more comfortable.

"So, not only are you going to leave me, but you are taking my clients as well?"

Bernie stood just inside the salon by the break room. Her timing couldn't have been any worse. Bernie looked to be fuming mad. Her eyes flashed and her mouth drew into a thin line. Every muscle in her body looked tight and ready to snap.

"Bernie, I thought today was your day off? Anita has been kind enough to see me since you didn't have any open times before the Christmas program." Sarah hopped down from the chair and hurried over to give Bernie a hug.

"I thought you knew I was coloring Sarah this morning." Anita's voice was barely above a whisper.

"Oh *pish*, don't apologize." Sarah stood between them, acting as a referee. "Bernie was off today and I needed my hair done. I will not be the cause of trouble between you two."

Anita didn't have the heart to tell her loving pastor's wife that she wasn't the cause. She was simply another log on the inferno.

"I just stopped by for a moment, to check in," Bernie said, crooking a finger towards Anita, indicating she was to follow.

Together they walked into the back room. Anita bit back tears, certain that she was about to get fired. *Would Bernie let her finish the day or would she have to leave before she could help Sarah?*

"Anita, don't mess this up. Noelle might have been one of your best clients, but Sarah is mine. I have written down exactly what I do on her and you will follow those directions. Is that clear?"

"Bernie, I would never do anything to hurt Sarah." Her voice trembled. "I would never do anything to hurt anyone. Not on purpose."

Bernie lifted one eyebrow and hissed, "Except for me, huh? Hurting me doesn't count I suppose."

"Bernie, I never meant to hurt you. I am grateful for this job. It's just I have dreams of my own." Anita reached for Bernie's arm, her eyes wide. She begged Bernie to understand and accept what she said.

Bernie glanced down at her watch, "I have to go, I have another appointment. I am not firing you, but things are going to change."

Anita watched as the woman stomped out the back door. Then she needed a moment to compose herself before going back out on the floor. All she wanted to do was curl up in a ball and cry, preferably at home under her favorite blanket. If she walked out the door and even looked at another human being, she would lose any composure she currently had. Leaning on the counter, she took a deep breath, and reminded herself that while she was here, her time was not her own. At the moment, her time belonged to Sarah.

Glancing at the color card in front of her, she reached out and grabbed the boxes of color and the 30-volume developer. She entered into an autopilot mode. She mixed color and chatted with Sarah, applied color and washed out bowls without even knowing what all she did. It wasn't until she began drying Sarah's hair that she seemed to wake up and that was when her nightmare truly began.

Normally, her client had a color of golden blonde, but as her hair began to dry Anita was horrified to find the woman's hair was now a *strawberry* blonde.

*   *   *

The rest of the day passed in a blur. Anita wasn't surprised when four of her clients cancelled their appointments, all with odd excuses and none of them agreeing to reschedule with her. Normally, after work she would sit in her own chair and dream of the future. Today she couldn't get out of the shop fast enough. After ruining Sarah's hair, she was certain that she was finished as a stylist. After all, who would come to her now?

She got home on autopilot, not really seeing the falling snow or the way streetlights glittered. Anita fixed herself a sandwich and grabbed a soda out of the fridge before curling up in her Grandfathers chair. Then wrapping herself up in her Grandmother's quilt, she let herself have a good cry. All she wanted was to help, to make people feel better and she had done the opposite today.

The light musical notes of *Amazing Grace* filled the room as her phone rang. She stared at the screen, trying to decide if she wanted to talk to anyone. She really didn't, but she also knew that she couldn't ignore the call either.

"Hello?" Anita hoped the person on the other end couldn't hear how fake the happiness was.

"Hi, it's Maggie. I spoke with you about doing the hair and makeup for the Christmas program tomorrow night?"

"Yes?" Anita sat forward in the chair, and held her breath.

"We have decided to go another route, something more simple. Thank you all the same."

"What are you saying? You don't want me?" A lump rose in her throat. She tried to take a sip of soda and almost choked.

"It isn't that we don't want you, it's simply we are going a different direction. Have a good night." *Click.*

Anita closed her eyes and leaned her head against the back of the chair, her sandwich forgotten on the end table next to her. She could call JoJo and accept the manager job. It was better than nothing. But that was a call she would make in the morning, tonight she just couldn't do it.

The tune of "Beauty School Drop out" from the musical *Grease* sounded from the phone that lay in her lap. That ring tone assigned only to JoJo. It seemed she would be choking on her pride and asking for that job sooner than she expected.

"Hey, Jo." Anita didn't bother to sound happy, JoJo could always hear through it anyway.

"Guess what!" JoJo was so excited. "I hired a manager today and she is amazing. Not that you aren't, but you are moving in your own direction."

Anita couldn't ask for a job now. "That is great." This time she tried to force some happiness for her friend. After all, JoJo deserved someone who really wanted to be there, not someone who was only there to get a paycheck. "I need to go, gotta get ready for the Christmas program tomorrow night."

"Right. Just wanted to share my good news, take care." With that, Anita listened to silence and tossed the phone to the floor.

Now the tears were falling harder, she didn't know where she would go when Bernie fired her.

The sweet sounds of *Amazing Grace* rang out from under the blanket she had pulled around her. Now what? Maybe it was Gabe, texting to say he was thinking of her, or better yet asking to see her. Picking her phone up off the floor, she tapped the screen to read the text. It was from Gabe!

Is it too late to call?

This was it, he was going to call and ask her to the party! Maybe this day would end on a good note after all.

She texted back and seconds later, the phone rang again. "Hi." This time she didn't have to force happiness into her voice. She sat up straighter in the chair and smiled.

"I am so glad you are still up. I wanted to call you and let you know I'm in Denver."

"Oh?" When had he left? Anita clutched at her phone, her last ray of hope fading. "When will you be back?"

"Probably not till next week sometime, I had someone I needed to see."

She wanted to believe it was work related but at the moment, that didn't seem possible. "I thought you would be here for the party tomorrow evening."

"This came up last minute and I couldn't say no. I haven't seen Jorja in a while and I have missed her. Are you okay? You sound upset."

He's there to see another woman?

"I'm not upset. I'm fine," she lied, and her voice cracked. "But I need to go, it's later than I thought." This time when she hung up the phone, she turned it off.

Who was Jorja? She must be someone special if he made the three-hour drive to Denver just to see her. Was she his girlfriend?

As she sat in the dark house, she began to realize just how alone she was. She had no one to turn to. The tears fell in rivers and her shoulders shook.

She didn't need to get up early in the morning and she couldn't handle any more calls. Grabbing a pillow off the floor, she buried her face and screamed. She wanted to box up Christmas. Not just her decorations, but the whole holiday. This month had gone downhill so fast.

After climbing into bed, she leaned over to turn off her lamp and knocked a stack of books to the floor. Sighing, she leaned over and picked one up. It was her grandfathers Bible. She smiled as she thumbed the pages to Psalms 102:7 and she read, '*I lie awake; I have become like a bird alone on the roof.*'

CHAPTER 5

Anita woke up with gritty eyes and a raw throat. *I guess this is what I get for crying myself to sleep.* Sunlight streamed through the cracks in her curtains. Of course the day would be beautiful. The Christmas program and party would be that evening. The sky was clear of clouds and the sun made the snow glare a brilliant white. It definitely looked like Christmas outside, but for the first time in years Anita didn't wake with a carol on her lips. She didn't want to turn on the radio and hear all the Christmas songs. She wanted nothing to do with the day at all.

After boiling water for her morning cup of cocoa, Anita picked up the Bible she had brought down with her that morning. She could sure use a fresh start, but she didn't know where to begin.

Sitting at her kitchen table, she flipped through the delicate pages and read a line from the book of Luke. '*But the angel said to them, "Do not be afraid. I bring you good news that will cause great joy for all the people. Today in the town of David a Savior has been born to you; he is the Messiah, the Lord.'*

Her Grandfather had highlighted this passage in yellow many years ago. She sat back in her chair, and wondered why this verse called to her today. Maybe she needed to pray, something she had only done in passing or when she felt desperate. She leaned forward and rested her elbows on the table, clasped her hands together. Desperation had moved in on her spirit during the night and didn't want to leave.

Lord, I know I haven't been reading my Bible or praying like I should. I need you in my life. I crave the joy I read about in Luke. Thank you for bringing a good person for JoJo and her shop. Lord, I don't know what is going on with

Bernie, but I ask that you help us work out our problems. She seems so alone, and so angry. I see that I am lonely as well and how it can make me cranky. It is hard for me to care when she's been so mean but I see it's not healthy for either of us. Thank you Lord for having Gabe share about his joy in this season. I needed a reminder of what Christmas is all about. Amen.

As she finished praying, a peace settled over her and a sense of direction she had been lacking when she woke. She would go to the church, not to do hair, but to see if they needed any help getting ready for the program. After all, the party wasn't the main event, the sharing of the Christmas story was.

After slipping on some old jeans and a flannel shirt over her t-shirt, Anita bundled up and headed out the door. With the hymn *Away in the Manger* humming in her mind and a smile on her lips, she was ready to face what was before her.

*   *   *

When she pulled into the church parking lot, Anita could see that several people were already there, setting up for the program. Stepping through the front door, her senses exploded. The scent of fresh pine filled the entryway, Christmas music filled the air, and silver and gold balls were hanging from boughs of fresh pine garland. Nearing the fellowship hall, she could almost taste the apple cider that simmered on the stove. All around her, people were busy, intent on getting their various jobs finished so they could move on to the next task.

Wandering around, she hummed and looked for a place to help. Outside one of the classrooms where those who were going to be in the program were changing into costumes, she heard the scratchy, deep voice of Bernie—and she was talking about her.

"Anita is the closest thing I have ever had to a child. When my husband died, I gave up ever having children. After she started coming in every week, I grew fond of her. I want to help her grow as a stylist, you know, be the best she can be. But she tends to get lost in her own head. I know that is what happened when she ruined your hair." Bernie's voice carried a whine Anita hadn't heard before. "If you come in on Monday, I will fix it for you."

Who is she talking to?

"Oh, it's ok Bernie," Sarah said, her voice grim. "I don't think that being hard on her is the best way to help her. I know personally I tend to get bristly when people tell me what to do, especially when it is something I am trained to do. Anita is a very capable stylist, but anyone can make a mistake and we need to remember to forgive each other so that we may be forgiven."

Anita wanted to see Bernie's face. She was sure Bernie wanted Sarah to agree that as a stylist, she was hopeless. While the pastor's wife hadn't exactly given a rave review, Sarah had said she was a good stylist.

She turned and walked to the little bathroom off the pastor's study. After closing the door, she sat on the lid of the toilet. Maybe Bernie wasn't the only one being hard on someone. Anita started to recall times when she had been judgmental towards the older woman's style and her techniques for hair. They both wanted what was best for the salon, they just had different ideas of what that was.

It also seemed that Bernie wasn't the only one that was lonely. After last night, she knew that loneliness was something she struggled with as well. Standing up, she turned the cold water on and splashed her face. She needed to make some changes if she wanted things to improve with her boss. Straightening her shoulders, she walked out of the bathroom and into the fellowship hall.

"Anita!" Noelle called out and waved her over. "I am so glad to see you. I hear you did Sarah's hair?"

"Yeah, I did." Anita tried not to panic, after all Noelle was her friend, and was happy with the lowlights she had done only two weeks before.

"I just wanted to tell you, I *love* her new look. She looks so much younger." Noelle gave her a big hug. "I know it isn't her normal color and you may get some flack from Bernie but it looks wonderful."

"Thank you for saying that, but if Sarah doesn't like it, well, she is one I want to be happy." Anita wanted to change the subject. "How can I help get ready for the program?"

Conversations ebbed and flowed around her, but she kept her attention on the hymns playing and the reason they were decorating the church in reds, greens, silver and gold. The delicate angel centerpieces were placed on each table and silver stars were hung from more garlands strung along the ceiling. Anita decided she would remain focused on why she was there and not what she had overheard from Bernie.

After a quick lunch of chili and cornbread, everyone finished their decorating and the actors gathered to get in one last practice before dressing for the program. Anita managed to avoid both Bernie and Sarah, and now she wanted to leave before her luck ran out.

*   *   *

"Jo, can you come over? I need to talk," Anita explained into the phone after she'd arrived back home a short while later.

"Sure, I can be there in twenty minutes." JoJo paused before adding, "Everything ok?"

"Yeah, I hope so. See you soon." Anita hung up and put the kettle back on. JoJo would want cocoa and a cookie when she got there. She turned on her favorite Christmas music and began singing, slightly off key and at full volume.

JoJo arrived and Anita gave her a huge hug.

"Wow, ok. What is going on with you? Last night you sounded like you were crying and today you are belting out Christmas music." JoJo's eyebrows rose in suspicion. "Is there someone I need to hear about?"

Anita laughed. "No, nothing like that, at least not yet. I wanted to tell you that I am genuinely happy for you. Finding a good manager is priceless in having a successful salon and you deserve that. You have worked hard for a long time and it is good to see it finally paying off for you."

"I don't know about it paying off yet, but thank you. I was a little scared last night to tell you. That is why I didn't ask what was wrong." JoJo looked sheepish before continuing, "I didn't want to know I had made you cry."

While they dressed for the party Anita gave a quick summary of the events leading up to that evening. While they took turns styling each other's hair, Anita giggled and didn't worry about the night ahead.

*　　　*　　　*

Anita saw Bernie sitting in the front pew during the evening program at the church. Afterward, Anita loss track of her in the mass exodus as the crowd headed toward the fellowship hall for the Christmas party. She hoped with so many people, she might avoid the woman, but somehow ended up running straight into her.

"Anita, really. You need to watch where you are going." Bernie spoke in a harsh whisper and snapped her fingers in Anita's face.

"I'm sorry, Bernie. Really I am." Anita spoke quietly. She didn't want to disturb any of the people around them.

"Oh Anita and Bernie. I'm so lucky to find you together."

Sarah's voice reminded Anita of angels in that moment. She had spared Anita any further pain caused by Bernie's sharp tongue.

"Anita, I must tell you that while this color isn't exactly what I would have chosen, I love it. So many people have commented on it. Even my dear husband told me he thinks I look younger than I have in years." She winked at the two stunned stylists. "And that, ladies, is saying something!"

"I am glad you are happy, S-Susan," Anita stuttered.

"Are you sure this is what you want? I can still fix this." Bernie looked incredulous, her eyes wide in shock.

"I am quite certain Bernie. I have fallen in love with my own hair, imagine that. I will be telling everyone to go and see this darling girl to get the best for

125

their hair." Sarah was so happy, she almost glowed. She patted Anita on the hand before moving on to the next group of people.

Anita stood motionless next to Bernie. It wouldn't do for Bernie to see how happy she was. Who knew what the older woman would do to ruin the moment.

"It seems that I may owe you an apology." It looked as though Bernie was choking on her words. "It appears you may be better than I previously gave you credit for. I would be willing to have you perform the managerial duties in the shop for a time to see if you truly are ready for those responsibilities."

"Really? Thank you, Bernie. I will work hard, I promise." The weight on Anita's heart lifted. She was walking two inches off the ground.

Anita lined up to get her bowl of chili from the food table. She had been dreading seeing Sarah and Bernie and that had turned out to be a wonderful thing. She hummed to herself when she stopped to put cheese and sour cream in her chili.

"Excuse me, can I get some of the cheese please."

She stepped aside and glanced back to see who was so pushy. "Gabe!" What was he doing here?

"Hello Anita." Gabe looked right into her eyes and gave her a heartfelt look so intense she almost dropped her bowl. "I decided that I had to be here tonight. You sounded like you needed a friend last night, so as soon as my class was finished today, I headed back."

"Class? I thought you said you were seeing another woman." Heat sprang up into her cheeks. "I meant to say *'a woman,'* not *'another woman.'*"

Gabe chuckled. "Jorja? She taught the class, but she is also my sister."

His smile lit up his entire face, and if she had been asked, Anita would have sang to the whole room at that moment.

*   *   *

Anita hummed as she prepared to add highlights to the hair of her current customer, and even Bernie seemed to be in a good mood as *together* they pulled out the coloring tubes.

It was December 24th and the shop was hopping. Both Anita and Bernie's styling chairs had been filled all morning. The other women waiting for their appointments chatted amicably while drinking hot-spiced cider. Anita caught her reflection in her mirror and smiled. *This is turning into a wonderful Christmas after all.*

I want my hair colored the same shade as Sarah," a woman from church proclaimed as she walked through the salon door.

Another woman entered behind her. "Anita, do you think you could give me one of those new fangled shorter cuts?"

Anita smiled. "Sure thing."

"I decided a hair cut would be my gift to myself this Christmas," the woman said with a wink.

Anita realized God had already given *her* several gifts. A restored relationship with Him through his son, Jesus Christ, and...the joy she'd read about in the Bible and had secretly craved. She was now on her way to managing her own shop, she had a date with Gabe that evening—yes, a *real* date, and happy clients.

He'd even helped restore her relationship with Bernie, a feat that until this week, she'd thought impossible. Now that she realized that Bernie cared about her and only wanted to genuinely help her, she wasn't afraid of the woman poking her nose in and offering her opinions.

Smiling, she sent up a quick prayer. *Thank you, God.*

Then, turning toward her mentor, she asked, "Hey Bernie, got a sec? What do you think of this new color shade? I could really use a second opinion."

About the Author:

Robin Gueswel is a member of the Northwest Christian Writers Association and helps lead its local branch, Penning on the Peninsula. She's always loved reading and writing, and is active running book tables at local conferences. In her free time, she loves hiking with her son and dog, Tumbler.

You can visit Robin at her Facebook page:

http://www.facebook.com/RobinGueswel

I used to make these cookies with my Grandma and my Mom. They are my favorite cookies to this date. I hope you enjoy them as much as I do. Love, Robin.

Grandma's Sugar Cookies

Prep Time: 60 min

Total Time: 3 hrs. 10 min

Servings: 60

Ingredients:

1 ½ cups powdered sugar

1 cup butter or margarine, softened

1 teaspoon vanilla

½ teaspoon almond extract (or lemon)

1 egg

2 ½ cups Gold Medal™ all-purpose flour

1 teaspoon baking soda

1 teaspoon cream of tartar

Granulated sugar or colored sugar

Directions:

Mix powdered sugar, butter, vanilla, almond extract and egg in large bowl. Gradually mix in the remaining ingredients except granulated sugar.

Cover and refrigerate at least 2 hours. Trust me, this is worth it.

Preheat oven to 375°F. Lightly grease cookie sheet.

Separate the cold dough in half. Working with half at a time, roll the dough so that it is 1/4 inch thick on a lightly floured surface.

Use your favorite cookie cutters; we always used ones that were 2" or 3" across. The bigger the cookies, the fewer you end up with! At this point you can either sprinkle them with granulated sugar or leave them alone. It depends on if you want to frost them after they are cooled off. Place on cookie sheet.

Bake between 7 and 8 minutes, until the edges are golden brown. Remove from cookie sheet. Cool on a wire rack before decorating.

O Night Divine

by

Debby Lee

DEDICATION:

With much love, I dedicate this story to my family. My husband Steven, and my children, Michelle, Devon, Toni, David, and Steffen, without your love and support this book would not be possible. I would like to extend a special dedication to those who rescued the Lewis County Museum from the abyss of ruin, and to those who work to keep it running.

ACKNOWLEDGEMENTS:

I would like to express my genuine appreciation to Darlene, Beverly, Carol, Jeri, Robin, and Julianne for including me in this anthology. Working with all of you toward this common goal is an experience I will treasure forever.

To Samantha Panzera, thank you so much for all the hard work and long hours you put into this book. It would not be possible without your efforts, your sacrifice, and your talent.

A special thank you to my beta readers, Jeneen Haley, Rita Hardenbrook, and Julie Zander, your input enhanced my story and helped make it what it is today.

CHAPTER 1

Karena Smith stopped moving, and breathing, to listen for the frightening noise. There it came again. A scraping sound, followed by a loud bang, echoed from outside and her stomach clenched tight.

Christmas music softly floated through the air of the Merriwether County Historical Museum where she worked. O Holy Night was one of her favorites, but the nights had recently become anything but holy. The exterior of the building had been vandalized twice in the past month. Several items in the museum had been passed down through the generations of her family, and then donated by her grandparents. This place meant a lot to her. She wasn't about to let the number of incidents rise to three.

Bang!

Bang, bang!

Driven to protect herself, she leapt from her chair and sprinted to the maintenance man's closet. There had to be some kind of weapon she could use among the tools and assorted junk. Finding nothing, she glanced around for something else. Her gaze rested on a large brass candlestick, adorned with a red bow, sitting next to an antique Nativity scene. She grabbed hold of the base and slowly made her way down the hall toward the back of the building.

Should she just call the cops? No way, for several reasons. One, the noise was probably nothing more than the loose rain pipe banging against the side of the building. Two, just last week she'd heard a noise and called the cops only to be told it was a false alarm. Three, She remembered one of the cops on duty that night happened to be her creepy ex-boyfriend, Detective Tim Gentry.

The last date she'd had with the detective, at the fanciest restaurant in town, culminated in a bad ending. First he'd chewed with his mouth open. When the meal was finished he burped loud enough for the waiter to look over and glare at them. Then he proceeded to pick his teeth and wipe his greasy fingers on his pants. The man was about as uncouth as a starving hog at the slops trough.

Karena quickly dismissed the notion of calling the police. She was probably over-reacting anyway. She moved forward to see what was making all the noise.

The antique door leading outside was locked, but before Karena slid the deadbolt aside, she peered out the grimy, ages-old window. In the bleak darkness, dense rain was the only thing visible. A twinge of fear wiggled within her mind.

Scrape.

Bang.

The sudden noise made Karena drop the candlestick to the floor with a startling clang. She plastered her body to the wall, placed a hand over her thudding heart, and tried to steady her breathing. Her imagination must be working overtime for her to be so jumpy. It was doubtful someone with malicious intent would strike when there were people in the building.

But that didn't stop her from wanting the criminals caught. A Christmas fundraising event approached and would provide some much needed funds. Still, the small museum settled in a tiny community in Merriwether County, Washington, could ill afford to repair additional damages by vandals.

With resolve, Karena reached down, picked up the candlestick.

A moment later, with her heart still thudding in her chest and fingers that shook, she reached for the door knob and shoved the door open.

A frigid gust of icy December wind blew in and snatched the air from Karena's lungs. Her fingers tightened around the base of the candlestick. She ventured outside into the night. Fat droplets of rain pelted her. Her red and green Grinch sweater was already getting soaked. Why hadn't she thought to grab her coat?

Karena shivered from the cold, and probably nerves, too. She made it several steps and then surveyed her surroundings. Darkness made it near impossible to see past the far corner of the building, but she wouldn't let that stop her. Determined to find the cause of the strange noise, she said a quick prayer for courage and crept forward.

The roof's overhang provided some protection from the torrents of rain and Karena clung to the side of the building as she proceeded. When she cast her eyes up toward the sky all she saw was an inky blackness. She blew out an exasperated sigh. How could she see what caused the ruckus when it was so dark out?

From somewhere in the distance a dog barked. Closer, a cat screeched. As it darted past her, its fur tickled her ankles. Karena yelped and dropped the candlestick yet again. Why hadn't she thought to bring the museums' cordless phone out with her, or at least her cell phone? Unfortunately, she'd left it on her desk to finish charging.

The corner loomed just ahead. If she could just get around it, quick enough, quiet enough, she'd have the element of surprise, and with luck, catch a glimpse of the prowler, if there was one. Maybe she could get a description for the police.

Bang!

The noise was closer now and Karena froze in place. A car drove past, and for a split-second its headlights illuminated the area. That's when she noticed the rain pipe had been secured in place with several large bolts. The rusty metal contraption wasn't the cause of all the racket. There really could be some creep out here. Maybe even the vandal the local press had dubbed the Merriwether Masher.

Karena had to get someplace safe, and fast! She turned and stubbed her toe on a rock. Her pain hardly registered as someone big and bulky grabbed her from behind. She screamed and lifted the candlestick to clobber the skunk. In one swift motion he grabbed it and yanked it from her grasp, while still managing to hold her tight.

"Let me go!" she cried.

"Take it easy, will you?"

She wasn't about to take it easy. Not by a long shot. She screamed again and bounced up and down in a valiant attempt to break free. Everything she learned in self-defense class went out the window. She tried to recall the maneuvers her friend Holly had taught her, but they jumbled in her brain like mismatched puzzle pieces.

Karena tried to step on his foot but missed and connected with the rock she had stumbled on a minute ago. Her toes reverberated with agony, but she fought on, in spite of it. She attempted to thrust her elbow into his solar plexus but connected with his sternum instead. Another cry escaped from her lips as pain zinged through her arm.

In the shuffle, Karena managed to turn and was about to shove her palm into his nose, but stopped cold. In the dim light, she stared at Dane Cassidy, the museum's security guard. Her high school crush.

* * *

Dane flicked on a flashlight.

"What are you doing? You scared the life out of me!" Karena yelled.

"I said take it easy." Releasing her, Dane picked up a chunk of old wood and tossed it into the recycle bin. It resounded with a loud bang and then he continued, "Some joker got into the recycle bin and tossed out all the broken pallets. I thought I'd pick up some of the mess before somebody comes out here and trips over it."

"I thought you were the Merriwether Masher, the schmuck who's been wrecking the museum. I nearly jumped out of my skin when you grabbed me." Karena tried to be angry with him, but his handsome, rugged face didn't make it easy.

"You about hit me in the head with that candlestick." Dane placed his hands on his hips and glared at her.

He still made a handsome picture, even with the furrowed brow and fire snapping in his eyes. Karena swallowed hard, twice, before the lump in her throat went down. Humble Pie sure tasted awful.

"I apologize, Mr. Cassidy, for trying to hit you. I honestly thought you were the one wreaking havoc around here. Why haven't we caught him yet?"

"Hey give me a chance, I've only been here a week."

"I'm sorry. I didn't mean to be rude."

"And I apologize for scaring you. I didn't mean to. Are you okay?" Dane's big green eyes now emitted genuine concern. "What are you doing here so late anyway? It could be dangerous with that creep lurking around."

Karena warmed considerably, in spite of the rain and chilly wind. "I was going over the account books again. I can't understand why our accounts don't show more of a profit. Something's wrong, but I can't put my finger on it."

"Why don't you go back inside? I'll take care of things out here. When you're ready to leave, let me know, and I'll walk you to your car."

"I'm fine, thank you, but I will go back inside now."

"Don't forget this." Dane picked up the candlestick and handed it to her. Karena noticed he wore no wedding ring. He was still single, after all this time?

"Thank you." Karena took the candlestick and headed back indoors. When she tried to close the ancient door, the old wood that comprised the door jamb made closing it a tough endeavor. Finally, with a good, strong yank, she got it to shut.

Images of Dane Cassidy permeated her mind as she walked back to her office. Memories floated to the surface. Shortly after high school graduation he announced he was leaving for Guam to do some missionary work. He cut out of their last date early. He also cut her heart to pieces when he boarded the plane and flew off for grand adventures, without her.

Through the years they had managed a few phone conversations, but their friendship lacked the closeness they once shared. It had been more than a year since they had spoken. Karena figured he'd settled down somewhere, with someone. That was all fine with her, he had abandoned her and broken her trust. The last thing she wanted was to give him a chance to do it all over again.

However, as Karena plopped into her desk chair, thoughts of Dane made a quick exit as worry over the museum's budget, and the Merriwether Masher, took center stage.

* * *

Karena stared at the numbers in the open account books on her desk until they began to blur. The museum's bookkeeper, a young girl named Bianca from New York, was long overdue in returning to work after some emergency leave. Karena would speak with her personally to see if they could make sense of it. With a deep sigh of resignation she closed the suspiciously thin ledger. She would go over it again tomorrow, and call the bank. Perhaps they would have some answers for her.

Karena slipped on her heavy coat and reached for her handbag. Before stepping through the front door she remembered to set the new alarm system. Then she got an idea. She would set a trap for the Masher. There had to be some way to lure him into the museum.

Then she could catch him red-handed.

CHAPTER 2

The next morning, Karena called the bank and asked to speak with Mr. Cowan, the man handling the museum's account. The receptionist informed her that Mr. Cowan was heavily booked with meetings and would be unavailable for most of the day.

"Do you know when he's going to be back? I need to speak with him, it's urgent." Didn't that man ever spend time in his office? Karena drummed her fingers on her desk. Patience may be a virtue, but it wasn't one she possessed. Her skin grew hot while she waited for the receptionist to jot down her message.

"Will you please tell him if I don't hear from him by lunch time today, I'll call him back before the bank closes at five?"

The receptionist concurred and Karena hung up the phone. She had a Masher to catch and right now, ensnaring this vandal seemed of greater importance than locating an elusive account manager.

Rising from her desk, she walked down the main hallway. She paused to stare at the plaques on the wall listing the founding pioneer families of the county. The day her grandparents had their names engraved on one of the name plates stood out in her memory. They had been so proud. A tear formed in the corner of her eye. Her grandparents, God rest their souls, would be so heartbroken to see the graffiti on the outside walls of the museum they had worked so hard to get up and running.

Karena had many happy memories of working in the museum when she was little, alongside her grandparents. Her grandfather had held a long standing seat on the Board of Directors. By his honorable character, and his good word, she had acquired her job at the museum. With her grandparents' demise, in her way of thinking, the reins had passed to her. She was certain they looked down from Heaven. The last thing she wanted was to disappoint them.

Mischievousness wormed its way through Karena's mind as she strode from her office to the museum's vault. She undid the locks on the safe and drew out some jewels that she had placed there earlier. They consisted of cheap rhinestones and costume jewelry, but Lord willing, they would help her catch the person responsible for the smashed windows and the graffiti slathered all over the building.

Hopefully, the items would act as a decoy to lure the villain into the museum. And because the police couldn't watch the place 24 hours a day, Karena and Dane would be waiting for him. All she had to do was convince Dane.

For more than an hour Karena worked on dragging a glass display case to the front entrance of the museum. She made a show of arranging the jewels inside the case. Then with her work complete, she went back to her desk and called her friend at the local newspaper.

"Hello, Holly, I need a favor. I'd like you to come to the museum and take pictures of some rare jewels, and print the pictures in tomorrow's paper."

"You have some rare jewels at the museum? Where are they from? How valuable are they, worth millions?"

Karena chuckled at her friend's enthusiasm. Rare jewels in the small town they lived in were something to crow about, but she couldn't hornswaggle her friend. "Holly, they're fake, I'm using them as bait to lure the Masher into a trap."

"Oh, I don't know if my boss will go for this. I'll have to ask him first. He won't take kindly to the paper deceiving the public like that."

"I wouldn't expect you to lie. Maybe you could write something like 'jewels found in depths of museum's vault, thought to be rare and costly, now on display at front of museum' or something along those lines."

Karena wiggled in her chair. The thought of misleading people did weigh heavily on her heart. To write up such an article would be asking a lot from her friend. It didn't exactly line up with Biblical principles, but desperation squeezed her heart.

"I'll pray about it, and I think you should, too," Holly replied. "Let's give it a few days and then we can talk about it more, okay?"

"No, Holly, you're right. I can't lie to folks like that. Ditch that idea. I'll think of something else."

Karena said goodbye, hung up the phone, and blew a deep sigh over her lips. Nothing seemed to go according to plan. At the end of the day she called the bank back. The receptionist gave her a song and dance about Mr. Cowan's kid getting sick so he had to leave early. Bianca hadn't shown up for work either, which irritated her further. The Board had hired the young inexperienced girl as a favor for a friend, but the decision had never sat well with her. She could only hope Bianca hadn't unbalanced the accounts too badly.

Karena locked up the museum for the night, remembering to set the alarm.

From there, she proceeded to her car and waited for Dane to show up for work. To kill time, she listened to the radio. The station's DJ played Christmas music and *"O Holy Night"* strummed over the airwaves, again. In early December what else could she expect?

When Dane arrived and climbed out of his truck, her breath caught in her throat and her skin tingled. Karena stepped from her vehicle and waves of unexpected emotion rolled through her.

An image of Dane carrying her books for her when she was a sophomore in high school popped into her mind. Old feelings for the man began to surface, but she told herself she was being daft and quickly tamped them down. She had a Masher to catch.

She approached him, and with excitement told him her plan.

"Are you crazy?" Dane exclaimed, staring at her with big green eyes.

"We need to do something," she cried. They couldn't very well let the Masher continue to cause trouble. The vandalism would probably escalate until the criminal destroyed the museum and all the artifacts in it.

"If your plan backfires in any way, and personally, I don't see how it *can't* backfire, at the very least you'll be in big trouble with the Board of Directors. Is that what you want?"

"Of course not, but Dane, if we can get a description of this monster, maybe find out who he is, we can turn the information in to the police. It will be good for the museum. I had hoped you would help me."

"What if he has a gun and shoots you?"

"He won't even see me. I'll stay hidden. Now will you help me? I need you to keep watch, lay low, and when he breaks in, we can call the cops."

"Promise me you'll think about this," Dane said as he held her by the shoulders and stared deep into her eyes.

"Okay." Karena gulped, said goodbye to Dane, and left the museum for the night. Despair hung like a rain cloud, but she wasn't about to give up. Maybe her plan would work if she ironed the wrinkles out of it.

Karena spent the rest of the week working on a room with a 1960's theme. She hung a framed Woodstock poster on the wall, and dressed a mannequin in a white peasant blouse and a green and blue tie-dyed maxi skirt. One kind member of the historical society had donated their entire collection of The Beatles, The Byrds, and Janis Joplin records. She gently placed them on a counter alongside the wall.

To Karena's delight, Dane had agreed to help her with her plan. But then again, she'd told him she was going through with it, with or without his help. So, with a shake of his head to indicate his misgivings, he consented. When she wasn't occupied with her work, she spread the word about the "jewels" on display at the museum. Rather than mislead folks about the value of the gems, she asked around for an appraiser. Of course, anyone actually appraising them would know they were fake, but at least it had created a buzz through town.

Mr. Johansen from the local jewelry store agreed to come to the museum and look over the jewels. He even told Holly that "if" the jewels were worth a lot of money he'd call some friends from Seattle to come take a look. This created an even bigger buzz amongst the small, close-knit community.

On Friday Karena was to set execute her plan. Thankfully, a reluctant Dane agreed to stay by her side the whole time. Even with Dane there, Karena wanted some extra assurance for safety sake. She called Tim Gentry on her cell phone. He was a good cop despite his table manners, or lack thereof. Tim agreed to come to the museum to speak with her.

"Will you keep an eye on the museum this weekend, please?" Karena told him she had set a trap for the Masher, and filled him in on the details. When she finished, she shuddered at his hard glare. For a few moments there was no response, and then he rolled his eyes and shook his head.

"And Dane is going along with all of this?" Tim asked.

"Why, I can take care of myself," Karena huffed.

"This criminal could be dangerous," Tim said, "and it's likely you'll get yourself *and* Mr. Cassidy hurt. I'll tell you what, I'll speak with my boss. I'll even do several drive by's and instruct the officers on duty to keep their eyes open."

"Thank you, Tim." Her precious museum and its invaluable artifacts were at risk. She felt grateful to both Dane and Tim for their help.

Tim pulled open the door of his car and got in.

As he drove away Karena couldn't help but feel vulnerable, but all the more determined. There was no way she would let anyone else do any more damage to her museum. Her grandparents had invested some heavy finances into the renovations and grand opening of the structure. That's one of the reasons Grandpa was elected to the Board of Directors. Every time the Masher struck, in Karena's mind, it was a blow to the two people who had helped raise her. She wouldn't give up.

Karena walked down the museum's main hallway. She paused and stared at the plaques on the wall containing the names of those who had contributed money to the building. She ran her fingers over the names of her grandparents.

From there, Karena strolled past the display containing Grandpa's old farm tools. She remembered the day he donated them. His face shined with excitement. Even though Karena had been only twelve years old, she'd been proud. If she had any say in the matter, the Masher's days of vandalizing were numbered.

CHAPTER 3

On Saturday night she and Dane crouched behind a piece of furniture. A baseball bat sat at her feet, just in case the Masher decided to strike. She prayed the vandal would make his move, and that God would protect her. What if, like Dane said, the creep carried a gun? Then what would they do? Maybe this wasn't such a hot idea after all.

An eerie quiet permeated the atmosphere. She wished the prowler would hurry up and break in. After all, she had to get up early for church in the morning.

"I guess I shouldn't be surprised that you work here," Dane said. "I am surprised that a girl as pretty and smart as you isn't married."

Heat rushed from her chest to her face. He thought she was smart. Nobody had ever thought that of her before.

"Thank you," she said with a smile.

"Your grandparents were wonderful people. My grandmother speaks very highly of them. I remember when we were in junior high they worked with my grandma on a quilt to be auctioned off at the annual museum pie social."

"That quilt brought in a lot of money for the country western exhibit." Karena warmed at the memory. She shifted her position to get more comfortable and nearly dropped her bat.

Dane chuckled. "What did you bring that for?"

"For protection, of course," Karena said, lifting her chin.

"Don't worry, I'll protect you," he replied. They gave each other a playful jostle. This wasn't such a scary assignment after all.

"Have you ever forgiven me for running off to Guam and leaving you here?"

The question jolted her like a streak of lightening. Her grip tightened around the bat while she thought of what to say. "Yes, I have forgiven you. I care about you deeply, and I don't wish you any harm, but I still don't trust you."

The hurt in his eyes caused her to scrunch down even lower behind the furniture. "I'm sorry, Dane, I—"

A loud bang startled Karena. It sounded like the same kind of noise she'd heard when she nearly clobbered Dane with the candlestick.

"Do you suppose the rain pipe broke loose?" she asked, gripping the bat tighter in her hands.

"I don't know. Let me check it out, I'll be right back. You stay put. Here, take my pepper spray, just in case."

"In case of what?"

Dane didn't answer. Instead he gripped his heavy flashlight like a club and took off into the darkness.

A moment later another bang resounded. Footsteps came closer. She trembled. A figure in dark attire entered the room. Dane wouldn't have walked back into the building without saying something. So, this person couldn't be him.

Right before the figure was nearly upon her, fear washed over Karena and she yelped. The pepper spray dropped from her hands and rolled away from her. She scrambled to locate the bat but in her panic, and the dark, she couldn't find it.

Strong black-gloved hands latched around her hair, giving it a violent tug. Karena screamed, hoping, praying, Dane would show up. While groping around the floor searching for the bat, she located the pepper spray. In her haste to subdue her assailant, she sprayed without aiming, and coated the display case with the noxious substance. After re-directing the canister toward the man who held her, he let go. Then he picked up the desk chair and hurled it through a side window, smashing it to pieces.

Karena threw her hands over her head to protect herself from flying glass shards. When she looked up, she saw the back of the intruder as he jumped out the window and took off into the night.

She scrambled toward the phone on the front desk and dialed 911. Then she hid beneath the desk and while she waited for the cops to show up, she prayed the intruder wouldn't come back. Where was Dane in all this commotion? She said a prayer for his safety, too.

A frightening thought sailed into her mind. Did this creep know what kind of car she drove? Or where she lived? If only the police would hurry.

Within moments flashing red and blue lights semi illuminated the interior of the building and Karena sighed deep with relief in spite of the eerie shadows bouncing off the walls. Two officers kicked in the front door and burst into the room.

Tim Gentry followed on their heels. Gun drawn, he hollered, "Merriwether County Sheriff, come out with your hands up!"

Someone flipped the interior lights on. Karena blinked a few times and stuck her hands in the air as if she were reaching for a chandelier.

"Please don't shoot me, I'm unarmed. The Masher went that way," she pointed at the shattered window.

"Did you get a good look at the suspect?" Tim asked as he flipped open his notepad and stood poised with pen in hand.

Karena thought for a minute. "No."

She was too worried about Dane to focus much on the Masher. "You have to find Dane. He was with me a few minutes ago, but went to check on a noise, and hasn't come back yet," she blubbered. If anything happened to him because of her hair-brained plans, she'd never forgive herself.

Loud, excited voices from the back of the building drew her attention.

"Dane, is that you?" she called.

Two other police officers drug Dane's unconscious body into the room. Blood poured from the back of his head.

* * *

"I didn't get a look at the guy. I went out to investigate the banging sound and noticed the rain pipe, which I just fixed, had been wrenched loose." Dane grimaced as a paramedic applied a bandage to his scalp wound.

Karena shrank against the far wall. Guilt seeped into her heart. This gentle soul had done nothing but nice things for her. What had she gotten him into?

"I'm so sorry Dane," Karena said. "Is there anything I can do to make it up to you?"

She wanted to wrap her arms around him to show him how much she cared, but she couldn't do that with the paramedic working over him. Besides, everyone was watching.

Dane stared back at her and then he smiled. Her heart skipped a beat, or two.

"Why don't you come over to my place on your next night off?" she asked. "I'll fix you a nice dinner." Karena hoped he appreciated her gesture of apology.

"Sure, I'd like that."

Her heart skipped another few beats. They made arrangements for him to come over to her house the following week. Then, the investigating officer interrupted their conversation.

Karena gave her statement to the police but continued to be distracted by Dane. She couldn't take her eyes off the man. He had been tall in high school, and sweet, but with the passage of time, he had grown taller, and sweeter. He hadn't even expressed one wit of anger throughout the whole ordeal.

Tim cleared his throat. "We're all finished with you here, Miss Smith. You're free to go."

"Okay, thank you. Dane, I'll speak with you about this on Monday. I hope you feel better soon." She reached for her handbag.

"Sure." Dane nodded.

Karena left the building and walked out into the night. She climbed into her car and said a prayer of thanks to God for protecting her, but part of her heart remained sad. She still hadn't caught the Masher. Would they ever catch him?

Sunday morning she sat in church with Holly, her friend from the local newspaper. Pastor Foster preached about a person's best laid plans and how, in spite of a man's plans, the Lord has His own plans. Karena let the comforting words tumble around in her heart. She had asked God for assistance in apprehending the criminal, but she grew weary of waiting on God's timing. Sometimes she wondered why He stretched her miniscule patience like a taut violin string before doing anything.

Soon the service ended and the congregation rose to sing *How Great is our God*. After service she chatted with a few older ladies and invited them to the Christmas event at the museum. Then she went to lunch with Holly. While eating burgers they discussed the break-ins and vandalism. Holly agreed to do a story on everything.

"I'll stop by the museum tomorrow morning and you can show me the damage. I'll even take some pictures."

Karena agreed, glad her friend found a Christian way to help. Maybe once the story broke, someone would come forward with some information that would identify the infamous Merriwether Masher.

On Monday morning a hard rain had begun to fall. Karena bundled herself up and opened her umbrella before stepping out into the deluge. Several roads were flooded, but she still managed to get to work early. She had to speak with the bookkeeper and the accountant at the bank before Holly showed up with her camera. Perhaps Bianca and Mr. Cowan had heard rumors about the Masher. They might have information for the news story.

Mumbling about the rain, Karena sprinted to the front door. She hoped Bianca and Mr. Cowan also had some information about why the books were in such a state of disarray. If the books weren't straightened out by the end of the day, she planned on going to the Board of Directors to voice a complaint.

The fine hairs on her neck tingled as she undid the lock.

When Karena stepped into the building, she froze. The glass case, which contained the jewels, was shattered. Pieces of broken glass covered the floor of the front lobby. However, inside the smashed remnants of the case, the jewels sat undisturbed. Obviously the Masher had struck again, but the note he left caused her blood to turn to ice in her veins.

So you thought you could fool me, huh?

CHAPTER 4

An hour later, yellow caution tape hung around the perimeter of the once glamorous display case. The crime scene investigator snapped pictures from all possible angles. Every time his camera flashed and clicked, Karena flinched.

"Miss Smith?"

"Yes?" Karena turned her gaze upward to stare at a police officer in uniform. He stood with a notepad in hand. He tried to coax her into elaborating on the details of her arrival at the museum that morning. Shock and fear caused her memory of the event to be sketchy.

How had the Masher known she would be there on Saturday but not Sunday night? Was it a fluke, or part of some sinister plan to drive her insane? A shiver coursed through her. Could the crook be somebody associated with the museum? But why would someone invested in the place go to such lengths to sabotage it? Why would anybody, for that matter?

When the police finished their jobs and left, Karena swept up the mess and went to her office. She dropped into her chair. Weary sobs wracked her body. Why were these terrible things happening so close to Christmas? The holidays were supposed to be a season of celebrating Jesus and being kind to each other. Not this sort of thing.

Her cell phone rang. It was Holly. Karena had forgotten she was scheduled to arrive that day. After explaining what had happened, Holly agreed to do a more in depth story of the events.

With any luck, they would get to the bottom of this before any more damage occurred.

"I hate to ask, but can it wait until tomorrow, Holly? My nerves are shot."

"Sure thing, take care of yourself. I'll pray for you, okay?"

Karena thanked her, ended the call, and set her cell phone on her desk. After taking some time to calm down, she walked to another office in the building. The bookkeeper had finally decided to make an appearance and Karena wanted a few words with the woman.

"Hey Bianca, we don't have all the ledgers here at the museum, but from the ones we do have, it looks like the accounts are out of balance."

"I have the others at home," Bianca replied.

"I told you I wanted those account books on my desk ASAP," Karena reminded her. A twinge of uneasiness swelled in her middle.

"I'm sorry, Miss Smith, but you know, my Aunt Gertrude died three weeks ago. I'm helping my uncle go through her things and deal with the loss."

Karena noted how dry the woman's eyes were for someone supposedly grieving, but forgave the absentmindedness anyway. After all, she had forgotten plenty of things in her lifetime, so who was she to judge? She trudged back to her desk, hoping to get some work done, in spite of the day's fiasco.

The following morning, Bianca had "forgotten" the account books again, and before lunch time arrived, she claimed she was sick and went home. Frustration boiled in Karena like molten lava at the core of an awakening volcano. The temptation to drive to Bianca's house and demand the book nearly overwhelmed her, but she had more urgent matters pressing at the forefront of her mind.

A large multi-author book signing party loomed on the horizon, the following Friday evening and she needed to decorate. In all the busyness of worrying over the books, and trying to catch the Masher, there hadn't been time.

First, she pulled a plastic tote of red bows from storage. She inspected each one, making sure they were arranged to her satisfaction, and not too squashed from being boxed up for a year.

Next she called the local book store to make sure enough books had been ordered for all the authors. The book store owner assured her that they would have plenty of books for the evening.

Karena pushed her anxieties aside and allowed herself to get excited about the event. With an extra bounce in her step she went down the main hallway and into the events room at the back of the museum. A flight of stairs went up to the second floor. She would have to remember to cordon off the steps so no one would inadvertently go up there and get hurt, especially the press, and the famous writers in attendance.

The county boasted some talented authors and they all came together for the fund-raiser to help the museum every Christmas. A silent auction for several pieces of antique furniture was planned. Several large baskets, heaped with goodies were donated by some reputable local businesses for door prizes and a raffle.

Her grandparents had dressed in period clothing and attended the party two years ago. It had been their last Christmas together before illness had claimed them both. Karena smiled at the memory as she set to work arranging tables and stringing ribbons and bows on the Christmas tree.

"Would you like some help with that?"

Karena turned to see Dane leaning against the door frame. A bright smile lit up his face. A lock of dark hair fell over his forehead, making him look just a wee bit mischievous, and she wondered what else he had in mind.

"Sure," she replied happily, "but I get to put the star on when we're done."

"No problem." Dane strolled over and with no effort, strung the red and gold ribbons at the top of the tree. When the evergreen was sufficiently covered with vintage ornaments, Dane held the step ladder for her. Karena climbed up and placed the Victorian era star on top.

She admired her handiwork as she stepped down. Just before she reached the floor, she paused to look at Dane.

"With you on that step we're the same height, and I wouldn't have to bend down to kiss you," he teased.

"Dane Cassidy, you behave yourself." Karena gasped. If he only knew how badly she wanted to kiss him. He placed his hand at the small of her back and reached for her hand.

"Let me help you," he said with a deep husky tone.

He was so helpful at everything, and he cared for the museum as much as she did. Her heart did a little flip and their eyes locked, their lips mere inches apart. For a moment, she thought they really were going to kiss.

But the front desk volunteer marched into the room and announced that Holly was there to do the in-depth story.

Dane stepped back and cleared his throat, twice. Karena fanned her face and thanked the volunteer for the information. The woman nodded and went back to manning the front desk.

"Thank you for all your help, Dane," Karena said.

"My pleasure," Dane said as she exited the room. His grin sent shivers of excitement through her and made her go weak in the knees. She was surprised her shaky legs carried her to her office where Holly waited.

"Wow, you're looking quite rosy. Why are you so happy?"

"I was just decorating the Christmas tree with Dane."

Holly didn't say anything more on the subject, but raised her eyebrows and smiled.

"Let's get to work." Karena sat down in her chair and pulled her notes from a file.

Holly asked several questions over the period of an hour regarding the vandalism, and Karena answered them the best she could. Then the subject turned to the off-kilter bank accounts. She squirmed in her seat and chewed on her bottom lip. Should she divulge her suspicions? What if she was wrong?

"I think the bookkeeper is up to no good," Karena finally admitted.

CHAPTER 5

On Wednesday night, two days before the author's event, Karena stayed late at the museum. The tables had been set up and covered with red and green tartan-print tablecloths. Large cedar centerpieces filled the room with an enchanting evergreen forest Christmas aroma. There wasn't much more she could do for the evening, so Karena set the alarm, locked the door, and stepped out into the cool night air.

"Hey there, Christmas elf, how are you?" Dane asked as he strode toward her.

"I'm fine Dane, thank you." Karena lifted her handbag onto her shoulder. It felt like lead, she was so tired.

"You're being careful around here at night, aren't you? Why don't you let me walk you out to your car?"

Karena noted the kindness emanating from his eyes. Heat rose from her stomach and flowed to her cheeks. Every time she conversed with this man logical thought flew toward the Heavens.

"Yes, I'm being careful enough. I'll be here late tomorrow night, too. Will you be at the multi-author book signing event this Friday?"

"Why, you need a hot date?" Dane winked at her.

Karena dropped her purse. "No, I, I just thought—" She picked up her purse and slung it back over her shoulder.

"I should be here early tomorrow night. I have a meeting with Detective Gentry in the afternoon, but that shouldn't take too long. I wish the museum board of directors would give me the okay to hire extra security for the event to help me keep an eye on things."

"You think we'll need extra security?" Karena asked.

"I'm worried the vandal might show."

"With all the people milling around, and all the press that's expected to be here, I don't think he'd try anything. But I guess you never know."

"I'd rather be safe than sorry," Dane replied.

Karena loved the logical side of him, his compassion, and concern for others regarding the event on Friday. Admiration swelled within her as she thought of his devotion to the museum and to catching the Masher.

Karena was unaware of how much time passed as quietness hung between them. She noticed that same dark lock of hair hanging almost to his eyes. He looked at her as though he could see into the depths of her soul. A warm tingly feeling coursed through her. The moon cast a soft glow over them and for a moment she yearned for his embrace, but she was too embarrassed to tell him that.

A light rain began to fall. Karena didn't care to be out in the chilly night air any longer. "I have to go Dane, thanks for everything. I'll see you tomorrow."

"Good night, Christmas elf, drive careful."

Dane chuckled and took a step back. She pushed the troubling thoughts of the Masher to the back of her mind as she got into her car and drove home.

On Thursday morning, the day before the big event, Karena was busier than ever. On her lunch break, she made time to call the police station. It would be nice if they were closer to finding the criminal.

"Merriwether County Sheriff's office, what can I do for you?"

"I'd like to speak with Detective Gentry, please," Karena said. The operator put her call through.

"Hi Tim, it's Karena. How is the investigation coming along?"

"We have a few leads, but I can't go into any details until we know more. I'm afraid that's all I can tell you for now."

"Dane is concerned that something may happen at the book signing this Friday night. What do you think?"

"I think you need to proceed as usual, but no more walking around outside at night by yourself. Got it?"

"Okay," Karena said. "Dane said he was meeting with you today. Please try to get something resolved, if possible."

"Of course,"

"Thank you." Karena hung up her phone. Both Dane and now Detective Gentry warned her of potential danger on Friday night during the event. An icy draft from somewhere drifted into the room. Karena shivered. She didn't want to think anyone would ruin a big fundraiser, but then again, some folks had hearts as black as coal.

Karena kept busy for the rest of the day making last minute arrangements with the photographer. A family of local musicians signed on to play some period pieces. Some of the instruments included three violins, a pianoforte, and a harpsichord. They would provide the guests with waltzes and a number of classical melodies.

Although this excited Karena, every now and then, the fine hairs on the back of her neck prickled. She chalked it up to nerves. There were so many little details to tend to, she did feel overwhelmed. She was grateful for the assistance of the front desk lady, who washed the front windows, cleaned around the one that had just been replaced, and swept the entryway.

Bianca refused to help, and furthermore, she now claimed she had misplaced the account books. Karena gritted her teeth and pushed forward with planning the event. She'd have to deal with Bianca later. With any luck the museum board would fire the woman.

The book store owner called and said she would be there in the morning to inventory the books. By afternoon the caterer would arrive and Karena needed to make sure enough cutlery, plates, and wine glasses were on hand. There were countless other details to tend to, and even with the help of the desk clerk, she had plenty to do and the afternoon passed quickly.

Long after it had grown dark outside, Karena decided to go home. She was tired and needed some rest. After shuffling the papers on her desk into a semblance of order, she grabbed her handbag, and plodded to the front door. She took a moment to punch the numbers into the security alarm system, but before she could exit she heard a sound.

Scrape.

Bang.

The first thought that crossed her mind was that Dane was doing something around the back of the building. He was probably cleaning up another mess behind the museum. Why did he have to make so much noise while doing it? Maybe that stupid rain pipe had gotten wrenched loose again. Feelings of uneasiness took the shape of centipedes and crept up her spine.

Common sense told her she was over-reacting, again. She should just leave, but she feared the Masher might have returned. Common courtesy told her to check on Dane and make sure he was all right and didn't need her assistance with anything. Fear got the better of her. She slung her handbag over her shoulder and headed to the back of the building. She was exhausted and longed to go home and crawl into a tub of hot water to soothe her tired muscles. Her mind needed a rest, too, but she was concerned for Dane's safety. As soon as she made sure he was managing okay, she could go home.

It would be nice to see him again, anyway. He always did know just what to say to chase away her fears.

With a kick of frustration she pushed the stuck door open and stepped outside into the darkness. Icy wind swept past her, and ruffled her hair.

"Dane," she called out, softly.

Silence filled the back alley.

"Dane, are you out here?" she spoke louder this time, hoping he would hear her and respond.

Worried that he didn't reply, Karena braved the wind and rain and sprinted to the back of the building. She did care about him, after all. She called, again, careful to keep her voice low. If she shouted she might cause some neighbors to panic and call the cops. The last thing they needed was another false alarm.

Where on earth was Dane? Had he gone around to the front of the building, or stepped into a side door?

"Dane Cassidy, please answer, if you can hear me." Her heart stopped beating for a second or two, and then began again. It pounded so fast she feared it would leap from her chest. Something was wrong, really wrong. In desperation, she dug into her deep reservoir of faith and said a prayer for his safety, and her own.

Karena rounded the corner and froze in her tracks.

There, by the dumpster, stood Mr. Cowan and Bianca.

"What are you guys doing out here?" Karena asked. Bewilderment and fear entwined themselves around her heart and squeezed like an anaconda as the pieces of the puzzle came together to form a terrifying picture of betrayal. Bianca and Mr. Cowan, together, were the Merriwether Masher.

Mr. Cowan pulled a knife from his trench coat pocket and in three short steps closed the distance between himself and Karena. She tried to maneuver around him, but Bianca blocked her path.

"How could you do this? Why do you want to ruin the museum?" Karena shouted while trying to sidestep the two. She was too angry to care if the neighbors heard the commotion. She hoped they did hear, and called the cops!

Mr. Cowan suddenly grabbed Karena by the hair at the nap of her neck and yanked her head back. He placed the sharp end of the knife against her jugular vein. Pain shot through her body. Panic shot through her heart.

A scream flew from her lips but the wind swallowed her pleas for help. Mr. Cowan kept the blade at her throat while Bianca held a cloth over her mouth and nose. It smelled awful. Bianca then tied Karena's hands behind her back and helped Mr. Cowan drag her into the building. She tried to jerk lose from their grasp, but she felt her mind slipping into a faint. There must have been some kind of drug on the cloth held to her face. One thought flitted through her head. Where was Dane when she needed him?

CHAPTER 6

When Karena's senses crawled back to consciousness, a length of rope bound her hands and feet. A rag had been crammed in her mouth to muffle her cries for help.

Determined to escape, she fought hard against the ties that bound her. The rope slipped a little, but it rubbed her wrists raw. Her skin stung at the effort.

Karena stopped struggling for a moment to take stock of the situation. After careful inspection of her surroundings, she recognized the room she was in. It was the tiny attic on the third floor.

If she could twist the binds a bit more, she could get free. From there she could get to a phone and call for help.

Tiny flames licked their way under the door. There was fire in the building. A hushed cry made its way out of her gagged mouth. She yanked hard on the ropes. Waves of blinding pain surged through her hands, wrists, arms and shoulders when the binds gave way.

Filled with a mix of urgency and relief, she threw the ropes aside. Then she pulled the suffocating cloth from her mouth. Gasping, she jumped from the dirty floor.

Karena stumbled for the door. She had to get to a phone and call the police before the fire consumed the entire building.

When she placed her hand on the old metal door knob it seared her skin, and she immediately jerked her hand back. She used the cloth from her mouth to hold over the door knob but it was of little use. The door was locked. All the pulling and pounding against the heavy wooden barrier did nothing to make it open.

Then wisps of acrid smelling smoke seeped into the room from under the door. The tiny flames were growing in size. She had to get out of there, and fast!

"Lord Jesus, help me," she prayed.

A window she spotted at the back of the room looked like an entryway to Heaven. She quickly maneuvered around a bunch of junk to get to it. She had to stand on an old trunk to reach the latch, but she managed to get it open.

"Well, I'll say one thing for you Lord, when you close a door you really do open a window." Now, all she needed was rope.

Karena climbed down and reached for the pieces of rope that had bound her. She tied them together but the length was far too short. There had to be something else she could tie to it to make it longer.

The open window had provided a few breaths of fresh air but it wasn't enough. A fit of coughing seized her. Her lungs ached. She had to get out of there before she suffocated, before the flames reached her. Maybe there was something in the trunk she could use.

After undoing the latch and lifting the lid she groaned with dismay. The only items in the trunk were ladies undergarments. Bloomers, stockings, chemises and such. She hated to do it, but she tore them into strips and tied them to the end of the rope.

Tears from the smoke blurred her vision as she tied the end of the rope to a turn-of-the-century radiator pipe. Closing the lid to the trunk, she stood on it again. Then she tossed the other end of the rope out the window. Now if she could just wiggle through the opening.

Karena poked her head out and sucked deep gulps of fresh air into her lungs. Working quickly now, as smoke poured into the room, she hefted herself up to the window frame and stuck her feet out. Praying the makeshift lifeline would hold her, she squirmed out the window.

Her arms ached, but she managed to shimmy down to the end of the knotted rigging. Panic crept into her heart when she realized she was still a good fifteen to twenty feet from the ground.

"Lord, please don't let me die here. Please save me, and the museum." She choked on the words as tears slid down her cheeks.

"Karena."

It had to be the Lord calling her. Only a few more minutes and then perhaps she would be in the arms of Jesus. Pain radiated in her shoulders from the exertion and her hands were numb from clutching the ends of a lacy stocking. The bloomers pulled taut and emitted a tearing sound.

"No!" Karena cried. She scraped her feet across the side of the building, trying to find a toe-hold, but nothing was there.

"Karena," the voice called again.

Twisting and turning while dangling in midair, she looked down to see Dane standing below her.

"Let go, and I'll catch you. Trust me," Dane shouted.

The sound of ripping fabric assailed her ears. The rope could give way at any moment. She had no desire to die, so in faith, she let go and felt herself falling. An involuntary scream flew from her lips.

Strong arms embraced her and then her body was slowly lowered to the ground. A pair hands gently caressed her face and hair and spoke soothing words to her. Then, she passed into blackness for the second time that night.

* * *

"Karena."

Someone was shaking her shoulders.

Strange.

She didn't think the Lord would shake her when she entered the Pearly Gates, unless she had been a really bad girl.

"Karena."

Someone called her name again, but it didn't sound like the Lord. It sounded more like Dane Cassidy. She slid her eyes open and stared into Dane's handsome face. Perhaps she was in Heaven after all.

Karena inhaled deeply and became more aware of her surroundings. She lay on a gurney with an EMT on one side of her, Dane on the other.

"Ma'am, you're lucky this guy caught you. Otherwise you could have died from the fall, or smoke inhalation, or the fire, or all three," the EMT said.

"You saved me?" Karena's insides turned to mush. Dare she admit it? She was falling in love with him all over again.

"Yeah, it's a good thing you're not heavy, otherwise I might have dropped you. Now, don't you worry about a thing," Dane said. "Detective Gentry arrested Mr. Cowan and Bianca, and the fire is out."

"My grandparents exhibits—" Another coughing spell took hold of her.

"The only area that burned was the small staircase leading up to the attic."

"But why would Mr. Cowan and Bianca do this?" Karena wailed as she pulled at the wires and tubes connected to her. Betrayal and anger consumed her common sense, but she was determined to face both of her attackers and demand an explanation.

"For the money. It's all gone. Mr. Cowan and Bianca embezzled it all. They vandalized the museum. They intended to set fire to it, blame the mysterious Masher for everything, and then skip town. The whole thing was a scheme to cover their tracks."

Now Karena was really mad. She sat up and climbed off the gurney. "Why?" she demanded. "Why would they steal all the museum's money?"

"Hey, take it easy." Dane wrapped his arms around her to steady her. "Bianca caught some funky disease when she visited overseas last year. She went to the bank for a loan for medical expenses but got denied. Mr. Cowan came up with the idea of embezzling the money, and said he'd take care of the books if she agreed to split the money with him."

"Why did Mr. Cowan want all that money?"

"He's just greedy, I guess." Sympathy and compassion were infused in Dane's tone.

"That is so wrong. Wait till I get my hands on them." Karena was so overcome with anger she hardly felt the pain from her overexerted muscles. A police car sat nearby, and she assumed Mr. Cowan and Bianca were in it. She tried to make her way there, to give them a piece of her mind, but her legs were just a bit unsteady. The world before her tilted and then spun.

"Whoa, there," Dane said. He embraced her, tightly. She appreciated the physical support.

The EMT tried to ask her a few more questions, but Karena brushed them off.

"I'll take her into the Emergency Room and see to it that she's checked out," Dane said to the EMT.

Karena leaned against his strong chest.

Dane continued, "They'll get their just rewards in prison." He gave her a gentle squeeze and nuzzled her neck. "Let's just worry about us. I thought I'd lost you in there."

"Oh Dane, the museum is financially ruined. We have no money. How will we manage to save it?" She cried for a long minute and Dane consoled her until her strength returned.

Pulling away, she wiped her eyes and squared her shoulders. Her grandparents would not want her to give up so easily. In their honor she would straighten out the bank accounts and build the trust fund back to its original balance, and then some. The museum would someday be financially secure again.

"We have a fundraiser tomorrow night. We can start there," she said.

CHAPTER 7

The following evening Karena and Dane danced to a waltz. Several investors had spoken with her already regarding a trust to keep the museum open. On Monday she would make some calls and find more folks willing to help.

She would build the funds back up no matter how long it took. She would have Dane's help, too, of course. But for now, she was content being held in his arms and dancing around the dance floor.

Dane placed a finger under her chin and Karena turned to meet his gaze. She ran her fingers through his soft dark hair. She toyed with the strands that fell to his forehead. A dreamy sigh escaped from her lips.

"Let's go outside. I have a surprise for you." Dane flashed a bright grin, and led her to the back door. The old frame and mechanism jammed for him as well. Karena chuckled.

"Remind me to work on that, will you?" Dane said.

"Sure thing." Karena followed him out into the starry night. She gasped when she saw two horses hitched to an old fashioned buggy decorated with evergreen boughs, holly, and big red bows. Long strings of bells adorned the horses' harnesses. A driver, in period costume, stood ready to chauffer them around, and Dane, ever the gentleman, helped her alight into the conveyance.

"Dane, this is wonderful," Karena gushed.

"I thought my Christmas Elf deserved a treat after everything she's been through."

"Thank you, Dane, for everything," Karena whispered as she snuggled close to him.

Dane wrapped her in a tight embrace. "This whole thing has made me realize I need to be honest with you, not hold anything back. I never want to be apart from you again. I love you, Karena."

"I love you, too."

The driver took the reins and chirruped the horses. The buggy and its occupants rolled down the street. They paused to admire a Nativity scene set up in front of a church and Karena voiced a prayer of thanks to God. It would take some time to restore the museum to its former glory, but without God's grace it would have been much worse.

Soon, they continued on their way and the clomping of the horse's hooves and the ringing of the bells filled the night with a joyful sound. Carolers from down the block added to the melody. They sang *"O Holy Night"* and for once Karena didn't cringe at the lyrics. These sounds were much different from the terrifying noises she had heard around the museum only a few weeks ago. It *was* a holy night, a night divine.

Dane smiled down at her and laid a tender kiss on her lips. And thinking of their future together, Karena could not have been more content.

About the Author:

Debby Lee was raised in the cozy little town of Toledo, Washington. She has been writing since she was a small child and has written several novels, but never forgets home.

The Northwest Christian Writers Association and Romance Writers of America are two organizations that Debby enjoys being a part of. She is represented by Tamela Hancock Murray of the Steven Laube Literary Agency.

As a self professed nature lover, and an avid listener of 1960's folk music, Debby can't help but feel like a hippie child who wasn't born soon enough to attend Woodstock. She wishes she could run barefoot all year long but often does anyway in grass and on beaches in her hamlet that is the cold and rainy southwest Washington.

During football season Debby cheers on the Seattle Seahawks along with legions of other devoted fans. She's also filled with wanderlust and dreams of visiting Denmark, Italy, and Morocco someday. **http://booksbydebbylee.com/**

HISTORY OF "O HOLY NIGHT"

The lyrics to this popular Christmas hymn were penned by a French wine merchant named Placide Clappeau in 1847 who attended church sporadically. Later, the music was written by a prolific Parisian composer, Adolphe Charles Adam. It became a popular hit and was sung in many Catholic churches during the holiday season.

On Christmas Eve, 1906, the very first radio broadcast took place. O Holy Night is said to have been the first song ever played over the airwaves. A Canadian inventor named Reginald Fessenden, from Brant Rock Massachusetts, played the hymn on his violin. The broadcast was heard over the North Atlantic coast and as far away as Norfolk Virginia.

Today, O Holy Night is still a favorite and has been covered by many musicians such as Glen Campbell and Celine Dion. It's still sung in Catholic churches, as well as many others, and it's still played over the radio. Only now it can be heard all over the world.

A True Christmas Present

by

Carol Caldwell

Dedication:

This story is dedicated to all you who think you have left God behind, only to find out he has been with you all along, waiting for you to look up.

Acknowledgements:

Thank you to Darlene Panzera who selflessly dedicated her time and resources to teach a class on short stories. Thanks also go to my classmates who read and reread each draft: Jeri Stockdale, Julianne Haag, Robin Armijo, Beverly Basile, Karen Deming, and Debby Lee. Thank you to Samantha Panzera for her work in putting together the anthology. I also appreciate the beta readers who braved my scorn by giving me their honest opinion: Evelyn Brix, Anita Allen, Lori Hanson, Elaine Bowling, and Verna Atkinson. Last but not least are Dianne Gardner and Pat Stricklin, my children's book critique group who let me run an adult story by them.

CHAPTER 1

Rebecca Blakeley's knuckles turned white as she gripped the phone. "Adam, you won't believe what Walker has done now. Can you come over?"

"Calm down, I'll be over ASAP."

Reb pressed off on her cell phone. Then she grabbed her winter coat, shoved her feet in fur-lined boots, and stepped outside onto the clear half acre in her front yard where her beautiful art studio was to be built. She stared at the spot that until today had been marked with stakes and twine, setting the boundaries of the studio. She tried to identify the emotions she felt. Anger? Disappointment? Frustration? Maybe all of them.

Adam, her son-in-law and contractor for the project, drove up in his battered blue truck. He glanced over where the studio was supposed to be. "Where are the stakes? What happened?"

Reb crossed her arms over her chest. "Sometime between ten o'clock last night when I went to bed and about an hour ago, Walker pulled them up."

"Are you sure it was him?" Adam asked. Reb thought he looked like he wanted to hit someone.

"I'm as sure as if I saw him do the deed. You know he doesn't want me to build this here and he threatened to stop me. Who else would do a juvenile prank like that?"

Adam raised his arms. "I have men coming this morning to dig the foundation. I've got to get the cement poured and set before the rains start."

"Can you tell where the stakes were? Walker left them in a pile by my front door." Reb hoped it would be a simple redo. "Can you just put them back?"

"I've got to measure to be sure."

165

Reb ran to get the used stakes and brought them to Adam. "I'll help you measure."

"I've got this. You go inside. It's cold this morning."

"Okay, but come and get me if you need help." She patted Adam on the shoulder and walked back inside. She should have started the project last summer, but she didn't have the money saved up until now. Adam gave her a family discount on his contracting fees, but the cost still chomped a big bite out of her budget. The studio would be a pay as you go venture.

This art studio was the result of years of dreams, planning and saving. The property was perfect. She had been praying for a studio since she was in high school but she gave up on God when He didn't answer. Now it was her turn to make the studio happen.

After her husband Oscar died she'd moved back home to Medford, Oregon where her roots were. She picked the house because of the acreage on the outskirts of town near her daughter and family, and spent months researching the effects of light on oil paint. With Adam's help, she laid out the studio so that the windows would be angled just right to gather the sun's rays into different corners during the day. The back half acre was full of beautiful evergreens and native rhododendrons, but they filtered the sunlight too much. The building had to be in the front. And her neighbor, Walker, wouldn't hear of it.

*   *   *

Several hours later Adam knocked on her door. "Stakes are back in the ground and I rescheduled the digging for tomorrow. The men will be here early. I want to get this done in one day so I don't have to pay for the equipment twice."

"Please, not before seven thirty. I don't want to alienate the rest of my neighbors." She gave Adam a hug. "Pass this on to Celeste and Becky. Oh and tell Becky that I'll call her to help me put up the Christmas decorations."

"I wondered why your decorations weren't up yet."

She smiled and winked. "I'm waiting for Becky to come and help. Last year we decided we would do it together. That daughter of yours has quite an eye for interior design." A spark of pride swelled her heart.

"She takes after her grandmother." Adam winked back and put his pen away, closing his construction folder. "Don't worry about the studio. I'll have my men start at a reasonable hour."

Reb stood at the door, watching Adam climb into his old truck. She didn't agree at first with her daughter's decision to marry him. Beautiful Celeste could have had anyone she wanted, someone with prestige and money. But she chose Adam, a kind man and an honest worker. He did what he said he would do, and a man with those qualities was hard to find, like Oscar.

Reb went to her dining table and began to address Christmas cards which she made from prints of some of her paintings. The doorbell interrupted her and she smiled. Every year she loved receiving piles of cards, piles so big they wouldn't fit through the mail slot. She swung the front door open expecting her usual mailman, but instead she found a man she didn't know in a gray overcoat.

"Rebecca Blakeley?" He reeked of garlic.

Coughing, she said, "Yes. Who are you?"

"Consider yourself served." He handed her a long white envelope, then turned around and left without another word.

She waved away the lingering odor as she closed the door, and turned the envelope over in her hand to see her name neatly typed on the front. Inside, she found a court order for her to *cease and desist building the art studio* in the front yard. No need to read further to know who filed the suit.

"Of all the gall!" she said aloud, and threw the papers on the floor. "That pompous peacock has done it!"

She growled as she grabbed her winter coat and shoved her feet back into her boots. The fallen leaves crunched under her steps as she strode across the yard to her neighbor's house.

The door opened before she even knocked. The familiar face that greeted her gave only a hint of a smile. "Hello Reb. To what do I owe the pleasure of your visit?"

She clenched her fists at her side and looked up at the still handsome grey haired man who stood half a foot taller than she did. "Walker, you have gone too far! How dare you sue me to stop the building of my art studio? I have every right to build anything I want on my property."

"I warned if you pursued this course, I would put a stop to it. That…that studio, as you call it, will be an eyesore. It will lower the value of the homes on the street, and it will stand in the way of the light I need for my orchids." Walker Rumpf narrowed his gaze and pointed in the direction where the sunlight illuminated his orchid display.   "Your orchids will grow anywhere," she said through gritted teeth. "I need the morning light to paint."

"Paint, ha! You call that scribbling you do on canvas painting? A monkey could do as much. Why even a child could do a better job." His blue eyes glittered with the intensity of an ice berg.

"Walker, you are cruel, you know that? I've called you names before, but I've never demeaned your life's work." Her face grew hot and her pulse throbbed at the base of her neck. She refused to be dismissed by his tone.

"I'm no more cruel than you are, my dear lady. I have nothing more to say to you," Walker informed her and slammed the door in her face.

"I will not abandon my dream," she yelled through the half open grilled porthole in the door.

Reb stood still for a minute, listening for a response. When she received none, she finally walked home. Collapsing on the couch, she screamed out loud to loosen the tumultuous storm within her. An orange cat appeared atop the back of the couch. Purring, he stepped, purring, onto her shoulder, and with one soft paw, he patted her mouth several times.

"Oh Mr. Bill, you understand, don't you?" She grabbed the six year old tabby and hugged him.

"Mr. Bill, Mr. Bill, Auk," came from the dining room where her blue and red macaw shifted back and forth on his perch, bobbing his head up and down.

She shook her head and smiled. "You Silly Bird. What would I do without you?"

Nothing could raise her spirits like her pets. They were her comfort when being alone flooded her heart. Without Oscar, just getting up in the morning became a struggle, but her pets gave her a purpose to rise and shine.

She picked up the phone and called Adam. "Walker has been busy again. He served me papers to stop building."

"Do they give a reason why?" Adam's voice was gruff.

"Um, let's see." Reb read down the sheet. "Just that the building is a nuisance."

"Do you want me to come back over?"

"No, I think I'll take this to my lawyer."

"Let me know what he says. Walker is becoming a real menace." Animosity came out loud and clear.

CHAPTER 2

Early the next day Reb opened the door inscribed David *Bruce and Associates, Attorneys at Law*, and moved into the plush dark wood and leather surroundings. Lawyers' offices always had the aura of success to put clients off guard. Their trick didn't work with her. She once did an internship in a law office, so while she respected them, she knew lawyers were just people, like David from her high school class. And he knew Walker from back in the day. *Strange how the world goes around, always coming back to where things started.*

She stepped up to the woman behind the front desk and announced, "I'm here to see David."

"And you are?" The secretary smiled cordially but didn't move.

"Rebecca Blakeley."

"I see, and do you have an appointment? Mr. Bruce has meetings all day."

"I talked to Mr. Bruce yesterday and he told me to come in this morning." Reb stiffened her back to stand straight and raised her left eyebrow. *Come on confidence, we can do this.*

"Oh Reb, there you are. Don't mind Miss Flattery. She's my guard dog." David Bruce, a year her senior, gave Reb a friendly hug. The laugh lines around his mouth belied the seriousness behind his hazel eyes. His high school physique had given way to a paunch, and his hair had grayed around the edges.

Reb followed him into his office, sat down and slipped the paper Walker sent her on the desk. "Thank you so much for seeing me. Here's the court order I talked to you about on the phone. I need to know what to do."

David picked it up and ran his gaze over the print. "I can see Walker thinks your building will be a nuisance. Hmm." He paused. "But this is supposed to be signed by the Court Clerk. Instead Walker signed it himself. Last I heard he wasn't elected to any city office."

"What does that mean?" Reb leaned forward.

"It could be his attempt to scare you, but I don't think it is valid. Let me make a few phone calls and I will get back to you."

Reb raised her brows. "Is that all?"

"I don't want to make a snap judgment. I want to be sure of the legal advice I provide you." He glanced up from the paper. "Are you aware of any covenants in your neighborhood limiting what you can do on your property?"

"No, I don't recall any covenants; however, I didn't check the deed before proceeding. Wouldn't the county planning office know all that?" Reb raised her voice. "If Walker is just trying to scare me into not building, I don't want to give him any satisfaction by taking this seriously. He threatened to *get me*—his very words. How can he get away with that? I want him to back off. Can I get a restraining order?"

"That's a different issue. Are you afraid for your life?"

Reb leaned back in her chair and rubbed her hands over her eyes. "No, he didn't say anything specific."

David got out a pad of paper and made some notes. "Have you already started construction?"

"Yes, sort of. Walker pulled up the stakes laying out the foundation and Adam had to put them back. They were to begin digging yesterday, but he postponed it to today. We secured all the permits before breaking ground. No one at the planning department questioned my floor plans or the location. We had to submit the exact measurements of the studio's placement on the property." *Be still stomach; I know I did what I was supposed to do.*

"When did Walker threaten you?" David laid his arms on the desk and leaned forward.

Reb hesitated. "I don't remember the exact day, but Adam was with me looking over the yard."

"Did you tell him you were going to build the studio?"

"I didn't ask his permission, if that's what you mean," she said, her voice rising higher than she intended. "Why should I tell Walker Rumpf anything I'm doing?"

"Since you are next door neighbors, I thought the studio might have come up in a conversation."

She blew out a breath and rolled her eyes. "Walker and I don't have conversations."

"My, how things have changed. Okay, I'll call you when I find out what is going on here. It's good to see you again, Reb." David stood up. She sat for a minute and then stood. She wasn't ready for the meeting to be over, but apparently David was.

"David, I really need you on my side."

"I know." He smiled and placed his hand on her back. "I'll do what I can."

They shook hands as he escorted her to the door. Could Walker possibly have a legal right to say what she could do on her own land? She needed help, but she didn't like to ask for any, and now she wasn't sure how to ask. No, she would not let that sham of a human wreck her dream. She shoved her shoulders back as she walked to her car. She'd build her art studio whether Walker Rumpf liked it or not.

*   *   *

A bell rang as Reb entered the door to her daughter's shop, *Flowers Galore*. Beautiful green wreaths and red poinsettias graced glass display shelves. The pine smell of Christmas filled the shop. Like her pets, the holidays always lifted her spirits.

It had been awhile since Reb came to the business as Celeste had a way of bristling when she did. All Reb ever wanted to do was help her daughter be successful, but Celeste made her feel like a bull in a china shop, telling her not to touch it, not to move it, and not to change it. She couldn't help if she looked at things with her artistic eye and instinctively knew what worked and what didn't. Celeste wouldn't take suggestions, at least not from her, and that led to many arguments. All Reb had to do was take a deep breath and before she uttered a word, Celeste would frown.

Reb looked around the shop and spied her daughter behind the counter tying bows. "Good morning, honey." Reb blew a kiss in her daughter's direction. "I saw my lawyer this morning and I thought I would let you know what's going on."

"Why did you go see him?" Celeste continued tying red velvet bows, not looking at her.

"Adam probably told you about Walker removing the foundation stakes. Well, now he has served me with fake papers to get me to stop building." Reb took off her coat and gloves and walked around the counter next to Celeste, picking up some ribbon.

"Here let me help you tie some bows."

Celeste frowned and pushed Reb's hands away. "I don't need your help, Mom."

Those words made a knot in her chest, but she didn't want to show it. "I know how to tie a bow. I'll do this while you can do something else."

"I don't have other things to do right now." Celeste stopped tying bows and focused on her mother. "Are you sure you want to get your lawyer tangled up in your spat with Walker?"

"What else can I do? Walker already has a lawyer—*himself*, and who knows what else he might conjure up. I want someone on my team."

Celeste drew in a deep breath. "Seems to me that getting David involved is unnecessary. I don't understand why you and Walker can't come to some compromise."

"I've tried," she choked out. "You don't know how hard it is to talk with that man." *Give me some credit here.*

"I know the kind of tries you've made in the past about other things," Celeste accused. "Your compromises are more like we'll do it my way or not at all."

"That's not fair. You can't judge everything I do by arguments we've had. You can't seem to let go of our differences over putting some of my paintings in the shop. You knew I needed to get some recognition when I moved back into town, but you were determined that a flower shop was no place for oil paintings."

"Mom." Celeste folder her arms across her chest. "You could have put two or three in for a short time. But you wanted to cover my walls with your art. There would have been no room for flowers."

Reb sighed, sorry for bringing up the conflict that would never be resolved. "You haven't been privy to my dealings with Walker. He is the stubborn one. Maybe I should get a restraining order against him."

Celeste said, "What good would a restraining order do? It would make him all the madder. Walker is a powerful man in town. You don't want to rile him."

Reb pursed her lips as she took in her daughter's prickly attitude. Seemed like she was getting hit from all sides. How could she make the situation right? *No, I've got to focus on this fight with Walker instead of getting pulled into Celeste's issues. There is time enough for that later.*

"Why shouldn't I rile him? He thumped his pointy finger on my chest while saying that he would 'get me' if I built the art studio. That certainly is grounds to get a restraining order." She tapped a finger on her mouth and closed her eyes. "Or maybe I can charge him with misconduct since he gave me that fake court order. Do you think that would get him disbarred?"

"Mother, you are grasping at straws."

"I know, but what am I going to do to stop him? He uses the law as if it were his play thing. That's his advantage. I need an advantage of my own."

"Please don't go off half cocked like you did the last time." Her daughter's voice resonated just above a whisper. "And don't do anything you'll be sorry for."

"Oh honey, don't get upset. I can handle myself." Reb held Celeste's cheeks and wiped away a tear. Celeste didn't pull away. *What a complicated person she is. When her heart seems to be stone cold, she shows she does care. Maybe there is hope for us after all.*

After handing Celeste a tissue, Reb picked up her coat and gloves. "I'll let you know what plan I come up with."

As she exited the shop, Reb braced against the cold wind. Celeste's words of warning stayed with her, even when she tried to shake them off. A tingling in the back of her neck would not go away.

Could Celeste be afraid that Walker will do something stupid or harmful if I take steps to stop him? Walker doesn't know how to lose well.

Reb shrugged and raised her chin. Her daughter was just wary of Walker's connections in town, that's all. He knew people that could make it hard for Adam to get work. Contractors work with bankers and real estate agents, and Walker had his fingers in all those pies.

The last altercation she had with Walker, the one that Celeste referred to, jumped into her consciousness. He kicked Mr. Bill when the cat wandered into his yard. She'd called the Humane Society, reported Walker as a menace to animals, and insisted that they arrest him. But she got in trouble when she argued with the woman sent to investigate. She recalled that they directed her to keep the cat at home.

This studio she was building was essential to her livelihood, and it would not be near Walker's property. Without it she couldn't produce the kind of art and number of paintings that would be her income. Yes, Oscar left her with investments, and what was left of his retirement, but that wouldn't last forever. She had to build up a cushion for her old age, and at sixty, that was approaching fast.

CHAPTER 3

When she returned home, Reb saw the beginnings of the foundation and an extra spoonful of hope graced her heart. *Yes, this is my perfect Christmas present. How I wish Oscar was here to put a ribbon on the door.* She caught herself wondering that if God had given her a studio what kind it would have been. *God, are you seeing this?*

That night Reb set her imagination to work. Walker might have some legal magic tricks up his sleeve, but she knew a lot of people in the Rogue valley who loved her art. She just needed to get them in one place and she knew just the place to do it.

The next day she drove to the Rogue River Gallery where her paintings were for sale. The owner was a friend and had the best location in Medford with a lot of windows bringing in light and giving passers-by a look inside at what awaited them. Reb appreciated Lorraine's long-time friendship, one of the few in town that didn't originate in high school.

As Reb entered the gallery, the sales clerk greeted her. "Mrs. Blakeley, how good to see you."

"Hi Fanny, I need to talk to Lorraine. Is she here?"

"Yes, she's in the back. I'll get her."

Reb waited for the gallery owner to appear, and did a quick inventory of which of her paintings were displayed. She saw three of the valley and one of Ashland. She needed to talk to Lorraine about moving them to the other wall. These paintings looked best from three feet away. *The oil of Jacksonville was missing.* She smiled. *Sold. Perfect timing.*

She considered the other pieces of art in the shop. Several outstanding sculptures of animals stood on pedestals near the front window. There was a new watercolorist in town whom she identified by the splashy globs of color with figures drawn in ink on top. *Different, but creative.*

Reb took comfort at being included in a world of artistic expression. Art could be expressed in almost anything and even though she chose oil paint for her medium, she liked different media and her studio would allow her to experiment. Yes, people loved the Victorian homes, fall leaves, snowy mountain tops that peppered her oils, but there had to be room for more. Her heart yearned to express the beauty she saw every day. She had a quote from Yeats framed in her bedroom. *"The painter's brush consumes his dreams."*

Lorraine Cortez, owner of the upscale art gallery, swayed her way into the large room. Her long Mexican patterned red skirt and white blouse made a statement, but Reb wasn't sure what the statement was. Lorraine was usually a more conservative dresser. They hugged briefly.

"Reb, how good to see you. What can I help you with?"

"First of all, I have to ask you about your new outfit." Reb tilted her head with her fingers alongside her cheek. "Is this a trend or a one time try-it-out-fit?"

"I just got back from Mexico with some primitive art." Lorraine pointed to a corner that displayed Paper-Mache sculpted figures and some acrylics in frames made from old wooden boards. "This is to draw attention to something different. Do you like it?"

"It's very colorful and it definitely will draw attention." Reb turned away from the new display. "I just noticed that my oil of Jacksonville isn't here. Did you sell it?"

"Yes, just yesterday. Got a good price for it, two thousand dollars. I planned to call you later today."

Reb's smile collapsed. "I thought the total was twenty-three hundred dollars."

Lorraine kept up the cheeriness in her voice as she walked behind the sales counter. "I had to come down a little. After I take my commission out, you still make thirteen hundred dollars on it. That is not bad in today's market. Is that what you came in for?"

She sighed. "Actually no. I came in for some marketing assistance. I have a... situation...that I want to avoid, and I need people clamoring for more of my art. I have several more paintings of Jacksonville, some of Table Rock, and of the Rogue River. I thought we could have a Reb Blakeley-artist-in-gallery-evening."

Lorraine broke into a smile. "What a great idea."

Reb's spark of an idea grew as she described it, relishing in the possibilities. "I could make some delicious hors d'oeuvres and bring wine. Maybe Celeste would furnish some Christmas floral decorations. We could have a drawing for one of my smaller oils."

Reb thought about what she would wear and how she would look waltzing among the crowd of art connoisseurs, wine glass in hand, and looking as delicious as her hors d'oeuvres. "Oh, and we'll have Christmas music playing in the background."

"My goodness, that sounds like a...a lot of work. Hmmm. When did you want to do this?" Lorraine's facial expression did not emanate the confidence for which Reb hoped and first saw. And gone was the cheeriness in Lorraine's voice.

"I could be ready in a week. How about a Friday night? People will be looking for Christmas gifts. We can make the evening very festive."

Lorraine pursed her lips. She took in a deep breath and let it out. "What would you need me to do? I have a couple of buying trips I need to schedule before the first of the year. This really is last minute."

"I can have some postcards printed up for you to send out to all your customers, especially the ones that haven't been in recently. Any reason to bring people into the gallery will be good for business. Minute Press has next day service." Reb bit her lip, and silently prayed that Lorraine caught her vision.

From behind the counter Lorraine rested her chin in her palm. "You are persuasive and I do need to get more people in here." She tapped her pencil. "Let me confirm with my calendar and I can call you tomorrow. If you'll wait a minute, I'll cut you a check for the thirteen hundred dollars."

While she waited, Reb fidgeted with her gloves, paced around the gallery, and stared outside. *Why did Lorraine suddenly act as if she wanted to change her mind? I would think she would be overjoyed to have an event that brings in customers. Keeping artists happy is essential for a gallery owner. And besides, I'm doing all the work.*

Lorraine returned, handed Reb the check and said, "I'll call you tomorrow for sure."

"Thank you." Reb flipped the large check into her bucket of a purse and left. She expected more help from Lorraine. They'd been friends for years and Lorraine had always been a supporter of her art. She needed to sell a lot more paintings to pay for the studio. Maybe she should think about other galleries. Ashland and Jacksonville were full of them. But first she would get this money to the bank before they got huffy on her mortgage and the art studio became a moot point.

The next morning Reb woke up with plans for the day already running through her head. December was spinning by and she didn't have any decorations up. Her twelve-year-old granddaughter promised to help, so the first thing on the list was to call her and arrange a time for Becky to come. The second item of the day which she checked off of her list was to order postcards from Minute Press for the evening at the gallery. Reb knew Lorraine would cooperate with her plans. The hesitation was just a ploy. Had to be. Determined to remain optimistic, she whistled as she dressed.

She looked forward to decorating her house since last Christmas when she and Becky talked about it. Becky showed an artistic bent that Reb was determined to nurture. She began digging into the storage closet to haul out boxes for her and Becky to look through. Reb sat on her knees reaching to the back when the phone rang. She mumbled and had to hold onto the closet door to get on her feet. *I'm not getting old, am I?*

"Hello?"

"Reb, this is Lorraine at the gallery. I'm afraid I have to back out of your plans for next week."

Reb couldn't have heard right. "What?"

"Something came up and I can't feature your paintings. In fact, I think you should pick up the ones I have here and take them somewhere else." Lorraine's voice had a catch in it. "I'm sorry. I've enjoyed working with you."

"Lorraine… Lorraine… Are you still there?" No. Lorraine had hung up on her. Reb grabbed the phone book and called the gallery back. "Lorraine, you owe me an explanation. You don't just end a long standing friendship without a warning."

"Reb, you have to understand business practices. There are people in town that more or less run things. If my landlord tells me to do something or he will kick me out of here, then I do what he says."

"Who is your landlord?" Reb asked, but she had a sinking feeling that she already knew.

"Walker Rumpf. He called and suggested that I would do better to get some new talent in the shop. Listen, I don't know what is going on between you and Walker, but I can't afford to lose my gallery."

"It's all right, Lorraine. Thank you." Reb's voice had no air to furnish anymore words with sound.

She dropped into a nearby chair. What else could she say to Lorraine? This wasn't her fault. Reb closed her eyes and leaned her head back. Life hadn't always been easy for her, but at sixty years old, she expected to see some dreams come true. She worked hard, but Walker was fighting dirty. Did he want to chase her out of town?

She took a deep breath and sat up. Nothing would keep her from her art studio. She reached for the phone book and looked up art galleries in Ashland. Why, she'd go to San Francisco if she had to.

CHAPTER 4

The knock on her door startled her until she remembered who was coming over, "Come on in, Becky."

Reb greeted her granddaughter with a long hug, and Becky announced, "I have the magazines I told you about. They have some great Christmas ideas." She spread them open on the dining table.

Becky had grown, Reb noticed, and presented a good mixture of her parents. She had her father's brown hair, but her mother's green eyes and button nose. Reb smiled inside. *Oscar, even if all else fails at least we did something good.*

Reb knelt on the floor. "First let's get all my decorations out so we can see what we have. I started emptying the closet, but you'll have to scoot back under the staircase to reach the other boxes."

Becky crawled to the back corner, and began sliding containers forward. "I found something, but I don't think this is a Christmas decoration."

"Bring it out and we'll see. I don't remember what I stored in there."

Becky backed out holding a plastic bag, from which she pulled a large, rectangular purse, late 1960's style, with blue, orange, brown, and yellow geometric shapes. "Oh wow, this is so cool. I love it."

Reb snickered and waved her hand. "That old thing. I haven't seen that purse for years. You can have it."

"Wow, thanks." Becky opened the purse and peered inside. "It's full of stuff."

"Let's see." Intrigued, Reb tried to remember what she would have left in the old bag.

Becky turned the purse upside down and her eyes gleamed at the assortment that fell out. Reb picked up a charm bracelet. "I'd forgotten all about this. I collected charms of things I did and places I went. Here is the Space Needle at the Seattle World's fair. This paw is for my dog Rusty; great companion. This one's for roller skating. Here's a paintbrush because I began painting early on. This one's for—"

Reb sucked in her breath and closed her hand around the small gold heart. Her thoughts catapulted back in time. A cold shiver ran up her spine. She tossed the bracelet to Becky, and said, "You can have that too."

Becky rummaged through the pile of candy wrappers, gum packets, mood rings and white lipstick. "What's this key for?"

"Oh my!" Reb covered her mouth and closed her eyes. There was a reason she buried the purse in the back of the closet. Emotions she bottled up eons ago threatened to explode. Why had she kept the key? All it represented was pain and sorrow.

"Grandma, are you all right?" Becky put her hand on Reb's knee.

When Reb opened her eyes, her sight was blurry. "That key...went to a box." She took a deep breath and let it out. For a minute she considered if she could tell her secret, but why not? Grandmothers shouldn't keep secrets from granddaughters. Besides that was a long time ago. "It was our mailbox. My boyfriend and I would leave messages for each other. We each had a key."

Becky stared at her grandmother. "Who, Grampa?"

"No, me...and...Walker." Her voice was barely audible.

"You and Mr. Rumpf?" Becky's jaw dropped.

"Yep, boyfriend and girlfriend, starting in the third grade."

"But you hate him now. What happened?"

"I don't hate him. He hates me. It wasn't always this way between us. I forgot how sweet he could be." She pulled a tissue from a pocket and wiped her nose.

Becky moved closer. "Why?"

"I don't know. After high school, he went away to fight in Vietnam and I went off to the community college and Woodstock. We didn't see each other again until we ended up as neighbors. When your grandpa died, I moved back to Medford. I didn't realize Walker lived in that house when I bought this one."

She often wondered why he still lived in his parent's house. Was she drawn to be near Walker without realizing it? Was God doing something? *And why now after all these years and so many unanswered prayers?*

Becky turned the key over in her hand. "What's Woodstock?"

Reb chuckled. She had not thought of Woodstock in a long time. "It was a celebration of life and freedom and music. We were a new generation, no longer interested in old ways, so thousands of people came together and partied." She reached out for the key and closed her hand around it. "I think I'll keep the key."

Becky dangled the bracelet through her fingers and found a silver square with *Reb* printed on one side. "Grandma, why do people call you Reb?"

Reb tilted her head back and laughed. "No one has asked me that for ages. Reb is short for Rebel, not Rebecca."

Becky crossed her legs and rested her chin on her elbows. "Why would people call you a rebel?"

"While everyone else wore skirts three inches below the knee, I wore mine three inches above the knee. Then when all my friends put on mini skirts, I wore skirts down to my ankles. I did what I liked, not what everyone else did."

"Did you rebel against God then too?"

She gave her granddaughter a sideway glance. "No, I've always gone to church. You know that. Why would you ask?"

"I only wondered. I don't hear you talk about Jesus much."

Reb stood up, her lips pursed. "We don't need to go there now, that's enough gabbing. We are far off track from our decorating."

*　　*　　*

When Reb and Becky finished, the house looked like a masterpiece. Strings of lights framed the front windows with greenery tied at the corners of the drapes. The front door sported a wreath on both the outside and inside. Every end table in the living room had an arrangement of candles and pine cones. Even the bathroom had a pine bough strung across the shower doors. Greenery and silver balls surrounded the mirror in the dining room, and tiny white lights completed the setting for the nativity scene laid out below on the buffet.

"What do you think?" Becky said. "Do you like it?"

Reb spun around and hugged her granddaughter. "I love it. Thank you for all of this."

"I had so much fun. Even your artificial tree is beautiful."

The tree sat in its usual place in the living room, polished off with lights and sparkling balls. Her favorite star adorned the top. As she stared at it, a ray of hope entered into her thoughts. "You know, I don't need an art gallery to show my paintings."

Reb snapped her fingers. "The house is so beautiful that I can have a special artist evening right here, and if I sell the paintings myself, I don't have to pay commission." She twirled around. "What a wonderful idea."

"Grandma," Becky said, her face aglow, "I could help serve food by carrying around trays. I could dress up as a French maid in a black dress and white apron with one of those little white hats. Your house will look like a foreign hotel."

"You would be so perfect." Reb hurried to grab paper and a pencil. She began a list. "Can we do this in a week?"

"Sure, if I help." Becky rubbed her hands back and forth in anticipation.

Reb's heart beat faster. "This will be so much better than having the evening at Lorraine's gallery."

CHAPTER 5

After Becky went home, Reb stood on her front porch, the key from the purse in her hand, and stared into space, reeling from memories. Why had she never thrown the key away? What good would it do now? Young puppy love, teen romances never were as satisfying as true abiding love, like the one she'd had with Oscar. They had a good marriage, cut short by a heart attack when he was only fifty. He was her rock, but also her encourager, caring for her as he did for himself. *He inspired me and my paintings glowed.*

His death left her without a soul mate. *God, why did you do that to me? I loved you once. I prayed to you, and worshipped you. And you left me alone.*

Her children were there for her, but they couldn't give the same comfort as having that warm body next to her at night with whom she could share the joys and troubles of each day.

Reb sighed and thought of her neighbor, *Walker*. His blue eyes still captivated her; they weren't always cold. She remembered the old tingling in the pit of her stomach when he was close. They had plans once too, and dreams. He always wanted to be a lawyer, telling her, even in high school, that she would look good beside him as he climbed the corporate ladder. He promised to take her to New York, dress her in fine silks, and put her on a pedestal. But those were his dreams, not hers. Reb had her own dreams that he didn't want to hear. She wanted to travel and paint the world. He liked her art then, but she didn't know where it fit into his plans. What happened to him?

She pulled on her winter coat, walked past the construction workers and got into her car. She headed toward the old elementary school on the other side of town where they had nailed their box to a tree. She doubted it was still there, but she had to see.

She tightened the collar of her coat as she got out of the car. The wind sent biting cold fingers down her neck and she chastised herself for not bringing her wool scarf. Reb glanced at the mothers and toddlers, all bundled up, playing. The school was gone now, replaced by a park, but the tree was still there. How fitting. The tree tilted a bit, probably from children climbing up. She walked around the trunk, leaning back to see how tall it had grown, and scanned the branches and base. Nothing. To think the box might still be there was a long shot. Probably best left forgotten, but the memories of this place screamed at her, and she cringed.

When she got home, the image of the box still pounded in her head, needing some kind of resolution. Maybe Walker had it. She stewed on that thought awhile, but then realized that she had a gala to plan. First, she called Lorraine.

"I'll pick my paintings up tomorrow," she told her.

"But tomorrow is Sunday. I'm closed." The sound of Lorraine's voice chaffed.

"Oh all right then. On Monday. Could you give me a list of your clients? Surely Walker couldn't stop you from doing that. I'm still going to do the Christmas sale, but at my house."

"I'll give you the names of people who have bought your paintings. More than that wouldn't be fair to the other artists. They'll be ready on Monday."

Reb pushed the off button on her cell phone, and flipped through the yellow pages. "Minute Press? I'd like to order some post cards." *They'll make good invitations.*

She ended that call and said to herself, *one more.* What would Celeste say? Would she be pleased to help or give a bunch of excuses? *I have to watch my tone of voice, not demanding. I'm not even sure how I sound demanding although she says I always do.*

"Celeste honey, how are you?"

"Fine Mom. What's up?" Reb heard her daughter's unspoken impatience.

"Did Becky share with you what she and I are planning? She's excited to be a part of it." *I hope saying that will make her more disposed to help.*

"She mentioned something about selling your paintings at home and that I need to find her a costume."

"Yes, well, Lorraine at the gallery backed out of an event I was going to have to ramp up sales of my paintings. I decided to have the same thing at my home. It looks so beautiful now that Becky gave the Christmas decorations her special touch."

"Great, but that sounds like a lot of work for you."

Here I go. "That's why I called. I do need help and I am hoping that you'll be available. It's next Friday evening. I plan to have finger food, wine and punch. I wonder if you would help Becky serve and maybe make some of your delicious taco dip."

Celeste paused before she answered, "Just a minute, I need to look at my calendar."

Reb heard breathing over the phone, and then Adam's voice in the background asked, "Were we going out Friday night?"

Reb's ears tingled. *OOPS.* She picked up a holiday cookbook while she waited and distractedly flipped through the pages. She heard mumbling background noises, and wondered what Celeste said to Adam's question.

"Okay, my calendar is relatively empty. I can help you and I'll be glad to make the dip. The evening might be fun. I can invite some of my friends too, if that's all right." Celeste's voice even sounded cheery.

"The more the merrier. Thank you so much." Reb slumped back in her chair and smiled contentedly. *Did Celeste really choose to help me instead of going out to dinner? What on earth changed? Maybe our relationship isn't as hopeless as I thought. Maybe I need to ask her to help me more instead of me always trying to help her.*

When she finished, her grumbling stomach reminded her she hadn't eaten lunch. An early dinner sounded good, and a left over turkey sandwich with her special orange-cranberry relish sounded even better. She was used to eating light, the side effects of being alone. She sighed.

The construction workers began to pack up for the day, and she wanted to see their progress. Stepping outside, she saw the wall studs and roof joists were up, giving the structure shape. Then she caught the foreman cleaning up. "Jose, how did things go today? Any problems?"

"No senora. Everything is well. We got foundation in and studs up."

"I can see the studio begin to take shape. When will you get the walls sheet rocked?"

"We do that on Monday or Tuesday." Jose turned his head toward the studio. "Building is not big, so it goes fast."

"Not until Monday, huh?"

"Tomorrow is Sunday; we not work."

Reb liked what she saw, but she had hoped it would have been more complete for the party. "Well, tell everyone thanks."

"Okay senora. Adios."

Sunday, a whole day wasted.

CHAPTER 6

She didn't always go to church, usually just on holidays, but Becky's question bothered her. *Did I rebel against God? True, I don't talk about Him much, if at all. But I know He's there.* That morning Reb needed to be in His house. Something pulled her.

The night before, her sleep had been fitful, so after church she took a nap. Mr. Bill woke her up by rubbing his face on hers. "What do you want Bill? Is there something going on, or are you hungry?"

She followed him into the kitchen. Gazing out the window she saw fluffy snow flakes drifting to the ground. Adam would be glad the foundation was in, since snow would have prevented the cement from setting up. She loved to watch snow fall. The world became so peaceful and quiet. *We'll have snow for Christmas.* Then she saw him, Walker, looking at the construction. *What is he up to now?*

She hurried to the front door to find out. "Walker, what do you want?"

"I'm just looking at your monstrosity. Are you going to name it? How about Reb's Insanity?"

She slipped on her boots and pulled her coat on. She approached him with her hands shaking in her pockets. "Walker, can I talk to you without you being a snapping turtle?"

"Sure, I'm listening." He backed up and folded his arms across his chest. She doubted he wanted to hear anything she had to say.

She hesitated. "I found the key today, in an old purse. I don't know why I kept the darn thing. Do you have the box?"

She pulled the key from her pocket. She could barely keep her hand still.

"Box? What box?" He wore his usual smirk as he pulled his chin in and moved his head around as if he was looking for something.

"You know very well what box. It isn't on the tree anymore. I looked."

"Oh that box. Yes…when they were going to tear down the school, I went over and found it, higher up on the tree than it used to be. I have it. In fact I opened it and found the last note I ever wrote you. You never took it."

His gaze bore into her and she felt the heat lazering in from his stare.

"I didn't know you left a note." Her voice wavered. "The last time I saw you, you were flying off to fight a war. You promised to write and never did."

She remembered that day as if she was in the middle of it right then. Strange, it was also at Christmas. She remembered going to the airport to say good-by and the heaviness that threatened to overwhelm her, the realization that her life didn't have a purpose anymore. She made promises to write if he'd send his address. Did he expect to die? Her chest constricted and she felt moisture trickle down the back of her neck. *You don't believe me, do you?*

"You didn't hear me tell you to check the box?"

She knew that look he gave her, one that accused by simply raising an eyebrow.

"Of course not. I was too upset. Why would I want to check the box? The love of my life was leaving and I didn't think I'd ever see you again." Her eyes began to water.

An admission she never wanted to make. Those days were so painful; she slept through them hoping they were just a dream. She had prayed, but God was silent.

"I guess that explains why you never came." Walker stomped around in the snow.

"Came where? What did your note say?" Her voice softened to a whisper and she held her breath.

"Nothing matters now. Water under the bridge." Walker turned and headed toward his house.

"What did the note say?" She reached out for him and snagged his coat. Her voice was louder, almost a cry. *I have to know.*

Walker turned toward her, but his eyes were downcast, not making contact and his lips curved up in a half smile. "I asked you to marry me, and if your answer was yes, you were to meet me at Ft. Lewis in Washington. I waited and you never showed. I supposed that was your answer."

Reb gasped. "Why didn't you say anything? You could have called and I would have come. I loved you. I wanted you to ask me. I waited for you. I thought you abandoned me."

She collapsed onto the snowy ground, with no strength to stand.

With a snort he turned back around and retreated into his brick fortress, his shoulders pulled tightly together. She watched him, not believing he could be so cold-hearted.

As she sobbed into her frozen hands, Mr. Bill found his way out of the half opened front door. He purred and licked her face, but even he wasn't enough to console her.

What if she had found the note? She would have run to him, but his parents wouldn't have sanctioned the marriage since she was a Christian. Would they have learned to love her? She remembered her passion for him. A million what-ifs tumbled around in her thoughts, everything for which she had prayed.

The bottom line was that her life would have been totally different. But how could she have lived without Oscar? He was her anchor. Maybe Becky would have told her that only God could be her anchor. Becky had a penchant of looking at life in ways Reb hadn't learned.

*   *   *

"I know it's here somewhere, Mr. Bill. When did I last see it? Maybe when I moved in here. Oh that was too long ago."

Reb brushed her hair out of her eyes as she rummaged in her dresser drawers and then in the top of her closet. She lifted out boxed treasures and sat on the floor to sift through the contents. Mr. Bill sniffed at each thing until he chose the box that he could make his bed. He settled in and began to purr. Finally her fingers found what she sought, a rose colored leather journal, her prayer journal. She carefully opened it to the first page dated September 1970. She read *this will be a record of my prayers so when I look back I can see God's faithfulness*. She had written down each prayer and a scripture reference for assurance. She had been so hopeful.

Reb had forgotten all about the journal until thinking about her relationship with Walker jiggled the memory. She flipped through the pages and counted the number of prayers about Walker that went unanswered, one, five, twelve, thirty-five. That's where they stopped. She recognized the sense of futility she experienced then. God was silent, but more than silent, she thought he didn't care and she gave up. Reb was aware of a familiar quickening that she had when she kept the journal. She lost it when she stopped writing and praying. God answered some prayers, but none that concerned Walker or an art studio. Now the art studio would become a reality. What did that mean about Walker? Should she consider caring for him again? But how could she when he was so cruel? Was God giving her a second chance and maybe a change of heart for Walker? Wasn't Christmas a time of second chances? Letting her mind wander over old wounds only made her heart hurt.

CHAPTER 7

The gala was set. Celeste found the black and white costume that Becky wanted at Value Village, left over from Halloween. Reb had a long list of RSVPs, and the food that she worked two days to prepare filled the dining table. Becky and Celeste decorated plates with sprigs of parsley, and cherries. *Celeste is quite talented at decorating too. I didn't realize that so much of me was in her.*

Mistletoe hung in obvious places. Reb looked in the mirror and saw that she was as stunning as she hoped to be in a black cocktail dress with red flowers at the waist. Christmas music wafted through the house and out into the neighborhood.

Celeste helped pile her hair into a French Roll, and sprinkled glitter over the top. Reb savored the feeling of her daughter's hands pulling her hair up. To her, Celeste's touch became an act of love. She closed her eyes and let her heart take it all in.

With Becky's help, Reb strategically positioned her paintings around the living room, hall, and dining room. Some hung; others were propped against a wall. She chose a small Christmas country scene as a door prize, one of her favorites.

"Welcome Mr. and Mrs. Mayor. Merry Christmas. It's so good of you to come. Councilman Whitfield, thank you for coming. Sheriff Jones, so good to see you and your lovely wife." She greeted guests as they arrived and clicked off in her mind people who might be influential in her battle of wits with Walker.

Becky walked around with trays of food and glasses of sparkling cider while Celeste kept the food replenished on the table. Reb was thankful for Celeste's help. *What a treasure she is. We might have our differences, but I would be lost without her.*

She stepped into a corner and watched people admire her handiwork. Satisfaction, that's what this was. All these friends had come out to support her, to say they appreciated what she did. Her efforts paid off and her dream studio was becoming a reality. Maybe God had heard her at last.

What was it about prayer that was so hard? When she was a little girl and she asked for a piece of candy, she got an answer right away. Prayer wasn't like that. How many times had she prayed for something important in her life and nothing happened? But here she had taken control, her efforts were being blessed, and a peace settled over her.

The guests came and went, but there always seemed to be a room full. She sold four paintings the first hour. One couple even argued with another over an Ashland Victorian home. They jacked the price up by half again in the bidding war. Her cheeks flushed. She promised to paint another one similar for the losing couple.

"Lorraine, you came after all. Thank you." She extended her hand and drew her friend into the dining room.

"Yes, Walker might have some say-so about who I do business with, but he can't direct my social life. I appreciated the invitation. No hard feelings?"

She shook her head, and smiled. She had no use for grudges.

Lorraine looked around the room. "There are some paintings I don't recognize. Oh, I like this one. It's unique."

She held up an oil of a wood-framed home on the banks of the Rogue River. The screened-in porch faced the water, and the faint light of dawn shone on the rusted screen creating a soft glow. The rocks in the river reflected a brighter light on their wet surfaces.

"If you look closely, you can see a child peeking through a window," Reb said softly. "That's Celeste. I painted it many years ago from a photograph."

"Why haven't I seen the painting before?"

"I thought I might hang onto the painting for sentimental reasons. Then I decided it is better on a wall where people can see the beauty of the dawn on the river." She smiled. "But I'm not going to let it go cheap."

Lorraine peeked at the back. "Forty-five hundred? I'll say that's not cheap. Hmmm." Lorraine swiveled her head as she considered. "But I have to have this. Can I write you a check?"

"Yes, you may, my friend. I'm happy it will be in good hands. Here, have a glass of wine."

"First I want to put this in my car so no one else grabs it before I pay you." She watched Lorraine move through the crowd with people's heads turning toward the painting. If she had been alone, she would have danced a jig.

When Lorraine returned, she picked up a glass of wine and whispered in Reb's ear. "I saw Walker in his front yard watching your house. Didn't you invite him?"

"He would have been a real kill joy," she said, and both of them burst out laughing. She glanced around the room and waved her hand at Celeste. "Have you met my daughter?"

"No, I don't think I have, but you've talked about her so much."

"Since you have her in your painting you should meet the grown up one. Celeste, this is Lorraine from the gallery. She just bought the river scene with you in the window."

Celeste said, "It's nice to meet you Lorraine." She turned to Reb, "You sold my painting?"

Reb raised her eyebrows. "I didn't know you wanted it. You should have said something."

"You never put it up for sale so I just assumed that you were saving it for me."

Lorraine put her hand on Celeste's arm. "I don't want to get between you two. I can reluctantly return it. It is an outstanding painting."

Celeste asked, "How much did you pay for it, if you don't mind me asking?"

Lorraine smiled as she said, "Enough."

"In that case, you keep it and I'll ask Mom to paint me another one." Celeste laughed.

Reb said, "You two had me going there for a minute. And yes, I can paint another one for my daughter."

Celeste headed back to the kitchen while Reb grabbed Lorraine's hand and gave her a tour of other paintings not seen in her gallery.

"Reb, you are so talented. I know the owners of several galleries in Ashland and Jacksonville. I'll give them a call to promote your work."

"That would be fabulous." She clapped her hands. *Thank you, God.* As she looked up, lights reflected and danced on the ceiling from the front window. "Do you see the lights on the ceiling? They are so pretty, but where did they come from?"

"Are they the Christmas lights around the front of the house?"

"No, I don't think so; they aren't quite right." She spoke slowly while something cold and sharp, like a knife, stabbed through her body.

Then someone opened the door and shouted, "Fire!"

Reb's wine glass shattered on the floor. Her studio, her beautiful half built dream was going up in flames. She couldn't move.

Someone yelled, "I'm calling 911."

In the faint distance she heard someone else call, "Mother."

A man jostled her as he ran past carrying the small fire extinguisher she kept in the kitchen. That brought her out of a stupor. She ran outside toward the garden hose and turned the knob, but water barely came out. She dropped the hose and started throwing snow on the flames. People around her were stunned. She motioned to them and pleaded, "Help! Help me!"

She couldn't believe what she saw. Red, yellow, and blue flames spiked up on each board, curling around them like a caress, and leaving behind a black charred residue. As she watched, she thought of Walker and how he had once caressed her heart, only to leave behind useless ash. Her hands shook as she scooped up snow to toss on the fire. The heat seared her face, yet she wouldn't stop. Her lungs heaved against the smoky cold air.

Someone else tried to get water out of the garden hose, but there was just a trickle. More were throwing snow, but their efforts didn't help. Several people came from the house with bowls of water. Sirens broke through the shouts.

Her spiked heels caught on pieces of wood covered by the snow and she fell. She was too close to the fire and her dress went up in a poof. The heat engulfed her. She felt hands grab her, pulling her away and covering her with cold. Then sirens blared and more hands lifted her onto a gurney and into an ambulance. Behind her somewhere she heard Mr. Bill yowl. Time stood still.

CHAPTER 8

She woke up with bright lights in her face and people pawing at her. "What's going on? What happened?"

A nurse patted her shoulder. "It's all right honey. Your dress caught fire and we're treating your burns. Stay still now. Are you in pain?"

She closed her eyes. "Yes, I have a headache from those awful lights. Can you turn them off?"

"I'm sorry. We need them on to see what we're doing. Keep your eyes closed."

She began to remember as she rolled her head back and forth. "My studio," she moaned. "What am I going to do? My dream…gone."

"Just be still, now. You'll be all right." The nurse turned to a man standing by. "Doctor, can we give Mrs. Blakeley something to calm her?"

*   *   *

Reb squeezed her eyes open to the dim light of a hospital room. She heard the door swoosh as it opened.

"Good morning, Mrs. Blakeley, I'm Dr. Stimple. I treated you last night in the ER. How are you feeling today?"

She grimaced. "I'm fine. When can I go home?"

The doctor flipped papers on his chart. "Luckily you only have an area of third degree burns on your thigh and leg. The rest are first and second degree. Your friends acted quickly, I hear, and covered you with snow. It not only put the flame out, but it cooled off the burn. You are very fortunate."

She frowned. *I don't feel fortunate.* "You didn't answer my question. When can I go home?"

"I want to keep you several days to treat the burns. Do you have anyone to help you at home? I want you on bed rest."

She turned her face to the window. "My daughter lives nearby. She can help if I need it."

"Okay, we'll see how your burns are doing tomorrow. You rest today." The doctor hung her chart on the wall and left.

Why God? Why did you bring me this far only to take away my dream? Don't I matter? You aren't fair. People always talk about you being so loving. How is this loving? Her soul ached. Rebuilding would be too much of an emotional investment. She couldn't do it, didn't even want to consider whether it was worth the effort. Walker had won. Anger rose up like gall, filling her throat and leaving a bitter taste in her mouth.

"Mom, are you awake?"

She turned her head away from the window to see Celeste and Becky standing in the doorway. She reached out her hand. "Yes, honey."

Reb's eyes began to blur and she quickly blinked the moisture away.

They carried a bouquet of red roses and placed them on the bedside table. "How are you feeling?"

She forced a smile for their sake. "I'm feeling fine, fine enough to go home. But they want to keep me longer. I just have one serious burn, the others are manageable." She cleared a spot on the bed. "Becky, you sit here."

"I don't want to bump you, Grandma." Becky's eyes were red.

"You won't. I need a hug." Even if Becky did hurt her, she wouldn't say anything. Her granddaughter's hugs were a sweet tonic to her soul.

"Mom, the studio is gone. Only a pile of ash is left." A tear slipped from Celeste's eye and trailed down her cheek. "I'm so sorry. Did the Fire Inspector talk to you yet?"

She shook her head. "No, what would he want?"

"I stayed there until the firemen left last night. The Inspector poked around in the ashes, and mentioned that the cause is most likely arson." Celeste shot her a pained look. "He said the smell of gasoline was still strong."

Reb nodded and turned toward the window. "He won. I can't start again."

The emptiness that started last night was still there.

Celeste touched Reb's hand. "You can prosecute him, especially since you were injured. You or someone else could have been killed."

"Yes. How could he have done this? What did I do to him to make him this hateful? We loved each other once."

Celeste nodded. "Becky told me."

She looked at Becky, and caressed her granddaughter's cheek.

They sat in silence until a nurse knocked on the door. "Flowers for you."

"Who are they from?'

"Let's see. The tag says, *Get well soon, Walker*. Where would you like them?"

All three of them stared at the nurse. Reb would just as soon see the flowers dumped in the trash, but she didn't like to waste pretty things. Finally she said, "Give them to someone who doesn't have any."

*   *   *

A week later, Adam drove her home. She had instructions on how to change the dressing on her thigh and leg, and demands from the doctor that she stay off of her feet. She patted Adam on the shoulder. "You are so good to me. Thank you."

"Becky will be over in a while. She can be your runner so you don't move around. Celeste will bring you dinner around five o'clock. Where do you want to sit?"

She smiled. "The couch will be fine. I have a comforter right here to put over me. I'll be quite cozy."

"Auk, cozy, cozy. Mr. Bill."

She laughed. "Be still, Silly Bird."

"Silly Bird, Silly Bird. Auk."

Mr. Bill jumped on the couch and curled around her feet. "You see Adam; I'll have someone to look after me." She picked the cat up in her arms and he licked her nose. "Did you miss me, Mr. Bill?"

Adam reached down for a hug and left.

Reb snuggled into the comforter and closed her eyes. Thinking made her head hurt. If only she could just go to be with Oscar. He made her happy and she hadn't felt that way in a long time. Not until the door bell rang waking her up did she realize she'd been asleep. "Come in."

"Grandma, it's me."

"Where's my hug?"

Becky bent down and Reb felt her light touch. "Now get us something refreshing to drink. There should be iced tea in the fridge."

Becky brought in the glasses. She pulled up a dining room chair next to the couch. Sympathy spread over her face. "Are you feeling better today?"

"I'm fine. I'll be over these burns and up in no time." Reb took a big gulp of tea.

"Grandma, I know you are really sad over your studio burning down. I brought you a card."

194

Reb smiled at the peaceful winter scene on the front. Inside, she read, "*If God shuts a door, whatever was behind it, wasn't meant for you. Believe that he closed that door because you are worth so much more than that.*"

Reb stared at the words, letting them settle in. Could that account for the years of unanswered prayers? A lump formed in her throat.

"I've been praying and I believe that God will answer your prayers, but maybe the art studio in your front yard wasn't what He planned for you. I believe He has something better." Becky's eyes looked so trusting.

Reb waved her hand as if to swat a fly. "God doesn't want to bother with me. He made that clear when He didn't stop Walker. I've tried to live my life as best as I know how, and I think God gave up on me a long time ago."

"I don't believe any of that. I know that God loves you as much as He loves anyone else. You know the verse: God so loved the world—"

"Yes, yes. I know what the Bible says. I just can't seem to make it work for me."

Becky moved her chair closer and leaned her elbows on her knees. "Grandma, did you ever ask Jesus to forgive your sins?"

She stared into her granddaughter's eyes. They were so clear and trusting. "Of course I did, when I was about your age."

Becky grinned. "That means all your sins are forgiven, even the ones you'll do next week. And God wouldn't forgive someone He didn't love."

"You are full of inspiration today, aren't you?" She looked down at her hands and picked at her nails. "Why don't you find something to watch on TV?"

Becky nodded her head. "Okay, call me if you need anything. But Grandma, you can't hide from God."

Becky took off for the TV room, leaving Reb with thoughts of her granddaughter's words repeating in her mind. '*Maybe he has something better. God doesn't forgive those he doesn't love.*' Did she believe that? The words to the song *Jesus loves me this I know* ran through her head. What made a twelve year old so sure of God's love? Becky sounded like a preacher.

She started to doze again when the doorbell rang. "Come in."

"Reb, are you okay?"

Mr. Bill raced to the door, arched his back and hissed. Reb's face contorted. She didn't see who entered, but recognized the gravely voice. "Walker, what do you want? Did you come to gloat?"

He stepped in, looking around to see where she was, and side-stepped the cat. "They said at the hospital that you had gone home. I wanted to see if you were all right. Did you get the roses I sent?"

"Yes, the roses were delivered. I hope someone enjoys them. Why would you care how I am?"

She moved to sit straighter but ended up pushing on her burn and flinched. Tears rolled down her cheeks. She hurried to wipe them away. "I know you torched the studio. How could you?"

He took off his hat. "May I sit?"

"Do whatever you want."

Walker's face had lost its hardness. He didn't look like a victor. "I'm sorry. I didn't mean for you to get hurt."

"Then why did you do it? What did you think would happen, that I'd stand and watch? Anyone could have been killed." She grabbed her glass of tea to wash down the bitter taste in her mouth.

He leaned back in the chair, fingering his hat. "Revenge, plain and simple." He paused. "There are things I need to say. Please just listen." He paused again as if he were searching for words. "All those years I kept track of you; when you married; knew each time you moved. When you had children, I thought they should have been our children."

Reb listened, her mouth opened. *I can't believe I'm hearing this. Is he insane?*

He rubbed a hand across his forehead. "By the time you moved back here, I hated you." His voice fell. "I blamed you for what I didn't have. I didn't want you to be happy. That's why I opposed the art studio."

His expression crumbled. "You know, I never married. My mother hated me for never giving her grandchildren."

"I didn't know that."

He lowered his gaze. "I watched the fire that night. I saw you run out and try to put out the flames. What a fiasco. In fact, I laughed. I wanted you to experience the loss that I've felt all these years. The revenge was satisfying. That is until you caught on fire. I dialed 911, but someone else had already called."

Walker's expression was that of one who had told his story, was done, and could say, "Oh well." The lack of regret was evident and Reb was repulsed.

The thought that he laughed at her pain made her nauseated. She turned her face away. She did endure a loss, and maybe it was a two-fold one. She lost two dreams.

"Are you going to report this to the police as arson?" His voice was soft, his eyes downcast.

The knife of his words cut through her heart. "Is that all you're worried about? Is that why you came over?" Her voice trembled. "You wanted to see if your precious reputation was intact. I can't believe you. I think you should leave now."

Walker got up without another word. She watched as he put on his hat and walked away. He looked like an old man.

CHAPTER 9

Celeste arrived at five o'clock with a plate of lasagna and a green salad. She also brought a copy of the daily newspaper. "You made the headlines, Mom."

She took the paper and read. "'*Local Artist Hurt In Studio Fire.*' Goodness, if I wanted publicity I wouldn't have chosen this way." She dropped the paper on the floor. "I'll read it later. Thanks for the dinner."

Celeste sat beside the couch as Reb picked at her food. "I thought you'd like the lasagna. It's your favorite. Aren't you hungry?"

"My appetite is on the fritz. Probably from pain killers. I could use some hot tea though."

She picked up the paper while Celeste was in the kitchen. The picture on the front page showed the ash heap in her front yard, a perfect description of her insides.

Celeste set the cup of tea on the coffee table. The steam spiraling from the cup gave Reb chills. Too much of a reminder of the fire that took away her dream.

"Has Becky been helpful?"

Reb picked up the cup and thought about the earlier conversation with her granddaughter, *where there is love there is forgiveness.* "Yes, she's been a big help."

Reb closed her eyes to gather thoughts together. "Honey, I need to ask you something. You were so nice to help me with the event last week. Given the bristly attitude that I encountered at your shop, I was surprised. What happened?"

"Mom, it is very simple. When you come into my shop, you treat me like a child that needs direction, not a business woman on the same level with you. But when you called and asked for help, a thing you never do, you let me know that you value me, that I had something to give you." Celeste sighed. "I guess the way you show love is not the way that I receive love."

Reb stared into her daughter's eyes as if she was seeing her for the first time, a grown woman. "I am so sorry. I never meant to treat you as a child. Will you forgive me? Maybe you will have to teach me how to show you that I love you."

Celeste reached out and squeezed Reb's hand. They shared a silence that mended a thousand hurts. If Reb could have jumped up in celebration, she would have. Instead, she let joy quietly flood her soul.

Then she leaned her head toward the TV room. "Becky, are you still watching TV? Your mom's here."

Becky came out rubbing her eyes. "I guess I fell asleep."

Celeste frowned. "A good nurse you'd be, falling asleep on the job."

"All right you two, scat. I need to change the bandage on my burn. I'll be fine." Reb accepted hugs from them and began to lift off of the couch.

"Auk, scat the cat, Mr. Bill, never married, call 911."

Celeste peeked into the dining room. "What did Silly Bird say?"

"Don't pay attention to him. He likes to make things up." She glanced at Becky who had her hand over her mouth. Had Becky been asleep or did she overhear Walker's confession?

*   *   *

The next morning the Fire Inspector called on her. "Mrs. Blakeley, I appreciate you seeing me while you're still recuperating. I thought you would want to know that we believe your fire was set on purpose. The scene reeked of gasoline."

"Thank you, but I suspected as much." Reb nodded her head slowly. "There wasn't anything in the studio that would cause a fire." *Except maybe the fiery darts from Walker's jealous glare.*

"Do you know who would have done this? I understand you had a disagreement with your neighbor." The Inspector held a small notebook in his hand with writing inside.

"Yes, Mr. Rumpf and I had some words over the building of the studio. But he's a respectable lawyer. I cannot imagine that he would commit arson." She looked straight at him. *Why am I protecting Walker?*

The Inspector put the notebook away. "If you think of anyone who might have set the fire, please call me."

He handed her his business card. She cleared her throat and placed the card on the coffee table.

"Of course I will. Thank you for looking into this."

Denying she argued with Walker would do no good. Everyone knew she had. But she couldn't bring herself to reveal his confession. Was she responsible for the sad turn his life took? She had to sort through a morass of emotions before she would know what to do.

*   *   *

That night she sat across the dining table from Celeste and buttered a piece of bread from the dinner her daughter brought.

"Mom, why didn't you tell the Fire Inspector that Walker set the fire?"

"What good would that do? What's done is done." She shook her head thinking. *God might have another way.*

"He should have to pay for what he did."

The look in Celeste's eyes touched her heart. She was comforted to know that her daughter cared about her, especially at a time like this. But her words reflected something else, perhaps a little pay back.

"By serving jail time as an arsonist? That wouldn't bring back the studio, nor would that teach him anything more than what he has already learned. He has suffered in his own prison for a long time."

Celeste got up and took the dirty dishes to the kitchen. Reb heard her daughter clanging plates and silverware into the dishwasher. Celeste returned to the dining room with her eyebrows knitted together. "You do know that what he did is not your fault. You are not responsible for his bitter soul."

"But I should have known his intentions." She flung her arms out to her side.

"You mean that he would burn the studio down? Didn't I warn you that he might do something?" Celeste sat and put her hands on the table in front of Reb.

"Yes, you did, but I never thought he would do something so dangerous. But…but I'm referring to before he left for Vietnam…that he wanted to marry me." Her voice dropped. "He thought I abandoned him and I thought he didn't care."

"If he really wanted to marry you, he would have asked you face to face. The message in the box thing was child's play. Adults don't make serious decisions that way."

Reb felt like she was a teenager getting a lecture from her mother. Celeste's voice had the sound of authority and wisdom. *She's going to do well with Becky growing up.*

Celeste stopped with a curious expression on her face. "You know it is strange to talk to you about someone else that could have been my father. And to think you loved another man."

Reb turned her head to the side, chin in the palm of her hand, considering what Celeste said. When she looked at her daughter, the room was brighter than before, like she just put on a pair of glasses.

When she spoke, her words were slow and determined. "I don't think there was a chance of that. You wouldn't have been you and I would be so miserable without you. I see now what God was doing all the time He said no to my prayers for Walker. Your father was the best husband for me, the best father for you, and God hand picked him. I never saw before how much God was involved in my life. I thought He ignored me."

She felt a heaviness fall away from her soul. She breathed in deep. "You are right. Thank you. How stupid of me to be led along by Walker's games. Why didn't I see it before? He's a true manipulator, so no wonder he's a good lawyer."

Celeste put a hand on Reb's arm. "Your skin is cold. Are you feeling alright? Do you need a sweater?"

"I'm fine, really fine." Reb smiled. "I'm actually better than I've been in a long time."

Then her daughter leaned over to plant a kiss on her forehead, and promising to check in on her with a phone call later, made her way out the door.

Where was God in this? If she mourned the fact that she lost an opportunity to marry Walker that would be like saying Oscar didn't provide her with a good life. But he did. She knew that God had given her a better husband than Walker could have been, and she wanted to believe He had a better art studio for her than the one she planned. *What kind of faith does it take to believe in something I can't see?* Did she want to believe just to get what she wanted? Or did she want God to direct her life where she would follow instead of lead? *God, please show me what to do.*

CHAPTER 10

The next day as Reb changed the bandage on her burns and dressed herself, both her wounds and her mood improved. She tied her hair into a pony tail and was ready to face the world. The snow had melted, but when she touched the window glass she could feel that the outside air was still icy. Mr. Bill wound around her ankles, meowing for his breakfast. "You are such a whiner and so impatient. You know I won't forget you."

She indulged him with a dash of tuna and some scrambled egg from her plate, a love treat for her confidant and best friend. But she wasn't so permissive with herself. She ate without taking time to taste her food.

Nights often had a way of sorting out the nonsense and leaving what was important. She thought about the job she had to do before Becky arrived. It was time to set aside the past and the thought of doing that gave her confidence.

She wrapped up in her heavy coat, fur-lined boots, and twisted the red woolen scarf Oscar had given her around her neck. Then she headed for Walker's house.

She knocked. "Walker, I need to talk to you." She waited, and then knocked again. "Please."

Finally she heard the metal lock turning and some grumbling as he opened the heavy front door. "What do you want, Reb?"

"May I come in?" Her insides quivered. *How long has it been since I've stepped into this house?*

Walker stood aside and motioned with his hand. "Sure."

She walked into a familiar but almost forgotten living room. The curtains were the same, the furniture was placed the same, and the dim lighting was the same. All was the same as when his parents were alive. Nothing had changed except the odor. The air wasn't fresh, but had the stale, moldy smell of an old person's home.

"The house still looks just like the day we graduated from high school," she commented.

"You're in. What do you want?" Walker looked bedraggled with stubble on his chin and hair uncombed. She had never seen him this way.

She leaned on the back of a chair. "May I sit? My thigh hurts when I stand."

"Why are you walking around on it then?"

"I wanted to invite you to dinner tonight. I didn't know if you'd answer the phone, so coming over was the alternative."

"What's the dinner for? Haven't we said enough to each other?" *He doesn't trust me. I guess the shoe is on the other foot.*

"I hoped that we could come to some sort of understanding as neighbors. I forgive you for burning my studio. I wanted to show that there are no hard feelings." She made sure the expression on her face was pleasant and that her voice was soft.

Walker let out a "Humph."

"That's all." She got up to leave. "I'll see you at six-thirty tonight."

She didn't look back as she walked to the door. However, her spine prickled, tempting her to turn around. As she closed the door her eyes met his and she smiled. She wanted him in good humor for dinner in case the news she planned to deliver gave him indigestion.

*   *   *

She was ensconced on the sofa when Becky arrived. "Will you please bring me my cell phone and the phone directory?"

"Sure Grandma. Is there anything else I can get? Maybe some tea. You look kind of worn out. Did you sleep okay?"

Reb chuckled. "Let me see if I can answer all your questions. Yes, I'll take some tea. Yes, I am tired. Yes, I slept well. And make the tea Lady Jane please."

She dialed Celeste. "I have a request for you. Could you please pick up two fried chicken dinners from the market, and bring them over about six o'clock? I'll pay you back."

Celeste laughed. "Are you having company tonight?"

"Yes, I am. What's funny?"

"You are recuperating. I didn't think you would be up to entertaining."

"That's why I'm not cooking. There's something I believe God wants me to do. I'll tell you later. See you at six."

She hung up and made another call. Then she lay back on the couch. Becky came in with a cup of tea.

She smiled. "This is just what I need. I'm going to rest, but while I do, will you set the table for two? Plates, silverware, napkins and glasses. Thank you."

Becky frowned. "Are you okay Grandma?"

"Yes, honey, I am. Just humor me please."

She sipped her tea. Mr. Bill snuggled up beside her and began to purr. "Is this a thank you for your special breakfast this morning? You always show up just when I need a bit of protection or comfort."

She remembered the lonely years after Oscar died when she needed a shoulder on which to cry. And one day Mr. Bill showed up on her doorstep as a scraggly, underfed kitten. "God must have sent you."

CHAPTER 11

She had added some plastic pine boughs, red bows, and white candles to dress up the table. Everything needed to be pleasant, at least outwardly. She wondered if Walker would have butterflies in his stomach like she did. She rehearsed what she would say, but couldn't imagine how he was going to respond. Would he be sorry or try to get her to take the blame for his actions?

The knock on the door was prompt at six-thirty. She opened it. "Please come in
 Walker."

Reb wore a red pant's suit because it was comfortable. Walker wore a red tie. His gaze told her that he still appreciated her beauty. "It looks like we both dressed for the season."

She took his overcoat and hung it on the coat tree. "Yes, red is fitting for Christmas."

She put her arm through his to balance her limp. As she ushered him into the dining room she noticed Walker glancing around.

"Is the cat out?" he asked nervously.

She snickered. "Don't worry, Mr. Bill is napping. He won't join us for dinner."

They both filled their plates with food and she asked if Walker minded that she say grace.

"Go ahead. This is your house."

"I didn't want to offend you, knowing how you used to dislike conversations about God."

"Doesn't bother me now. I've grown up."

After thanking God for the ready-to-eat meal, she cleared her throat and spoke in a matter-of-fact way. If she could keep her voice even, she would get through this.

"Will you please forgive me for ignoring your requests for me to put my art studio someplace else? I was not a good neighbor and I want to be a better one." Her whole body relaxed.

She took a bite of chicken and coughed. Coming from somewhere, the pungent smell of gasoline overwhelmed her. Washing her food down with water, she tried again. The second bite was fine. She closed her eyes and tried to clear her imagination.

Walker put his fork down. "Are you all right?"

"Yes, I am. Something went down the wrong way." She thought, *was that gasoline smell coming from him real or imaginary?* She repeated her question to him.

Walker didn't answer right away. What was he thinking? She looked at his eyes and saw a far away gaze.

"Forgive you?" His speech was slow at first. "You ruined my life. There isn't enough forgiveness in all of heaven, if there is a heaven, for that."

Walker's voice was taut and a purplish red spread over his face as if his tie was too tight.

What could she say? She wasn't expecting that kind of a response from him. In fact she didn't know what she expected out of Walker, but that wasn't it. She closed her eyes and drew in a deep breath.

"God has been showing me that I need to ask forgiveness for what I did wrong. And that's what I'm doing. But I am not responsible for what you think, and I did not ruin your life. You did that yourself."

"God? What's he got to do with this? You are the one who rejected me."

"I will not take on that role because it isn't true. You can't make me feel sorry for you." She softened her tone. "If you really wanted to marry me, you would have stood up like a man and asked me face to face. You had plenty of opportunities."

She started to take a bite of chicken, but put her fork down.

Walker leaned his body across the table. "You knew I loved you. How many ways did I have to tell you?"

"I guess that's the question, isn't it? You should have proposed and offered me a ring." She leaned back in her chair and crossed her arms. "What did you plan if I showed up at Fort Lewis? Were you going to whisk me off to some Army Justice of the Peace?"

She had tried to control her voice, keep it calm, but now the pitch rose to a squeak that made her cough. She grabbed her napkin and covered her mouth.

"What would you care? You were always doing the unexpected. Isn't that why everyone called you Reb the rebel?" Perspiration beaded up on his forehead.

She leaned forward, gripping the edge of the table. "You didn't think I'd want a wedding?"

He picked up a roll and took time to spread some butter, not looking her way. "You probably didn't deserve the white dress that goes with one."

She gulped. "What? Are you suggesting what I think you are? Who do you think you are? Did you even know me?" Her breathing came faster.

"Everyone gossiped about you and your shenanigans. I tried not to believe what they said, but you know the saying: 'where there's smoke there's fire.'"

She bowed her head with her fingertips supporting her forehead. "You and I never—In fact, I never—I was a virgin on my wedding night."

She frowned at his smirk. *Were you always so stupid?*

That was enough. She would not be insulted in her own home. Disappointment rocked her. She had wished that Walker would relent, would forgive and forget. But he had gone too far. Sweat trickled down her neck and her eyes stung. She held on to the growl that was forming in her throat.

Her chair tipped backward as she stood up. She limped over to the coat tree, yanking Walker's coat free from the hook. She faced him with a locked-in stare. "My husband respected and loved me for who I was. He believed in me. I am truly sorry that you allowed bitterness to carve your soul into a block of granite."

Walker's mouth gaped open, but words didn't find their way out. He stood and shuffled toward the door. Just then Mr. Bill woke from his nap and in an orange flash, jumped onto Walker's shoulder, and bit him on the ear.

"Yeouch. Get that cat off of me!"

As he tripped forward out the door, she said, "Expect a visit from the police. I told the Fire Inspector you burned the studio down."

CHAPTER 12

After Walker left, Reb went back to the dining table and finished her dinner. She was famished. Taking her dishes into the kitchen, she took the key off of the buffet and threw it in the garbage. *Some keys lock us up in our own prison and some keys set us free.*

Then she called Celeste and asked for a ride to church. They never rode together and Reb often missed, but there was a new burning inside of her, a longing pulling her to a place she would find contentment. *I've found my forever rock.*

*   *   *

Adam helped Reb into the front seat, while Celeste and Becky were in the back.

"I have something I want to show you after church, Reb. I got a new issue of *Architectural Digest* yesterday and there is an article about building an art studio over a garage. I think the design is just what you're looking for, if you want to grant the studio another try."

"I might, Adam. If the insurance company pays off, I could have enough to begin again at least. I'd like to see it, anyway. I have a new perspective on the studio, some new thoughts."

She was comfortable with her family around her. She mused about how plans changed in a short time. "I liked the idea of selling my paintings without paying a gallery fee, and I couldn't have done that with the studio I designed. There wasn't enough space to paint, display and sell. I hate to think that maybe Walker did me a favor."

207

"Mom, you were going to tell me about the chicken dinner last night. What was that all about?" Celeste leaned forward to hear better.

"I invited Walker for dinner. I wanted to apologize for not being a good neighbor. God showed me what forgiveness should be, and your encouragement helped. Besides, I needed to make a few things clear to the gentleman. But it turned out he wasn't much of a gentleman. The police want to talk to him about a matter of arson."

"It's about time." Celeste's voice held a hint of laughter.

"Some things were just never meant to be." Reb closed her eyes and thought of the past and what could have been, then she let go, of Walker, of Oscar, of the studio she planned. She was ready for the future now as she reached out to what would be ahead with God leading.

She leaned back in the seat and closed her eyes. She again thought of Becky's words. *Yes, God did have something better in mind all along.*

*   *   *

Christmas Eve day she and Adam stood beside her garage bending over building plans. Adam pointed to the drawing. "Here you see the stairs going up to the studio."

"Will the steps be wide enough to carry large canvasses down?" she asked, concerned.

"We can make them as wide as you need them to be. And here we'll insert roof sky lights so you'll have light whatever time of day you're painting."

"Oh Adam, this will be so much better than the studio I designed. There will be space for painting, for display, and even for walking around. No more commissions."

Adam said, "I just need to take the plans into the city planning department for their approval. I don't expect any problems. I know several people there who are easy to work with." He paused. "I can get a crew together next week to start taking down the garage roof."

Celeste peeked out the back door. "Hey, dinner is ready."

Reb turned to wave at Celeste. "Be there in a minute."

Adam rolled up the drawings and patted her on the back. "You will finally get your art studio."

She beamed. "Yes. My dream becomes real." *But more than that, I have found what I always needed, a relationship with my Lord.*

That is a true Christmas present.

About the Author:

Carol Caldwell writes children's and women's Christian fiction. Her background includes an English degree from the University of Southern California. She is a member of the Northwest Christian Writer's Association, and has attended conferences with SCBWI. Tari Books, an imprint of PDMI Publishing, published her first children's book, "Princess to the Rescue," in August of 2015. They have a contract to publish a sequel. Carol lives in Washington State with her family and two dogs.

Visit her at: **http://authorcaldwell.blogspot.com**

Create your own prayer journal

Select enough paper to fill the pages. Cut paper to 8 ½ X 11 inches. Fold in half to 4 ½ X 5 ½

Glue folded pieces back to back making a "book".

Trim edges for a clean even look.

Trace book onto chip board or matt board for a hard cover.

Cut 2 pieces of chip board or matt board.

Select decorative paper to cover and cut 1 inch larger than the chip board or matt board.

Trim corners of decorative paper straight across.

Score paper to fold easily.

Using double sided adhesive tape, secure the paper to the chip board/matt board, folding one side at a time.

Tuck in corners.

Add double sided adhesive tape to front and back of paper "book".

Secure to decorated front and back.

Tie ribbon to back as a place mark.   Enjoy! Love, Carol Caldwell

Christmas Gone Awry

by

Jeri Stockdale

Dedication:
For Jeff, James, Justin, and Joy

Acknowledgements:
I want to thank my friends and family for all their support and encouragement during this endeavor. A special thanks to my son, Justin, for ensuring I had peaceful writing times. An enormous thank you to my mentor and friend, Darlene Panzera, for freely teaching our small writers group the tools to hone our skills as writers, so we can better share the message God puts on our hearts. I've grown from the process of finishing my first story and I'm thankful for God's guidance and for the friendships He's forged with; Bev, Carol, Robin, Debby, Julianne, and Darlene. May all who read our anthology be blessed by the work of our hands, hearts, minds, and spirits.

CHAPTER 1

Emma Keller couldn't breathe as the school principal lurked in the corner of the classroom, intently observing her performance as she moved from desk to desk helping students with their homework. Soon she would land the fourth grade teacher's position she had worked so hard for. Or she wouldn't. Either way it was time to tell her family she'd decided to pursue a career as a teacher, even though her father wanted her to become an engineer.

Over the past few months, her job as a teacher's aide had crystallized her goals. And when Carol Holden announced she'd be taking maternity leave, Emma hadn't wasted any time turning in the application for her position. Her heart skipped a beat just thinking about the possibility of having her own class. She'd wanted to be a teacher ever since she'd been a little girl. Playing school with her dolls and stuffed animals had been an obsession. After all the hard work in high school and college, and the disappointments she'd faced, her dreams were within her grasp. Finally.

After the principal left the room, Emma's shoulders relaxed and she smiled as Brittany, one of the quieter students, finished the math problem on her own. She loved seeing the light in the students' eyes, the understanding that dawned from the work and the explanations Emma shared with them one-on-one.

She glanced around the room, observing the variety of paper snowflakes taped to the window, the small desktop Christmas tree with its tiny flickering lights, and the gold tinsel garlands decorating their whiteboards. The smell of cinnamon and nutmeg was strong today, wafting from the tasty hot apple cider permeating the classroom. Angie Jorgenson, the enthusiastic red-haired fourth grade teacher Emma worked with, made each holiday a special celebration. *I can't wait to decorate my own classroom. I only hope I can make it as fun for the kids as Angie does.*

The school bell startled her as it rang its raucous call to end the day. Emma handed a child the lunchbox he'd forgotten under his desk. The fourth grade students chattered as they hurried to put their notebooks in their backpacks, grabbed their jackets from the coat hooks, and headed out the door for home. Angie stood by the door for their daily send off, dressed in splashes of green and red Christmas print and wearing lipstick the color of holly berries.

"Boys, pull up your pants! We don't need any frozen fannies falling to the ground and breaking on the way home, do we?"

The sound of the children's laughter resonated throughout the classroom, spilling into the hallway. Each day ended the same. Miss Jorgenson had a million zingers and her students loved them. They loved her. Besides, their excitement was building now that December was here. Each day brought them closer to Christmas with its celebrations and traditions, and the anticipation was palpable.

"Bye, Miss Keller. Thank you for helping me." The tentative voice broke into Emma's thoughts and warmed her heart.

"You're welcome, Brittany. Just work a few more of those problems tonight. If you need help we can go over them again tomorrow. Okay?"

Brittany nodded, smiled, and hurried out the door to catch her bus.

"You're good with the kids, you know," Angie said, giving her a look of approval.

"I want to be," Emma was unable to keep the uncertainty out of her voice. *Why am I so unsure of myself, even after I've been working as Angie's aide for months?*

"When is your interview for Carol's teaching position?" Angie asked.

Emma hesitated. "It's a week from tomorrow, on Friday."

"Have you told your family?" Angie cocked her head to one side and arched her brow.

"I plan to tell my mom and dad as soon as I get home." Emma frowned. "Then I'll get ready for that silly blind double date my sister arranged."

Angie shook her head, her large hooped earrings with silver Christmas bells twirling and tinkling with the movement. Her reddish auburn hair, piled high on her head with curls framing her face, blended well with the festive decorations around them. "Hey girl, you told me you were bowing out of that one. You need to find a man on your own."

"I agree, but Bree was insistent and laid a guilt trip on me. Her new boyfriend has a friend named Randy. The Navy just transferred him here from San Diego. Besides, it's only one date."

"*Humph.* We'll see," Angie said, her tone wary.

They were preparing assignments for the next day when Mrs. Dalton, the teacher from the classroom next door, popped her head in the door. "Emma, can I ask you a big favor? I really need help getting papers graded today."

Emma hesitated and before she could open her mouth to speak, Mrs. Dalton continued, "Thanks hon. I appreciate it. Helping me will look good for your interview too, although I heard three other teachers put in for Carol's job. See you in a few!" Mrs. Dalton popped out just as quickly as she'd popped in.

Emma's shoulders sagged as an encyclopedia-sized weight of worry bore down on her.

"Don't mind her, Emma." Angie shot her a look of concern. "She's a busybody. You can still tell her you can't stay today. And you have as good a chance at getting the position as anyone."

"No, I'll stay. I need all the endorsements I can get and I don't mind helping. I don't need rumors spread about how I'm not a team player, especially before an interview."

"What about your date?"

Emma shrugged. "I can finish the grading and still make it to the restaurant on time."

*   *   *

Emma took one look at the three-inch-high stack of papers she was to grade and groaned.

Mrs. Dalton must have been procrastinating. Or saving them for her to do. A social studies test to grade and math assignments due back to the students tomorrow. After Emma finished, she shook her head in frustration and hustled to her car.

I am running so late. Bree is going to kill me!

Twenty minutes later, when Emma finally arrived at Anthony's Pizzeria, she pulled her black jacket tight around her to ward off the cold breeze. Despite the chill and the fact she was late, she held the door open for an older couple who were also coming in for dinner. She exchanged smiles with them while her stomach churned with anxiety over whether she and her date would hit it off. *I hope he's nice. And cute.*

Then a young family with a sweet curly-haired daughter were leaving. She held the door open longer, stalling for time. *I just don't want to do this.*

Nine years ago her heart had raced when Greg, a senior, noticed *her*, a freshman, and asked her to the prom. But after the dance she learned he had rigged it as a double date to get close to Bree. Emma's face grew hot as she remembered the humiliation. When she returned to school the following Monday and walked past Greg and his friends, they teased her about being so gullible. Their laughter had followed her down the halls.

Casting off those thoughts, she realized she couldn't stand there and hold the door open all evening. She drew in a deep breath. *Lord, please don't let this be a repeat of that awful experience.*

Keeping her word to Bree, she braced herself and walked in. The smell of pizza with its rich flavor of garlic, basil, and oregano was not as welcoming as usual. Her appetite was gone. As her eyes adjusted to the darkened room, she noticed the light emanating from the single red candle on each table set for four, complemented by sprigs of holly. Cedar boughs and festive wreaths brightened the rough wood beams and dark paneled walls of the pizzeria. Another reminder Christmas was coming. Clanging glasses, excited chatter, and bustling waitresses completed the scene.

The place was packed. Where was Bree? And their dates? Emma spotted her sister waving to her. The two men seated beside her were grinning as Emma walked toward them.

Great. Now I'm on display. She awkwardly dodged busy busboys, cheerful waitresses, and hungry customers to reach their table.

"I'm sorry I'm late. I couldn't get away from work any sooner."

"Great first impression, sis," Bree scolded. "We couldn't wait for you any longer so I went ahead and ordered for everyone." With a smile Bree introduced, "This is my boyfriend, Shane, and his friend, Randy. Gentlemen, this is my little sister, Emma."

Emma nodded hello to both men, but an uneasiness crept up her spine as her gaze met Randy's. Although he was smiling, his eyes weren't.

Is he sizing me up? Is this dislike at first sight?

Observing her date, Emma did some sizing up of her own. Randy's short dark curly hair complemented his piercing dark eyes, his olive colored skin gave him a permanent tan, and his large biceps enhanced his slender build. His exotic look added to his attractiveness, but it didn't shake the uneasy feeling that had hit her.

Bree and Shane whispered and laughed, acting as if they were the only couple in the room. *This is so awkward.* Emma could understand why Bree liked Shane. He was tall with dark wavy hair and soft brown eyes. His pleasant manner exuded likeability, but he could hardly take his eyes off of Bree. Worse, Emma saw that Randy was also staring at her tall blonde, model-like sister.

Emma couldn't help but glance down at her own straight brown hair, and modest turquoise sweater. She knew it wasn't good to make comparisons, but sometimes the differences between her and Bree just smacked her in the face. Knowing that kind of thinking would get her nowhere, she decided to at least try some conversation. "So, Randy, where are you from?"

Her date leaned forward just inches from her face. "I served in the Navy in San Diego, but I'm from Los Angeles."

"Oh, do you miss L.A.?" Emma asked.

"No. You'd be surprised how bad it is." Randy's expression darkened as he clenched his fork tighter.

Emma leaned as far away from him as she could without being obvious. *Why is he so angry?*

"I didn't mean to upset you," Randy said. He shrugged his shoulders. "Los Angeles is a hard place. It's crowded. And unfriendly." He sighed. "Sorry. I don't have a lot of good memories from there. And I had a bad day at work. My Ensign was breathing down my neck all day." Looking at Shane, he said, "But this guy had my back. Thanks, buddy."

Shane nodded and Randy's face relaxed as he leaned back in his chair, watching her with new interest. He was smiling again, but the look in his eyes made her wary.

"That's enough about me for now," he said. "What about you, Emma? You're a teacher?"

"No, Randy," Bree said, breaking off her conversation with Shane and jumping in before Emma had a chance to speak. "She's a teacher's aide. She went through college and got her teaching certificate, but she's at a job she could have gotten without all that work. Well, I guess that's something she can tell you about." Bree smiled. "Another time."

Emma gripped the cloth napkin on her lap. She fought to stay in control of her emotions as heat rose in her face. Bree's digs had gotten worse lately. Emma didn't know why. But she suspected it had something to do with the fact that she still had a chance to pursue her goals, while Bree did not, now that she was a single mom and had to take a job to make ends meet. Emma slowed her breathing to calm down and looked for a way to change the subject.

"At least *I'm* getting promotions at the lumberyard," Bree continued, her face smug. "I started as a cashier right after high school and now I'm working in the office part-time. When my boss retires, I'm hoping to move up to assistant manager."

Emma ignored Bree and looked at Shane. "Where are you from?"

Shane pulled his arm away from Bree and leaned over the table toward her.

"Virginia. Beautiful state, but so is Washington with all the beaches and waterways around Puget Sound. And mountains and trees. It's got everything."

"Yeah, it's got everything, all right. Gray clouds, gray skies, rain, and more rain," Randy complained.

"But Randy, it's not like that year round," Emma said. "We need the rain for the trees. We are the Evergreen State."

"The ever green state? Ha! Should be the ever gray state." Randy paused for a moment and studied her. "You really like this cold, damp place?"

"Yes, I do." Emma sat straighter and looked into Randy's face. "And it's not wet all the time."

"Let me guess. You haven't lived anywhere else, have you?"

"Well, no."

"Then I rest my case," Randy said, acting as if he'd won an argument.

"I have to agree with you, Randy," Bree butted in. "Imagine being content with this place when you've never been anywhere else in the world. In high school, I travelled quite a bit to cheerleader competitions so I saw a lot of the country. Emma could have done the same with her choral groups. They had competitions in Oregon and California, and even DC, but Emma didn't go to any of them. I can't imagine passing on opportunities like that."

Emma's insides burned. "That's not the whole story."

"Well, why don't you tell it then?" Bree's shimmery black blouse and gold necklaces caught the light of the fire from the stone fireplace, giving Bree a richness and confidence Emma did not possess.

She swallowed hard. "I really didn't want to share my life story."

"Why? Cuz there's not much to tell?" Bree's laugh rang hollow. Her digs reminded Emma of painful moments between them stretching back to childhood. *When had things changed between them?* "I shouldn't have to say anything, but just to set the record straight, I did want to travel. I felt bad that I missed out on those trips. I had mono. And it hit me hard. I barely had the strength to go to school and do my homework. I still practiced with my choral group, but I didn't bounce back enough to go on those trips."

"You did have mono, but you were such a homebody. I didn't think you wanted to leave your comfort zone."

"I can't believe you're talking to me like this." *Especially in front of two men we barely know.* "Let's just drop it."

"Okay. Whatever." Bree slipped her arm through the crook of Shane's and sat back, smiling and sipping her diet coke through a red plastic straw.

Emma turned to Randy again. "You should give the area a chance. You've only been here a few months." She didn't know why she was even trying to convince the man of Washington's finer points.

"Maybe I could bear it if I had someone to keep me warm on dreary nights." Randy looked directly at Emma and she broke eye contact. She could sense he was waiting for her reaction. She looked down at her pizza, her hair falling forward and successfully hiding the blush she felt rising up her neck and cheeks. She didn't want to show her revulsion, and hurt his feelings, but she also didn't believe in giving anyone false hope.

"Well, we're not going to agree on the weather so let's change the subject," Emma said. Her voice sounded high and unnatural to her. She turned toward Shane, trying not to notice Randy's reaction. "What are your plans after the Navy?"

Shane cleared his throat and glanced at Bree. Was that uncertainty in his eyes? "My hope is to make the Navy my career, work myself up the ranks like my father and grandfather did before me, then retire from the military and have a job in the State Department in DC."

"That's wonderful," Emma replied.

Bree shot Emma a dirty look. *Was she jealous?* Bree whispered in Shane's ear and giggled, starting another private conversation with him, and leaving Emma on her own with Randy once more. Emma glanced at him. He sat there rigid, with arms crossed, and she could envision a stamp entitled, 'worst date ever' in bold red letters smack over a photo of his face. She banished the thought and decided to try small talk one last time.

"What about you, Randy?" Emma asked. "What do you want to do after the Navy?"

Randy gave her a cynical look, and the hint of a smile briefly passed over his face, as he unfolded his arms and leaned toward her again. "Me? I don't know. The Navy seemed like a good idea, but it's different than I thought. It's difficult to see too far ahead. Better to take one day at a time, don't you think?"

"Sometimes, but if there's a goal you really want, often you have to plan and work at it to achieve it." Emma sipped on her soda and was conscious of Randy's gaze lingering on her.

"Maybe you're right." His eyes gleamed as though a new thought had occurred to him.

I wonder if he took what I said the wrong way. I hope he doesn't think his plans should include me.

Emma glanced at the digital wall clock at least a hundred times as the minutes slogged by, slower than a slug crossing the sidewalk. She drummed her fingers on her knees beneath the table.

Why am I even here? My pizza tastes cold and disgusting. Bree knows I don't like green peppers and pepperoni, but she ordered them anyway.

"I hate to break up the party," Emma said, interrupting Bree's conversation with Shane. "But I really need to get home. I have work early tomorrow."

Bree frowned and her mouth twisted into the tight pout of a little girl. "Oh Emma, you're such a party-pooper. Let's stay just a little longer." Bree turned her attention back to Shane without giving Emma a chance to answer.

Why doesn't anyone listen to me? Emma sighed. *It doesn't seem to matter what I say or think.*

"What is wrong?" Randy grabbed her hand and she jerked backwards in her seat. His actions were as welcome as those of a rattlesnake.

"Nothing," she replied as she pulled her hand back and read an incoming text from her phone.

"Bree, we need to go. Mom needs help with Carson."

"Who's Carson?" Shane asked.

Bree stared at her. Obviously, her sister had not told him she had a son, but Emma kept her silence.

Bree laughed it off. "Oh Shane. Just family matters."

Before anything else could be said, Emma stood to leave. With reluctance, Bree stood as well. Both men tried to help them with their coats. Bree required much help and Shane gladly complied. Randy approached to assist Emma, but she held up her hand to stop him. "No, I've got it," she said, and slipped her jacket on unaided.

"As you wish, Emma." He relented with a displeased look as he took a step back and shoved his hands in his pants pockets.

Several other customers were leaving too. Bree and Shane were ahead and out the door, while Emma was stuck with Randy behind a slow-moving family with three busy children in tow. Randy put his hand on the small of her back and his touch made her skin crawl. A tall, blond man was holding the heavy oak door open for an older couple, presumably his parents, the family resemblance unmistakable. He stayed longer, holding the door open for other customers as well. He smiled at Emma, and his blue eyes sparkled as their gaze toward one another held for a brief second. He continued to hold the door open for her and Randy too. She was grateful. However, Randy was not.

"Stop making eyes at my girl, or you will regret it," Randy said in a low, menacing growl.

The smile faded from the blond gentleman. No anger in response, just concern.

Concern, for me? Emma wondered. She was shocked at Randy's behavior, his words, and how he rose to his full height to intimidate someone who was being kind. Maybe this was more than just the excuse he gave of having had a bad day. Something was not right with him.

"Randy. Let's go." She gave Mr. Blue eyes an apologetic look and took Randy's arm to divert his thoughts and appease him. Once outside she let go of his arm and tried to stifle the panic that was rising in her. She was frantic to find Bree and Shane, and walked with quick short strides toward the parking lot. She relaxed a little when she saw them by Bree's car. Emma's car was parked nearby.

"I'd like to see you again," Randy said, following her as she hurried toward her sister.

"Uh, I don't know. I'm really busy, especially with Christmas coming."

"We could do something for Christmas," Randy replied with a hint of desperation.

They came to a stop beside the cars and Emma faced him.

"I'll be busy," she repeated.

A spark of anger flashed in his eyes, but it was gone as quickly as it had appeared. "Alright. We'll see."

"Oh, are you two making plans to get together again?" Bree asked, invading the dying conversation. "I have the perfect idea."

Randy turned, and Emma vigorously shook her head toward Bree, and prayed her sister would stop.

Bree ignored her. "Why don't you and Shane plan on joining our family to watch the Christmas ships from the beach on Saturday night?"

Randy, Bree, and Shane all smiled in agreement. Emma's stomach lurched. Apparently, they didn't feel the need to consult with her. A wave of hurt, anger, shock and disbelief all rolled into one and washed over her, nearly knocking her down.

How could Bree do this to me? How do I get out of this? Lord, I know I haven't been listening to you lately. Please help me. Show me what to do. Angie. I'll talk to her, Lord. And I will straighten out this mess at the family dinner tomorrow night…when I tell them about my possible new teaching position.

CHAPTER 2

The following day, after her work at the school, Emma hurried into her family's home, closing the door more abruptly than she intended. The cold wind whistled and propelled her forward. Ginger, her large, loving, Husky-German shepherd mix, met her at the door.

"Whoa, down girl." She hugged her big furry friend, and directed Ginger's body away from the three ceramic angels set on the entryway table. Her wagging tail was a constant danger to any home decorating attempt.

"Brrr. Sorry I'm late," Emma apologized. She pulled off her woolen gloves and black jacket and threw them over the back of the sofa as she headed for the dinner table. The satisfying smell of a home cooked meal made her stomach rumble, and she realized her skimpy lunch had caught up with her. Just as she was going to sit down she noticed that her mother wore a stern look on her face.

"What is it, Mom?"

"Please put your belongings away. It would be nice if you could at least make it home on time for a family dinner." Emma let out a deep sigh, left the table, and grabbed her clothes to drop off in her attached apartment.

Her three-year-old nephew, Carson, laughed. "Mind your mommy, T-Em."

Bree and her parents chuckled. Emma returned just as Bree commented, "Isn't he the cutest thing ever?"

His proud grandparents nodded in agreement.

Emma smiled and silently agreed as she looked at Carson's golden hair and huge blue eyes. *It's too bad he isn't as nice as he is cute.*

When Emma sat down at the dinner table, the rest of her family already had their plates filled with fried chicken, mashed potatoes, and gravy. Carson banged on his plate and jumped up and down in his chair. No one but Emma seemed to care. Ginger settled down under the table, her favorite place during family dinners, especially when Carson was visiting.

"Carson, please settle down and eat," Emma said, as she helped herself to the mashed potatoes and gravy.

"No!" Carson yelled. He slammed his little fist on the table, flipping a spoon in the air that flew into the bowl of gravy, and splashed its contents all over Emma's shirt.

"Oh, Carson!" Emma said. She jumped up, ran to the kitchen sink, and used her napkin to wash off the greasy gravy splatters. She looked back at her family for support, but all she received was cold silence.

"Aren't you going to correct him?" She wanted to scream, but Emma controlled her voice, and waited for a reasonable answer.

"Listen, Emma, he's my son and I will correct him when he needs it. We agreed to ignore his tantrums so he will stop doing them. He'll grow out of it soon enough."

"Mom, Dad? Do you agree with this?" Emma asked as she sat back down, moving her chair further from Carson.

"Yes, Emma. We do," her mom replied. "Without a father, you know it will take all of us to help Carson work through these behaviors."

"Dad, you too?" Emma asked.

"Well, yes, hon," her father replied with some hesitation. "We have to go along to get along sometimes."

"He has to be corrected, and learn right from wrong," Emma said. "If you let him do whatever he feels like, he is going to run right over everyone. It's easier to teach a child good habits from the beginning than to break bad ones."

"That's not what his therapeutic counselor said," Bree retorted. "He's a professional and we're following his guidelines. If you were a real teacher I'd take what you have to say more seriously." Bree smiled. "But…you're *not*."

Emma couldn't believe what she was hearing. Once again she was discredited and her opinion ignored. She saw a hint of a smile on Carson's face as well. He'd won another round. The boy hummed while he played in his mashed potatoes with his fingers.

"Well, what if I was a real teacher, Bree? Would you listen to me then?"

Her dad finished his chicken, wiped his hands on his napkin, and leaned forward. "What are you talking about Emma? I thought you decided to go back to school to become an engineer."

"Dad, I know you think it would be a good career path for me, but my heart isn't in it. I really like working with children and helping them learn."

His brow furrowed, but he didn't speak. Instead, his face reddened and he clasped his hands together in front of him as if in prayer. He had a fiery German temper when provoked, but this time he appeared to restrain himself. He was an engineer by profession, and Emma knew he was disappointed she was rejecting his plan.

Meanwhile, Bree choked on her food as she laughed. "Emma, you may like children, but it's obvious you don't know the first thing about working with them. Your philosophy is all wrong, and you're too timid when it comes to speaking in front of a group. How would you ever be able to control a classroom? You're the one who told us about your awful student teaching experience. You barely passed."

Emma's heart sank as she saw her mom nod in agreement with her sister.

Memories of Mrs. Gunner, her assigned teacher for her student teaching experience, still filled her with dread. The woman had it in for her from the first day they met. No matter what Emma did, Mrs. Gunner had been critical to the point that she was afraid to do anything. The students caught on and laughed at her requests or ignored her altogether when asked to follow the rules.

The final blow was the day Mrs. Gunner unexpectedly put her in charge of the classroom and left. Emma tried to quiet the class so they could work on a math lesson, but they grew loud and silly, and were out of control. Then the door opened abruptly and Mr. Tennison, the principal, walked in, accompanied by Mrs. Gunner. Emma had been terrified by their stern looks.

"What's going on here, Miss Keller?" the principal asked. The children fell silent and Emma stood, paralyzed, by the teacher's desk. She caught a smug smile on Mrs. Gunner that told her she had somehow been set up.

She went to the office with the principal, like a child ready for a scolding, and perhaps, a dismissal. The principal's words had shown concern, but his main point had been that you can't be a good teacher if you can't control the class. She'd left his office unsure of her fate.

If it hadn't been for a few nice teachers rallying to her defense, she would have failed out of the program. It wasn't until much later that she learned Mrs. Gunner had treated other student teachers in the same fashion. Emma could only suspect that Mrs. Gunner was insecure, feeling threatened that a good young teacher would one day take her place. That's when she realized she *could* still be a teacher.

Emma's thoughts snapped back to the present when she heard her dad clear his throat. She realized her family was waiting for her to answer. "What happened during my student teaching is in the past," she told them. "The reason I've been working in the school is to see how I would do in a classroom again."

The looks of disapproval caused her to shrink into her chair.

"And?" Bree demanded, lifting a skeptical brow.

"I have done much better working with Angie as an aide in her classroom," Emma said with a soft voice. "I have a job interview next week for a teaching position that starts in January and goes through the rest of the school year. I'm hoping the position becomes permanent."

Her father grunted, and said, "Just promise me, if this teaching job doesn't work out, you will pursue another career that will provide you with a good living. There are engineer positions all over this county, but if you don't want to work for the government, you could look in Seattle, at places like Boeing."

Disappointment hit Emma like a punch to the stomach. *I thought they'd be excited for me, or at least, encouraging.* "I can't make that promise, Dad. I want to stay open to possibilities, but I was hoping for some helpful suggestions for my interview and for landing the teaching job over the other candidates."

"Well, if there are other candidates, you can kiss the job good-by," Bree said with a snicker. "I'm sure they're more experienced than you are. They're probably just giving you an interview as a professional courtesy since you work at the school."

Her dad nodded. "You do your best. If you can't handle the interview, you'll know it's not meant to be. After all, handling a classroom full of children is a lot more pressure than talking with a few adults."

"Well, why don't we leave these life changing subjects behind and decorate the Christmas tree," her mom broke in, her tone an octave higher than normal. "Dad already has the lights strung."

A kaleidoscope of flashing lights greeted them as they shuffled in tense silence to the family room. Emma's heart softened as they placed ornaments on the fresh cut pine tree from Olsson's Tree Farm. Apparently, her family's hearts did too, and the previous tension soon disappeared as they decorated together. Bree was as nice and considerate as when they were young girls and Emma wished it could always be this way. The girls laughed at their early attempts at handmade ornaments, especially when they considered how artistic their mother was, a painter with her own art studio. Other special ornaments reflected a rite of passage or hobby they enjoyed.

As they decorated the tree, Carson played with the classic train set that had magically appeared each Christmas for the past twenty-five years. When Carson got tired of the trains, he zoomed around the room, with his arms extended, and played airplane. "Plane crash!" he yelled. Then he dove into the plush couch several times, making explosion sounds with each collision.

"Plane crash into tree!" he yelled as he headed straight for the festive looking Christmas tree.

Emma intercepted and lifted Carson off the ground all in one movement. No one else seemed to notice the near calamity. "Let's find some crayons and a coloring book for you. You can make Christmas presents for your mom and grandparents."

"Yes. Christmas presents. I want Christmas now," he said in a whiney voice that shook her nerves. Emma settled him down at a small folding table nearby, with crayons, blank paper, and coloring books, hoping he'd stay busy. At least she could keep an eye on him. She returned to the boxes of ornaments, where she found the sparkling birds and delicate angels they'd collected over the years.

"How's life at the lumber company, Bree?" their dad asked. He inserted a battery to make a red cardinal ornament chirp *The Holly and the Ivy*, while their mom hummed along to an instrumental version of *The First Noel* from the radio.

"Business has been slow on the lumber side, but now, we're selling lots of Christmas tree and lawn decorations, tools, and gift cards. After the holidays we'll have markdowns and I'll get extra hours helping with the inventory."

"That's good, honey. Doesn't sound like you'll have hours cut."

Their mom gripped the bow she was making tighter. "Of course they won't cut back her hours. They need her there. We are so proud of you. Whatever you do turns out so well," their mother gushed. "Remember all those dance recitals you had? That experience helped you become head cheerleader. Although, I dare say you would've been voted in just on your looks. And every Christmas I think about your senior year when you were selected to be St. Lucia for the downtown festivities. You were just perfect with your beautiful long blonde hair and ocean blue eyes. How exciting that they'll be calling up all the past St. Lucia girls at the Christmas bonfire celebration tomorrow night. It brings back so many wonderful memories!"

As Emma placed a tiny shimmering angel on a branch of the long needle white pine, her brown hair fell forward, reminding her that even her looks were different from the rest of her family. She closed her eyes for a moment, took a deep breath, and sighed. *Has Mom ever gushed over me like that? I don't think so. I worked hard and did well in school, but I can't even remember my parents or Bree saying they were proud of me. Why does it seem Bree can do no wrong and I can do nothing right?*

Her family had been this way for as long as she could remember. She'd thought that, as adults, they could move beyond the favoritism she'd grown up with. Apparently, she was wrong. How she longed to have her dreams embraced and supported by her family.

"Well, what did you think of your date, Emma?" her mom asked.

The question brought Emma back to the present, but her emotions had welled up like a tiger ready to pounce. "Mom, it was terrible. I don't plan to see Randy again."

Her mom sighed. "What was so bad about him? You couldn't have gotten to know him well on one date, could you?

"I think you can tell a lot in one date, Mom."

Bree whipped out her cell phone and cut in. "Look at this great picture of Emma and Randy. Isn't he good looking?"

Their mom leaned over to see the photo. "Yes, he is really good looking." She looked at Emma with approval.

Emma looked at it too. He was a good looking guy. Bree had even caught him smiling, but her stomach churned at the thought of him. "Why did you even take this? You knew the date wasn't going well."

"First dates aren't always the greatest, sis. He may have been having an off day. He did say he'd had a bad day at work. You gotta give a guy a chance. I'm sure the next time will be much better."

Mrs. Keller clapped her hands together. "There's going to be a next time. Wonderful! There's nothing wrong with a second chance, Emma. You don't want to give up too soon. I would like to have more grandchildren before I'm too old to enjoy them."

Mom! I wish you wouldn't say things like that. I have plenty of time."

"Time waits for no one, young lady. Look at all the wonderful guys Bree has been with. It's a shame… Oh, never mind."

"What? What mom? It's a shame I'm not as beautiful as Bree? It's a shame I don't have a troop of admirers like she does? Don't you realize most of those guys have been losers?"

Her mother, father, and Bree all gasped and each one stared at her. Even Carson stopped coloring in his *Things That Go* book to watch the grownups in his life.

"Emma!" her mother exclaimed. "That's uncalled for. You're just jealous."

"Okay, I'm sorry. I shouldn't have said that." Emma hung her head to hide the hot tears that threatened to fall. The walls were closing in as negative feelings assaulted her.

"Well, little sister," Bree spoke up. "If you want to make it up to me, just agree to be at the family bonfire to watch the Christmas ships tomorrow night, and spend time with Randy."

"I'll be there." Emma saw the look of triumph in her sister's eyes, but refused to let it disturb her. *Yes, I agreed to the bonfire, but not for the reasons you think. I'll see Randy, for the last time, with God's help, and Angie's. Hopefully, I will do well and the evening will help me land the teaching job. And maybe even win my family's approval.*

Guilt passed over her for not sharing with her family her role in tomorrow night's festivities, but she couldn't take the chance of being laughed at again. She already had enough self-doubt without heaping more on her head.

Ginger sauntered over, wagged her tail, and placed her head in Emma's lap. It was almost like Ginger knew something important was about to happen.

CHAPTER 3

It was a little after seven in the evening when Emma arrived breathless at the beach with Ginger. The huge bonfire was already roaring and the welcoming wood smoke smell rode on the shifting breezes. The whole community milled around the seashell strewn beach and waited for the Christmas ships to arrive in the bay.

Emma hated arriving late to anything, but she knew her family already had a patch of beach claimed, with folding chairs, a smaller campfire for roasted marshmallows, and blankets to huddle under to protect themselves from the sea breezes and cold December air.

Laughter punctuated the waves gently rolling onto the shore. A perfect night for the annual festivities. There was no low fog to dampen the view or spirits of those attending. And a cloudless sky filled with stars and constellations was a reminder of the immenseness of God's universe.

Emma searched for her family, while Ginger became the local greeter for both children and adults alike. Ginger's beautiful blue eyes and the defined markings on her soft coat drew attention whenever Emma took her out in public. Her gentle manner won her friendship from those who met her. After they'd walked in circles, it was Ginger who spotted their family and pulled at the leash to let Emma know where they needed to go.

The evening was just as Emma had envisioned, except the family circle around their campfire included Shane, whom she'd expected, and Randy, whom Emma had hoped would take the hint and not come. *No Carson, though. Probably with a babysitter so he won't disrupt the evening. Too bad to exclude him from a family event. Bree probably hasn't told Shane about him yet.* Determined to make the best of one of their annual Christmas traditions, Emma forged ahead with Ginger who led the way.

"Hi everyone! Sorry I'm late. I decided to bring Ginger." *Lord help me.* Emma had a sick feeling in the pit of her stomach. Everyone greeted her, and when Randy saw her, his face lit up until he noticed Ginger.

Randy leaned over and whispered to Bree. Bree's forehead wrinkled and she nodded her head and asked Emma, "Can you keep Ginger away from Randy? He doesn't care for dogs."

"Oh sure," Emma said. She had to chuckle inside. Once again Ginger was her protector in a way she hadn't anticipated. She sat in a red canvas chair a little removed from Randy, and Ginger stuck by her side like Velcro.

After some conversation with her folks, Emma grabbed a sharpened stick by the fire. "Who wants s'mores?"

Her parents shook their heads no, but Bree and Shane were agreeable. When she glanced at Randy he smiled, but his gaze remained hard. He sprung up with eagerness to join her at the campfire and was about to speak when there was a cry and a crash. Ginger had darted between Emma and Randy, and dragged the chair, still tied to the leash, with her.

"What?" Randy cried. He jumped back when Ginger snapped at him.

The dog's hair stood on end along the ridge of her back. Her growls continued, low and guttural, and she kept her eyes on Randy even though he'd backed away. Randy swore and Emma was relieved that his words were carried away by the wind.

"Ginger, no! Bad girl!" Emma called out, but her rebuke was only half-hearted. She grabbed Ginger's leash and tugged the dog to her side. Everyone else had jumped to their feet.

Furious, Bree demanded, "Emma, why did you bring the dog? What a disaster!"

"Me? I didn't know she'd act like this. Ginger loves everyone." Emma lowered her voice slightly so Randy couldn't hear. "Maybe it means something, that Ginger doesn't like Randy."

An air of defiance settled on Bree's face. "Oh nonsense. You did this to sabotage any possibility of this working out between you and Randy. And after all the trouble I've gone through for you."

Emma's mouth hung open in shock. *How could Bree twist the situation around like this? Why was she pushing this relationship on her?*

"The least you can do is see if Randy is all right and apologize."

Emma glanced toward Randy and watched him sit back down. Her parents and Shane spoke with him and tried to make light of what happened.

Bree took Ginger by the leash and Emma steeled herself for the encounter as she walked toward the small huddled group. "Randy, are you all right? I am so sorry. Ginger is usually a gentle soul, but she is protective of me."

Randy's hood fell back off of his head and she was surprised by his striking good looks. His features were fine, but his short curly hair framed them, giving him a classic Greek look. For a fleeting moment she wondered if she'd been too harsh in her appraisal of him, but the memories from their blind date were too strong to overlook her first impression of him.

Randy's countenance softened. "It's all right. Maybe you can make it up to me?"

Emma drew back at the suggestion.

"That's a great idea!" Bree called from across the campfire.

Before Emma could respond, Randy vaulted from his seat, totally cured of his affliction. He took her hand.

"Emma! Emma Grace? Well, how are you, hon?" Angie said, her booming voice announcing her arrival.

She gave Emma a big bear hug, which forced Randy to drop her hand. Emma could have hugged Angie to death. She'd showed up just in the nick of time and Emma was relieved to see Randy slink back to his chair.

"Mom, Dad, everyone, this is Angie, my friend from work." She couldn't help but smile as she finished her introductions.

Angie's energy was infectious. They laughed and told stories, and best of all, Angie stayed by Emma's side. A short while later, Angie checked her cell phone for the time. "Well, I hate to interrupt our visit, but Emma and I have to be on stage in five minutes."

"What?" Emma's mom said in a confused voice.

"No time to explain, just listen and enjoy," Angie said as she grabbed Emma's hand and they took off for the stairs.

A makeshift platform complete with podium, microphone, and stage had been assembled a few yards away. Emma's stomach lurched as she ascended the stairs and clutched the podium. *My future is dependent on every word I speak.*

Emma cleared her throat a few times, but a lump made it hard to swallow. She took a deep breath and looked over the crowd. "Ladies and Gentleman, welcome to Paulson Waterfront Park and our annual Christmas festivities. Tonight we celebrate the Scandinavian heritage of our local community and the traditions of those who now call Paulson their home. First, we'd like to introduce our local dignitaries. Mayor Lindquist…"

"Is that Emma?" Bree asked, her tone incredulous.

Emma glanced at her sister and parents who stood within ten feet of the stage. She smiled as she overheard their reactions.

"Why, yes dear. I believe she is speaking, and doing a good job too," their mom said with surprise in her voice.

Her family and the dreaded date moved closer to the stage to hear, along with many others who'd previously been relaxing on the beach. Angie stood nearby to offer a smile of encouragement.

"Thank you to all our distinguished guests," Emma continued. "This year we have a special treat for you. I would like to ask all former St. Lucia's of Paulson to please stand on stage with us."

As the former St. Lucia's came on stage, it was apparent by their numbers that this tradition had remained important to the women who had participated in the event over the years. Some held the hands of their young children. Others were gray-haired grandmothers who glowed in the limelight. All took on a regal look as they stood on the stage to be presented.

Emma shook off the inferiority that rose up within her as she stepped to the microphone again. "Thank you all for your service in years past and for coming forward today. Let's give them a hand." After the applause waned, Emma continued, "We would like each of you to come to the microphone one by one and give your name, the year you were St. Lucia, and where you now live." As each woman shared, Emma stood to the side of the stage. Angie winked at her.

Her heart beat rapidly with nervousness and joy. All was well. Emma walked with purpose toward the podium to direct the next part of the program. She was halfway to the microphone when her shoe caught on an electrical cord. She fell in slow motion, heard the gasp from the crowd, and shame flooded over her as she hit the floor. Physically, she was okay, but she wished she'd been knocked unconscious. Oh, the humiliation! She slowly rose with help from Angie and the mayor. She tried not to cry, and vowed to shake it off, to carry on.

Then, from the front of the crowd, where most of the St. Lucia women stood, she heard a voice say, "Well, that's my sister for you. Once a clutz, always a clutz."

Snickers resonated through the air and memories of her senior year flooded back. It reminded her of the time she had to use crutches to climb the risers for the final choral concert of the year. She'd lost her balance when she took the stairs wrong, heard a gasp, and realized all eyes were on her. She'd become so self-conscious she didn't watch where she was going. Down she fell, and people rushed to lend aid, in front of all the parents and her peers. Now it had happened all over again.

I really am a clutz. She walked to the podium and took a deep breath. "If I were a comedian, I could say it was part of my act, but I definitely didn't plan to fall on my face... None of us do, but sometimes it happens, and I guess we all have to learn to just get back up, brush ourselves off, and keep going."

Much to her surprise, the crowd clapped and cheered. There was a connection, an understanding of the words she'd spoken from the heart.

She relaxed a little. "Thank you. Please help me welcome the three finalists for St. Lucia for this year. They are all remarkable young women who are a credit to our community. This time next week you will know who will represent us, not just for our Christmas festivities, but also for the next twelve months at special events around the Sound."

When she'd finished, Angie was right there. She intertwined her arm with Emma's and walked with her back to the family's bonfire. It was only eight thirty, but it seemed like a lifetime ago that they'd stood and chatted before the program.

Emma's family welcomed her with smiles and words of encouragement. Her mom came toward her with outstretched arms. "Emma, dear. I didn't know you could speak so well. In spite of your little mishap you recovered and finished strong." Emma was shocked to hear her mom's praise, and when her dad said, "Good job," his smile of approval meant the world to her.

Only Bree and Randy hung back without enthusiasm for what she had accomplished. Angie noticed. "Okay, you two," Emma's mentor said to them, "I don't know what your problem is, and it shouldn't be any of my business, but if no one else will speak up, I sure will. Bree, you are her sister. Why on earth you think it's okay to ridicule her in public, or private for that matter, is beyond me. How could you try to undermine your sister when she's working so hard to reach for her dreams?"

Bree only rolled her eyes, then turned her back on Angie and spoke quietly to Randy. Angie looked as if she was ready to wage verbal war, then changed her mind. Instead, she turned to Emma's parents and Shane. "Thanks for supporting Emma. I think she and I should take Ginger for a walk."

Cheerful Christmas music of *Jolly Old Saint Nicholas* announced the entrance of the Christmas ships. Colorful lights outlined each boat as they came into view in a processional line around the bay. Emma watched them sail as she and Angie walked along the path above the beach. Angie's quick pace betrayed her frustration, and Emma's short legs couldn't keep up with Angie's long gait.

"Slow down a bit, please," she said, and stopped to catch her breath. "You were something else. You lit into them faster than fireworks starting a grassfire."

Angie chuckled. "Now you sound like me, honey. You better watch the company you keep."

"Believe me. I'm trying to do just that." They both laughed and continued their walk.

After a while, Angie calmed down. She stopped, leaned over, and stroked Ginger's soft fur. "I love that beautiful dog of yours. What a sweetheart!"

"So are you, Angie. You rescued me tonight. In more ways than one," Emma confided.

"Well, that was the plan, hon, but I didn't do much. God is your help in time of trouble. I saw that by the words you spoke after you fell. No wonder you've had a hard time pursuing your goals. Your sister enjoys making life difficult for you. Funny your parents are blind to what she does. And Randy. I'm glad I arrived when I did."

"Me too. Even a minute later and I may have been forced into another uncomfortable situation."

"Thank you for filling in for Principal Hargrove," Angie said. "His cough sounded terrible on the phone."

"Well, I have to admit I was nervous when I agreed to be the MC for the event, but I've never spoken so well in front of a group before. I just hope my fall didn't hurt my chances for the job. Is it possible to feel triumphant and embarrassed at the same time?"

"I suppose so. Try not to fret about it. Ultimately, God's ways and His timing are perfect. We just need to be in tune with Him."

"I like that, Angie. I will mull that one over. God's ways and His timing." Another reason she admired Angie. The woman was a voice of wisdom, so different from the foolishness she normally heard. Emma's thoughts had turned more toward God since she and Angie had become friends. Maybe God had brought Angie into her life for some greater purpose.

She and Angie shared a smile, and then Emma looked down the cobbled path to the next bench set under a tall bright lamppost, and gasped.

"What?" Angie asked.

"That's him."

"Him, being Mr. Tall, Blond, and Handsome?"

"Yes." Emma couldn't tear her gaze away from him.

"He has a dog too," Angie observed.

"Is it possible this is God's timing?" Emma asked in awe.

"Yes, it is. I don't believe there are coincidences in God's world. I think it would be a very natural step for you to walk Ginger down the path and meet the gentleman who held the door open for you at the restaurant. Just leave it in God's hands."

"Just leave it in God's hands," Emma repeated as she walked toward the man leaning against the bench. He talked to his German shepherd while he watched the line of Christmas ships turn around and head off into the distance.

"Ginger, come on girl." Emma spoke a little louder to make sure she didn't startle them as she approached. His dog stood erect, and whined with a wag of his tail.

"What is it, boy?" The man looked up. Then his gaze met hers and he said, "It's you."

"Yes," she replied.

His dog strained at the leash to meet Ginger. "Hey Luke, what are you doing?"

The man pulled Luke back to his side, but the dog couldn't take his eyes off of Ginger and he continued to whine.

Emma laughed. "Well, our dogs seem to like each other."

"Yes, they do. That's a good thing. I'm Nathan, by the way. Or Nate. I answer to both." He smiled and his gaze didn't leave her face.

"I'm Emma. Nice to meet you…officially, Nathan-Nate." They both laughed. "I wanted to thank you for, for holding the door for me, us, the other night. I'm sorry for what Randy did."

"No need to apologize. It wasn't you."

"*Brring. Brring.*" Her phone rang and she glanced at the caller I.D.

Oh no. It was Bree. She ignored the sound. She would call her later. "I'm sorry. Where were we?" she asked.

"You mentioned your boyfriend," Nate said.

"He's not my boyfriend. My sister fixed me up with him on a blind date."

"I see."

What did Nate *see?* Emma wondered. Could he see into her very soul? If the eyes are the gateway to the soul, he was already there.

"Are you okay, after the fall you took on stage?" His look of concern melted her heart.

"Oh, you saw that, huh?" Her face grew warm and she was relieved the lamplight wasn't any brighter.

"I thought you recovered in an inspiring way."

"Inspiring?"

"Yes. Inspiring. I was inspired." He looked up at the stars and laughed. "And impressed. I think most of the crowd felt the same way."

"Thank you, Nate." Emma's heart filled with hope. Hope about her job and career, hope about her parents, and hope about Nate. *Didn't God want to give us a future and a hope? Wasn't that in the Bible somewhere?*

She wanted to ask where he worked and if he'd grown up here…when her phone went off again. She tried to ignore it but more texts rolled in, and her phone buzzed relentlessly.

"Looks like you're busy, Emma. It's nice to meet you, but I have to run. I work nights right now." Nate smiled, pulled Luke to his side, and walked away.

He was a little abrupt. Was it because of the interruption or because it's late? She looked after him wistfully. *Did I miss my opportunity?*

He turned back to wave with a sheepish grin. "I hope to see you around."

Emma waved and watched him a moment longer. Her smile faded as his figure receded into the darkness.

Angie shot to her side the moment he was gone. "Well, girlfriend, how did it go? When do you see him again?" she asked, full of excitement. She bounced up and down like a kid at a candy counter.

"I don't know, Angie. My phone interrupted us several times. When the texts rolled in Nate said he had to go to work. He 'hopes to see me around,' whatever that means."

"Honey, if it's meant to be, God will work it out for you. Don't force it. And don't be discouraged." Then Angie frowned. "Who called?"

"The first time it was Bree and I just ignored her call. I don't want to talk to her right now. Let me see who sent the other texts." When Emma looked at her messages, she scoffed with disgust.

"Bree gave Randy my number. Good grief. He says he's sorry for what happened and we just started off on the wrong foot. He thinks we were meant to be together. He even says if I don't go out with him, he may go AWOL because it won't be worth staying in the Navy without me by his side. Angie, what is wrong with him? He doesn't even know me and I don't want him to."

All trace of humor left Angie's face. "He's trying to manipulate you emotionally. He is immature or unbalanced, or both. I'm not sure there is a way to let him down easy. I saw the way he looked at you, like he already possessed you."

"What should I do?" Emma didn't know whether to be angry or frightened.

"Well, you certainly can't agree to date him just to keep him from going AWOL. You need to end it, and make sure your sister knows to stop interfering in your life."

"I've tried, but maybe I haven't been clear." She bowed her head for a moment in thought. "I know what I'll do!" Emma texted Randy, with an emphatic 'no' to his request. Next, she texted Bree and said she was done with Randy. There would be no more dates, family gatherings, or anything that included him. She was also on her way home now, so they were not to wait for her.

Emma's last act of defiance and decisiveness was to block Randy's number from her phone. *I will no longer try to do things that only please others. I will be true to myself. And I won't let Bree run my life. I will move forward, even if I don't know what my life will look like.* Her thoughts turned to the teacher position she wanted so badly. *Will the school board members think I spoke well...or will they only remember my fall? They could say I choked under pressure.*

Her spirits began to droop. Then she thought of Nate. She wanted to see him again. She'd met him twice in the small downtown area of Paulson. Maybe she'd run into him again if she were in town more often.

Am I working with God, or wanting Him to bless what I do? Until she received a sign that told her otherwise, it was the best plan, the only plan, she could think of. For the first time since college, even though there were obstacles, she could see a future and a hope.

As Emma and Ginger left Angie and followed the illuminated path toward home, her heart sang a familiar half-forgotten song with bold clarity. "Your Word is a lamp to my feet, and a light to my path."

CHAPTER 4

The Coffee Cozy bustled with activity when Emma stopped in for an apple spice chai tea. For three days she'd come after work to the small business area in hopes of seeing Nathan again. The day before, she'd overheard that a young substitute teacher had been hired for a job at the middle school. There was hope. But today the harsh sound of ground coffee beans and the strong smell of brew assaulted her senses. Customers were louder than usual, drowning out the calm Christmas music in the background.

After enduring the elbow to elbow crowd of unknown faces to pick up her order, she left the confined space. She'd had her fill of chai tea, pastries, and secondhand books. Disappointed Nathan didn't appear, she slipped outside.

"Hey girl," Emma said as she slipped Ginger's leash off the post. "Maybe we should go to the park and walk on the beach. Do some sightseeing, huh?"

Ginger wagged her tail and danced around, excited for their walk to continue. Emma turned to go, tea in one hand, Ginger's leash in the other, when she bumped into someone.

"Hey, watch where you're going!"

Emma's body stiffened at the sound of the familiar voice. *She's the last person I want to see right now.* "I'm sorry, Bree. Guess I was distracted."

"Interesting I should run into you here. You haven't returned any of my calls or texts." When Emma said nothing, Bree continued. "I wish you'd think about someone besides yourself. Randy is hurt, distraught actually."

"What about me, Bree? Doesn't it matter if I'm hurt or distraught?" Emma said, her voice raised. "Why does Randy matter more than me? I'm your sister."

"You've blown this entirely out of proportion." Bree's face was red, and her silver St. Lucia medallion necklace reflected the sunlight into Emma's eyes to serve as a reminder of who was in charge. "You never gave him a chance. Even when you agreed to the date, you had a bad attitude about it. Everything is a mess because of you. I think he will go AWOL if you don't give him another chance."

"So, if he goes AWOL you would blame me?" Emma shook her head. "Why would I want to date someone like that? And why would you want me to?"

"Never mind. You just don't get it."

"No, I don't. Why don't you tell me?" Emma looked Bree in the eye, and dared her to come clean.

Bree broke eye contact and glanced away. "Forget it. I need to go. I'm meeting Shane for dinner."

Before Emma could say another word, her sister turned and disappeared into the sea of Christmas shoppers. Stunned by the unwelcome exchange, she turned away from the park. "Come on girl," she said, as she glanced at her dog. "Let's get out of here."

Emma and Ginger walked toward home, but stray negative thoughts crept through her mind. *When did I become such a pushover? God, please help me. Give me strength.*

She turned left onto Holly Street, and walked through old neighborhoods decorated with colorful flashing lights, manger scenes, blow up snowmen, and a Santa Claus. As she tried to clear her mind she heard singing. Christmas carols. The sound came from the old church on the hillside. The sign said *Paulson Community Church*. She had seen the aging structure with the tall white steeple from the park, and when she'd driven by she had thought it was an historical site, especially since it had its own private cemetery. She didn't realize an actual congregation met there.

The songs were familiar. She stood outside the door and quietly sang along, while she watched the sun set over the bay. One lonely light flashed slowly on and off in the distance, a beacon of warning for boats not to stray off course. *Am I off course, Lord?*

"You sing well."

Emma stepped back, startled.

"I'm sorry. I'm Peter Hill. I didn't mean to surprise you. I'm the choir director. And you are?"

"Emma Keller."

"Nice to meet you, Emma. Why don't you join us tonight? I know a good voice when I hear one, and we are desperate for another soprano."

Unsure, Emma looked down at Ginger.

"Oh, it's fine," the choir director said. "Bring her in. We're not too formal around here. We'll warm up our voices a bit more, and then we'll walk through the neighborhood and sing Christmas carols. I can even offer you a bribe of hot chocolate and homemade Christmas cookies at the Pastor's house."

Emma smiled. "It sounds fun. And I can't very well pass up homemade cookies."

"Great! We'd love to have you."

*   *   *

They sang their way through the neighborhood, and families turned on lights, opened doors, and thanked the carolers for their songs. Emma remembered the few times their youth group caroled when she was in high school, but this was different. There were no cliques. The people around her seemed genuinely glad she was there.

She'd met Amy, Bruce, Mrs. Nordine, Charlotte and Sam, and others whose names she couldn't remember. This group had purpose. They joyfully shared music that told of the Savior's birth and the hope His coming gives to the world. She knew this was something she'd been missing. *God is answering an unasked prayer, a need of my heart.*

On the last street, a baritone voice joined theirs. Emma turned and was surprised to see Nathan at the back of the group. His tall form stood out, and his voice joined in, adding a richness to the carolers' music. Her gaze locked with his and he smiled. His blue eyes mesmerized her. She smiled back and turned to face the front to finish a hoarse version of *Joy to the World*.

There was no discreet way to join Nathan, but Emma was in awe that when her effort to find him failed, they had met again. *Was this God's hand? Thank you, Lord.*

The last home belonged to the pastor and his wife. They provided hot chocolate and an assortment of Christmas cookies. Smells of chocolate, cinnamon, and fresh pine intermingled, and the fire in the hearth crackled heartily, creating a warm welcome that made Emma feel at home. They laughed together, visited, and even Ginger was openly welcomed and given a few dog treats. Emma's heart skipped a beat when, in the middle of a bite of sugar cookie, Nate joined her at the food table.

"So, what brings you to my neck of the woods, Emma?"

"The caroling," she said smiling. "Do you go to the same church as these people?"

"Yes, I do. I've been there ever since cradle roll."

Emma tried to understand. "Cradle roll?" she repeated.

Nathan laughed. "It means I've been here ever since I was born. You've never heard of that?"

Emma shook her head and sipped her hot chocolate. "No, I haven't. But I really like the people I've met here tonight. I was taking Ginger for a walk when I heard Christmas songs. I stopped outside the church and sang along. Pete heard me and invited me in."

Nathan chuckled. "Good ole' Mr. Hill. He has a way of bringing in strays, especially ones who sing well." He leaned over and ran his hand over Ginger's silky coat. "So, you have great taste in dogs, can speak in public, and sing," Nathan said. "What other hidden talents do you have?"

"I'm not sure they're talents. I like to eat sugar cookies and help children learn."

"You're a teacher?"

"I'm an instructional aide at Paulson Elementary School, but I have an interview for a teacher's position on Friday."

"If I were in charge, I'd hire you in a second. I bet you're great with the kids."

"Thanks Nathan. I hope so. It's been my dream for a long time to be a teacher. What about you? What are your hidden talents?"

"Me? I also like dogs, singing, and eating sugar cookies. If left alone, I can eat an entire tray of cookies by myself." He laughed. Taking her arm, he motioned to the others gathering their coats. "Looks like it's time to go."

Emma wished the evening didn't have to end. As the carolers headed out, hearts and stomachs full, they sang *We Wish You a Merry Christmas* to the Pastor and his wife. Then the group broke off in different directions to return home, and Emma realized Nathan had also drifted away. Spotting him several feet ahead, she called, "Nate!"

He turned toward her, a question in his eyes. She hoped she didn't sound desperate.

"I wondered if you would like to meet me at the St. Lucia's Festival on Saturday afternoon?" she asked. "I'll be at a booth with my students to pass out food for a few hours, but then, maybe we could hang out."

"Sure, Emma. I'd like that." His blue eyes sparkled, lighting up his whole face. After they went their separate ways, Emma wanted to skip home but she contained herself, and kept pace with Ginger. She hummed and thanked God for His ways. Life was good.

CHAPTER 5

The next afternoon, Emma stood in the back of the classroom, lost in thought. *How could one day drag on so long? I should be enjoying our class Christmas party and our last day of school before break, but all I can think about is my job interview.* Emma wiped down the table used for the cupcakes and other goodies they'd given to the students. The children were noisy as Angie called out numbers for Christmas bingo. Emma practiced answering possible interview questions in her mind while she swept the floor of crumbs, sprinkles, pieces of cut paper, sparkling sequins, and misplaced stickers.

She glanced at the clock on the wall. Two o'clock. Twenty more minutes of games before early release. *I better double check the time of my interview.* She walked toward her bag behind her desk when Angie called her.

"Miss Keller, I need you to take Sara to see the school nurse. She has another pesky nose bleed."

"No problem, Miss Jorgenson." Emma went over to Sara with Kleenex in hand. "You know the routine, Sara. Hold your head up, use the tissue for pressure against your nose and you'll be fine."

They walked down the hall together, and heard laughter and Christmas music from several classrooms. Games of duck duck goose, musical chairs, and hot potato were in full session. Glancing down at the small hand tucked in her own, Emma noticed Sara seemed a little down. "You know, I used to have nosebleeds as a kid."

"You did?" Sara asked, arching one little brow.

Emma nodded. "They're embarrassing. And they always seem to happen at the worst moment."

"Uh huh." Sarah pressed the tissue tighter against her nose.

241

"They're nothing to be ashamed of though, and you will outgrow them."

"That's what my mom says."

"Your mom is right. Here we are, Sara." She handed Sara over to the school nurse who gave the child a sympathetic nod.

"Thank you, Miss Keller," Sara said, as Emma turned to leave.

Emma looked back and smiled at the little girl. "You're welcome, Sara. Merry Christmas."

"Merry Christmas to you too!"

The time was two fifteen. She hurried down the empty hall, and her heels click-clacked on the floor with an echo reverberating to the classrooms. *I have to check my paperwork for the interview.*

She made it to the room in time to help hand out Christmas crafts and goodie bags to each of their students, and make sure no one left any backpacks, coats, or gloves behind. As the students lined up and waited for the dismissal bell, their lively chatter was contagious. Miss Angie, with Santa's helper cap and blinking light necklace, began to sing a robust, if slightly off key version of *We Wish You a Merry Christmas* and the children joined in.

This class is so much fun! I'll miss them, but I have to get that job. Maybe someday I'll be a great teacher like Angie.

The bell rang, and a second later the room exploded with students who raced for the bus, their parent's car, or toward friends for their trip home. Warnings by the teachers to walk went unheeded. Then, silence. The building, which teemed with life only minutes earlier, was deserted. The kids were gone. In full vacation mode.

Angie shook her head. "That's something else, the way they can disappear. Better than a Houdini trick."

"I need to see what time I disappear from here for my interview." Emma walked to her bag and rummaged through it. She looked, then looked again. "The paperwork's not here." She shuffled through her papers in a frenzied manner. "I can't believe I forgot it. I think my interview time is at 3:00 or 3:30." *This isn't like me at all. Maybe the stress from Bree and my family, and Randy, has gotten to me even more than I thought.* "I probably left them at home beside my computer. What do I do now?"

"Calm down, Emma. Take a slow deep breath." Angie placed a hand on her shoulder. "You can call the admin office to check on the time, or call home first and see if your family can find it for you."

"I'd rather not call the admin office. It won't look good if I can't even remember my interview time. It means I'm disorganized, or the job isn't important to me."

"Good point. Try home then."

Emma pulled her cell phone from her bag, quickly called the home number, and prayed her mom or dad were home to answer.

"Keller residence."

"Bree, is mom or dad there?"

"Nope, that's why I'm answering the phone."

"Why are you there? Never mind. I need you to do something for me. It's really important."

"What is it?"

"I need you to go into my apartment, and next to my computer should be some paperwork from the school district. Look at the top page and tell me the time of my interview."

Emma heard the sound of her apartment door opening, then Bree's voice say, "Ginger. Down, girl." Some rustling sounds followed. "Here's the paper," Bree said. "Let me see. It says to be at the Administration building, Room 135, at 3:30."

"You're sure? Is there anything else?"

"No. Just normal bureaucratic paperwork."

"Okay, great. Thanks, Bree."

"Glad I could help."

Emma hit 'end call' and paused.

"What is it?" Angie asked.

"Oh, nothing really. After all our fights, Bree was actually helpful."

Angie cocked her head to one side. "I can finish up here. Why don't you head over to the interview a little early, just to make sure you're on time."

"Okay." Emma looked at Angie and understood what she meant. She saw it was 2:45 now. She gathered her belongings, shoved some papers and a water bottle into her bag, grabbed her keys, and hurried through the door. "Thanks, Angie. Please pray for me!"

"You bet I will!" Angie called after her, the last words Emma heard as she left the building.

*   *   *

Her stomach nervous, Emma pulled into a parking spot in front of the admin building with high hopes. The time was 3:10. She had wanted to arrive by 3:00, but heavy traffic had slowed her down. She hurried to Room 135, only to find a testing lab, and the door was locked. *Well, that can't be right.*

She ran back to the front door to find the building directory. Personnel was in Room 235, so if she were one number off that would make sense. Maybe they had meeting rooms for job interviews or perhaps those rooms were next door. She took the stairs as fast as she could in high heels, not trusting her future to the slow rickety elevator.

Out of breath, she reached the door to personnel. The time was 3:20. She pushed the heavy door open, and was met by a single employee behind the counter. She wasn't smiling.

"May I help you?" the woman asked.

"Yes. My name is Emma Keller, and I'm here for a job interview for a teacher position."

"Running a little late today, are we?"

Emma didn't appreciate the condescension from the office secretary. "It's not 3:30 yet, is it?" She saw a clock that said 3:25 and relaxed a little.

"No, but your interview, Miss Keller," she said as she looked down her glasses at her interview list, "was for 2:30. You missed it by one hour."

"I what? I…I was told 3:30. Are they still here? Can I still interview?"

"I'm afraid not. You were the last interview of the day. They waited until 3:00, and then left. They won't be back until after the first of the year. There's no one left in the office but me. And I don't do interviews."

As she turned away from the counter, Emma's knees buckled and threatened to collapse. *I missed my big chance. There is no way I'll be considered for the job when I couldn't even make it to the interview.* The three Christmas elves poised on the oversized bookcase seemed to laugh at her as she left the office. Tears sprang to her eyes, but she didn't care. Her vision was blurry as she gripped the dark mahogany railing and plodded down the stairs. Each step echoed, and pounded defeat into her very being. Pushing open the heavy door, she left the cold lifeless building.

"Merry Christmas, Miss!" the janitor called after her.

She nodded her head and walked on. Her Christmas spirit had vanished along with the chance for the job. When she climbed into her car, it hit her. *Bree! Had she misread the time, or did she give me the wrong time on purpose? I have to see the paper with my own eyes.*

It was possible the wrong time was written down, and the personnel office had messed up, but she couldn't say anything to anyone until she saw the paperwork. She wanted proof one way or another.

CHAPTER 6

The first thing Emma did when she got home was to look for the paper. Tears flowed again as she searched for the stack of forms by the computer. They weren't there. With an anguished cry, she flung herself onto her bed in despair. *What am I thinking? What does it matter now, whether it was Bree's fault or not? I didn't get the job. I didn't get the job.*

She grabbed her grandma's quilt, a bright colored pineapple design, and wrapped it around her. She wanted to feel the arms of the Godly woman whom she could not touch again in this lifetime. The quilt gave comfort as she remembered the one who had lovingly entrusted it to her, a keepsake made by her ancestors. Her grandmother was the one who had taken her to Sunday School as a child when she could, and had talked to her about God. Where was He now? She muffled her cries into her pillow so her family wouldn't hear through the thin walls that separated them.

Ginger pushed her nose in between the pillow, the quilt, and Emma's face. Emma wrapped her arm around Ginger's body and let her soft loving presence ease her pain. *Why God, why? I thought I could see what I was supposed to do. I just don't understand.*

When she was all cried out, Emma rose from her bed and walked in defeat to the bathroom sink. She washed her face with cold water and stared at her reflection in the mirror. She saw her red rimmed eyes, tear stained face, and felt the pain of an oncoming headache. Then a thought hit her. *I have to leave. I have no future here.*

She had thought she'd be content to live here forever, raise a family, and teach. But not now. *Maybe life has been so hard because I'm not supposed to be here. I can put in for teacher openings in other counties or even other states. If those doors close then maybe it's a sign from God. Maybe I'm not cut out to teach.*

* * *

"What do you mean you're leaving town?" Her dad's face flushed red with anger as he paced the living room floor before dinner. "No daughter of mine is going to just give up and run away."

Emma braced herself. *I am twenty-three years old and he still treats me like a little girl.*

"Dad, I'm not doing either. I just think it's time for me to try something different." Emma clasped her hands together, tense from the realization she wasn't emotionally prepared for this conversation.

"You haven't thought this through. And now you've upset your mother."

Mrs. Keller sat at the kitchen table and cried into a Kleenex. "Right before Christmas, too."

"I'm sorry. I know my timing could be better, but that job meant a lot to me. I need to move on with my life and I don't see it happening here." *I can't tell them I suspect Bree sabotaged my chances for the job. That would really ruin their Christmas.*

"Promise me," her dad said. He took her hands in his and sat close to her. "You won't take any action on a job somewhere else until at least after the New Year." He looked into her eyes. "Give yourself some time to calm down and think about your options."

"Dad, I can't promise anything to anyone right now. But I will think about what you said."

"Maybe that's all we can ask for. That, and maybe for you to patch things up with your sister."

"*What?*" Emma shook her head. He had no idea what he was asking.

The front door flew open and Carson ran full speed into the kitchen, and captured three Christmas cookies from the cheerful snowman cookie jar. Bree hustled in, arms loaded with shopping bags that she dumped onto the couch.

"Great sale at Macy's," she said. "Thought I'd show you on my way hom—" She stopped and looked at everyone. "Did I interrupt something?"

"Your sister's leaving town," their mother informed her. Her hunched figure showed her distress. She blew her nose again.

"So, you didn't get the job after all?" Bree put her hands on her hips and wore a smug look. "Well, you know the old saying Grandma used. 'If you can't stand the heat, get out of the kitchen.'"

"Bree, stop." Their dad paced the floor and shook his head. "You two need to put your differences aside."

But Emma couldn't let it go. Not now. She moved closer to Bree, eyeing her like a serpent. "Tell him."

"Tell him what?" Bree asked. Her voice sounded all-too-innocent.

Emma swallowed hard under her sister's penetrating stare. It was almost as if Bree dared her to make an accusation. "You sabotaged me, didn't you? You gave me the wrong time for my interview."

"Well, that's quite the fantasy! Don't you think you should have proof if you're going to blame me for your problems?"

"I don't know what you did with my paperwork, but I know you gave me the wrong time. You ruined my chances for this job. Why?" Emma placed her hands on her hips too, and waited for an answer.

"Girls! This is ridiculous." Their mother jumped between them and looked from one to the other. "Emma, I think you need to apologize. A grown woman like Bree wouldn't do such a thing. Of course, Bree, you would help your case if you weren't being so antagonistic."

"I'm done. There's no point trying to talk," Emma said.

"Please!" her mom cried.

But her anger had gotten the best of her, and she walked quickly back to her apartment. There, she locked her door and her heart. Her spirit sank even lower as she realized she hadn't been honest with her father about giving more thought to her future before applying for jobs elsewhere. *I'm leaving. And there's nothing you can do to stop me.*

Turning on her computer, she began a job search.

*   *   *

"All right, everyone. Gather around the booth." Emma collected permission slips for each child to participate, while Angie's booming voice called the students to attention, and each of them listened for her expectations for St. Lucia's Fest. "We'll split up in a few minutes. You all look like you were just transported here from another country," Angie said, making the children giggle. "The dancers will meet in the town square in fifteen minutes. The rest of you will work in the booth. We'll hand out hot apple cider, krumkake, and lefse with butter and cinnamon to customers. And no licking your fingers. We have wet wipes. Got it?"

The children nodded.

"We'll also have a jar for donations so we can raise money for more special events. And when St. Lucia arrives in the longboat, we'll send some of you to help her give out saffron buns from the baskets we have sitting under the counter."

A few children jumped up and down, and Emma couldn't help but smile as she stepped forward to talk. "Before we get started, let's see if we know the answers to a few questions. Who was St. Lucia? Just call out if you know."

"Lucia was a young girl who brought food to the Christians who were in hiding in Rome," one girl said.

Emma nodded. "Good. Where were they hiding? And why?"

A little boy raised his hand, waving his arm with vigor. "They hid underground to keep from being killed."

"That's right," Angie said. "What does the name Lucia mean? And how does her name relate to how she helped Christians?"

"Her name means light," a small voice replied. "But that's all I know."

"Good job," Emma replied. "Lucia was a young Christian girl, who secretly brought food to the persecuted Christians in Rome who lived under the city in what were called catacombs. Why did she wear a wreath of lit candles on her head?"

No one answered. Angie looked at Emma.

"It was so dark in the catacombs she needed a light to guide her way," Emma explained. "And yet, she wanted her hands free to carry as much food as possible to the hungry people, so she wore a wreath of candles on her head. She also died for her faith. We remember her today as we do every December, because God used her to bring light into a dark place. She had a heart of love, and she risked everything to do what was right." Emma was encouraged by her own words to the children. St. Lucia's story was an inspiration and a reminder to be light in the dark corners of life.

"Thank you Emma," Angie said with a smile. They saw a number of families, couples, all ages, milling around, and walking toward the booths. "Now it's time to get ready," Angie instructed. "Man your battle stations."

The students scattered. Some took their places behind the counter in the booth, while others hurried off for the town square dances.

*   *   *

The crowd grew as Emma and Angie watched over their students.

"This time I tend to agree with your father," Angie said, as she and Emma poured cups of cider for the children to hand out. "Even though I could ring your sister's neck for what she did, you don't want to make a life changing decision as a reaction to her dastardly deeds. You need to think it through. Pray it through."

Emma's body stiffened and her throat tightened up. Fearful that Angie would no longer be supportive, she carefully chose her words. "I do hear what you're saying, Angie. But I think I need to get away. Maybe a short term assignment will help clear my head." Emma moved to the end of the booth to clean up some spills. "There are a couple of temporary positions in Eastern Washington open, probably because they're in a small town—"

Emma's words died on her lips as the faces of Bree and Randy abruptly appeared at the side door as harbingers of grim tidings. Shane stood back a respectable distance, shuffled his feet, and looked down as if embarrassed.

"Bree. Randy. What are you doing here?" Emma asked, her voice stilted.

"We're hanging out like everyone else," Bree said. "Thought we'd stop by. Randy wanted to see you. He just got out of jail for going AWOL. I didn't know he was already in jail when I talked to you about it. But I did tell you it would happen if you didn't see him again."

Why can't they leave me alone? Against her will, Emma's eyes filled with tears. And Randy saw it. She stood there, unable to move or say anything. The image of a relentless tide came to mind and a weariness settled on her, sapped her strength, and paralyzed her will.

"Oh Emma, I knew you felt something for me," Randy said.

Before she realized what was happening, he had taken her hands in his and pulled her toward him. He hugged her. And during this moment of confusion she looked up and saw Nathan, not even five feet from the booth, turning away, a look of disappointment in his eyes.

Mortified, she struggled out of Randy's hold and pushed him away. "No. You misunderstood."

Randy's smile vanished and his eyes darkened. His hardened look sent chills down her spine. "What do you mean?"

"I'm sorry, Randy," Emma said, her voice firm, her hands clenched into fists. "I think you have misunderstood from the beginning, thanks to Bree." She glanced over at her sister and saw her smirk. "There is *no* future for us."

Randy's face turned red. "Yes, I see that now."

"Do you? Really? When I say no, I mean no. And I've said it in a hundred ways. We are done!"

Randy's face morphed into a monstrous distortion as rage took control of him. He raised his arm with a clenched fist.

Is he going to hit me? Her body tensed, and she raised her arms to protect herself. Nothing happened. The side door slammed shut, and Randy was gone. She watched him jostle people as he stalked away from the booth. Bree scowled and went off in a huff after him.

Emma's legs and hands shook as she leaned against the counter, barely able to stand. For the first time a heavy weight of fear settled on her. *What if that's not the last I hear from him? Why does he persist in all this unwanted attention?*

She cast a glance at Angie, who was busy waiting on several customers. *I've got to pull myself together. Why, God, is this happening? I've lost Nate. He saw me with Randy and he gave up. He'll probably never come back.* Despair hit her like a punch in the stomach. *I really thought we might have something special.* Tears welled up again. *I've messed up everything. I have to get away.*

"Excuse me, Emma. I'm sorry." It was Shane, hands in his pockets, barely able to look her in the eyes.

"What is it?" she asked as she wiped her tears with the back of her hand.

"I'm supposed to remind you that you're babysitting Carson tomorrow night for Bree. She has her company Christmas party at eight o'clock."

Emma shook her head in disbelief. "She finally told you about Carson?" Shane nodded.

"My sister has a lot of nerve expecting me to babysit after everything she's done."

"I wouldn't blame you if you cancelled." Shane hesitated, then said, "I think you ought to know, Emma."

"Know what?"

"All your sister sees when she looks at you is the person she's always wanted to be."

"What do you mean?"

"She's jealous of you. You're smart, pretty, successful, and you haven't made all the bad choices Bree has made. She's taken advantage of your kind heart to try to bring you down to her level."

Emma nodded, but she was puzzled. "But why did she want me to date Randy?"

"She thought a 'bad boy' type of guy would knock you off your pedestal of perfection, as she calls it. She's not happy, so she doesn't want you to be happy either."

"Thank you Shane. I appreciate you telling me."

"No skin off my nose. Bree and I are done. Or we will be, after tonight. I'm breaking up with your sister. My mom used to say 'beauty is as beauty does.' I understand that saying now. How a person acts makes them beautiful, not their appearance. And just for the record, I didn't realize what a creep Randy was when I first met him. I just tried to help out a fellow sailor who was new in town. I'm sorry you ended up in this mess."

Emma nodded.

Shane turned to leave, then paused and faced her again. "Emma. Keep reaching for your dreams. God is with you."

What? Is Shane a Christian? I didn't expect that from him. Her respect for him immediately grew, but he disappeared before Emma could say anything more. The immensity of his words played and replayed in her mind, even as she handed out more food and drink.

Bree. Jealous of me? She's always been popular, has won all kinds of awards, and has all the praise and support from mom and dad that she could ever want. Meanwhile, I've tried so hard to feel accepted, and I still feel like a failure.

Images of recent family conflicts and disastrous events in her life flashed through her mind. She held her breath as the guilt and responsibility settled down to rest in its rightful place. As if a light had switched on for the first time, her mind poured over her role in each of the difficult times.

I let my dad think I would consider engineering. I went along with Bree on the blind date fiasco. I'm the one who forgot the interview paperwork and relied on Bree to give me the details. I've blamed others for the bad moments of my life, and never saw the role I played in them too.

She turned away from the counter and pretended to be busy, while different childhood memories came to mind. *Why didn't I invite Mom and Dad to the science fair? Or to the Senior Choral Concert?* There were times when she could have spoken, shared more of her dreams, stood up for herself, but she didn't. *Why? Because I didn't want to rock the boat. Because it's what I thought everyone wanted. Because I didn't want to inconvenience them. This mess is partly my fault because I thought if I pleased others it would help me be accepted. But you can be kind and still stand up for yourself. I didn't.*

She stifled a cry, caught it in her throat, and grabbed a napkin to blow her nose. Her legs, her whole body, trembled. *But God is with me, isn't He? Lord, forgive me. I wanted the approval of others when I should have been trying to please you.*

Angie slipped away from the customers and took Emma's hand. "I saw the troublesome trio stopped by. Good riddance to them. Do you need to go?"

"I— I think I should," Emma said, as she took off her apron and pulled her purse out from under the counter.

Angie placed her hand on Emma's shoulder and quickly prayed, "Lord, please guide and protect Emma. Help her do what's right. Amen."

Emma shifted her feet, uncomfortable the prayer had been said in public for all to hear, but at the same time, God's peace settled on her with the gentleness of a dove. He would guide her. She gave Angie a tight appreciative hug and then melted into the sea of faces.

Horns blew and caught the crowd's attention. They announced the arrival of St. Lucia in the longboat, escorted by torch wielding Vikings. While many moved toward the shoreline, loud festive music drew Emma's attention to the town square. Children in Norwegian costumes performed traditional dances for the remainder of the crowd. A few of them, her students, smiled at her. She paused to watch their joyful exuberance. *I may not feel like dancing now, Lord, but your light will guide me in the dance you've called me to do.*

With one last look toward the bay she turned, and walked away from the celebration.

CHAPTER 7

Emma stopped at her house after a few hours of Christmas shopping to drop off presents, change clothes, and pick up Ginger. She found Carson there, playing with the train set, cookie crumbs around his mouth. Her parents were limp on the couch. Their exhausted faces showed they were no match for Carson. She needed to talk to her sister about many things, and that included her son, but Bree had ignored her calls and texts, and stayed away from their house to avoid her. She didn't relish the idea of a confrontation, but now that she understood her sister's motives, she needed to set Bree straight once and for all. Tonight. After her evening of babysitting.

At Bree's apartment, Emma found Carson's pajamas under his pillow. "Time to get ready for bed, buddy," Emma said, and tried to sound more enthusiastic than she felt.

"No, no, no, T-Em. I'm a big boy."

"What?" Emma asked.

"I don't go to bed early any more. My mom said so."

"Really? What happens if I catch you like this?" Emma grabbed Carson in her arms as he bounced off his bed. "And what happens if I tickle you like this?"

They both laughed as she fell on the bed with him. Ginger hovered nearby in her protective stance. Her dog appeared unsure if this was a game or if someone needed help.

"Tell you what. Since you're such an old guy now, let's get your pajamas on, brush your teeth, and I will give you a really long story time before you go to sleep. Unless you're too old for stories."

"Oh no, I still like stories!"

"Okay." Emma laughed. "It's a deal?"

"Deal," Carson said.

* * *

When Carson was almost asleep, Emma pulled the covers up and placed them gently under his chin. Mr. Beaver, his stuffed animal, was already in his nightly embrace. Emma bent over and picked up some stray clothes and toys, and put them in their bins. Then her gaze swept over the room.

A Christmas candle? In Carson's room? She walked over and found a lighter on the shelf beside the decoration. *What is Bree thinking?*

The thought of what could happen horrified her. She checked the shelves and scanned the room for signs of any other lighters or matches. When she didn't find anything else, she picked up the candle and lighter, called Ginger out, and closed the door behind her. She carried both items to the kitchen and placed them on the counter. Then, she thought better of it, and put the lighter in a childproof container and placed it on top of the refrigerator. *Something else to talk to Bree about.*

While she waited for her sister to come home, Emma settled down on the couch. Ginger laid at her feet, content. A small Christmas tree decorated with white lights and blue balls stood in the corner with wrapped presents stacked around it. Emma was sure most of the gifts were for Carson or Bree. Emma knew she couldn't say anything to her sister about overdoing the gift giving. Her sister would say it was none of her business.

She picked up the T.V. control, and repeatedly flipped through the channels, a habit she'd picked up from her dad. She decided on *Gone with the Wind*, and shook her head at Scarlet's misdeeds. Scarlet reminded her of Bree a little too much.

Ginger interrupted Emma's thoughts with a growl. The dog rose up, bounded to Carson's door, and barked nonstop.

"What is it girl?" Emma asked. Her body tensed as she sprang up from the couch.

Smoke billowed out from under Carson's door. *God help me!* Her heart pounded in her chest and a thrumming sound rushed through her ears. *I've got to get Carson.*

Emma grabbed a pillowcase from the laundry basket, quickly wet it, and tied it around her head to cover her nose and mouth. *Hurry.* She felt the door. *It isn't hot. Thank you, God.* She opened it and went in, crouching close to the floor where the air was still good.

She focused on Carson in an effort to ignore the loud crackling, the aggressive flames, and the swirls of acrid smoke that threatened to engulf them. Her eyes stung and she broke into a sweat from the heat. The fire illuminated the room, devoured the drapes, and promised to move across the walls and ceiling toward her young nephew.

As she scooped up his sleeping form, Ginger darted across the room. Her ferocious barking was directed toward the patio door. Emma glanced at the opening and froze. A dark silhouette stood outside holding a gas can, and he splashed its contents onto the deck. He stopped and watched her, and an insidious smile spread across his face.

Emma gasped. "Randy?"

"What did you expect, Emma? That I would just walk away? You will pay for blowing me off!" His angry voice was defiant, his face taut, and his eyes held a gleam that sent a shiver throughout her body. His lips were curled back, making him look like a rabid dog.

She hesitated, unable to move. *What do I do, Lord?*

Randy took a few steps toward her and she instinctively took a step back, hugging Carson's small frame to protect him. Just then, Ginger charged, and Randy kicked at her. She leapt at him and knocked Randy onto the floor of the wooden deck. The gas can flew out of his hands.

"Get this she-devil off me!" he screamed.

His face changed from threatening to fearful. He wrestled with her, and used his arms to protect his head. Ginger snapped at him and grabbed onto his arm. Then she let go and hovered over his body. She growled, hackles raised, and sharp teeth snapped just inches from his face.

This is my chance. Her heart in her throat, Emma shifted Carson into a better position and rushed past the flames. *Thank you, Lord.* Sweat trickled down her back as she made her escape.

"Fire! Fire!" she yelled until her voice was hoarse.

Frantic residents ran from their apartments. Mothers and fathers held on to their crying children. A baby's screams protested the night's disturbance. And elderly couples fussed as they helped each other hurry to the grassy commons away from the threatening fire.

As the urgent sirens grew louder, Emma realized someone else had already called for help. Two fire engines and an aid car screeched to a halt in the alley by the ground floor apartment. A police car arrived just as quickly, with lights flashing.

Firefighters and Emergency Medical Technicians converged on the scene around her and Carson. Firefighters raced to unwind their hoses and spray the fire full force. Emma's body trembled and her knees began to buckle. Someone gently took Carson from her arms. Another took her hand to lend support, and she heard a far off voice ask if she was all right. She nodded. Then she was led away from the fire, but turned toward Ginger and Randy.

"Ginger, come!" she called as two police officers approached Randy. Ginger released her hold on Randy and ran to be with her.

As in a dream, Emma watched the officers lift Randy to his feet. He jerked his arms away from the officers' grasp and tried to run. One officer tackled him and the other cuffed his arms behind his back while he was held face down on the ground.

Rolling smoke obscured her view intermittently, but Randy shouted her name and what sounded like a threat. A shiver of fear shot through her. As the officers pulled him to his feet again and led him to the waiting police car, one officer carried the gas can away from the burning building.

Lord, how could I have not seen this evil standing next to me?

*　　*　　*

A bullhorn alerted residents to evacuate and Emma watched fire fighters move with precision from one apartment to the next, pounding on doors to make sure everyone had gotten out. Residents stood around or sat on the grass in shock and disbelief. Some shivered in pajamas, others pulled coats tight around them. Many were barefoot. Trancelike, they watched the fire burn their homes and belongings. The firefighters hustled as the savage flames shot high in the sky, first in one place, and then another, while high arched streams of water worked to douse and control the inferno.

The EMT firefighter who carried Carson laid him gently on the ground. Thankfully, Carson was a heavy sleeper, and was only now stirring from what, Emma thought, seemed a blissful if bumpy slumber.

As he woke, he cried, confused and scared. "What's going on?" he said as he struggled to stand up. Fear showed in his little face and sleep filled blue eyes. Then he saw Emma and his body relaxed when she sat by him and held his hand. He shifted his attention, with new interest in the uniform and equipment of the man who sat with them. He reached up and touched his badge.

"Will you help me out by trying my equipment for me?" the firefighter asked.

"Okay," Carson agreed.

The firefighter slipped a small oxygen mask over his face and then he took Carson's pulse. Emma met the man's friendly gaze and gasped. "Nate?"

His eyes widened. "Emma. Are you all right?"

"Yes. I'm okay. But you? You're a firefighter?"

"Yeah." He put a blood pressure cuff on her. "I should've told you sooner. I keep odd hours and get called in for emergencies. I've been called away during some of our conversations and just before we were about to meet at the St. Lucia's

Fest. Maybe it would help if you gave me your phone number. Can we talk later?" he asked, his expression hopeful.

"Yes," she said, nodding. "I'd like that."

Nate finished taking her blood pressure. "You're fine, Emma," he said as he put the cuff away and smiled. "In more ways than one."

"Thanks," she said, and her face grew warm. She looked down at Carson, partly to hide her embarrassment.

"And this little guy," he said, as he high-fived Carson, "is going to be just fine too." Nate removed the oxygen mask from Carson, who'd pretended to be Darth Vader while the two had talked.

"I'm not so little," Carson said, crossing his arms over his chest.

"No, I guess you're not." Nate laughed. "You're very brave. Will you take care of someone for me?"

Carson nodded and Nate handed him a stuffed animal, a Dalmatian with a firefighter's hat. "Your name is Spot," Carson declared.

He hugged the dog to his chest, then grew quiet as he watched the grey smoke billow up into the sky. Emma wondered if he was remembering Mr. Beaver.

"Emma, do you know how the fire started?" Nate asked, his face filled with concern.

"It was Randy." She could barely say his name. "H—he started the fire with a gas can and threatened me." Quietly she added, "He started the fire right outside Carson's bedroom." She couldn't hold back the tears or speak any more.

"Emma. Carson. Thank God you're all right!" Her mom picked up Carson and held him close.

Emma's dad was right behind her mom. "We heard the sirens and got a call about the fire."

"It started in Carson's bedroom, but I got him out," Emma told them.

"Oh, thank you, Emma. Thank you." Her mom cried and gave her an intense hug.

"I need to check on the others," Nate said, and placed his hand on her shoulder. "But don't leave until I have your number."

Emma smiled. "You can count on it."

Nate nodded his good-bye to Carson and her parents, and moved among other residents to take their vital signs and make sure they were okay.

"What a nice young man!" her mom said. "A firefighter in the family would be grand."

"Mom. I barely know him." Emma paused. "But I do like him."

A flurry of activity, a commotion of sorts, drew the family's attention. "Out of my way. My baby! Where's my baby?" Bree bumped into an elderly woman in her frantic search to find Carson.

"Bree! We're over here. Carson's fine," Emma yelled.

Carson was still in his grandma's arms when Bree arrived, eyes wild and haunted. She grabbed Carson and hugged him tight. "My baby. My sweet boy. Thank God you're okay!" she said. Tears welled up in her eyes. "No thanks to you."

Startled, Emma realized Bree's comment was directed at her. "*What?*" she asked.

"You," Bree accused. "It's your fault. Disaster follows wherever you go. I should have known better than to have you babysit him. I was told the fire started in my apartment. Did you forget to turn off a burner on the stove?"

"Breann Noelle Keller!" Their father's voice boomed like the sound of thunder, and his eyebrows shot down like lightning bolts. The intensity of his voice stilled every movement and quelled every word. "Your sister saved Carson. Who knows how many people owe their lives to her this day!"

"Thank you, Dad," Emma said, glad for once to have her father on her side. The support enabled her to stand taller and look Bree directly in the eye, as she said, "Bree, we need to talk."

Their mom took Carson in her arms, and both parents stepped away.

"I don't see that we have anything else to talk about," Bree said. She shifted her weight from one leg to the other and fidgeted with her bag.

"You set me up with Randy because he was a 'bad boy,' and you continued to push us together because you saw him as a way to bring me down."

"I don't know what you're talking about," Bree said. She flung her blonde hair off her face and looked everywhere but at her. "You didn't have a boyfriend, Shane was trying to help Randy, and I thought it would be good for you."

"Good for me?" Emma paced the ground in front of Bree and the frost crunched the grass beneath her feet. You pushed me toward Randy, you pushed me away from teaching, you ridiculed me when I was the MC, and you made me miss my job interview." Emma came to a stop directly in front of her sister. "How is any of that good for me?"

Bree clenched her fists and shouted back in defiance, "You've misunderstood everything."

"No, Bree." Emma shook her head to clear it of self-doubts. "You twist things around, and make something look good when it's bad. I'm not falling for it. Not anymore."

Bree hesitated for the first time. "You're indecisive. You needed someone to give you a push in the right direction."

"From now on," Emma said, shooting her sister a look of warning, "I'll make my own decisions."

Bree fell silent, as if for once, she didn't know what to say.

Am I getting through to her at last?

"Excuse me, ladies. I'm Detective Mack Thompson," a tall slender dark-haired man interrupted. He flashed his credentials. "Are you Emma Keller?" he asked, as he looked from Emma to her dog.

"Yes sir, I am," Emma said.

"And I'm Bree, her sister," Bree said, butting into the conversation. "My apartment caught on fire, while *she* was supposed to be babysitting my son."

Emma bristled at Bree's accusatory tone.

Detective Thompson cleared his throat and looked at his notes. "My understanding is that the fire started in the bedroom by the deck?"

"Yes," Emma said as she nodded. She saw Bree's look of confusion.

"And what did you see when you entered the bedroom to rescue your nephew?" the detective asked.

"I had just picked up Carson, and my dog charged across the room. She barked toward the outer wall where the drapes were on fire." Emma took a deep breath. "I realized the sliding glass door was open, and I saw a man standing on the deck holding a gas can."

"Can you identify the man?" Detective Thompson asked.

"Yes. Yes sir, I can." Emma tried to calm her nerves before she choked out, "It was Randy. Randy Roberts." She glanced at Bree and saw her sister turn white as a sheet.

"What? Randy started the fire? In my apartment?" Bree said. "He tried to kill you and my baby boy?" Her sister bent over and buried her face in her cupped hands.

"Miss Keller," Detective Thompson continued, "we've already run a check on Mr. Roberts. He's the main suspect in a couple of arson fires in the Los Angeles area, but there hasn't been enough proof to charge him. You and your nephew are lucky. There were fatalities in the other two fires."

Bree lifted her head, her expression full of remorse. Detective Mack wrapped up the questions with Emma and then he slipped away, leaving her and her sister alone.

"You're right," Bree admitted. "I have been jealous. And because of it, I did some terrible things. I didn't think it would come to this. I didn't know what Randy had done. Or what he was capable of. I can't believe I almost lost Carson. And you. I'm so sorry! You must believe me."

Emma saw for the first time in a long time that her sister was genuinely sorry. She put her arms around Bree as ash from the fire drifted down like snow around them. The dying embers of the fire glowed in the distance. *Was this the real Bree? Lord, please help me to forgive her. And to love her in the way she needs.*

"God is good. He's taken care of us," Emma said, as she stroked her sister's hair.

Bree cried into her gloved hands. "I lost Shane tonight too. He said he's done, that I'm manipulative and spiteful. No one has ever talked to me like that." She laid her head on Emma's shoulder and continued to cry as their mom, dad, and Carson surrounded them. They huddled together like a football team at halftime. And they *all* cried.

Head bowed, Emma prayed, *Lord, let my family see the hope you can bring into our lives.*

CHAPTER 8

Emma thought the picturesque little church belonged on a postcard. As she walked up the stairs, Nate held her hand. The light coating of snow, with flakes still falling, was a gift to usher in Christmas day and the early Julotta service they were attending. Behind them were Emma's parents, followed by Bree who held the hand of her sleepy-eyed pajama-clad son. Emma scanned the faces of the other people who walked in. She was supposed to meet Nate's parents for the first time today.

Mr. Hill stood at the door to greet them. "Good morning and Merry Christmas!" he said. "Emma, you are just the person I hoped to see this fine day."

"Merry Christmas to you too, Mr. Hill. Is it about joining the choir?"

"No, no. Not at all. I want to know if you're still interested in the teacher's position you applied for to fill in for Mrs. Holder?"

She couldn't believe her ears. *Is he serious?* "Why, yes, but how do you know about that?"

"I work for the school district." Mr. Hill smiled. "If you still want the job, it's yours."

Emma couldn't speak. She looked from Mr. Hill to Nate and heard the excited voice of her mom, already making plans.

Nate laughed. "Mr. Hill is the Assistant Superintendent for the school district, Emma. You didn't know?"

"No, I didn't." She turned back to Mr. Hill. "Yes, I accept the offer. Thank you. Thank you so much. But I don't understand why you're offering the job to me. I missed my interview."

"Emma, I knew you were one of the four candidates. I also realized you didn't know my position in the district. That allowed me to get to know you a little when you joined us for Christmas carols. I saw your public speaking skills at the beach bonfire and how well you handled the situation when things went wrong. I also heard your explanation of St. Lucia to the children on the day of the festival. And I was impressed by your quick thinking during the fire. Emma, you have a good head on your shoulders. You are a resilient and kind person, and your references speak highly of you. You truly have the heart of a teacher. We will do an official interview, but I've already made up my mind."

Emma smiled and shook Mr. Hill's hand. "You don't know how much this means to me. You just gave me a great Christmas present."

"You earned it, Emma."

She nodded. "Thank you sir." Emma walked with an extra bounce in her step toward the old wooden pews and fingered the shiny St. Lucia medallion necklace Bree had insisted on giving her. *How am I going to sit still?* She could hardly contain herself with the exuberance exploding within her. She saw some familiar faces in the pews, including Angie, who smiled and winked at her.

When she sat down beside Nate, she glanced around the church and noticed the candles for the first time. Hundreds of lit candles. All over the church sanctuary. The light and warmth emanated from them, and touched her very soul. *God's peace is in this place. Thank you, Lord.*

Nate held her hand, his caring support adding to her contentment. Carson snuggled against her. Bree sat close, and leaned forward, eager to learn, and Emma was pleased to see what she hoped was a new openness to God. Even her parents were smiling, and seemed happy to be there.

"O holy night, the stars are brightly shining." The congregation sang the words with reverence and conviction.

Nate leaned over and whispered in her ear. "Don't worry. I turned off my cell phone. I'm all yours."

Emma smiled and caught the joy in his sparkling blue eyes. *Lord willing, maybe you are.*

About the Author:

Jeri Stockdale is a member of ACFW and the Northwest Christian Writers Association. Instilled with a love for learning and teaching others, she has incorporated her life experiences into her inspirational women's fiction and historical fiction stories. When not writing and caring for her family, she works with a discipleship ministry at her church, oversees a menagerie of pets including dogs, cats, and horses; and enjoys gardening, nature walks, small towns, and researching family history.

Visit Jeri at: **http://www.jeristockdale.com/**

Ginger, Emma's faithful companion

Animals were my first friends. They helped pave the way for me to overcome the type of childhood shyness that severely limited my life until I opened my heart to God. My relationship with God and with my loyal animal friends inspired me to write my first novella, *Christmas Gone Awry*. It's the story of a quiet young woman struggling with faith who needs courage to stand up for herself. Emma's dog, Ginger, a beautiful husky-German shepherd mix, is a supporting character in my story. I was inspired by my daughter's dog, Sasha, who is a sweet-tempered delight within our household. I decided Sasha would be the perfect model for Ginger, best friend and protector to my main character, Emma. For my story, I was motivated to share my connection between humans and animals, and in particular, between a girl and her dog. I wanted to share how a beloved pet can be not just a companion, but a friend who accepts you without reservations, forgives your faults, and rises up to your defense when needed. God works through all of creation, so aren't animals another beautiful way God uses to speak to us? I hope you will enjoy reading about Emma and her canine friend, Ginger, as much as I enjoyed creating their characters and giving them a significant role in each other's lives.

God's blessings! Jeri Stockdale

All I Want For Christmas

by

Beverly Basile

Dedication:

To my husband and world's best chiropractor, Tom, my creative and crazy son, Gianni & his lovely bride, Mikaela, my witty and sarcastic twin daughters, Lacee & Tori, and my energetic and humorous sons, Chris and Matthew. Thanks for all your encouragement toward seeing this dream become reality.

Acknowledgements:

Thank you Lord for inspiring me to become an author and leading me to Darlene Panzera whose coaching, equipping, and editing gave me the tools I needed. You are amazing, Darlene! Thanks to you, Samantha, for your sweet presence and expertise on promotion. I couldn't have done it without both of you. Seriously. Thanks to Darlene's husband, Joe, for letting seven newbie and experienced authors invade his home every month during the past one and a half years for our Start to Finish Class. Joe, you have no idea what you've rocket launched to the world!

CHAPTER 1

Janee Peters strolled into the boardroom with a song in her heart and an attitude of expectancy. She'd dressed in a tailored navy blue suit and Gucci heals bought special for the occasion. Confidence permeated her every step.

Today was the opportunity of a lifetime; an entry position as a public relations agent with William Robert & Associates, better known as WRA, a prestigious advertising firm in Seattle. It had taken her two years since she graduated from Harvard to land this working interview. Settling her grandmother's affairs back home in Massachusetts had slowed down her job search.

"You must be Janee," said a man with dark hair and sideburns. He extended his hand toward her. "Brent Dodd, vice president of public relations. Welcome."

"Good morning, Mr. Dodd. It's an honor to be here. I look forward to working with you." She returned his enthusiasm with a broad smile.

"Call me Brent. We're informal around here. The president wants everyone on a first name basis."

His gaze dropped toward her professional attire. He gestured toward her shoes. "Dress code is business casual except for when we meet a client. Feel free to wear jeans or slacks, and flat shoes if you desire."

Janee looked down at her Guccis then back up to him. "Oh. Yes sir, I mean, Brent. Uh. Sorry."

Where is the nearest hole I can crawl into? Lord, please help!

A rush of heat washed over her face as she realized her Neiman Marcus suit and spiked heels were over the top for this corporation.

She squeezed her fingers into fists at her sides.

Aghhh! How could I have missed this? And after all the searching I did in second hand stores to find this outfit. Seattle is so unlike Boston. Oh well, I'll do better tomorrow.

She remembered her very first day back at Harvard. She'd walked on campus and immediately realized she was way out of her league. The students wore expensive name brand clothing which she couldn't afford. Her tuition wasn't paid by family wealth. Academics and financial need landed her the scholarship and grant.

She let out a quiet sigh and was about to ask about the account she was being assigned when someone from behind brushed her aside and pressed in between her and Brent. The intruder reached out his fingers for a handshake. "Breennnt. Good to see you. Hey, I'm looking forward to winning this account for WRA. Thanks for giving me the opportunity to demonstrate I am the man for the job."

Janee froze.

I know this man. I recognize his manners…and the voice…

She looked into the face of her competitor. And her jaw dropped. Stunned, she let out a small gasp.

This can't be. It is. Simon Wesley.

He stood six feet tall, with strawberry blond hair, dressed in Docker pants and a plaid shirt with the top button left undone. The perfect look to fit in with WRA, which made her own attire stick out even more.

Simon turned to look at her. He appeared both shocked and amused at the same time.

"Janee Peters? What are *you* doing here?"

She took a half step away from him.

Brent raised a brow. "You two know each other?"

"Yes. We were in the same program at Harvard a few years ago," Simon explained as he quickly took the lead ahead of her. "She's been trying to keep up with me ever since we sat next to each other in our marketing class."

Just my luck. Of course it would be him. I knew God would catch up with me sooner or later for not going to church regularly.

"Hello, Simon," she said, unable to keep her frustration out of her tone.

Brent glanced back and forth between them. Then cleared his throat. "I have good news and bad news," he said. "You are both competing for a public relations position here. By the end of the week, one of you will be joining our firm. May the best man or woman win. Good luck."

Janee looked Simon squarely in the eyes. "We'll have a friendly and *fair* competition like old times, won't we Simon?"

"You bring the best out of me, Janee." Simon grinned. "Only the best."

"Looks like we have some fun days ahead," Brent said, and gestured for them to take a seat.

Janee and Simon pulled out chairs across from each other while Brent sat at the head of the twelve person table.

"Rainy Day Coffee is the client for whom you will be preparing a marketing plan. A fairly new upstart company, their long term goal is to become the largest distributor of coffee in the Northwest. They have asked us to develop a marketing strategy that will increase their sales and visibility."

He looked at Janee and Simon. "Both of you and other senior members will be working on this project. This will give you an opportunity to present WRA with fresh, creative marketing ideas. Show us your best."

Janee's head was spinning. Although she heard what Brent said, her thoughts kept drifting back to her nemesis sitting across the table.

What is Simon doing here? Is he stalking me? How did he know I was applying for this job? How could he have found the same opportunity as me?

Janee snapped herself to attention and refocused on Brent's every word.

"Let me show you where you'll be working this week. Follow me." Brent led them out of the board room and down the hall past the executive suites to the public relations department. It was a large room with full length windows on the far side overlooking the Puget Sound. Twelve cubicles divided the room with two desks, computers, and phones in each square.

"This will be home for the week," Bret continued. "You'll be working together in close proximity, so keep it friendly, will you?"

Worst set up imaginable! I have to work with my desk opposite Simons. Are you kidding me? This is not good...not good at all.

Bent handed them each a folder. "Review these stats on their company, as well as their budget, and begin work on a proposal. Tomorrow morning, at nine o'clock you'll present your plan. I don't expect perfection given the short amount of time...just give it a shot. Any questions?"

"No problem, Brent," Simon said, nodding his head with confidence. "I got this."

"This is going to be fun, Brent. You won't be disappointed," Janee said.

Brent looked at his watch. "It's ten o'clock now. We will have lunch together with all the department heads in the boardroom at noon. They will each give you a brief description of their services which you will incorporate into your plans. Lunch is on us."

Turning and giving them a final wave, Brent left the room.

Janee began to rearrange the contents on her desk. She placed the pens, pencils, paper clips, and other supplies in the top drawer. She moved the phone to the far right corner out of her way. Then she sat down and wiped her hands slowly across the clean, smooth, surface. Satisfied that everything was in order, she opened the Rainy Day Coffee folder and began to read through its contents.

Now if I can get Simon off my mind the same way I eliminated the distractions off my desk, I'll be in good shape.

Janee sat in silence for a moment and visualized herself permanently working at this firm. Her day dream was spoiled when out of the corner of her eye she sensed Simon staring at her. When she looked up, he grinned at her with a mischievous smile.

She rolled her eyes in annoyance. *Oh, I can't wait to show him he can't beat me this time.*

Janee recalled how Simon had stopped by her table in her marketing class at Harvard. He pretended to borrow a pen from one of her team members. Then he lingered awhile and "listened in" on their group project. The next morning in class he was the first to volunteer to give his group's presentation. Only it wasn't his idea he delivered. It was hers. He had copied it. Unfortunately, after the professor finished giving a raving review of Simon's work, her presentation came off like an unwanted piece of candy at Halloween by a trick or treater who had already eaten too much sugar.

This desk arrangement is not right. She began to squirm at the close proximity between her and Simon, and looked around the cubicle to see if there was a better place where she could shift her desk and computer to.

Worse, former feelings of resentment surfaced in her heart and competed with teachings she'd learned from years of Sunday sermons.

God, I know I've forgiven this man. Why are these wounds just as fresh today as they were back in college?

Janee got up and pushed her desk and computer to the opposite side of the cubicle so she could face away from Simon. Then she sat down in her chair, relaxed her shoulders, and re-opened Rainy Day Coffee's file.

She could still feel Simon's gaze follow her every move.

He won't shake me. I won't let him. God is with me.

A silent war descended down on the space. The only sounds were the clicking of keys on keypads and quiet conversations of other employees in their work stations around the room.

During their lunch Simon kissed up to everyone and acted as if they were his
next door neighbors. He interjected into the discussions at hand as if he'd worked for
WRA for years. His jokes and know-it-all attitude were polished and conniving.

He is so smooth. Just like his father, Allen Wesley, richest man in Massachusetts who will stop at nothing to get what he wants. Neither of them can be trusted.

Great set up. Umm, God, is there a reason this shyster has been placed into my life again? Look, I could use a break. Simon has everything. The entirety of my possessions can be stored in the trunk of my car. So, I'd really like to get this job here without a whole lot of trouble included in the package. Do you think you could lend a little helping hand?

Five o'clock came. Quitting time at WRA and Simon had disappeared. Now was a good time to quietly slip out and avoid any more encounters with him for the day.

Janee saved her work on the computer and shut it down. She put her files in her briefcase, grabbed her coat and umbrella, and walked toward the main lobby.

"Goodnight, Tami," she called to the young secretary. "It was great meeting you today. I look forward to seeing you again tomorrow."

Tami smiled back. "You, too, Janee. Good luck getting this job."

"Thanks." She walked past the large receptionist desk beneath the corporate logo in the lobby, and feigned confidence as she walked out of the office toward the elevator.

Then, unable to help herself, she reviewed the past interactions with Simon like scenes from a bad movie.

The way Simon bribed his way right into the internship she had applied for by taking Professor Nelson, department chairman of Communications to lunch at The Wooden Keg.

Prime Rib, grilled onions, and Porter Beer bought his way into a national software company for the best internship any public relations student could ask for. She was the waitress who had to deliver the food while he smoozed his way into the position. When the food was served and the transaction sealed, Simon insulted her still more by not leaving a tip.

Janee knew she couldn't compete in that game. Prestige and money opened doors for the Wesley family, whose name influenced people all over the East Coast.

She punched the button inside the elevator of the 32nd floor of the Columbia Towers and the doors closed. Then she rode down to street level.

Simon has everything he wants. He doesn't need this job. This position is perfect for me. This is where I will begin new. There is nothing left for me back in Massachusetts. I've got to get this job. I need this job. But, what if this firm hires him instead of me? If they get wind of his daddy's influence, will they want the notoriety of having a son of the "Wesley" family work for them? Ugh! Simon will not *steal this job from me. I won't let him. No matter what the cost.*

She stepped out of the elevator and hurried across the expansive, tiled marble floor to the revolving exit door of the building.

To her dismay, someone pushed in quietly behind her and squished into the small compartment that was designed for one person, not two.

The brief moment of solitude was rudely interrupted by a tortuous, familiar whistle which rang in her ears, sending chills down her spine, and dread in her stomach. She knew the measure. Simon always whistled the tune before he devoured his prey. She turned her head to look back at him.

"What are you doing here, Simon? Gonna try and beat me out of this position too?" She poked him in the chest. "Just so you know, I have every intention of getting this job."

"Still think the world revolves around you, don't you, Janee? Look, Sweet Cheeks, they only invited you here to satisfy the requirement that two people compete for the spot. *You* are a fill in. *I* am the hire. By Friday the job will be mine. Why don't you pack your princess totes and return to waiting tables where you belong." He looked down his nose at her. "The corporate world is not for you. You were raised on the other side of the tracks. Poor folks don't know how to run with the rich."

Simon is a beast. Why does he have to be on the same career track as me? Where is his sense of humanity?

"How did you find out about this job and how did you know I would be here?" she demanded.

"You think I tracked you here?" he retorted. "You've *got* to be kidding. Do you think for one moment that I would want to be in the same locale as you? My home would never be near a trailer park. Sharing the same continent with you is too close in proximity for me, Janee." He chuckled. "Hmm. Have you ever considered moving to Mongolia? I hear the climate there matches the temperature of your heart."

Janee grimaced. "You're just insecure, Simon. You're worried that you're going to be beaten by a woman. Admit it. You are threatened by me," she said. "For your information, you're going to lose this one, frat boy."

The two of them stumbled out onto the wet sidewalk. It was cold, dark, and raining outside. A stark contrast to the sweet sounds of Christmas music she heard on the streets and the warm holiday cheer emanating from storefront windows adorned with colorful Christmas lights and shiny garland.

Janee buttoned up her overcoat and opened her umbrella. She tilted the top of it toward Simon as if to push him away from her and create distance. To her dismay they both walked in the same direction.

Janee quickened her pace to get away from him. She wished she had brought tennis shoes to walk the three blocks to the garage. Instead, she clicked along in her stilettos, pushed her purse behind her shoulder, and braced against the wind. She climbed the stairs to the second floor of the parking garage and scanned the concrete shelf for her vehicle. Then she spotted her car and crawled into the front seat, closed the door, and shut her eyes.

Only four more days to put up with this buffoon. On Friday, it's bye-bye to this pebble in my shoe. I'll be a self-sustaining woman and upcoming leader in my field. No more poor Janee. Living in Washington will be the new start I need.

CHAPTER 2

Janee put her keys in the ignition and started the car. The motor purred like a well-tuned treasure.

It's you and me, Betsy.

Betsy was the pet name for the much loved and reliable 1960 Chevrolet Impala Janee drove across the country. She didn't bring much more with her besides the car, a suitcase, and tip money she'd saved from her earnings at the Wooden Keg.

Although the car wasn't as pretty as its former days of glory, it was very dependable. Janee inherited Betsy from her grandma who died during her senior year of college. Even though the seats smelled a bit musty, the interior was immaculate. Her grandma had never driven much further than five minutes to town.

She and Grams had spent countless hours together cruising along inside Betsy. Trips to the grocery, bank, church, visiting friends in need, and picnicking at the lake. They were fond memories.

"Who knows, Betsy, with a fresh coat of paint and some sprucing up...you could wind up in the Smithsonian. But I don't think I could part with you. It would be like parting with Grams. Having you keeps her close to me."

Someday, however, I'm going to buy a new car, a beautiful BMW Convertible...navy color with baby blue leather seats. I can see it now. Roof down, wind in my hair, care free and money in the bank. It's going to be good.

Owning a new car wouldn't make her happier. But having plenty of money would give her the freedom to buy new things without having to worry about not being able to afford it.

Janee's early childhood was wonderful. Her parents had been smitten with their firstborn and only child. They'd thought her dark, curly locks, emerald green eyes, and pearly complexion were heavenly. They heaped love on her like a child spraying whip cream on a cup of hot chocolate and they spent as much as they could afford on her with a construction worker's salary. She had frilly dresses, hair ribbons, beautiful dolls, and a designer bedroom furnished with matching dressers and a canopied bed. Every girl's dream.

But her happy life was rudely interrupted when her daddy was diagnosed with cancer. Her mom took over as the breadwinner, but working two cleaning jobs was not enough to pay the hospital bills and living expenses. Phone calls from the bank about late mortgage payments would bring her mother to tears. Janee didn't want to repeat the past and lack in finances. After her father's death, her mother's health went downhill from exhaustion. She died not long afterwards. Then Janee's grandma took over raising her.

Janee started the car and pulled out of the garage for the commute back to the Cedar Inn. The day had gone fairly well despite Simon's best efforts to demoralize her. She liked the people, the casual atmosphere, and the working conditions at WRA. The prospect of landing this job in the heart of downtown Seattle thrilled her. Coming up with a great marketing plan wouldn't be difficult. She'd proven she could compete with Simon back at Harvard so why should this week be any different?

The headlights of commuter traffic blurred together.

I really hope I can do this.

"God," she whispered. "I truly need your help. I haven't talked with you much lately. Can you hear me? Even though my Sunday school teachers told me that you love me and have a wonderful plan for my life, I still wonder how anything good could still come after losing Mom, Dad, and Grams."

Overcoming the loss of her parents was more than any little kid should have to endure. But to lose again…made her wonder about God's goodness and feel like an orphan. She had no other living family members left. She was it. Just her. The last of the Peters family.

Grams and Janee hadn't been rich but they'd had enough money to pay the bills. There had never been a lack for deep conversations, tasty meals, clean clothes, or a warm home. She had fond memories of playing poker on Saturday nights using M & M's for chips. Her grandma would always cheat and bring out a secret stash of candy whenever she started to lose.

I miss you, Gram. I miss cooking together, going for walks, attending church, and pigging out on cookies.

She pulled into the Fauntleroy ferry dock and paid for a ticket to Southworth at the toll booth.

"Make sure to get into the far right lane," the attendant instructed.

Slightly distracted, Janee didn't register his directions and instead, followed the car directly in front of her and parked in the left lane.

When the ferry started to load, she moved forward in line. Then after she parked her car on board, she reclined her seat, put her head back, and shut her eyes to take a brief rest.

Knock, knock, knock. She was awakened by a loud rapping on her driver side window.

"Miss...wake up...you need to get off the boat."

Janee jumped to attention, looked up, and gazed out her window into the eyes of a handsome man about twenty-five-years-old. He was a ferry worker in a yellow raincoat who was over six feet tall with sandy brown hair. Most striking, was his strong rugged jawline and kind eyes.

"Sorry. Didn't mean to startle you. The ferry has arrived. You need to get off."

She looked around and saw that the cars ahead of her had already unloaded. Her car was the only one left holding up the line. Embarrassed, with heat flooding her cheeks, she started her car and began to drive off the boat.

"Now unloading for Vashon Island," droned the overhead speaker.

"Vashon? No! I'm supposed to be getting off at Southworth." Janee pounded her steering wheel.

She rolled down her window and called out to the same ferry worker.

"Excuse me, there must be a mistake. I'm supposed to be getting off at Southworth," she said, unable to suppress her panic.

"Southworth?" He raised his brows then tipped his head to the side and looked at her curiously. "Uh...You're on the wrong boat. You new to the area?"

She stifled a groan. "Yes."

"Drive off, turn around at the end of the dock and wait in the lane marked for Southworth. Next boat is at seven-thirty."

Ugh. Of all the dumb things I could do.

He waved her on and continued to offload the other cars.

Janee made certain to get in the correct lane this time and waited for the ferry to Southworth. A few hours later she finally arrived back at the Cedar Inn.

She walked down the garden path that led to the front door and entered the grand, old white farmhouse with black shutters and a covered, wrap-around porch. The Inn's golden retriever, Shelby, escorted her inside with a happy disposition and a wagging tail.

"Hi, Mrs. Martin," Janee greeted the short, overweight innkeeper.

"My, you're home late. How was your first day at work?"

"Everything went well till I found out my competitor for the position is someone I know from back East. He's not a nice guy. Kind of lost my footing when I saw him. Oh yeah, on the way back I got on the wrong boat and wound up on Vashon Island instead of Southworth. Oh well...I won't make that mistake again."

"Sounds like a little sweet with a little sour. Don't worry your pretty, little head. It will all work out. Leftovers are in the refrigerator. Make yourself a plateful and warm it in the microwave. I'm going to lock up. If there is anything else I can do for you, just let me know."

"Can you write me a winning proposal?" Janee asked.

Mrs. Martin smiled. "Sorry, I can't help with that."

Janee thanked the woman and reheated a quick dinner of roast beef and mashed potatoes, and sat down at the table to enjoy the meal and a quiet moment. Then, tired from the long day, she shuffled her way upstairs.

After she changed into her pajamas, she plopped down on her bed, and opened up her laptop like a college student pulling an all-nighter.

I can do this.

***

The next morning Janee got up, showered, and dressed for work. As she was coming down the stairs, the scent of coffee and baked goods filled the air. Closing her eyes, she drew in a long, slow whiff of the delicious aroma.

Yum. Smells like Gram's cooking.

Janee was putting her coat on when Mrs. Martin called from the kitchen. "Eggs are almost done, Janee."

"Sorry, Mrs. Martin," she hollered back. "Wish I had time because it sure smells good. I can't afford to be late and have got to catch this ferry."

Mrs. Martin hurried to the living room and passed her a small, brown paper sack. ""You're going to wither up into a bag of bones if you don't eat," the innkeeper replied.

"Here, take these hot, fresh, cranberry-orange scones. The recipe has been in my family for generations."

Janee smiled. "Thank you."

Mrs. Martin looked outside the big picture window and warned, "Sometimes the ferry gets off schedule when it is foggy outside. Regularly scheduled boats can be late and some runs can be cancelled. Don't be surprised if things are not as they should be."

"Really? Oh boy. I had no idea."

Janee scooped up the scones, her keys, and her overcoat, and raced out of the Inn letting the screen door slam behind her. With breakneck speed she flew to the ferry dock, and by the time she arrived, cars were almost finished being loaded. She rushed down the dock at 25 mph.

"Whoa, slow down," hollered two ferry workers. They used a downward motion with their hands to urge compliance.

Janee decreased her speed and noticed the ferry worker was the same man she encountered the night before. She tried to scrunch down in her seat to avoid being noticed by him. But to no avail.

Oh my gosh. Now he's caught me speeding.

When she parked the car he looked at her with a teasing smile and mouthed, "Newbie."

Janee rolled her eyes and nodded back at him and said, "Yes."

She pulled out her notes and began rehearsing the proposal. Ten minutes into the crossing, the ferry slowed to the pace of a jellyfish, drifted in the water, and stopped.

"Your attention please," the captain's voice announced over the speakers. "We are having engine problems and will be delayed for a short time of repair. Estimated time to arrive at the Fauntleroy Dock is nine o'clock."

Oh, no. That's when my proposal is to be presented. This can't be happening.

Janee fumbled in her purse for her cell phone and called Tami to report that she would be delayed.

This is not good.

CHAPTER 3

"Sorry to keep you waiting, Brent. I wasn't planning on the ferry breaking down this morning," Janee said, as she seated herself at the table to the left of him and scooted in her chair. Simon was seated right across the table from Janee to Brent's right. He shot her a scornful gaze but she dismissed it like water off a duck's back.

"What do you have for me, Janee?" Brent asked, his words short, clipped, and abrupt.

Undeterred, Janee enthusiastically began. "I've got a great idea for the Rainy Day Corporation. The up and coming market of new buyers for coffee are predominantly young, adult women. I suggest that they offer discounted coffee at their shops during finals week to all students at the University of Washington, community colleges, and private universities. In addition, Rainy Day Coffee could sponsor study hall in their cafeterias, fraternities, and sororities with free drip coffee and cookies. This will introduce their products to a targeted market and help create brand loyalty to a younger clientele."

Brent rubbed his chin. "Great idea, Janee, but unfortunately you're just a bit behind schedule. Simon made the exact same proposal as you did this morning. His was on my desk first thing while you waited for the repair on the ferry."

"But…"

That wasn't my fault. And how could Simon have stolen my idea?

Simon grinned, his face smug.

Brent looked approvingly at her competitor, then turned back toward her. "I'll expect a fresh idea from you by tomorrow morning."

Janee glanced to the side and let out a sigh.

When she looked up Simon had his hand cocked in the shape of a small pistol. He made a clicking sound, released the trigger and mouthed, "Bang. You're dead."

Stay calm, Janee. You've got this. Don't let this monster derail you. This job is worth fighting for.

"Keep developing your idea, Simon," Brent said. "You might want to call some schools and work out the viability of your plan."

They all rose from the table and moved back to their offices. Janee sat down at her desk, booted up her computer, and went to work drafting a new idea.

A rustling noise erupted behind her and she turned to look. Simon had pulled out boxes of cookies, sweet breads, and cake pops which he brought in to work to share with the employees.

He looked over at Janee and gloated, "This is going to be good."

Janee squirmed in her chair.

Simon is schmoozing again. He's going to try and work his way into the hearts of all the staff here at WRA and influence management's decision. If only they knew his true nature.

Simon got up from his desk and paraded his tray of assorted goodies around the room to show off his generosity to everyone in the firm. "Help yourselves, everyone. I've got plenty for all. I'll put it in the break room along with a fresh brew of Rainy Day Coffee. My treat. Eat up."

Employees rose from their desks and followed him to the break room.

"So Simon, what brings you to Seattle?" the graphic design artist asked.

"How do you like the Northwest? I heard you moved here from the East Coast," a copywriter interjected.

Happy laughter and light conversation flowed from the break room but Janee denied herself the pleasure of joining them.

I refuse to eat one morsel of his bribery.

***

She was finally able to relax after she parked her car on the ferry dock that night. The soft golden hue of the streetlights warmed the cold, misty evening. Janee watched the walk on passengers quietly converse with one another as they stood outside and waited for the boat. Some had their umbrellas up but most didn't. They seemed at ease with the elements.

Oh, the peace and serenity of the Northwest. I love this place. The rain isn't as bad as I've been told. People here seem so content with this commute. No heavy traffic, honking horns, or impatient drivers.

A ferry with double car decks docked which Janee had never loaded on before. It was white and green with open air windows cut out along each side of the steel boat on the lower deck. Passengers could feel the breeze in these windows and stick their heads out a bit to look down at the water's surface and listen to the water lap against the side of the ferry as it made its way across the sound. A drawbridge located on the dock was lowered to the level of the ferry deck so cars could drive onboard. On each side of the ferry was a steep ramp leading to the second car deck.

I don't want to drive up there to the second level. What if my car rolls back? I hope I get to park on the first level.

When Janee drove her car on board, a worker pointed for her to go to the far left lane and drive up the ramp to the second level of parking.

This is scary. I can't see over the top of it. What if...

Janee slowly drove up the slope. Just as she neared the top of the ramp, the car in front of her stopped. Janee put on her brakes but they failed. Her car rolled backward and crashed into the front fender of the Mercedes Benz behind her.

Oh, no.

She tried to pull forward but couldn't because their bumpers were stuck together. She parked her car, set the emergency break, and got out to inspect the damage.

The driver of the Mercedes stormed out of his car and got right into Janee's face.

"What are you doing?" he hollered.

She winced and took a step back away from him.

Quick on his feet, a hooded ferry worker came over to usher the angry driver away from her.

"Calm down, sir. Take a breath," he said. The hooded ferry worker turned toward Janee. Their eyes locked. "You? Again?"

Janee wilted. This was the third time she had run into the handsome ferry worker under less-than-desirable circumstances.

"Leave the cars where they are till we dock," the ferry worker explained. "We'll offload all the other cars first then see about disconnecting your two fenders."

He looked at both her and the other driver and said, "You better call some tow trucks."

Janee looked at the vehicles and cringed.

This is more damage than I thought. Now my insurance premium will go up.

Her thoughts raced and she wished she could wake from this nightmare.

Wonder how much this is going to cost me. Why do I keep running into this ferry worker? Why did he have to be so cute with his sideburns and wavy hair? Oh...Betsy! What have I done to you?

"Do you both have insurance?" the ferry worker interrupted.

"Yes," she and the driver answered in unison while nodding their heads.

Janee looked over at the angry man. "I'm so sorry, sir. I didn't mean to damage your car. Why don't we go upstairs and exchange information."

"I guess accidents do happen," he replied testily.

Unfortunately for her, they happened far too frequently.

***

Janee was quiet while riding home with the tow truck driver.

How am I going to afford to pay for the repairs on my car? The insurance is not going to pay for the damage. The deductible is $1,000. I'll have to pay for the expense out of my own pocket. I only have two thousand dollars in my checking account and I need to pay Mrs. Martin. What if there isn't enough money? This accident could blow my budget.

"And we know God causes all things to work together for our good," whispered the still small voice within her.

Could she trust this voice?

Mrs. Martin dropped Janee off at the ferry in the morning and coached her how to catch the bus from the Fauntleroy Dock to work.

"Make sure to get on the east side of the street not the west. And take the 51 going north," the widow advised.

"Ok, Mrs. Martin."

***

Janee's third day appeared to be going smoother. No glitches with the directions and no broken down ferries. She rehearsed her proposal in her mind and pumped herself up with positive thoughts while commuting to work.

This is going to be a good day. The boat is on time and my proposal is a winner. I just know it.

Her spirit lifted higher when she heard Johnny Nash's song, *I Can See Clearly Now the Rain Has Gone* playing in the lobby of WRA.

Surely this is a sign.

All anxieties aside, she entered Brent's office. "Good Morning," she greeted. "I've got a great proposal."

"Let's hear it." He gestured for her to take a seat.

Janee placed her file on his desk and scooted the chair in closer. "Rainy Day Coffee can promote their delicious brew at community events that are sponsored by the Chamber of Commerce, the Rotary, the Elks Club and non-profit organizations. To be more visible they can take the marketing to a grass roots level. For example: Thanksgiving. Thousands of shoppers will be out on Black Friday in the wee hours of the morning. Rainy Day Coffee can be out front and center spreading the joy of the season by handing out free coffee at the malls and downtown shopping areas."

When Brent didn't respond, she continued, "Instead of throwing loads of money into radio and newspaper, our clients can advertise by giving. Their audience will already be in a festive mood. Free cups of coffee complements of the Northwest's best coffee company will only add more joy to the holiday events."

Janee searched his eyes for affirmation. Instead there was a long pause, during which her stomach nearly fell to the floor.

Finally, Brent rubbed his forehead and let out a long breath. "I don't know how to tell you this, Janee. I really appreciate your peppy attitude. But we tried a similar idea in the past and discovered that it simply won't work in the indoor shopping centers. Mall management won't allow free beverages to be given away because it takes revenue from the other cafes and fast food businesses located there. Plus they don't want to pay janitors to clean the mess from thousands of paper cups and potential spills. Sorry."

He pushed away from the table and gestured for Janee to return to her cubicle. "Give me a fresh idea tomorrow morning. Good luck, kid."

Kid? Did he just call me, Kid?

Her chest tightened as she stifled a groan.

Two more days to wow this firm. I've got to do this. I can do this. I will do this.

CHAPTER 4

"Fifteen hundred dollars to repair Betsy? I mean, my car?" Janee spoke loud enough to wake the dead. "You've got to be kidding me. That's more than my car is worth." She looked toward the kitchen and saw Mrs. Martin standing in the entryway wiping her hands on her apron and listening in on the conversation.

"Yes, Maam," the voice replied on the phone. It was the rep from the auto repair shop. "What do you want me to do? Fix it or send it to the junk yard?"

"Junk yard?"

I can't let Betsy go to the junk yard.

"Just fix it," Janee said glumly, then hung up her cell phone.

Is any of this worth it? All I wanted to do was get a decent job, make a good living, and start a new life.

She looked up toward the ceiling. "Is that too much to ask, God?"

Mrs. Martin gave Janee a curious look. "Is everything all right, dear?"

Janee shook her head. "No."

Once I pay the car repair and rent, I'll have $250 left. My total net worth right now is $250. It doesn't even look like I am going to get this job. If I don't get this job, I'll be out on the streets… Homeless.

It will be a "Silent Night" for me when that happens.

Janee sat down at the dining room table with her chin in her hands and looked off in the distance. Her mind drifted back to Grams and the kitchen table back home.

She could almost hear her grandmother's voice say, "Don't worry, Sweetie, when troubles come. God will take care of everything."

A scripture verse she had memorized when she was a teenager came to her mind, 'My God shall supply all your needs according to His riches in glory.'

I need your provision, God. Now more than ever.

Peace began to trickle in her heart.

Mrs. Martin appeared in the doorway with a steaming bowl of hot soup and a plateful of fresh baked rolls. "Here, darlin." She placed the food in front of Janee and looked at her with eyes full of compassion. "Take your coat off, eat, and rest a bit. Don't worry, it will all work out."

Janee picked up her spoon, stirred the contents in her bowl, then perked up with the first taste. *Comfort food.*

"It's absolutely delicious," she said.

"Beef barley soup," the widow replied. "It's my mother's recipe. And she got it from her mother. Been in the family for generations. It's a favorite here at the Inn."

"I don't think there is any bad food served here. This is so tasty I think I could eat two bowls full."

"Good. There's plenty. And it's time you eat something. You are always on the run."

A lump rose in the back of her throat as she thought of how much Mrs. Martin reminded her of Grams. Both of them were so good at encouraging. Had God sent Mrs. Martin into her life to guide her? Was it all part of his plan? If so, she thought Grams would approve of their relationship.

After finishing her dinner, Janee walked to the living room, sat down on the couch, and picked up a real estate magazine. Flipping through the pages, her heart stopped when she saw a picture of a cottage in the country. The property was beautifully landscaped with flowering bushes, fruit trees, and green acres. There were hanging baskets on the covered porch overflowing with colorful blossoms.

She imagined herself living in such a place and married to a handsome, reliable, down-to-earth man who was handy at repair. They had two children. A boy and a girl, and a loyal Golden Retriever. Chicken eggs were gathered daily and homemade meals were prepared with the fresh fruits and vegetables raised from their garden.

Janee startled when Mrs. Martin came to her side and stood over her. She was wringing her hands and looked a bit nervous.

"Is there something wrong, Mrs. Martin?"

"Janee, dear. I know you are busy with your new job and all but I was wondering if I could ask a favor from you? My neighbor tripped in a pothole out on her property today and sprained her ankle."

"I'm sorry to hear that," Janee replied.

285

"Me too. She has a small farm down the road and needs help with her animals and meals. Her son, who lives with her, would normally help but he's had to work a lot of overtime lately. I told her I could help take care of things if I found someone who could cover for me. Do you think you could lend me a hand by helping out around here some? In exchange for your work, I'll give you room and board."

Janee gasped and a wave of relief swept over her.

Manna from heaven. A second chance. God's intervention.

"I would be happy to help, Mrs. Martin. When do I begin?"

***

Janee hummed as she made her way through the hallways of WRA to Brent's office. Full of renewed hope from Mrs. Martin's offer, she cheerfully greeted Simon and Brent who were already seated at the boardroom table. Gone was the dark cloud of yesterday. Present was the smell of victory.

"Morning, Janee." Brent didn't stand this time but gestured for her to take a seat beside them. "What have you got for me?"

Janee handed him her proposal. "Brent, we're going after the senses. Rainy Day Coffee will donate thousands of pounds of coffee next year to schools, clubs, and non-profit organizations. Places like food banks, the Salvation Army, Toys for Tots, and homeless shelters. We'll awaken people's senses when they hear the coffee dripping, smell it brewing, and taste its delicious flavor."

"Look, Janee. Poor people don't buy expensive coffee," Brent lectured.

"But business owners and community minded people do," she responded. We're going for goodwill, visibility, and charitableness. Rainy Day Coffee's presence will be seen at all the local events throughout the year such as Christmas tree lighting festivals, Moms Night Out, and Fourth of July celebrations. Their logo will be seen on promotional materials such as t-shirts, hats, and banners. Coffee baskets can be given away at silent auctions and used for raffles at fundraisers."

Brent frowned and crossed his arms. "It's too expensive."

"Advertising dollars will be better spent by giving," Janee responded. "People will experience the coffee firsthand instead of just hearing a jingle about it on the radio."

"I'm going to be blunt, Janee," he said with a huff. "It is not going to work."

Simon leaned his body toward Brent and shook his head at her like it was a bad idea.

"No professional company is going to want to spend money on an advertising campaign that is not going to have an immediate return on their investment. Non-profits are so desperate they will take donations from anyone. I'm afraid your campaign will hurt Rainy Day's image. Sorry, but Simon's ideas have clearly—"

"Excuse me, Brent," Tami interrupted. The secretary stood at the doorway with a sense of urgency. "Your wife just called and said you need to go to Children's Hospital. Your daughter's stomach ailment has been diagnosed as appendicitis. Her stats are good but she's being prepped for surgery."

Brent grabbed his jacket and left the room with great haste.

"I will pray for your daughter, Brent," Janee called after him.

He didn't reply and Janee's heart sank. She knew the pink slip was coming. If it wasn't for this family emergency, she would be packing her bags this instant. The public relations consultant job at WRA was lost.

Janee plopped into her chair.

"Umm, I'm not quite sure what to tell you both," Tami said. "No one on the executive staff is here right now to cover for Brent. I guess the two of you could probably take the rest of the day off. Someone from our office will get back to you."

After Tami left the room, Simon stood up and walked toward Janee. "Game over, Dorothy. Time to get on the bus and go home to Toto and Kansas." He reached into his briefcase and pulled out a newspaper. "Here's a copy of the classifieds. You'll be needing this." He dropped the paper in her lap.

Salt in the wound. Crushed, Janee closed her eyes and blinked away the tears so Simon wouldn't notice.

I've done my best. But my best... isn't... good... enough.

Simon had beaten her...again. She looked away from him, gathered up her things, and slipped out the door.

***

Janee's bus dropped her off at the top of the driveway to the Cedar Inn. Dark gray clouds had formed overhead. She lifted the collar on her wool coat to cover her neck and braced against the cold wind.

The slow walk down the driveway toward the gate gave her time to regenerate from the day's disappointment. She reflected on how no matter what difficulty she had experienced in her life, she had never gone one day without food or shelter.

"Home so early?" Mrs. Martin greeted as Janee came through the front door. "You look sad. What's wrong?"

"I don't think I'm going to get this job, Mrs. Martin. Brent shot down my idea and was about to fire me when he got interrupted by a family emergency. I think the pink slip has been postponed till he gets back. I guess I have the weekend to start looking for a new job."

"Don't worry," Mrs. Martin said. She placed her hand gently on Janee's arm. "The good Lord closes one door and He opens up another."

Janee walked over to the closet and hung up her coat. Shelby came and stood by her. He forced his head under her hand making her pet him.

"Did you see how those gray clouds are forming in the sky?" Mrs. Martin asked. "Snow is in the air. I can feel it. The weather forecast is calling for five to six inches of snowfall tonight."

"Really? That's funny, I was just thinking on my way back from work it felt like it would snow. The air tonight feels just like it did in Massachusetts right before a snowfall. My grandma and I lived in a small town close to the mountains and we got a lot of snow there."

"Well, we shall see if the weatherman is correct, won't we? Why don't you go sit by the fire. I'll make us some tea and we can talk about what needs to be done around here."

"Sounds good."

Janee's cell phone dinged in her purse. She pulled it out and looked at the text message from WRA.

"Simon and Janee. Due to the fact that heavy snow is forecast for tonight and Seattle transportation is not set up to handle such conditions, we ask that all of our employees remain at home, work via the internet, and wait out the storm. Stay safe. Our firm's president, William Robert, will step in for Brent on Monday. Meet him in his office at nine o'clock. Tami. PS... Enjoy the snow! Be happy! Build a snowman!"

"Build a snowman? I don't feel like building a snowman. And I don't feel like waiting around to get fired," Janee mumbled.

She unloaded her briefcase and looked at the classifieds Simon had given her.
Somehow she just couldn't get over the fact she'd lost to him again. She threw the paper into the fireplace, sat down on the couch, pulled her feet up under her legs, and watched the light snowflakes fall outside the big picture window. Shelby walked over and put his head on her knees.

What am I going to do? Get a position as a waitress while I look for a job in my field? How long can I work for Mrs. Martin before my money runs out?

CHAPTER 5

Friday morning, Janee assumed all of Mrs. Martin's responsibilities since she wasn't going to WRA that day. Setting out breakfast for the guests was a welcome distraction. Today she felt like she was a resident at Cedar Inn instead of a guest.

Mrs. Martin left her with a list of chores to complete. After she finished cleaning, Janee looked around the kitchen.

Hmm. Cookies sound really good right now. I bet Mrs. Martin wouldn't mind if I baked some. I wonder if she has chocolate chips.

Janee searched through the pantry and found all the ingredients. She had prepared this recipe so many times while growing up, it took her no time to get a batch into the oven. Soon the aroma of fresh baked cookies filled the air.

"Ho, Ho, Ho! Anybody here? Hello? Hel…lo? Knock…Knock…Where are you, Aunt June?" a voice called from the front of the inn. "Did you bake me cookies? You shouldn't have."

Janee poked her head out of the kitchen to see who was making all the noise. A man walked into the living room, carrying a freshly cut Christmas tree. He left the front door open letting cold air into the warm house. A trail of snowy footprints led right to him. The delivery man set the tree down and stuck his head out from behind the branches.

Janee gasped. *No way.* There standing directly in front of her was the ferry guy.

"What are you doing here?" Janee asked, startled yet pleased.

"I was about to ask you the same thing," he said with a grin.

"Sooo…what's with the tree? Are you one of Santa's elves?"

"Yep. Where is Aunt June?" he asked as he looked around the room. "Hey, aren't you the crazy girl who doesn't know how to drive on a ferry?"

Janee laughed. It was one of the first times she had laughed since she came to Seattle.

"Aunt June?" Janee asked. "Are you looking for Mrs. Martin? Is she your aunt?"

"Yes."

"Mrs. Martin is over at her friend Maggie's house."

"She is helping my mom?" asked the ferry worker.

"Wait a minute. Maggie is your mom?"

They both chuckled as their conversation mimicked Abbott and Costello's, 'Who's on First Routine'.

"I'm filling in as the temporary innkeeper while your aunt helps your mom," Janee said. "Sorry to hear about your mom twisting her ankle."

"Yeah, me too. She sprained it pretty bad. Hey, I thought you worked somewhere over in Seattle."

"I do. Or I should say, I did. Or rather I still do." She frowned. "That is till Monday."

"Oh. Sorry." He quickly changed the subject. "By the way, my name is Bryan Thomas and is that chocolate chip cookies I smell? You know as innkeeper you need to pay your hired hands. Cookies will do."

She laughed. "Nice to meet you, Bryan. I can afford your rates." She reached out her hand to shake his. "I'm Janee Peters. Would you like some coffee to go with those cookies?"

"'I'd prefer some milk, thanks." He rummaged through the refrigerator. "I'll help myself."

Bryan was even more handsome up close. Wavy brown hair, dreamy blue eyes, broad muscular shoulders, strong arms, and big hands. He wore hiking boots, blue jeans, a forest green rain coat, and he smelled of fresh pine. And his jaw had a six o'clock shadow.

He grabbed a handful of cookies, dipped one in his milk, then popped the whole thing in his mouth. His hands were dotted with melted chocolate chips.

Janee handed him a napkin.

"Thanks. Great cookies. Mind helping me out for a minute with this tree?"

"Yeah, sure. Why not."

They both walked to the living room. The tree stand waited in the corner between the fireplace and the big picture window. When she went to grab the tree his hand brushed hers and heat rose into her cheeks. She hadn't had many relationships in her past but couldn't deny she found herself attracted to this man's looks and casual, laid back attitude. In the past, she hid her awkwardness by convincing herself she didn't have enough time for boyfriends. She was too busy with school or work.

Bryan held the tree steady while Janee crawled beneath the limbs and screwed the large bolts of the base into its trunk to hold it secure.

When they finished, they stood side by side, and gazed at the eight foot pine tree to see if it was straight.

"Perfect," they said in unison.

They looked at each other in surprise then awkwardly glanced away. It felt like eternity passed before either of them spoke.

"Gosh. Time's flying. I've got to start moving to put dinner on the table." Janee dusted her hands and moved toward the kitchen.

"Job's not done yet. We need to water the tree," Bryan said.

She went to the cupboards and started to remove plates and glasses. Bryan filled a pitcher with water at the kitchen sink.

"How's the car?" he asked.

"It should be repaired by Monday. I hope the garage does a good job."

"If there's anything I can do to help out, let me know."

"I think the interior needs to be vacuumed and it needs a new wax job for winter," she teased.

Bryan laughed. "What's for dinner?" he asked.

"Pork chops and scalloped potatoes. Should I put on an extra plate for you? We have plenty."

"Sure," he said, holding her gaze. "I'd love to."

"Great."

Janee's heart soared as she and Bryan enjoyed dinner together with the other guests at the inn, and her pulse raced even faster when he lingered around afterwards and offered to help with the dishes.

"Hey, tomorrow's the annual Christmas Boat Festival. For the past fifteen years, my mom, Aunt June, and I have gone to the Port Orchard waterfront to vote on the best decorated boat. It's always the Saturday before Christmas. But with mom's sore ankle they won't be able to come. Would you like to join me? There will be a high school marching band, Chistmas lights, and carolers. Santa will make his grand appearance aboard the local fire truck." He chuckled. "And if you've been good enough this year, maybe he'll give you a candy cane."

"I don't know," Jane said, her tone wistful. "I'll have work to do around here, like clean up dinner dishes."

"Great idea. I'll come over for dinner and help you with the dishes so you can finish early. Any other excuses?"

She gazed into his deep blue eyes and said, "Not one."

He grinned. "I'll see you tomorrow night then."

Janee's heart fluttered with excitement.
I wish it was tomorrow right now.

***

The next evening after all the kitchen chores were done, they bundled up with winter coats, knit hats, and gloves. Mrs. Martin loaned Janee a pair of rubber boots and wool socks to keep her feet warm and together they rode in Bryan's vintage 1950 Chevy truck to the waterfront. Fifteen minutes later, they got out and walked alongside the old storefronts. Bake shops, bike repair, second hand stores, a library, and restaurants lined both sides of the road.

"What a quaint town. I feel like I'm going back in time," Janee said, looking around. Strings of Christmas lights draped across the street from store to store. Snowman banners and red and white candy canes hung from the street lights. Janee gestured toward them and said, "Looks like they are straight out of the sixties."

"Some people think it's a little bit outdated."

"Not me. I find it very refreshing because it doesn't feel overdone. I like the simplicity of small towns but I also enjoy the fast pace of cities. You have the best of both worlds here right next door to each other."

Bryan glanced around at the decorations then settled his gaze on Janee and said, "Yes, I do."

Janee's heart pounded.

"Oh my gosh." Janee gasped and placed her hand over her mouth.

"What's wrong?"

"I didn't know there was a Rainy Day Coffee Store here," Janee said. She pointed to the shop just ahead. "That's the company I was hoping to get the account for."

An elderly woman walked toward them and called out, "Bryan Thomas? Is that you? Long time no see. I never forget a face, why I remember when you were a cute little boy in my kindergarten class."

Bryan gave the woman a nod. "Good to see you, Mrs. Johnson. How are you?"

"Just fine, son. Had a hip replacement last year but look at me today. I'm still getting around. Parked my cane on the coat rack. Thankfully I don't need it anymore. I don't move as fast as I used to but I'm still getting around."

Mrs. Johnson continued to talk. This time about her pet, caramel-colored poodle, Gingerbread, who was in her arms dressed up like Santa's favorite reindeer, Rudolph.

"Bryan," Janee said, touching his arm. "I've got to go check out this store and buy something hot to drink. I'll catch up with you in about five minutes or so. Would you like something?"

"No. But thanks."

Janee excused herself and walked into Rainy Day Coffee.

As soon as she opened the door to the café, the scent of fresh roasted coffee washed over her and she drew in a long, deep breath.

Yum. I love the aroma of coffee. I remember as a child smelling this first thing every morning when I got up for school.

Rainy Day Coffee was packed full of customers. Movable wood tables for two and four lined each side of the cafe. It was set up so tables could be arranged to accommodate large and small groups. Vintage pictures of the historic town hung on the walls. Umbrellas of different designs, shapes, and sizes hung in all kinds of positions from the open rafters of the dark cedar ceiling. There were happy customers everywhere who were laughing and carrying on small talk. Janee got in the back of a line of people and looked at the menu.

This is a great place. It's so wholesome. I could easily see myself working with this company. If only I didn't blow their account. But it just wasn't meant to be. She frowned as she remembered her last conversation with Brent. He wasn't happy with her proposal and was about to tell her so before he was interrupted by the family emergency. *If only she could change his mind.*

Janee moved forward in the line that led to the baristas. Just ahead of her was a man with dark hair, about forty years old, dressed in a three-quarter length black wool coat. He looked at the menu which hung on the wall and then darted his gaze about the shop looking at all the customers. Then he turned and looked at her.

"What's a pretty girl like you doing with a sad look on your face? Is it too long of a line? Don't worry. It moves fast," the stranger said.

"Oh, was I frowning? I'm sorry. I guess my face gave away my disappointment. I drove out from the East Coast a couple of weeks ago and have absolutely fallen in love with this area. I was hoping to get a public relations position with a firm here but it looks like I'm not going to get hired for the job."

"Oh, I'm sorry to hear that."

"Maybe I should sit on Santa's lap before he leaves for the North Pole and tell him all I want for Christmas is this amazing job," she joked.

"Hey, it couldn't hurt," he said. "What do you like about the Northwest?"

"The people here seem to be so at ease with themselves. They're not caught up with the hustle and bustle of life. Just look at how relaxed everyone is in this shop."

He looked around and nodded. "You're right about that. I've lived out here all my life and never wanted to move."

"This shop is great," she said and gestured toward the décor. "I love the comfortable, hometown feeling. With a little bit of marketing, it could become the number one coffee chain in the region."

"Funny that you should say that," he commented. "I've always liked this shop. I've drank a lot of coffee here over the years and have enjoyed many conversations with friends and family. So what's your background?"

"I graduated from Harvard a couple of years ago with a degree in communications and I'm looking for a job in marketing," she explained. "One that will help me support myself and just maybe…" she said with hope, "let me buy a convertible."

He laughed. "Well you won't be able to drive a convertible with the roof down much in the Northwest. You know we get a lot of rain out here." He reached into his breast pocket and pulled out a business card. "I like your enthusiasm and spirit. We could use someone like you in our company. Here's my card."

Janee took his card and put it in her purse.

"Give our human resources department a call," the man continued. "Mention my name and tell them that I recommended you contact our company."

"Oh, thanks. That's really nice of you. I'll call."

Janee paid for her drink and went outside to join Bryan. He was standing quietly by the door waiting for her to come out.

She stood close to him and said excitedly, "Guess what?"

"What?" He tipped his head and looked down at her face.

"I met a man standing in line at Rainy Day Coffee. He gave me his business card and told me to contact the human resources director. He said he might have a job for me."

"That's great, Janee. Really great," he said warmly. "You should definitely check it out on Monday. But right now, let's go down to the docks and vote on our favorite Christmas boats. Time for some fun."

Bryan looked across the busy street filled with a loud marching band, drummers, and floats, then he took her hand. "Hold on, I'll find us a way through."

He made his way between the marching band and a float and was nearly clipped by the head of a tuba. Janee almost got stuck in an angel's wing from the Angel's Rejoicing float. They joked and laughed about the incident while they made their way down to the Marina. And as Bryan continued to gaze at her, she couldn't help but smile. Maybe there was hope for a good life in the Northwest after all.

CHAPTER 6

Monday morning, Janee trembled as she entered WRA's office with a lump in her throat. All morning long she had coached herself that she would be professional and not cry when she got the pink slip. Simon, however, walked in like a cat who just swallowed the canary and it crumbled her resolve.

"Come in, the both of you. Good to see you this morning," William Roberts greeted. "Take a seat."

Janee and Simon sat opposite each other, and the president stood at the head of the table.

"I just want to let you know I haven't spoken with Brent since he left on emergency leave. Tami tells me his daughter is doing fine, but he left in such a hurry, I didn't get to discuss his thoughts regarding your employment here."

Janee and Simon leaned in toward him.

"However," he continued, "I reviewed both of your proposals Friday night and thought they were noteworthy enough to merit Rainy Day Coffee Corporations review."

"Great," said Janee.

"Glad to hear that, Will," boasted Simon. "I know *my* plan will take the coffee shop to new heights."

"Your ideas were emailed Saturday morning to Sean Lewis, president of Rainy Day Coffee, along with an invitation for him to join us this morning. Sean is eager to meet you both."

"So you want us to *re*-present our plans?" Simon asked indignantly. "But, Brent—"

"Don't worry about Brent," the president interrupted, with his hand up in the air. "Sean mentioned on the phone that he has someone else in mind who could potentially do this job. Make it good so we don't lose this contract." William raised his brows and gave both her and Simon a direct look. "Are we clear?"

"Yes, clear," Janee and Simon said in unison, each of them nodding their heads.

I have a second chance. I have a chance! Janee's heart leaped and she looked around the room with renewed energy.

"Here he is now." William moved toward the door, and Janee turned her head to look.

It's him.

There in the entryway was Sean Lewis, the same man who Janee spoke with while waiting for her coffee at the Rainy Day Coffee Shop. William reached out and shook his hand and began introducing him to Simon and Janee. When he saw Janee, his face lit up. She smiled back at him and her pulse quickened. Excitement began to mount.

"It seems we've met before," he said, his gaze upon her. "Yet I don't know your name."

She stood up, smoothed her jacket, and moved toward him.

"Janee Peters."

He gave her a firm handshake and said, "I didn't expect to see you here this morning. Small world, huh?"

"Yes, I had no idea when I spoke with you on Saturday that..."

Out of the corner of Janee's eye she saw Simon's gaze dart back and forth between her, Sean, and William with a look of worry on his face.

Janee smiled. "I'm excited to discuss my proposal for Rainy Day Coffee with you in detail."

"Okay everyone, let's all take a seat and get to work." William gestured for everyone to move back toward the table.

Sean sat beside Janee and took out his notes.

"The first idea I read was about donating to college students. Whose idea was that?"

"That was my idea, Sean," Simon boasted. "Great idea, isn't it?"

"Well, Simon, we do see college students coming into our shops with their books, laptops, and ear buds. However, they don't spend a lot of money, and they stay a long time."

"That may be true, however once they graduate they'll have plenty of money to spend in your shops," Simon said.

"The idea is not right for our company at this time." Sean frowned. "Your approach, if applied, would not generate the immediate return in revenue we need so we can invest in opening more shops."

Simon leaned in toward the executive. "Look, Sean. You'll be missing the boat if you don't reach them now. Free cups of coffee and cookies will create lasting memories for these *poor* college students." Simon put his hand on his chest and looked over at Janee with a poor puppy dog look. "Now I wasn't a poor college student, but I know a lot who were."

Janee winced slightly at his put down. Then she squared her shoulders and sat up straighter, refusing to let him get the better of her. Not this time.

"With your great tasting food and coffee, and your savvy shops," Simon continued, "these students will be looking forward to spending more time with their friends, family and business associates at your cafes in the near future. You will build brand loyalty with them."

A note of tension penetrated the room. William shifted in his seat. Sean rolled his eyes and let out a huff. Then the muscle along the side of Sean's jaw tightened. He raised his eyebrows at Simon and looked down his nose at him.

"I'm not sure you're hearing what I'm saying. It's Simon, right?" he asked. "I'm confident we'll get these students eventually. But right now our company needs to see immediate growth. We want to make more money, increase our visibility in the region, and open more shops in the next few years. Rainy Day Coffee needs to become a household name. That's our goal."

William cleared his throat. "Would you like to tell us your thoughts on Janee's proposal?"

"Sure," Sean said, leaning forward, his hands clasped together and an eager expression on his face. "Your proposal, Janee, had a completely different approach that I have never considered before. I see visibility in your plan. A lot of visibility. We want that. We need that. How would you implement it?"

"I'm glad you asked, Mr. Lewis."

"Sean. Call me Sean."

"Mind if I stand up?"

"By all means." He gestured for her to take the floor.

Janee stood and walked over to the dry erase board at the front of the room. She picked up a marker and drew a few stickmen and then an arrow toward an increased amount of stickmen with an additional arrow connecting to an even larger number of stickmen.

"My plan, Sean, is to identify and reach out to community leaders. These include festival managers, business networking groups, Chambers of Commerce, and non- profit organizations. We will offer complementary coffee and cookies, and gift cards to support their events. We can donate to their silent auctions and raffles."

He began to nod his head with interest. "I'm listening."

"During this process, we'll develop relationships with leaders and their volunteers, and Rainy Day Coffee's name, logo, and influence will be seen in high pedestrian traffic everywhere."

Sean stood and moved toward the board next to Janee.

She moved her marker from the small number of stickmen toward the larger groups. "Reaching out to the few will in fact get us seen by many more."

"Yes, I can see that."

"It's a win for the non-profit organizations, festival organizers, and the less fortunate. And it's a bonus for Rainy Day Coffee who will spread goodwill, gain in visibility, and generate more connections. All at a minimal cost compared to other forms of advertising."

Janee glanced at William who began to nod his head in agreement with Sean and an air of expectancy descended upon the room.

Simon crossed his arms over his chest. He looked at Janee, and his mouth tensed. Her idea was gaining ground, and she and Simon both knew it.

"We can follow up with the new contacts," she continued. "We'll send out informational packets explaining all the additional catering services Rainy Day Coffee has to offer." She hesitated, then looked directly at Sean, and asked, "What do you think?"

Every head turned toward him. The room grew quiet.

Janee's heart pounded in her chest and she barely dared to breathe as she, too, waited for Sean's reply.

Then the corners of Sean's mouth lifted into a slow grin that lit his face as he turned to look at her. "You know. I like it. I like it a lot. Grassroots promotions. This would be good for us. Having a good name in the community will go a long way. Sales will follow our good reputation."

He stood up and reached his hand across the table toward William. "I'd like Janee to spearhead this account."

"What?" Simon demanded, a look of utter disbelief etched across his face.

Janee closed her eyes for a brief moment, then looked toward heaven and smiled.

Thank you, God.

"Looks like we've got work to do, Janee," William said. "Great job this morning. I'll touch base with you in a little while, after Sean and I wrap things up here."

Janee walked over to Sean and shook his hand. "I look forward to working with you."

"And I, you, Janee. Happy to have you working on my account."
"Thank you very much. It will be an honor."

CHAPTER 7

As Janee stepped outside onto the sidewalk in front of William Robert Associates at the end of the day, a light dusting of snow fell gently from the sky. She stopped and breathed in the cool, crisp, winter air. And the warm glow of the city lights reflected the joy that swelled in her heart.

This is my city.

Last minute Christmas shoppers hustled in and out of stores, and food vendors hawked their last hotdogs and pretzels for the day. Janee lingered, savoring the sights and sounds. She heard the song, "*It's beginning to look a lot like Christmas*" from a nearby car radio and began to whistle it all the way to the bus stop.

Best Christmas present ever, I get to work in the job of my dreams and live in a beautiful city.

Janee flipped through a Penninsula Real Estate magazine while on the ferry home and tore out a picture of a small cottage with hanging flower boxes for sale.

This is exactly the kind of place I've always wanted. I can't wait to buy a home just like it.

As she looked out the large windows on the ferry and gazed over the water toward Port Orchard, the silvery lights from cozy beach homes sparkled off the ripples of water on the Puget Sound. She leaned back on her bench seat and relaxed, waves of peace rolled over her for the first time in a long while.

I'm finally home.

***

A loud stove buzzer went off in the kitchen.

"Janee, can you please check on the turkey?" Mrs. Martin called from the dining room where she was setting the table for Christmas Eve dinner.

"I'll help," Bryan replied, jogging toward the kitchen. "Here, let me lift that bird out of the oven for you." He put on the mitts, reached inside, and placed the turkey on top of the stove.

Janee's heart melted. *What kind of a guy helps his mom, his aunt, and me?* She'd been so accustomed to doing things herself most of her life, but she now found she liked the two of them doing things together.

"Thanks, Bryan."

When Bryan closed the oven door he turned around to look at her, and gave her a broad smile.

"Anything to help a pretty girl like you," he teased.

"Why sir," she said with a southern bell accent, and with a curtsy, she winked at him. "I don't know what we'd do without you."

He tipped his invisible hat toward her. "Oh, I imagine you'd survive…now that you've finally figured how to drive onto the ferry."

They both laughed and Janee and Bryan couldn't stop gazing into each other's eyes. Her heart pounded wildly in her chest as Bryan stepped closer and whispered in her ear, "Anytime you need me. I'll be there." He reached out and took her hand and held it tenderly. "Any time."

Good to know, she thought, bursting into a smile. Because she was falling in love with him more and more each day.

"Hey, what's going on in there? It's awful quiet in the kitchen," Aunt June called. "Seems like I can't find any good hired help around here these days."

Bryan and Janee laughed. "Coming," they said in unison.

Resuming their duties, he put the turkey on a platter and Janee filled up the gravy boat and grabbed the mashed potatoes. Together they walked out to the dining room.

The table was set with fresh cut evergreens, candles, pine cones, and was trimmed with ribbon and shiny glass ornaments. Instrumental Christmas music played softly in the background reminding Janee of warm, loving Christmas's in the past.

The scent of roasted turkey, fresh rolls, and spiced cider filled the room and the heat from the blazing fire in the fireplace wrapped around Janee like a warm blanket.

"Let's all take a seat, everyone," Mrs. Martin said excitedly. Bryan pulled out a chair for Janee and sat beside her.

"God is so good," Mrs. Martin said, beaming at them. "We have so much to be thankful for. Family, friends, health, home, food on the table and our

Savior." She indicated for them to all join hands, and took one of Janee's in her own. "Let's pray."

Bryan reached for Janee's other hand. "Aunt June, may I say the blessing?" he asked.

"Of course," his aunt said with a nod. "Please do."

They all bowed their heads. "Our heavenly Father, we are thankful for your Son Jesus who came to earth to save us from our sins and give us eternal life. We are grateful for your abundant provisions, for helping Mom to heal and especially for bringing Janee all the way to Washington to bless us with her beautiful spirit." He squeezed her hand and wouldn't let go. "Amen."

Janee looked up from the prayer at Bryan, whose eyes glimmered with hope. She squeezed his hand back. As she gazed around the table at her new family, she couldn't contain her happiness.

"I have to tell you all right now—thank you. Thank you for accepting me into your lives. My heart is so full it could burst," she said. "I haven't felt this way since the last Christmas I shared with my grandma. Honestly I was beginning to wonder if I would ever experience this much love again."

Shelby, got up from his resting place and walked over to the sweet couple and rested his chin on their entwined hands. He looked up at both of them and whined his approval. Bryan's Mom and Mrs. Martin smiled at them too.

"We're so blessed to have you here, dear," Mrs. Martin cooed. "There will always be a seat at my table for you."

"Yes, a seat right next to me," Bryan said, his voice soft.

Janee's heart skipped a beat, the way it did every time he looked at her, and she teased with a southern drawl, "That's the best seat in the house."

About the Author:
Beverly Basile is a current member of Northwest Christian Writers Association and has written her first book, "All I Want for Christmas," and loves to encourage others through inspiring stories. When she is not working, you can find her hiking and glaciating mountains, cycling on the Olympic Peninsula, or drinking a split shot white chocolate mocha (extra whip please) and savoring time with her family and friends.

Beverly studied Speech Communications at Central Washington University and worked in her field for the Washington State Senate, Concerned Women for America, and World Ambassadors. Her chiropractor husband coached her in the sport of triathlon where she became a nationally ranked triathlete with USAA Triathlon. Together they have raised and homeschooled five children in the Pacific Northwest.

https://www.facebook.com/Beverly-Basile-100271153702543/?fref=ts

Recalling Life's Memories Hanging on the Christmas Tree

I love the Christmas season and each year I look forward to taking a break from its busyness by sitting down on the couch with a cup of creamy hot cocoa and extra whip cream. During this time, I watch the glistening tree lights and reflect on God's goodness represented by the tiny ornaments carefully chosen throughout the years to adorn the tree.

Like the golden yellow glass Christmas bear. I bought this ornament to remind me of the year I was spared by God from getting eaten by a black bear while living in a remote area. I am thankful to be alive.

Or the fragile green Gumby ornament. This one was given to my husband, Tom, by one of his patients who felt badly when she heard him tell her his childhood memory of how he lost his Gumby doll forever when he accidentally threw it up on the roof of his house while playing. He never told his dad what happened because he was afraid of getting into trouble. She showed him kindness when she went out of her way to buy a new Gumby for him.

And there is the handmade manger scenes made out of popsicle sticks by my children when they were little. Each time I see these ornaments, I am reminded of the wonder of Christmas and Jesus, the Son of God, Savior of the world, born in a stable.

Or the miniature kerosene lantern. This one takes me back to the stark cabin I lived in the summer I visited Gustavus, Alaska. Each morning before going to work at the lodge, I would have to hike a quarter of a mile out of the woods to get to the rustic restroom and build a fire to heat the water in the tank for the shower. Sometimes I resorted to taking a cold shower because it took too long for a hot one. Brrr... One night I almost burned down the cabin when I tipped over the lantern. Oops.

Perhaps this year you would like to start a tradition of saving memories on your Christmas tree. Go out and buy yourself an ornament that reminds you of something that has occurred in your life. Tell the story to your friend, family member, children, or grandchildren. Sharing experiences with loved ones draws our hearts closer together...which is one of the reasons I love Christmas so much.

Beverly

Made in the USA
San Bernardino, CA
06 December 2016